SOULWEAVER

B.G. LYRAX

Soulweaver
Book two of the Crown of the Alchemist series

Published by Blu and Gihon Creative Media, LLC.

For more information, email hello@bluandgihon.com.

Print ISBN: 979-8-9933048-2-3

E-Book ISBN: 979-8-9933048-3-0

Visit us today at bluandgihon.com to learn more about us and to view our artwork and other creative projects.

For more Crown of the Alchemist, follow and read our digital webcomic for free by going to cota.bluandgihon.com/read.

TABLE OF CONTENTS

N
W
E
S
Othalgar Port
Othalgar
Velkhamore
Lanzamire's Keep
The Ironpeak Mountains
Ravencroft
Blacktalon Thicket
Galathar's Hollow
Caandemium
Salisna
Lulgirm
Redwind Port

PROLOGUE

THE OTHER SIDE

"This is absurd."

A draekis male swathed in shimmering white scales glanced curiously at the hooded figure beside him as the man spat those hate-fueled words. The hooded man was staring straight ahead at a bulletin board, almost as if he did not even realize the draekis had heard him, or that he had spoken aloud at all.

The notice board in front of the pair was plastered with pages of all sorts. Newspaper clippings, missing person signs, and job requests surrounded one large wanted poster that was pasted directly in the middle.

The wanted man's illustration boasted long white locks and a smug expression, devilishly handsome in nature. Under his perfectly sculpted chest read a bone-chilling name: *Solomon*.

"The bounty is way too low. I'm worth way more than that," the hooded man groaned. "And 'dead or alive'? They aren't even trying that hard to kill me! They don't even care if I'm alive or not!"

"Please lower your voice, Master Solomon," the draekis pleaded, bowing his head in apology for making such a request. "We're in Ravencroft. If you were to draw any attention to yourself now, we'd be in a world of trouble. This is Dirigent Gihon's territory."

"Which is precisely why the bounty is so insulting," Solomon insisted in a furious whisper. "This is my own hometown. The first place I ever ruined. The one person on Tevus who hates me more than anyone else governs this pathetic little croft, and he can't even offer more than a few thousand gold for my head?"

"You are worth more than that, Master," the draekis assured.

"I know. Agares, you're the only one I trust around here. Do you realize that?" Solomon asked, turning from the bulletin board and starting off down the street.

Ravencroft was a sleepy town of few residents. Located in the protective thistles of Blacktalon Thicket, a swamplike biome that featured alchemically-enhanced defenses against outsiders, very few would find themselves able to access the village at all. Public knowledge of the residence remained sparse, with one of the only publicly-known features being the Corvid Athenaeum: a private school for alchemy that had all but closed when the previous Keeper, Arvien Marleogne, died.

Arvien's son, a transmuted raven zoa by the name of Gihon, had inherited the Athenaeum but suddenly closed it, having no interest in raising a new generation of alchemists.

Something had caused a change in Gihon's spirit a few years ago, something that Solomon had still yet to understand.

It must have been because of me. He's breeding a little army of alchemists to put an end to my truthseekers, my devoted followers of the Verutian Order. I am, after all, the focal point of everyone's life.

"You don't trust the others?" Agares asked, bringing Solomon's mind back to the present. "All of us homunculi were made by you, to obey you. Why would they betray you?"

"It wouldn't be the first time. You lot aren't my first creations, you should realize. There were more before you. A lot more."

"Naberius?"

Solomon tensed.

"Yeah, Naberius was my first homunculus. I was angry at Gihon, so I made a little version of him that I could boss around. Naberius is usually off doing his own thing, but he's still somewhat obedient. He's the one who drew out the Zenluvians from hiding at my command, by backlashing their kingdom. He's been feeding me intel on the Deepwood and Zenluve for a while now."

"Do you miss having Gihon around?"

Lightning shot through Solomon's veins, boiling his blood, and he whipped around to face the white-scaled draekis.

"That's a ridiculous question and you're a fool to think such a thing, Agares!" Solomon seethed. "It's just a little hard to be creative when you don't have a soul, so I made a lot of you look like people I know."

"Like Allocer?" Agares continued curiously, seemingly ignorant to Solomon's outburst. "You made her in Queen Edelein's image."

"I did that to get a rise out of Gihon. That's all. And I regret it constantly, because Allocer is by far the most infuriating homunculus I've ever dealt with, and that includes answering these infantile questions from your scaly ass. For the record, I was thinking of you, not that bitch of a woman."

"Me?" Agares asked, his steps faltering.

"Eraroth, an old friend of mine. Long ago, way before any

of this," Solomon gestured vaguely around him. "We were kids. I suppose you're meant to look like how Eraroth would have looked if he'd grown up."

"What happened to him?"

"He was sick. I don't want to talk about it," Solomon turned away, continuing to walk towards the outskirts of the town.

Is that why Master Solomon built his following around his healing alchemy? He lost his childhood friend to an illness, and the lost souls that find him remind him of Eraroth? Agares wondered silently, following behind his master as they slipped behind an old wooden building.

In the shadows of the dilapidated shed, three figures lurked with hungry eyes. Aim and Kimaris rose to their feet as their master pulled off his hood. Allocer remained seated on top of an upright wine barrel. The lioness leaned casually with one arm on her propped knee, second leg swinging down beneath her.

"Master," Aim and Kimaris greeted Solomon with a bow.

"Allocer?" Solomon's eyes narrowed at the lioness' disobedience.

"I don't bow," Allocer scoffed. "Especially not to men. *You* should be bowing to *me*."

Right. Homunculus clones take on exaggerated negative traits of their references. Making her in the image of a queen gave her an ego of one.

"I don't care," Solomon spat. "I created you. Bow."

"Make me," Allocer taunted.

Irate, Solomon grabbed the back of the lioness' head, ripping her off of the barrel and throwing her onto the ground. Allocer caught herself with her palms pressed into the dirt, wincing as she felt a muddy boot press onto the nape of her neck.

"Bow down, kitten," Solomon growled from above her. "I am your creator. Your god. I don't want to hear another word of backtalk. Got that?"

"Should we intervene?" Agares whispered to Aim and Kimaris, who both shook their heads in denial.

"There's no stopping Solomon when he gets like this. Plus, Allocer has had it coming for a while. I'm just surprised he hasn't killed her yet," Kimaris shrugged.

"She's useful to us, that's the only thing keeping her alive. We can use her against Gihon," Aim added. "Kimaris has some good ideas for that, actually. They'll be a lot more vulnerable once they follow us into the swamp."

Agares looked out at the thicket that loomed ahead, drinking in Aim's words as Allocer and Solomon continued to fight in the background.

"Do you really think it's going to work? The plan?" Agares asked Kimaris as Aim turned her attention back to the fight breaking out.

"Solomon's plan? Maybe."

"The thing with the Dweller."

"Oh, yeah. I think so. We don't need to kill it, we just need some of its water. From how Solomon described it, the thing's pretty damn wet, so, it should be fine. We'll be in and out of this wretched place by tomorrow."

"What about Gihon? Is he going to fall for it?"

"That? Absolutely. They won't even realize what we're doing until it's too late," Kimaris assured with a dry laugh. "The Queen's cure made them overconfident, and it'll be their downfall."

"Just kiss already, you two!" Aim called out, drawing the two men's attention.

Aim was speaking to Solomon and Allocer, who were at each other's throats. Solomon was clutching Allocer's neck as he lifted her from the ground, the lioness digging her sharp claws into his shoulders in return as they exchanged fiery glares.

"Naberius would be a better leader than you," Allocer choked, coughing as Solomon tightened his grip.

"When I'm done with you, I'll send you back to Zenluve with him, and the two of you can leave me alone and never bother me again. I'll be rid of you soon enough, and you two can be the disgusting little freaks you are, far away from me."

"You're kind of hot when you show authority like that, big boy," Allocer teased.

Solomon let out a loud groan, dropping Allocer to the ground.

"Like I said," Aim repeated dryly, "just kiss already so we can get a move on. We're losing daylight, and your dumb brother will be catching up soon."

CHAPTER 1

ONCE MORE

Within a mere week, what was originally meant as a culture exchange between two unfamiliar lands had already descended into a newfound chaos that threatened the safety of millions across the material plane.

Zenluve, the reclusive kingdom cloistered away in the mysterious Deepwood, had finally decided to embrace alchemical technology as their last-ditch effort of restoring peace to their homeland after a rampaging phantasm ended the lives of six brave fighters in a single moment.

With no other choice but to blindly trust the Society of Alchemists in Caandemium, the Queen of Zenluve had introduced her noble Zengarde warriors to Dirigent Gihon Marleogne, offering a chance to study crystallized leyline energy in exchange for his assistance. The malice of alchemy himself, however, decided to interfere with the foreign newcomers during every step of their turbulent journey.

Gihon's estranged and exiled elder brother Solomon Marleogne proceeded to outwit, overwhelm, and manipulate his way into acquiring both of the Zenluvians' leyline crystals. Now, with the intention of using them to fuel an array strong enough to wipe out a quarter of the continent, Dirigent Gihon and Queen Edelein have been scrambling to make sense of their situation and hunt down the homunculus called Solomon before it's too late.

Solomon's most recent attack on the entourage left Gihon's home in disarray, hardly even a roof over their heads, as the party regrouped the morning after.

Gihon found himself distracted from his usual reading as quiet chatter began to resonate around the house, indicating the stirrings of his students and the Zengarde. From his position seated in a large armchair in what remained of his living room, he noticed Jinn and Zander having a stern, yet quiet discussion together, which seemed to be normal for them. Everett, looking significantly improved after Jana's potions and some deep sleep, rummaged through the kitchen to pack some rations into bags for the others. Luthro approached Gihon with a quick bow before taking a seat on the couch next to him. Setting his book down, Gihon turned to face his student, who seemed eager to speak.

"Solomon will likely be expecting us," Luthro started. "He won't be in the town itself, correct? He knows he would have better luck escaping us if he buried himself deep in the marshlands."

"Yes, that is correct," Gihon confirmed as Luthro smiled confidently. "He is likely going to hide himself away in the thicket that surrounds it, hoping the land favors him over us. I suspect he may still have some tricks up his sleeve, so we need to stay on high alert."

"The swamp is quite large, and the density of it may make him hard to track. Do you suppose he is heading for the leyline's most condensed point?"

"The potent leyline energy that the heart provides would be likely to aid him, but the underground dungeons may not provide enough space for the Gates to operate. The theory is possible, but not guaranteed. What should we do about that?" Gihon asked warmly, pouring into his student and elevating Luthro to a position of leadership. Noticing the opportunity, Luthro straightened up his posture confidently.

"We still have the relay stones, so I propose we split into groups again. Half of us can explore the dungeons, while the other half take the surface," Luthro suggested.

"Excellent. Well done, Luthro," Gihon laid a hand on Luthro's shoulder affectionately, standing to address the others. "Everyone, Luthro and I have agreed to lead two separate parties of– where is Queen Edelein?"

Jinn sighed, turning to Zander with a knowing look. Zander folded his arms across his chest and bluntly stated, "She's asleep."

"Still? Is she unwell?" Gihon asked. "The sun is high in the sky at this point. We're losing time."

"That's what I said," Jinn agreed in exasperation.

"She needs rest, or do you care not for the wellbeing of your Queen?" Zander snapped at Jinn, whose ears flattened backwards in disagreement, teeth clenched in a silent snarl.

"Of course I do, but we cannot simply wait around for her to wake up. She never sleeps this late. Are you sure she's even in there?"

"She's in there. I can feel her presence. If she snuck out, I would know."

"You mean, sneaking out as she does all the time?"

"Alett lets her get away with it."

"Don't bring me into this!" Alett exclaimed from the table in the dining room, out of sight and likely tinkering with bombs.

"Fine," Zander sighed, irritated. "I will retrieve Her

Majesty."

The Ehret turned and started up the stairs, giving the room back to Gihon to explain the situation once more. Turning to his student, Gihon nodded, and Luthro stood to address the group.

"Solomon is going to be expecting us to follow after him, and it is likely that he has accommodated for that," Luthro started, eyes flickering around the room. "That being said, I believe the best course of action is to split into two links again, to cover more ground. I will be leading a group that will explore the dungeons surrounding the heart of the leyline, and Master Gihon will take the rest of you in a clockwise search through each quadrant of the swamp to locate any traces of Solomon. We can use the relay stones to communicate if either party runs into significant troubles that require backup."

Zander returned down the steps, a yawning Edelein in tow behind him. She stretched her arms over her head, looking around the room and meeting the curious gazes of her companions.

Gihon approached her, his eyes scanning her body in a cautious and concerned manner. "Edelein, are you feeling alright? Jinn says it's unusual for you to sleep in like this."

Edelein groaned and turned to him with a slight twitch of her eyebrow followed by a gentle smile. "I'm really fine, Gihon, just a little sleepy today. Probably the remnants of your Fortress Black, or whatever."

"The effects of the Fortress should not be lasting this long. Perhaps I should give you a physical evaluation to see if–"

"I'm fine!" Edelein laughed heartily, punching his arm. "Stop being a worrywart. Can't a girl get some sleep without a room full of worried bodyguards?"

Something is off about her. I am unsure as to what it could be, but I can feel it. Or am I just in my head after seeing that homunculus clone of her? Gihon wondered, lost in thought as his eyebrows furrowed. *Perhaps I am overthinking. After all, she did use a lot of energy yesterday. Sleeping in a bit more is to be expected.*

Luthro cleared his throat, drawing the attention of the others. Gihon snapped himself out of his silent spiral and nodded to Luthro, indicating for him to continue.

"Your autowagons were destroyed by that phantasm a few days ago, so we will have to travel on foot. Admittedly, this is an oversight on my part. I would have called for drivers rather than taking the train here with the other Corvid Athenaeum students. Anyways, if we leave now, we can arrive in town by late afternoon, and get an hour or two into the swamp before making camp. We have no time to waste if we want to accomplish this."

Pointing around the crowded room, Luthro continued, "Spira, Nora, Lylia, Jinn, Alett, Nephvir, and Cari, you're with me. Zander, Edelein, Everett, Thorne, Jana, and Mandus will go with Gihon. We will–"

"Did you just separate everyone by how much you like them?" Mandus interrupted with a laugh. "Damn, am I really that low on the list? I thought we were best friends."

"I considered the natural affinities of each fighter, as well. By putting you on the surface team and Spira on the underground team, you will have open spaces to sprint and Spira's hardlight can illuminate the dungeon. Though, rather than personal preference, I would say… compatibility of personality."

"Ah, you put all the loud and annoying people on the other team. Got it."

"That's not how I would describe it."

Jana looked down, nervously fiddling with her hands. "Am I annoying…?"

"Look what you did, Luthro. You made Jana sad."

"I never called anyone annoying. Mandus, stop instigating.

This is why you're on Team Gihon."

Gihon stifled a laugh as the drama unfolded between his students. "Don't worry, Mandus, Team Gihon is the better team anyway. We have the Lion Queen of Zenluve."

"Master Gihon, don't pick sides!" Luthro gasped, wounded.

Gihon ignored his student's outcry and changed the subject to prevent further escalation. "Time is wasting. Everett, are the bags packed? We will be rationing for the next few days, so everyone is aware," Gihon ignored him and changed the subject to prevent further escalation.

Everett nodded, hoisting several bags over his broad shoulders. Without another word, Gihon walked outside and motioned for the others to follow.

"You won't mind traveling on foot, will you?" Gihon asked Edelein, who looked up at him curiously.

"I love the outdoors, and I'm a natural-born hunter. Frankly, I would rather walk to Ravencroft than have to take another autowagon. Fresh air is lovely at this time of year," Edelein responded warmly. "Your people call this month Al-Nadi, yes?"

"Yours do not?" Gihon asked.

Edelein shook her head. "We understand the Caandemite Trade Calendar, but within the comforting arms of our Deepwood, Zenluve follows our own calendar system. Six weeks in a month, five days in a week. Right now, the Deepwood is approaching the end of the Faehunt season, when the Summer Court brings hot weather with their arrival into our realm. The current month is Titanom, and then our calendar resets back to Alderom as the weather begins to cool once more back into the temperate climate we are used to."

Edelein drank in Gihon's curious expression as he listened to her explanation, reading his curiosities further.

"The Deepwood is located within the Summer Court's

territory, so fae aren't incredibly uncommon. The Winter Court is further north, in the mountains. We… aren't on great terms with them."

"The Unseelie enjoy tragedy, as I have come to understand from the old tales. They are not exactly the type worth befriending," said Gihon.

Edelein nodded.

"Correct. Nephvir got on bad terms with them before joining us after he broke a mercenary contract to retrieve their Crescent Shadow, the scythe of shadow-stepping he now wields. They've wished for tragedy to befall us for years, but they are unable to enter the Deepwood to enact it."

"Do you not worry that they can reach you now that you've left?" Gihon asked.

"We're half a world away. Even if they did, my Zengarde and your alchemy students could fend off whichever fae Neph pissed off. The only tragedy they'd get would be their own death."

"So you named your calendar after the Seelie Court, then? Titanom, after the Seelie Queen Titania?"

"Just the faehunt season. The other months are named after the Great Ancestor Alderich's sons," Edelein concluded.

"How fascinating. Fae are but a myth around Caandemium, having been pushed out by our rapid developments and industrialization. Our land is not the most conducive for a fae habitat anymore, so I believe they would have all either left or died out. Hundreds of years have passed since the last sighting of one," Gihon explained. "Though I cannot say it surprises me, considering that your existence was also a tall tale to us Caandemites until we received that letter from you."

"We do heavily associate ourselves with the fae, beyond just our calendar system. I feel that naming a few months after them is the least we can do, for all they've done for us."

"Would it not be easier to just use the Caandemite Trade Calendar, if you have to learn it anyway? It has been accepted and utilized worldwide, after all."

Edelein shrugged.

"Easier, sure. Though, the same is said for speaking Common. Should every nation abandon their culture in favor of the standardized trade language?"

"You make a convincing argument for culture," Gihon admitted. "I have studied other languages in my lifetime, however I must admit that Common is my mother tongue. I find it a bit hard to fully relate to people like you in that sense."

"Common is as a mother tongue to me as well. We in Zenluve speak a secondary, traditional language called Aldersprak. My ancestors spoke this language, and we use naming conventions from it, though Common is what we teach in most schools," Edelein explained. "I had private tutors myself, all of whom spoke Common."

"What does Aldersprak sound like?" Gihon asked.

"Words you have heard, such as Ehret or Zwitet. My surname, von Luvemann, means 'of the lionfolk.' *Mankmal dein noige bekomz da baeste von du*, Dirigent."

The Dirigent looked down at the Queen, silently waiting for her to interpret the phrase.

"Sometimes your curiosity gets the best of you, Dirigent," Edelein translated with a coy smile.

Gihon laughed gently, unprepared for her comment. "Alright, alright. Perhaps I should not press further, Your Majesty."

A gust of wind kicked up, blowing through the lioness' blonde locks as she admired the Dirigent from beside him. She was silent, lost in thought, but her eyes were warm.

After a beat of silence, Gihon found himself looking over Edelein once more. Subconsciously, he found himself checking for any possible symptoms of illness or ailment, but the Queen seemed normal in every sense. Catching his stare, she chuckled. "What, do I have some dirt on my clothes, or something?"

"Are you really cured?" Gihon blurted out, too quickly to stop himself. Her smile faltered for a moment, and she tilted her head, confused.

"Of course I am. I told you before, I'm fine. Why are you so worried?"

"Why are you *not*? Blight is a terminal illness. Are you not concerned that Solomon's cure was a fake?"

"Because I've never felt better in my life. Whatever he did, I feel better now than before I was blighted, entirely. Please stop worrying. It is unbefitting of you."

"Your Majesty, with all due respect, you are under my protection as the Dirigent of Ravencroft and chief escort during your time in Caandemium, and I've already managed to lose both leyline crystals presented by you. Certainly, my impression on your people is currently subpar, at best. If the blight takes over your soul under my watch, an all-out war would break out between our lands. Please allow me the courtesy of fretting, just a bit."

"When I first met you, I thought you were stoic, you know?" Edelein laughed. "It's only taken me a few days to realize that you have a lot of strong feelings tucked away in that big chest of yours. How you manage that stoic impression to others is beyond me."

Strong feelings... Gihon faltered for a moment as Edelein's words echoed in his mind.

Gihon cracked a soft smile, letting out a small sigh. "Perhaps you're right. All this worrying has ruined my reputation. All right, I'll let it go for now. But if you start to feel anything off, let me know, alright?"

Edelein nodded, satisfied with the compromise as they

began their journey to Gihon's hometown. "Yes, of course, Dirigent Gihon."

Gihon followed closely behind Edelein as she looked around the small town of Ravencroft, drinking in the sights. Behind them, Mandus and Jana chatted quietly together, comfortable in their home, while Everett, Thorne, and Zander quietly investigated the new area.

Luthro stood at the head of the secondary group, offering a polite bow to his master.

"I will take the others westward, to head toward the dungeon entrance," Luthro relayed. "We should part ways here if we want to make good time."

"Understood. You have the stone, so if there is any trouble, be sure to use it immediately," Gihon replied.

"Take care of Eddie, you guys!" Alett waved. "If I find out that she has even a single scratch by the time we get back, you're all dead!"

The owl-boy was puffing out his chest in a manner of faux intimidation, trying his best to impersonate Zander's gruff demeanor. Edelein laughed and waved at her friend

Straightening up from his bow, Luthro escorted his allies into the shadows of Blacktalon Thicket. Cari had a grimace on her face as her boot sank into the soft, muddy soil of the looming bog ahead, hardly comforted by the reassuring smile that Luthro offered her. Spira, Jinn, and Lylia were unbothered by the terrain as they began to wade through effortlessly, while Nora and Alett continued to follow behind and chat happily with each other. Nephvir covered the group's flank, looking around uneasily, though keeping his anxieties to himself.

As the first team vanished into the swamp, Gihon began to lead Edelein and the others to the northern gate.

"So this is your hometown, huh?" Edelein asked as they approached the town outskirts, the croft's border lined with a dark and murky marshland ahead.

"Born and raised. Hatched, technically. You'll likely see a few ravens around here at some point. But yes, this is the town that Arvien poured her life into. My Athenaeum is here, a little ways outside of the town itself. We cannot dally here, but I will tell you about it as we head forward. There are things you should know about the swamp, as well."

Zander placed a hand on a nearby tree and turned to Gihon. "Something is unusual about this place. It feels like the Deepwood, but the land does not speak the way that the Deepwood does. It feels… cold, in a way. I do not care for it."

"I do not believe I have previously mentioned this, but Ravencroft sits atop a leyline not unlike the Deepwood, though much smaller in scale. As with the Deepwood, its energies seep into the land here. However, Arvien has restrained the power to the borders of this swamp, in an attempt to protect the leyline from outsiders. It is likely that the familiar feeling you are experiencing is the suppressed leyline energy. It simply does not 'speak' to you because you are a foreigner. The land can be hostile towards newcomers."

"Is that something we should be concerned about?" Edelein asked.

"No. I know these lands well, and spent my entire life as a resident here. I will be able to navigate us. There is no reason for the land to turn against me," Gihon affirmed, stepping deeper into the woods.

"I must say, charming as it is to be in your hometown, I don't think I care for it," Edelein continued, lifting a foot from the mud and shaking it out, disgusted. "I don't mind being in nature by any means, but as far as said nature goes, I cannot say that I enjoy mud."

"Don't piss off the living swamp, Eddie," Thorne snickered. "Just ask Everett to carry you. Or Gihon."

Edelein spared a quick glance at Gihon, who was looking at her with a subtle bemusement.

"Nope," Edelein looked away, blushing slightly. "Not doing that. I'm going up. That way, I'll be able to scout ahead and not get covered in mud. Everyone wins."

"Queen wants uppies?" Thorne laughed.

"Shut it, Thorne. You know I mean the treetops," Edelein rolled her eyes and grabbed a low-hanging bough, hoisting herself upwards into the tree. Crouching on a large branch, she looked down at the others.

"You can keep wading through mud and water. I'm going up to scout out some higher ground for us to rest tonight." Lifting herself higher, Edelein vanished into the leaves.

"Lions aren't supposed to climb trees, but fine," Thorne shrugged, continuing to walk onwards.

"She should avoid going too far. The marsh favors me, not you all," Gihon started, before a voice snapped from above him.

"I can still hear you, you know!" Edelein called from the treetops.

Gihon pulled a small golden medallion out of his cloak, holding it out for the others to see. "These medallions disable any of the array traps nearby, ensuring we don't get lost. Only myself and my students have these, so stay close to us."

"What happens if we don't?" Thorne asked, eyeing the medallion curiously.

"Best case scenario, you end up back at the town."

"Worst case?"

"Worst case, the Dweller finds you, buries your body under the swamp and pickles your corpse for later consumption." Gihon shrugged nonchalantly, pocketing the medallion and continuing to walk deeper into the swamp.

"Hold on, back up. You can't just drop something like that on us like it's nothing. What the hell is the Dweller?" Thorne ran after Gihon, anxiously staying close.

"Stay close to the alchemists and you'll never have to find out. To put it simply, though, the Dweller is a creature created by Arvien made to protect the leyline. It preys on people bold enough to venture in the swamp without a medallion."

A loud screech sounded overhead, causing Thorne to jump nervously. Looking up, a raven flew from the trees with an alarmed caw, likely startled by Edelein. Gihon laughed at Thorne's reaction, as Thorne sighed in defeat.

"I told you, ravens."

"Who was that, your cousin?" Thorne remarked, Gihon staring back in silent disbelief at the comment.

"I could banish you to walk without me, and deal with the Dweller."

"N-no, I'm good. Are there… any middle case scenarios? Anything less horrifyingly nightmarish than the Dweller?"

"Oozes."

"*Oozes?*"

"Sentient masses, also created by Arvien. They won't eat you, but they will probably kill you."

"Great, so you're leading us headfirst into a nightmare swamp full of unfathomable horrors, with the only hope of surviving being a piece of gold that only *you* get to hold onto?"

"Correct."

"I think I should be the one holding the medallion."

"Absolutely not."

Thorne fell into an uncomfortable silence, pondering the group's choices that had led them to this moment.

"Are there any fae here?" Thorne asked after a moment.

"Fae? No, there aren't. Why?" Gihon looked down at him, confused.

"It's just… I got lost in the wilderness once." Thorne admitted sheepishly, his head on an anxious swivel. "The fae saved me. Otherwise, the Deepwood would have killed me. I was just a kid at the time."

Gihon's silence urged Thorne to continue.

"The Deepwood is pretty hostile, like this place, though it's naturally occurring and not created by your psychotic mom. No offense. My parents, uh… they got into a pretty bad fight, which wasn't unusual for them, but it was nastier than normal. I ran off. I didn't… I didn't want to deal with them anymore. The yelling, throwing things, all of that. I wanted to run away, so I tried. I took off into the forest, and got lost within an hour or two. When the sun set, I realized I had no idea where I was, and even worse was that *no one* knew where I was."

"You find yourself anxious in unfamiliar, hostile territories," Gihon confirmed, and Thorne nodded.

"A fae girl found me that night. She was from a hunting party of the Summer Court. A sylph, I think. She flowed like the wind… she found me there, lost and alone. She wanted to help me get home, but her party was looking for her. I don't know how, but she gave me her powers to manipulate the wind; she pointed me in the direction of Zenluve and told me to change the wind until I could smell home again."

I could only dream of meeting the fae in person. I could see why Thorne ended up developing an ego surrounded by his power, especially when you consider that he's using it as a defense mechanism to protect that lost child inside of him. Gihon thought to himself as Thorne continued.

"As you can probably tell, I made it back home. If you're *really* smart, you probably also figured out that my parents got divorced very shortly after that. I guess they decided giving up on each other was better for their kid."

"Do you feel anxious that your tracking doesn't work here?" Gihon asked.

Thorne nodded. "I'm sorry, Gihon, but your hometown sucks. I hate this place. There's no balance of good and evil here. It's just… all evil."

"It is not evil," Gihon countered, "it is protective, warding off those who do not belong."

"So why would Solomon be here, then?"

"The medallions. He has one as well."

As darkness began to consume the land, sun dipping into the horizon, Edelein stuck her head down from the treetops, ponytail swinging down by Gihon's face. He looked up and saw her upside-down above him.

"There's a clearing of dry land up ahead. Let's make camp there for the night."

Gihon nodded, and Edelein flipped down next to him, landing on her feet.

"Something about cats and feet, right?" Gihon asked with a sly smirk.

"Oh, so you're a comedian now?" Edelein retorted playfully.

Ahead of them, the trees parted to reveal the open clearing that the Queen mentioned. Everett wasted no time dropping bags and beginning to set up tents for everyone, grateful to be on solid land. Jana began to rummage through the bags, looking for rations to prepare. Edelein turned to Gihon, holding out her hand. He stared down at her extended palm, confused.

"The medallion, please," Edelein motioned for him to hand it over. "I'll be taking the first watch tonight, because frankly, this place freaks me out a bit. I would like to patrol the area tonight to scan for dangers."

"Alone? That's unwise. I should accompany you."

"That defeats the purpose of standing watch. If no one sleeps, the watch is pointless. Please, Gihon, let me be useful. I used to patrol the Deepwood all the time. I'll be fine. If anything happens, you'll be the second to know about it."

"Second? Not first?"

"You can try to be first, but Zander's got the best Seventh Sense in Zenluve's history. He can usually detect danger *before* it happens. He'll likely know about it from my energy before I could even say a word to you."

Gihon sighed, handing the medallion to her. "Fine. You can take the first watch. I know how stubborn you can be, Your Majesty."

"Thank you, I– stubborn? How dare you!" Edelein scoffed, taking the medallion from his hand and pocketing it. "The audacity."

Jana waved at the two, calling out to them from the welcoming fire she kindled.

"Master Gihon!" Jana said, "I have some food ready for you and Her Majesty, please come sit!"

"Are you hungry?" Gihon asked Edelein, who stared back at him with a deadpan expression.

"I've been walking and climbing trees all day. Of course I'm hungry. Come on, let's go eat. Let's see if they packed any birdseed for you."

Edelein set off towards the fire where Jana sat preparing

portions bread and cheese. Zander approached from the outskirts of the camp, holding a wet and wriggling bag. Tossing it down by the fire, several fish spilled out, some of which still flopped around desperately.

"Fish. Eat," Zander huffed, sitting down next to Edelein.

"Nice work, my Ehret!" Edelein beamed, as Zander turned away to hide his expression. "Did you just catch these?"

"They are… still alive," Zander pointed out. "Yes, I just caught them."

"We didn't bring any fishing materials. Did you use your hands?" Mandus asked.

"Everyone has such intelligent questions today," Zander grumbled sarcastically. "Of course I used my hands. Have you never fished without a pole? What kind of zoa are you?"

"One with technology and a deadbeat dad who never taught me how to fish," Mandus replied. "I guess…I don't really get out much at all. Can you show me how to fish?"

"No," Zander huffed.

"Come on!" Mandus pleaded. "I've always wanted to go fishing with a father figure."

"F-father figure?!" Zander stuttered in disbelief, his nose scrunching into a displeased snarl. "Absolutely not. Isn't that what Gihon is for?"

"Gihon, will you teach me how to fish?"

"Of course, Mandus. With poles, though. I'm not the type to grab at a slippery creature with my bare hands. I fear I'd make a fool of myself that way," Gihon responded casually, staring into the fire as he roasted the fish that Zander brought. "I lack the elegant grace of our feline friends."

"You are all pathetic excuses for zoa," Zander muttered.

"Apologies, did you want to be the one to cook the fish? Or did you plan to eat them raw?" Gihon smirked as Mandus' face illuminated with delight.

"Whoa! Master Gihon's getting fired up," The fox-boy laughed.

"Can you two go five minutes without jabbing at each other?" Edelein asked, laying down on her back and crossing one leg over the other. "You worked together. I'm proud of you. Don't ruin the moment, and finish cooking my dinner."

"You're such a little princess sometimes, you know?" Gihon chuckled, turning the fish skewers over.

"That's what I tell her all the time," Zander grunted. "For a Queen, you still act like the little Crown Princess I once knew."

"How old was she when you met her?" Gihon asked.

"Twelve. I was eighteen. This little punk had a chokehold on the whole castle, being King Alderis' only kid. I cannot begin to tell you the amount of times I had to drag her back to her lessons," Zander dared to crack a small smile, tousling her hair gently as he reminisced on simpler times.

"It's not my fault that mathematics and history were so boring!" Edelein pouted, taking one of the roasted fish and biting into it with bright eyes. "Not the arts, though. I wish I could have just studied those all day."

"Which arts?" Gihon tilted his head as he watched her eat.

"Music and dance. I've touched many instruments in my lifetime, but the flute was my favorite. Ballroom dance, however, was my strongest class. It's been years since I've last danced, but I love a nice waltz."

"Did you really try to run away from history lessons?" Gihon laughed.

"More mathematics, but sometimes, yes." Edelein admitted. "History was a little boring for my taste. Mathematics was… difficult."

"Mathematics is all logic. I suppose that checks out for you, then, with your free-spirited mind. I could help tutor you, if you'd like. That's one of my favorite subjects," Gihon mused.

"Absolutely not! I'm never touching it again. I'm the Queen, I don't have to!"

Gihon laughed, his eyes meeting Zander's. Zander seemed lost in thought for a moment, his eyes darting between Gihon and Edelein before settling on the fire.

Ahead of them, Mandus, Everett, and Thorne approached and sat on the other side of the fire.

"Tents are done," Everett stated, grabbing some bread out of Jana's hand.

"Hey!" Jana yelped, trying to grab it back, but Everett held it up over her head.

Thorne and Mandus laughed, Gihon smiling warmly as he handed skewers of fish to them. He looked over at Edelein, who had fallen asleep next to him, fire illuminating her peacefully sleeping face.

So much for taking the first watch, Gihon mused, ignoring the pulling ache in his chest.

CHAPTER 2

THE DUNGEON

Brushing aside dried-out vines and undergrowth, Luthro revealed a small and dark opening between two jagged stone formations. The hole seemed to lead underground, the air inside musty and unwelcoming as the thicket they had waded through to get to it.

"Hang on," Alett paused. "This entrance clearly hasn't been touched by anyone for quite awhile, with the amount of vegetation growing around it. You really think Solomon would be in here?"

"There are a multitude of entrances," Luthro explained. "This one is the closest to Ravencroft, so I would not expect him to choose to enter here. However, each one leads to the same destination, so we would benefit most from taking the closest entrance we have access to in order to catch up to him, rather than investigating each entrance throughout Blacktalon Thicket for any signs of him."

"I suppose that makes sense. I simply cannot help but feel

that no living soul would go down here," Alett sighed.

"He doesn't have one, remember?" Spira added. "Nothing bothers him or creeps him out. If you're scared, you might still be able to catch up with Master Gihon."

Alett opened his mouth to deny the accusation, but Spira had already squeezed into the dungeon's entrance. The lightbound alchemist was able to see as clearly in the dank underground as she could on the surface, summoning a hardlight shield to illuminate the cavern for the others.

Jinn hopped down after her, extending his hand to assist Lylia, Nora, and Cari. The ground underfoot was made of solid stones, offering a single advantage as opposed to staying on the surface. Alett followed them in, leaving only Nephvir and Luthro standing in the mud outside.

"Something feels very wrong about this," Nephvir spoke quietly.

"You seem a bit quieter than usual," Luthro noted. "What do you think that feeling is coming from?"

"I cannot say for certain. Instinct," Nephvir replied. "This whole swamp… it fills me with a sense of dread that I have not known before. I am no stranger to darkness, and yet, the shadows of this place feel colder than usual. Almost as if they beg me to leave."

Cryptic as always, Luthro thought.

"You don't have to come if you aren't comfortable," Luthro assured the Zenluvian warrior. "I've come to learn that your instincts are usually worth noting. Alett felt uneasy, as well."

"No, no," Nephvir denied with a wave of his hands. "All is well, alchemist. The surface is just as foreign to me as this cavern is. We should stay together."

"Hurry up, Luthro!" Spira called from inside.

With a sympathetic look, Luthro clapped a hand on Nephvir's shoulder. The fellborn seemed appreciative of the gesture, following behind as the group reunited and oriented themselves.

The dungeon had an ominous aura to it, reverberating echoes of water droplets on the stone floor resounding like the ticking of an invisible clock. The air was cold and damp, hidden from the sunlight above, bringing about an early winter's chill. A faint scent of patchouli clung to the walls, mixing with the dungeon's natural odor of mildew and mycelium for a unique blend that was unfamiliar to the trained senses of the Zengarde.

"This is the most direct path to reach the heart of the leyline," Luthro explained, sensing the uneasy energy rippling through the Zengarde. "Unpleasant, yes. But it beats wading through mud, does it not?"

The group began to walk behind Spira, the alchemist's tall figure silhouetted by the light shield she held in front of her. The light from her alchemy revealed colonies of fungi and moss growing in crevices of the walls, the stones slick with wet lichen that soaked up the damp air. After a quiet moment, Lylia asked suddenly, "Do you have fae here?"

"Fae? No, we don't," Luthro responded, curious about the elf's sudden query. "Why?"

"This dungeon. I can feel the faintest trace of a fae somewhere in here," Lylia explained.

"Currently?" Alett asked.

Lylia shook her head, unsure. "The presence is faint, so I couldn't even tell you what type of fae it is. Something about this place just feels like there was a fae here. Or is."

"In the Deepwood, we have clans of elves that dwell within their own tribes," Alett started to explain as he drank in the curious expressions of the three alchemists.

"I am from one of such tribes, yes," Lylia continued. "The Brightwood tribe. Elves often commune with fae, due to our lifespans and general disdain for modern societies. I was barely even two-hundred when I left for Zenluve, so I have less experiences with them than my tribe did, but I know a fae when I see one."

"Why did you leave?" Nora couldn't help but ask.

An uncomfortable silence passed through the Zengarde for a long moment before Lylia answered, "They were massacred by a beast right in front of me. I was the only survivor."

"The Deepwood can be a terrifying place," Jinn added in what seemed to be an attempt at empathizing with Lylia. "The creatures that lurk–"

"That monster was no Deepwood beast!" Lylia snapped. "I've told you all a hundred times, I know the Deepwood inside and out. That thing was not a local species!"

As Jinn held up a hand apologetically, Nephvir whispered to the alchemists, "No one has ever found a single trace of the monster Lylia described. Some people… do not believe her story at all."

"That's so awful," Nora whimpered. "Poor Lylia."

"We should be wary of her warning, though," Nephvir added. "I would rather not encounter any fae, if possible. They do not like me very much."

"The Summer Court loves you," Alett laughed. "They think it's hilarious that you stole your scythe from the Winter Court."

"Yes, and now the Winter Court wants me dead. We all know this. Moving on," Nephvir turned and stared straight ahead as they continued to walk.

"I can sense some unusual presences in here, but none of them feel like a homunculus," Jinn stated, honoring Nephvir's request for a change in subject. "I do not believe that Solomon has entered this underground area at all."

"Still, we should check on the heart of the leyline and ensure everything is in order. Even if he's not here now, that doesn't mean he didn't come here at any point, or that he won't. There's no other reason for Solomon to be near Ravencroft," Spira replied.

"Spira is correct," Luthro added. "It would be better to go and check on it, to make sure it is secured. As for the unusual presences, I imagine that would be the oozes that guard the dungeon."

"I've read about such creatures. Little sentient balls of slime, yes?" Alett asked. "Where there is one, there are many. They attack by overwhelming their foes and squeezing into your… orifices."

Luthro nodded. "Technically, ooze is a colloquial term for a general classification of amorphous shape-changing creatures. Mimics, for example, can be classified as an ooze. You are correct, though. If we encounter any, please be mindful of your bodies' apertures. The ones that reside here were made via Master Arvien's high-caliber alchemy. Originally a colony of eukaryotic cells designed to maintain ecosystems, it turns out that they can be used as sentries for protected domains such as this one. They are controlled through chemical messaging, similar to ligand receptors of our own cells."

"If we were to provide a different chemical aroma, would it change the oozes' behavior?" Lylia wondered aloud.

"Yeah, but good luck cleaning the whole dungeon. The stench of ooze has been soaking into the rocks for years," Spira explained. "No getting rid of it."

A small yelp came from Nora, the young alchemist hopping up onto one foot as a rock began to quickly crawl away from beneath her. The cat zoa's tail was fluffed up in fear as the movement startled her, only setting her foot down when the creature was out of sight.

"Was that one of them? It looked like a stone," Alett pondered. "Camouflage?"

"Yes. Alchemist oozes are designed to blend into their surroundings, so the ones down here are the same greyish color as the floor. Please be careful," Luthro instructed. "Nora, are you alright?"

Nora nodded uneasily. "It just surprised me, that's all. I think I stepped on it."

"Why didn't it attack?" Jinn asked.

Luthro produced a small golden medallion from his pocket, extending it out for Jinn to see. The wolf zoa took it curiously, eyeing the sigil embossed onto it. The emblem was sleek and geometric, appearing to resemble a shield wrapped in the wings of a raven. As Jinn handed it back to Luthro, the alchemy student explained. "These medallions protect us from Blacktalon Thicket's protective measures. Members of the Corvid Athenaeum possess these, and it allows us to traverse freely through the swamp."

"Fascinating," Lylia murmured.

"Something's wrong," Jinn added suddenly.

The rest of the group turned to look at him expectantly, waiting for the zoa to elaborate. Alett's eyebrows furrowed, before turning to look ahead. "Jinn's right. There's someone up ahead!"

"Is it Solomon?" Spira asked, picking up the pace at the front of the link.

Jinn stopped as the group approached a fork in the dungeon hallways. Spira had started to go down the right hall, but Jinn was hesitating in front of the left.

"Left!" Jinn barked.

"Left? The heart of the leyline is to the right. Left is a dead-end," Luthro explained.

"Those oozes are attacking someone down the left hallway," Nephvir added, agreeing with Jinn. "It feels off, though. Why would someone be down here at all?"

"That's what I'm wondering," Spira stated. "A trap,

perhaps?"

"I'm going," Jinn huffed, turning and heading down the left hallway at a quick pace.

"It's not a good idea to go alone!" Nephvir exclaimed, taking off after Jinn.

The rest of the Zengarde followed suit, never the type to abandon their allies, leaving the alchemists to follow along behind them in befuddlement.

The pathway opened up to a dead-end room as Luthro predicted. There was a quick flash as they entered the space, and the link could barely make out several squirming grey masses of varying sizes as they crawled about. A whimpering young boy cowered in the middle of the room, with slicked black hair and wearing simple dark clothes.

What was that flash? Luthro wondered.

"Oh, absolutely not," Nephvir muttered, drawing his scythe and vanishing into shadow.

"Nephvir! Where did you go?!" Luthro hissed, pulling out his pocketwatch and preparing to strike the oozes that surrounded the boy.

"Wait, Luthro, something isn't right," Lylia instructed. "That odd presence, I feel it again. One of these oozes is fake."

"Lylia could be right," Alett added. "That flash was a changeling. There's a fae in here. Whether it's malicious or not, we can't be sure, but it definitely doesn't want to be seen."

Spira held out her medallion, stepping forward. The oozes slinked away, recoiling from the alchemist as she approached.

"Little boy, did you see anyone else in here?" Luthro asked from behind Spira.

The child nodded, trembling. "T-there was a creature in here… it was about the same size as me, but covered in black fur. It had glowing red eyes and… and long arms… it turned into one of those blobs when you guys showed up..!"

"A puca," Lylia realized. "A shapeshifting fae. Little troublemakers, more often than not. Jinn, can you escort this boy out of the dungeon?"

"How did you get in here?" Luthro pressed.

"I-I'm lost," the boy admitted.

"What is your name?"

The boy hesitated. "Kow."

Kow? What a strange name, Luthro thought.

"I'm Luthro. Kow, my friend is going to bring you back to the surface, alright? You can trust him, I promise," Luthro assured.

"I am… Luthro," Kow repeated shakily.

He's quite shaken up, Luthro noticed.

"Kow, come along with us. Jinn will keep you safe," the alchemist insisted.

Kow nodded, following behind Jinn as the wolf zoa led him away from the oozes. Jinn turned around for a brief moment, confirming, "Luthro, continue onwards with the others. I will be able to track you, so no need to wait for me."

"Understood," Luthro replied, tossing his medallion to the zoa.

"It is getting late, so we should avoid heading too far in before making camp for the night," Spira added.

"No way, we have to sleep down here?" Nora whined. "It's so gross!"

"I'm with Nora on that," Cari agreed.

Not interested in listening to their complaints, Jinn placed one hand on Kow's shoulder and urged him gently into the hallway. As the two vanished into the shadows, the group turned their attention back to the oozes crawling around along the edges of the room. They seemed desperate to avoid coming close to the medallions, opting to slink against the walls instead.

"Alright, puca, we know you're here," Lylia spoke into the darkness, eyes carefully tracking the movement of each ooze. "We mean you no harm. This place is not safe for the fae."

The oozes continued to squirm around, unresponsive to the elf.

"Spira, do any of them look different to you?" Luthro asked his classmate, knowing her lightbound eyes were capable of seeing things beyond his own human vision.

Spira shook her head, adjusting her star-shaped sunglasses. "They all look the same. If there's really a fae changeling, it's a damn convincing one."

Lylia crouched down, trying to get a better look at the creatures ahead of her. "They really do all look the same. I was certain there was a fae here, though."

A long beat of silence passed before Alett asked, "Is there a possibility that the changeling was Kow?"

The only sounds were the droplets of water and slimy wet oozes as everyone stopped to consider the possibility. After a moment, Lylia stood up and sighed, "Probably."

"And we left Jinn alone with it?"

"We did."

Another beat, broken up by cold rhythmic drops.

"Should we turn back and go after him?" Alett asked.

Lylia pondered it, but shook her head. "Pucas aren't usually violent, and Jinn is strong enough to handle one if it were. Our only concern is making sure that the Jinn that returns to us is the real one. Jinn is fast, so he'd be more likely to catch up to us than us to him. Let us continue forward to find an open space less riddled with monsters and set up camp for when he returns."

"I think we should trust Lylia," Luthro agreed, to the elf's relief. "There should be a good place to rest about a half mile from here, if my memory serves."

Leaving the squelching noises of the ooze swarm behind them, the link pressed onwards and doubled back to the previous fork in the hallway. Luthro led the group into the right entrance instead of the left this time, walking beside Spira as she illuminated the path ahead. Everything looked the same as any other hall within the dungeon, damp and lined with fungal growth that seemed to stretch endlessly ahead.

After about ten minutes of walking, the group found themselves in the large open room that Luthro had promised, a suitable campsite. Although the space was the same mossy stone composition as any other part of the dungeon, the walls were lined with old torches, and a fount of running water poured from the east wall. The rushing fountain masked the distant sounds of oozes, offering a much more pleasant atmosphere as well as a fresh drinking supply.

"We can rest here for the night," Luthro explained, igniting an array that was carved into the wall. The array sparked each torch, several small fires sputtering to life and illuminating the area. The connecting chain of arrays landed in the center of the room, where a bonfire sprung to life in a modest stone firepit.

The flames helped to warm up the room from the damp chill that plagued the dungeon, drying the stones with a heat that lapped up the cold moisture. Cari sighed in relief, removing her puff-sleeved jacket and relishing in the warmth on the bare skin of her shoulders as she remained in the signature fitted sleeveless shirt that marked a Zengarde's standard uniform.

"I hope Neph comes back soon. He's missing out," Cari said, closing her eyes and leaning back on her palms.

"Where exactly did he go?" Nora asked.

"He doesn't like to be perceived by most anyone, really, but especially the fae. If there's a fae around, he usually hides until he's sure they're gone. He should be back soon," Cari explained.

"As we've mentioned, Nephvir is the sworn enemy of the Unseelie Court. If they catch wind of his location, it could be incredibly dangerous for us all. It is for the best that he flees when fae are around," Lylia added.

Footsteps echoed from behind the group. Assuming Nephvir had returned, they found themselves surprised to realize that Jinn was the first to reconvene with them. Jinn sat down beside Cari, extending his palms to the fire gratefully.

Jinn, normally one to welcome silence, looked around curiously as he met everyone's uneasy gazes. "What?"

"Say something only Jinn would know," Alett said.

Jinn blinked silently, confused. The longer he hesitated, the more wary the group became. "Did something happen while I was gone? Oh, look, it's Nephvir. Let's all be weird towards him, instead."

The link followed his gesture, looking over the fellborn as he returned from the shadows on the other side of the room. Nephvir sat down beside Jinn, not seeming to notice the unusual energy rippling between the Zengarde.

"Nephvir, the others are acting strange," Jinn commented.

"Strange? They are always strange, are they not?" Nephvir replied.

"Jinn, we believe that Kow was the true fae spirit, not one of the oozes. We need to ensure that you are the Jinn we know, and not a changeling," Lylia clarified.

"Why would I be a spirit? I am Jinn," stated the wolf zoa.

"Jinn's acting kind of weird," Nora muttered.

"True, but, he also kind of always acts like this," Alett whispered back. "It really is hard to tell if this is normal Jinn or not."

Jinn's ears flattened, dark blue eyes flitting to each of his allies. "I did what you asked and brought the boy back to

Ravencroft. That is all. There is nothing amiss."

Nephvir let out a small laugh, a rare sound to come from the softspoken fellborn. "You are acting a bit strange. Are you really not a puca? Should I leave again so you cannot see me?"

Is Nephvir joking? He's usually more skittish around fae, Lylia wondered silently.

"This is the last time I will do anything for you people," Jinn growled, annoyed. "Save your own little boys next time."

"Jinn, what do you think of your brother?" Alett asked suddenly.

"It's like you are *trying* to get under my skin. It is working," Jinn retorted.

"Alright, time to play a game," Alett addressed the others. "Is Jinn annoyed because we're bugging him with questions, because he hates his brother and doesn't like talking about his family, or because he's secretly a changeling and doesn't know the answers?"

"Jinn, you would make this a lot easier for us if you'd just give us a straight answer," Lylia sighed. "Tell us *one* thing about yourself. That's all."

"I have no interest in talking about myself."

"Look, it's easy," Spira added. "I'm blind and can only see through the Plane of Light. My elder sister is named Justice and is an Inquisitor for the Church of Prima Luma, and it's cool as hell. Luthro, your turn."

"I'm, um… left-handed, like Master Gihon, and set to inherit the Corvid Athenaeum as the future Dirigent of Ravencroft, despite not being a Marleogne."

"And you're a nerd," Nora added with a snicker.

"I knew I should have put you on Mandus' team, you little punk," Luthro retorted and rubbed his temple. "You spend too much time with Mandus and not enough time with Jana. But… yes, I suppose I have an affinity for academics."

Jinn remained silent, refusing to indulge his allies.

"Jinn, we really don't want to have to do this. Please," Cari pleaded, drawing her whip. "Just one answer, or we have to fight. I don't want to fight you."

"I wouldn't want to fight me either," Jinn shrugged. "You're rank ten, I'm rank three. I'd destroy you."

"New game!" Alett exclaimed. "Would the fae know Jinn's rank?"

The room fell quiet as the group tried to decide if the information would suffice.

"We have a tendency to walk in formation," Nephvir commented. "High ranks in front, low ranks in back. Fae are rather intelligent, so they may have noticed this habit."

"Neph, if you think he's a fae, why are you still here?" Lylia asked gently. "Aren't you worried that he'll recognize you and report you to the Unseelie Court?"

"I do not think he is a fae," Nephvir replied. "He said the boy left. If he had been replaced with a fae, where would the real one be?"

"The boy did leave. I came back on my own," Jinn insisted.

"It is difficult to believe that a notoriously troublemaking spirit would leave us alone…" Lylia sighed under her breath. "I cannot deny, however, that Jinn does seem fairly normal."

"How about Jinn tells us a secret about himself? Something that there's absolutely no way a fae would know," Nora suggested.

"None of you know my secrets, and I intend to keep it that way," Jinn retorted. "I could say anything, and you'd be none the wiser."

"Wait, Nora might have a point," Alett realized.

The alchemists looked at Alett expectantly, urging him silently to continue his train of thought. The owl-boy stood up to address the room and eagerly began to reveal his epiphany. "Zander and I are experts at discerning truth from lies. You have to be, when you're close to our beloved and ever-so-mischevious queen. I know enough about Jinn to where if he were to say something personal, I'd be able to recognize his tells and cross-reference it with my knowledge of Zenluve's social constructs and history to determine if he's telling the truth, something only Jinn himself would know."

Nephvir chuckled quietly again. "That would work, I think."

"I will draw my blade against every one of you," Jinn growled.

"I thought you might say that," Alett said with a coy smile, rummaging through his satchel and producing a small vial. "Amobarbital sodium, mixed with a little bit of my dad's special techniques. One drop of this and you're spilling a lot more than just a single secret. Oh, and don't forget, I'm ranked above you, and you're not one to betray orders from a superior."

Jinn gritted his teeth, clearly uncomfortable by the position he'd been thrust into. As soon as his muscles tensed to leap up, Alett had already thrown a razor-wire bomb at his ally with lightning-fast reflexes, entangling the wolf zoa before he could react.

"I figured you'd try that," Alett crouched down, waving the vial in front of Jinn's face. "Last chance, buddy."

Jinn's face turned beet-red, the humiliation of defeat rising to his cheeks. His eyes darted around for a moment, before he finally sighed and relinquished his ego. Muttering under his breath so quietly that it was nearly impossible for an untrained ear to hear, Jinn murmured, "I had a crush on Edelein when we were kids. Briefly. Very briefly."

Alett pondered Jinn's words for a moment before his eyes lit up in delight. "Oh, Jinn, it is you! I never doubted you for a second."

"You absolutely doubted me, several times," Jinn replied. "Undo the wires now, Zwitet Alett."

"You're right. It's fun to mess with you, though," Alett snickered, pulling the razor-sharp cables free with his thick gloves.

"How could you tell it was him?" Luthro asked.

"As I mentioned, I cross-referenced what I know about Zenluve and about Jinn. None of us had mentioned Edelein by name since he had returned, so a fae wouldn't know her. Plus, Jinn and Eddie are the same age and grew up in similar circles as nobles, so the comment about being kids adds up. She's told me before that on two separate occasions, Jinn had openly disregarded her at galas when she tried to talk to him. From what I know about our Dritet, that seems like plausible behavior for handling his infatuation."

"The first time, yes. We were six years old. The second time she approached me, we were fourteen, and I had long since realized that she was an annoying rich brat who had no business being near someone like me," Jinn started, but cut himself off as he realized what Alett said. "Hold on, you said the fae wouldn't have known Edelein's name. Do you mean to tell me that I could have just told you her name and you would have realized that I was never a fae? Why the hell didn't you just do that?!"

"Because this was way more entertaining!" Alett laughed, dodging a thrust from Jinn's scabbard. "Come on, admit that it passed the time way better."

"I am never speaking to you again, Zwitet Alett," Jinn spat, cheeks flushed red.

"The more information you provided, the easier it was to assure your legitimacy," Luthro explained, offering a handful of dried meat to the wolf zoa as a peace offering. "Plus, there's no shame in admitting a childhood crush. I admire your bravery and cooperation, Dritet Jinn."

Jinn took the food with a swift swipe and a harsh glare.

Lylia placed gentle hands on his arm, healing the thin cuts left by Alett's razor wire. Jinn was silent, but seemed grateful for the relief from his stinging wounds as they closed.

"Alett, I must ask, where did you get the amobarbital sodium from? Did you synthesize it yourself?" Luthro wondered aloud as the group began to wind down for the night.

"It's made by synthesizing malonic acid with urea derivatives for a temporary sedative effect. Acquiring the derivatives isn't too hard," Alett replied.

"Why do you have it? Was it really for a makeshift truth potion?" Luthro continued. "Why would you have thought you needed such a thing?"

The sedative effect would decrease resistance and depress neurons firing, making the user more likely to answer questions truthfully by forcing him to suppress his inhibitions. Unethical, but effective, Luthro added silently.

"I didn't," Alett answered.

"What?"

"I didn't think I'd need amobarbital sodium."

"So why do you have it?"

"I don't."

Luthro sat in silence, eyebrows furrowed. "You lied?"

"Yeah, it was a bluff, or potentially a placebo if it came to that. I'm good at identifying if someone is telling the truth. That doesn't mean I have to tell the truth all the time myself. A little white lie had put everyone's doubts to rest, so it's no harm, no foul, right?"

"I suppose so," Luthro concluded after a long moment.

Lylia warmed her hands in front of the fire beside the two men as they chatted, lost in thought. The chill in the air, though banished by the fire, seemed to still cling to the walls around, leaving an unsettling feeling in the pit of Lylia's stomach.

"Alett," Lylia whispered after their conversation had died down. "Something isn't right. Why would that fae leave us alone? It isn't characteristic of a puca. The little things love mischief."

"Perhaps it was spooked from the oozes," Alett theorized. "We helped it, after all, so it wouldn't want to mess with us."

"They would still do it, though. Puca are the type to do so. Us helping them doesn't change anything. If I had to guess, I would hypothesize that helping one would make it *more* likely to follow along for fun."

"Is there a possibility that it wasn't a puca?" Alett asked.

"It was definitely a puca," Lylia confirmed. "The boy, Kow, was small with sleek black hair. Pucai tend to prefer changing into creatures with a similar composition, though they could hypothetically become anything. When they're in an animal form, they often shift to things such as ravens or black dogs."

Nephvir sat up suddenly, looking towards the direction the group had originally come from. "I hear something. Stay here, please, I'll be back in a moment."

"Is going anywhere alone ever a good idea?" Cari muttered.

"It is not, but he does it anyway," Lylia replied as Nephvir vanished into the shadows of the hallway unilluminated by firelight.

A quick moment later, the lean fellborn returned, awkwardly running a lavender-colored hand through his long black hair in embarrassment.

"Look, um, I apologize for leaving," Nephvir mumbled, sitting down by the fire and pulling out his pocket-sized notebook.

"You always run off at odd times, so it doesn't really surprise us anymore," Cari shrugged. "Did you find whatever you heard? You came back pretty fast."

"Heard? I didn't hear anything," Nephvir responded, confused.

Wariness rippled through the air around the group at Neph's

befuddled reply, Lylia's quiet explanation ringing clearly in their minds.

Pucai tend to prefer changing into smaller creatures with sleek black hair, said the voice in everyone's head as they looked over Nephvir's wiry frame, glossy dark bangs partially obscuring his face.

"Neph, tell us a secret," Lylia demanded.

"What? Is the campfire bringing out the team-bonding time?" Nephvir joked. "I'm not really interested in talking about myself."

Here we go again, the party all thought in dismay.

"Who is your mother?" Lylia asked.

"My mother? Why?" Nephvir grumbled, seeming to dislike the topic. "She's a jaded old woman who blames me for her problems, when my father is the one she should loathe. Former Tardonian missionary turned street beggar."

"Who is your father?"

"The lying Red Mantis assassin bastard who plane-shifted his way into my mother's bed, leaving her with nothing but a bastard shadow-plane devil of a fellborn. Which is me, before you ask. Are you done now?"

The Zengarde seemed to relax at Nephvir's disgruntled comments, his attitude lining up with his story.

"See, Jinn? That wasn't so hard," Alett teased.

Jinn growled in response, laying down and turning away.

"That still doesn't answer Neph claiming to hear something, and then immediately coming back and denying it. What did you see over there?" Cari pressed.

"Cari, I really don't know what you're talking about," Nephvir sighed. "I didn't hear anything, and there wasn't anything unusual in the hallway. I've been gone this whole time, for Ethereus' sake. I understand that I am a creature of shadow, capable of disappearing without a trace, but did you really not notice?"

Realization hit Cari at that moment. Looking around at her allies, she found similar expressions that indicated that the others had just put the truth together as well.

"This is the real Nephvir. The entire time we interrogated Jinn, the puca was sitting right next to him, learning everything about Jinn's mannerisms and sharing the only fact we will probably ever get him to share. The next time that thing shows up, it is going to be a *lot* more convincing," Lylia shuddered.

"Absolutely not. Run me through with my own sword and let the creature take my place if it comes back, because I am not telling you anything about myself ever again," Jinn refused, shaking his head.

"That's the spirit, Jinn," Alett sighed.

CHAPTER 3

AN ALLIANCE

Crackling fire met golden eyes as Solomon gazed into the flames, lost in thought as he passed a gold medallion between his fingers. Agares sat beside him, the campfire reflecting on his scales and illuminating him with a warm glow. Aim was preparing the campsite at Solomon's command, with no interest in engaging in conversation. Solomon sat in silence together with Agares for a minute before he finally spoke.

"Something feels odd about the swamp right now, Agares. It's annoying me. I caught wind of Gihon and the Zenluvians finally entering the territory, but they won't be able to catch up to me here. Why am I so frustrated about this?"

"The leyline is torn, that's my theory," Agares suggested. "You're commanding it to keep Gihon away from you, and Gihon's commanding it to bring him to you. It's a conflict of interest."

"I've got the crystals, though." Solomon countered. "In the event of two opposing medallions, the swamp has no choice but to side with the one with more leyline energy."

"You don't suppose the leyline has been angered by what we did to the Dweller, or do you?" Agares asked.

"The Dweller will be fine. It's licking its wounds in the Sea of Miracles right now," Solomon replied, producing a vial of deep red liquid. "We retrieved the water and the blood, so we'll be leaving tomorrow anyway. Assuming everything goes according to plan, Gihon and the others will be stuck here without even realizing that we've left. The swamp won't help them because they don't know what they're looking for."

"What if it–" Agares started, before a new voice interrupted them both.

"Ugh!" Allocer groaned, walking over to the fire and sitting on Solomon's lap. "I hate camping. I hate the swamp. This sucks."

"I've realized why I'm so annoyed. It's you," Solomon moaned in irritation. "I should have never made you."

"I don't understand why we can't just go kill them right now. You're so insistent on being discreet and evading them," Allocer whined as Solomon pushed her off, opting to sit on the splayed-out tail of his coat to keep herself off the ground.

"I told you, I need them both alive. The Zengarde, you can kill if you want to. But Edelein and Gihon stay alive."

"Why?" Allocer moaned, throwing her head back in dismay. "Once they figure out our plan, they're bound to catch up anyway."

"Because Gihon is essentially unkillable, and I need Edelein to ruin Gihon first to make him vulnerable."

"No one is unkillable."

"You don't know him. Us Marleognes were created with an exact purpose in mind: me, the unstoppable force, and him, the immovable object. Trust me, your venom arrays won't kill him. He is truly the only bigger pain in the ass than you."

"Master Solomon!" Kimaris called out, entering their camp as he returned from the murky woods ahead. "There's a phantasm up ahead. I have no idea how it got there. It's headed eastward at the moment."

"So? Go banish it," Solomon leaned back on his hands, uninterested.

The Dweller protects the thicket from phantasms. After the damage we did, it wouldn't be unheard of for a phantasm to get in.

"Aw, are you scared?" Allocer teased, leaning over and tracing her finger along his chest.

"Scared? I couldn't care less about the damn thing."

"So go get it, then, big boy."

"No, Allocer, Solomon is right," Kimaris admitted. "I could have banished it myself, and I should have. I just thought to report it to our leader. I trust Solomon to handle issues… but I'll go back."

"Kiss-ass," Allocer rolled her eyes as Solomon stood up, pulling his coat out from underneath her with a swift tug.

"You were right to trust me. Frankly, I'd like to see more of that from some of you." Solomon glanced down at Allocer, who was pouting up at him. "I'll go handle it, because I would like a moment of respite away from you all. You damn homunculi are a pain."

"You're a homunculus too…" muttered Allocer.

"Yeah, yeah. I know. But I'm better than you all," Solomon waved a hand, facing out into the darkness. "I'll be back in a bit, so don't go anywhere. That's an order. I'm looking at you specifically, Allocer. Don't move."

A red array glowed across Solomon's palm as a small flame sprung up from it, illuminating the swamp with a dim light as he worked his way through the mud in the direction Kimaris had returned from.

He said it's headed east, but why? There's nothing eastward… Ravencroft is north, and the heart of the leyline is southwest of here. Is it just rampaging in any direction? Solomon paused his thoughts in realization as his feet continued to trudge through the marshy ground. *Wait, Kimaris was right to get me for this. If the phantasm runs into any of Arvien's defenses like those careless oozes, it'll end up blighting a chunk of the entire swamp. With the medallion, I could get to it quicker and more safely.*

Solomon's other hand clutched onto the medallion as he walked, thinking, *Come on, bring me to this stupid thing before it's too late.*

The homunculus could feel what seemed to be the ground shifting underneath his feet, a familiar feeling for a native to the area as the swamp responded to the medallion. Dropping low to the ground, Solomon peered through the underbrush to lay eyes on the phantasm as it creeped noiselessly through the trees. The creature's head had no features, only a large eye in the center of its chest that glowed a dim violet as the inky black monster's long limbs worked through the thicket in silence.

An assassin shell, Solomon realized. *Entirely silent, virtually undetectable. Thank God for this medallion... at least Arvien was good for one thing. I never would have found it otherwise. It's prowling, though... after what?*

Following the path of the creature, Solomon's heart dropped in realization as a familiar blue-and-white figure perched in a tree, facing away with her bow over one shoulder as her tail swished back-and-forth.

This is a joke. You're joking. How the hell is Edelein here? The rest of the group is miles away. Did she come out this far on her own, in the middle of the night? Did the swamp move her closer to me? Is the leyline really not on my side? He wondered in dismay, gaze moving from her figure back to the assassin shell that was approaching. *Shit, I can't let this thing kill her. This is a conflict of interest. The best plan is to try to get the jump on the phantasm while it's focused on her and banish it quickly. If I distract it, she'll run back to the others and they'll find me.*

Solomon kept his center of gravity low as he approached from behind the phantasm, trying to catch up to it before it reached her. The creature stopped moving suddenly, the eye on its chest beginning to glow brighter.

No, no, no, no, no. Plan B, Solomon realized as he recognized the action. *It's going to snipe her. I need to get her out of here immediately or it will kill her..!*

Acting swiftly, Solomon leaped into the air, his feet pressing against an array in midair as it launched him forward. Hearing his movements, Edelein turned around to see Solomon barreling towards her through the air as his body collided with hers.

The lioness let out a yelp as a blast of energy whizzed past them, incinerating the bough she was crouched on as she tumbled into the mud, a large and heavy homunculus on top of her. Their eyes locked in a surprisingly mutual fear for a brief moment before Solomon slapped his hand over her mouth.

"Scream and we both die," he stated, keeping her pinned underneath him.

Edelein squirmed from under Solomon, trying to push him off.

"I'll let go of you, but you have to promise not to scream for help or try to bite me," Solomon growled as she continued to struggle. "Seriously, can you stop that? We're about to be killed right now if you don't quit it. That thing's got about fifteen seconds before it'll shoot again."

Edelein stopped moving, azure eyes quivering in fear as she looked at the man on top of her.

"I'm going to let go of you now, okay? It's very important that you don't make any loud noises. Nod if you understand."

The Queen nodded weakly as Solomon lifted his hand from

her mouth and helped her sit up, brushing some of the mud off of her back as she cleaned off her ears.

"Something about cats and feet, huh?" Solomon chuckled to himself.

"What is wrong with your family? It wasn't funny when Gihon said it, either."

"Gihon made the same joke? You mean, *Gihon* made a joke? My brother Gihon? Ethereus be damned, what have you done to him?"

Edelein huffed, ignoring him. "What are you doing so close to our camp? Is this another one of those clay things?"

"We can chat later. Stay low– ow!" Solomon began, before wincing in pain as Edelein grabbed at his wrist in the same way that Zander had done before. "No, I'm not clay! You're the one far from your camp. I think the swamp moved you away."

A second beam shot out suddenly from the darkness, Solomon summoning the Divine Sword in time to slash through and deflect the energy.

A phantasm?! Edelein realized silently. Staying low, the Queen pulled herself through the mud to where her bow was stuck, tugging on it until it dislodged. Frantically wiping it off, she uncovered the array that Gihon etched for her, sighing in relief when she realized the array was still intact.

"Solomon, why the hell is there a phantasm here? What did you do?" Edelein asked, drawing her bow. An arrow of light formed as the array activated, and she fired it into the darkness where the beam had shot from.

"You think *I* did this?" Solomon retorted, brandishing his sword.

"Quite frankly, yes!" Edelein hissed, charging another shot. "What other alchemist is stupid enough to cause a backlash in the middle of this wasteland? Also, the phantasm isn't making any sound, almost like it doesn't want my friends to know about it! You set me up!"

The phantasm charged forward, swiping large claws at Solomon. He deflected them, and the claws dissipated upon touching the sword. It reared back again, thrashing its head in silent agony. The eye on its chest began to glow as it charged another beam of energy, but Edelein stopped it in time with another light arrow.

"*Me*, stupid?" Solomon laughed, shaking his head as he deflected another beam. "I implore you to use your tiny little cat brain for a second. If I summoned it, why would I be fighting it? It's silent because it's an assassin shell, and again, you are not as close to your friends as you think you are!"

"Perhaps you're trying to win me over with your heroic acts, I don't know!" Edelein griped, annoyed. "Just use your magic sword and kill it, then!"

"I'm working on it!" Solomon snapped, rushing at the phantasm. It backed up as he approached, expertly dodging his slashes as if it were expecting them, before vanishing into the shadows. "I can't stand you, you know that?"

"Took the words right out of my mouth. How cute," Edelein rolled her eyes, pulling back another arrow.

"Assassin shells fight best when they are unseen. When it disappears like this, it could be circling anywhere around us as it prepares another strike. Stay behind me and cover my back," Solomon informed her, his sword at the ready to deflect another beam.

Edelein turned around, pressing her back to him as she tried to locate the beast.

"This way!" Edelein called out with a moment to spare as another beam shot towards them, Solomon twisting in front of her to deflect it as Edelein ducked around his side, firing a light arrow into the darkness.

"I heard the arrow hit," Edelein confirmed.

"We need to lure it out of the shadows. I can't banish it this way," Solomon instructed.

"I'm all ears, if you have an idea. It doesn't seem like you do, though."

"You are such a brat, has anyone ever told you?"

"Frequently, actually. It's wildly inappropriate for you to say, considering my status."

"Can't you track it? Aren't you supposed to be some kind of legendary hunter?"

"It is as you said; the assassin shell is clearly designed to be undetectable. I'm trying, but it's moving around us quickly and entirely without noise. It's– this way!" Edelein cried, turning around again and ducking behind Solomon before firing another quick shot.

A new voice rang out from behind them, both Edelein and Solomon turning around in unison at the sound.

"Master Solomon, look out! Incoming!"

Whizzing between them, a lance shot out at high speed, narrowly missing Solomon and Edelein as it launched forward and into the shadows. The creature stumbled in silent agony, and Edelein watched as the lance-wielding homunculus rushed past both of them, grabbing his lance out from the phantasm's body.

"Kimaris!" Solomon gasped as his servant pulled the lance out. Just as fast as he arrived, Kimaris was gone, disappearing into the night.

Solomon looked back at the direction Kimaris came from for a split second, baffled, but realized the situation at hand. Bright light began to glow from the shadows ahead of them as the phantasm began to thrash, the hole glowing a bright white and violet as light spilled out from it. Dispelling his sword, he ran towards the phantasm in a panic and pressed his hands against the hole as the creature continued to thrash in pain. An array formed underneath his hands against the shell of the phantasm as he continued to press his hands against it.

"Edelein, run!" Solomon screamed, turning to look at her over his shoulder. His eyes were filled with panic, genuine terror reflecting in his gaze as it locked onto hers. "Get out of here!"

Edelein was frozen in place, staring back at him in denial as she tried to process his words.

"Run!" He repeated as the light began to glow brighter, spilling through his fingers.

She turned, trying to run, but her feet would hardly move. It felt to her as if she was moving in nightmarish slow-motion, helpless. Edelein urged her feet to move, willing and begging for an escape as the mud dragged her down. Turning to look back, she saw Solomon desperately pressing his hands deeper into the phantasm, trying to contain the oncoming blight. The creature thrashed as the shell began to expand, inflating as darkness started to consume Solomon.

"Go!" He mustered, but it was too late. A flash overtook them, Edelein shutting her eyes tight as the sting of the reality shell pierced her body.

Edelein squinted as her gaze was met by a blinding, endless white. Solomon was collapsed on his knees in front of her, facing away as he banged his fist against what she presumed would be the ground.

"Dammit, dammit, dammit!" Solomon cursed, beating the ground beneath him in agony. He was yelling fully, seemingly unconcerned with being seen or heard anymore.

"Solomon, what happened? Are we dead?" Edelein asked, looking around in confusion.

"Worse. We're trapped. Permanently."

"What do you mean?"

"I *mean* we're stuck here, with no way out. I'm doomed to spend eternity with you."

"Where are we, exactly?" Edelein gasped, the air around them growing thicker and harder to breathe in.

Solomon sighed. "To put it simply, we're inside the phantasm."

"Inside the– what are you talking about?" Edelein's eyes widened, trying to wrap her head around Solomon's words. Solomon gestured for her to turn around, to which she gasped as she saw a wounded creature on the ground behind her. It was alien in appearance, in a way she could not find the words to describe, though rather sad-looking as it breathed heavily, laying on its side. It did not seem to acknowledge the two new residents of its void.

"That's the thing that attacked us? It appears to be dying…" her words trailed off as she eyed the creature, its heavy breathing becoming the only sound within the expansive nothingness.

"Look, cub, I'm not Gihon. I'm not going to sit here and explain how alchemy works to you. I have no urge to seduce you with my intelligence, unlike him," Solomon retorted, approaching the creature and placing a hand on it as an array lit up underneath its body.

A few moments later, the creature melted away into nothing as it was returned to the Sea of Miracles, and the air began to clear up again.

"It's okay to admit that you don't know something," Edelein prodded.

"You little… fine. Since I'm stuck here for eternity with you, I might as well get along with you. Sit down, I'll explain it," Solomon patted the ground next to him.

Edelein sat apprehensively, eyeing him. "I was going to say the same thing. There's a million others I'd rather be stuck here with than you, but the least we can do is try to not kill each other the entire time. Right?"

"Fine. Truce. For now. No promises that I won't try to kill you in a decade, or perhaps a year… maybe an hour."

"Tell me where we are, Solomon," Edelein demanded as Solomon groaned.

"I'm sure you know the basics about phantasms, right? A misstep in alchemy that draws in extraplanar energy, oftentimes creatures. It swaps a living being of ours with a living being of another plane, coating them in the reality shell to keep the matters from touching. That poor thing got dragged in by the backlash, coated in a reality shell, and set loose on a terrified rampage through our plane."

"Right. Gihon explained that much."

"And you know about blight, obviously, as you've lived through one."

"When the shell breaks, the energies mix, resulting in an explosion that drains life from its surroundings. I've got the gist of it."

"When Kimaris pierced the shell, the energy began to spill out. When I pressed my hands against it, the array I formed was an attempt to patch the hole enough to stop the explosion. However, you probably know that energy can neither be created nor destroyed. I stopped the energy from moving outwards, but by forcing it back inwards with nowhere to go, the phantasm imploded instead of exploded. The thing I didn't account for was the shell expanding to account for the explosive energy."

"So that's how it consumed us?"

"Pretty much. The phantasm as we would know it is not technically a phantasm anymore, but what alchemists call a reality sphere. The shell expanded to form the sphere, a bubble of alternate reality, which is what we are currently stuck in. There's no way out from the inside."

"But from the outside?"

"They can be broken from the outside, yes. However, that requires someone not only to have enough knowledge to do it properly, but also to find us. Need I remind you, we are currently in an endless labyrinth, far away from anyone."

"Oh, you're so dramatic!" Edelein laughed. "Gihon's going to find us. We're fine."

"Gihon isn't coming, you damn wench!" Solomon snapped. "You're expecting him to find an invisible bubble in an ever-changing, constantly moving giant swamp full of predators. We aren't technically on the material plane anymore, so I don't want to hear a damn peep about your Zengarde, either. They can't track you in here. Gihon's not some hero of legend, either, but a plain old zoa. He is not going to rescue you from this. It's like finding a microscopic, invisible needle in a haystack the size of a continent."

"You really believe we're stuck here, eternally damned? Nothing to be done, and only you to thank for bringing me here?"

"This wasn't my doing, you damn cat!" Solomon griped. "You should be thanking me for the fact that you're alive at all, even if my useless bastard of a brother is helpless to do anything about it."

Edelein sighed at his attitude. "Why is it that you hate Gihon so much? I thought siblings were supposed to love each other. Yet, I cannot decide which one of you despises the other more."

Solomon groaned, leaning back on his hands as he looked up into the endless void. "You want the tragic backstory, huh? Fine. We've got an eternity to kill. Close your eyes and I'll paint the picture."

The homunculus looked at her from the side of his eye as she stared back at him, unwavering.

"Or don't close them, I guess. You do you."

Edelein rolled her eyes before indulging him, closing her eyes as he began to speak.

"I don't know how much you already know, but Arvien, our master, created us to be her children. Cursed with infertility, Arvien devoted her life to the studies of alchemy. She did a number of horrible things within Ravencroft, but her strongest passion was creating artificial life. Drawn by her desire to be a mother, Arvien built her first kid: our eldest brother, Perath. He died not long after, so she made me. She created a little seven-year-old kid to follow her around, to learn from her, and yet… I was never enough.

I don't have a soul, which I'm certain you're aware of. Homunculi are artificially created humans, and you cannot artificially create a soul. Arvien programmed me to love her like a child loves his mother, and yet she could not offer me the same love in return, for I was incomplete in her eyes. As I grew older, Arvien began to see me as an apprentice rather than a son.

A few years later, she had taken to a little young raven from the local population. She would go out and feed the fledgeling daily, until one day she convinced it to follow her inside the Athenaeum. It never left her side after that. I always felt she loved that stupid raven on her shoulder more than me, and on one wretched day five years later, she proved me right.

I was seventeen when she made Gihon. The soul inside of that raven meant more to her than her own son, so in her wickedness she decided to make that raven another one of her children. When she transmuted him, he was a few years younger than me, a stupid little teenage bird boy, and yet she cherished him greater than anything.

Gihon took after Arvien better than I ever could. Following her around in a little suit and tie, drinking in her teachings, reveling in her affection. I was cast aside, worthless in her eyes. As little Gihon grew up, he became more of a punk, dyeing his hair and loosening his ties. As you've seen now, he's lost his ties entirely in favor of showing off his chest. You know how strong pectoral muscles are in birds? It's stupid. I hate him. I was created with the perfect form, and yet somehow everyone thinks he's better than me."

"Solomon…"

"I know, I know. Anyways, Gihon became the perfect child, the perfect apprentice, the perfect everything. He followed Arvien like a shadow, and she would praise his ability to pick up her techniques faster than I could. When she introduced him to the Bookkeeper instead of me, that was when I finally realized my place. Arvien had no interest in me. Gihon was inheriting a piece of the Black Armament, his stupid Fortress Black, and I got nothing. I was some old toy she was no longer interested in using. So… I left.

I heard a few years later that by some miracle, Arvien managed to conceive a child. A real one. I knew it would be a matter of time before Gihon became the old plaything like I did, and I was ecstatic to have someone to commiserate with about Arvien's questionable parenting skills. Not long after, I heard about her death.

I met with Gihon once more after her death, where he told me about Arvien's Hourglass. It turns out, the entire time, she was trading her lifeforce for knowledge, ever pursuing more and more. From the Bookkeeper she bartered an hourglass that would teach her the secrets of the universe at the expense of her own life, no stone left unturned. The more she learned, the more the sand would fall. As the hourglass reached its final granules, Arvien finally understood the gravity of her knowledge, taking it to her grave with her. She locked herself away to prevent herself from learning anything new, sending Gihon out in her stead. She traded those last few grains of sand to have her daughter, Hiddekel. Born of Arvien's true blood. Raising Hiddekel is what killed her. Arvien died doing what mattered most to her… loving someone that wasn't me.

I tried to point out the hypocrisy to Gihon, showing him that she chose the baby over him, trying to incite the rage in him that I had felt for all those years. Yet, he continued to side with Arvien, ever the steadfast one. Plus, he had some reasons to be upset with me, I'll admit."

"Because of Othalgar?" Edelein asked.

Solomon's face twisted. "He told you about Othalgar?"

The Queen nodded.

"Damn. Yeah, because of Othalgar. So we, uh… parted ways after that, accepting our differences. He still blames me for what happened there."

"So why are you trying to do it again?"

"What?" Solomon laughed, astonished. "I'm not doing another Othalgar. I know how to open the Gates this time. Well… I'm pretty sure I do."

"He's not going to let you."

Solomon gave a dry laugh. "Well, he can just come try and stop me, huh?"

"You know that if you try to open the Gates, you risk destroying Ravencroft the way you did to Othalgar, right?"

"I know the risks, princess. I've accounted for them. There's also the fact that using that much energy, regardless of if it works or not, brings the risk of a backlash just from sheer energy output alone. If I leave the Gates to open fully, it will probably blight everyone anyway. It's okay, I never really cared about this town. Since we're trapped for eternity, I might as well admit that I'm not even–"

"You really are a sociopath."

"I genuinely, literally, cannot feel empathy without a soul. Let me get one and maybe I'll pity those people one day. Maybe."

"I find it hard to believe that you are wholly incapable of

caring. You saved me back there, didn't you?"

"'Saved' is a strong word, considering you're trapped in here with me now."

"You tried to help me," Edelein looked at him curiously, Solomon avoiding eye contact as he stared at the ground. "There's a part of you that cares."

"I tried to save you because my idiot brother would destroy everything I've built if you died. Also, I have a personal motive for keeping you alive. You're going to make Gihon snap one day, and I want to see it happen."

"I would never hurt Gihon. I'm his ally."

"You're more than his ally," Solomon paused, looking at her confused expression. "No way, you still haven't realized it?

"What are you talking about? I won't let you speak poorly of him."

"Oh, so he's got you wrapped around his little finger too, is that it? You're just as smitten by him as he is by you. You little freaks," Solomon laughed.

Edelein's ears perked up, a rosy tint painting her cheeks. "Smitten?! You're disgusting, Solomon. I am a Queen, sworn to my duty, and I would never–"

"Is that why you've refused to take a husband?" Solomon questioned, and Edelein's eyes widened. "You're so sworn to duty, but you've refused the zoa transfiguration for years now. You know your Royal Court is waiting on your command to bring you your perfect lion king, and yet, you refuse them year after year. Is that a part of being sworn to duty? Or is it because you've wanted to find love on your own, being dictated by your little emotions?"

How does he know that? Edelein wondered.

"This is besides the point, Solomon," Edelein continued anxiously. "What do you mean by me being Gihon's downfall? I would never hurt him."

"Darling, you don't have to," Solomon laughed. "He will hurt himself over you. Gihon's never been in love. He's been devoted to work his whole life. He doesn't know how to care about someone the way he's begun to care about you. He's in uncharted territory, and it terrifies him. He's never been lost like that before. Because of you, he's become a little ball of nerves, and it's getting in the way of his work. It's hilarious. Therefore, I must keep the little Queen alive, so I can make Gihon more vulnerable."

"I think you're saying that to make yourself feel better, because you don't want to admit that you knew my death would hurt your brother. You don't need a soul to have a basic understanding of love, right? You said you were made to love Arvien, despite not having a soul."

"That's not a choice, though," Solomon countered, "not free will. That's programming. Being forced to love someone isn't truly loving them."

"But you know how it feels to care, and to be hurt. That's human. You're closer to the thing you so desperately yearn for than you even realize."

Solomon paused, gold eyes flitting up to meet Edelein's gentle gaze.

"You're… kind. You have the makings of a good leader," Solomon mumbled reluctantly, looking away again.

"See? You're not all bad, Solomon. Even though you're willing to kill thousands, you're doing it because you want to feel alive the way that others do. It's almost noble, if we overlook the criminal acts."

Solomon laughed, brushing a white lock of hair out of his face. "No, I'm definitely pretty bad. I'll admit to that."

Edelein chuckled, meeting his laughter. As silence fell between them, the air felt a little less awkward. After a moment, the Queen spoke up.

"Your homunculus, Kimaris. He showed up earlier and caused the shell to break. What was that all about?"

"Kimaris is a useless idiot," Solomon stated, annoyed. "He was probably the one who summoned the phantasm, showing up so he could try to cause a blight to kill you, not realizing it would have killed me too. Even though I've told him, *repeatedly*, to keep you alive. Sometimes homunculi get wretched ideas into their heads and go off on their own."

"Like wiping out cities to get a soul?"

"Yeah, like wiping out cities to get a soul. I told you, us homunculi are pretty bad. Surprisingly enough, Kimaris is one of the better ones."

"There's more? I mean, other than the crazy fire lady and the draekis with the clay?"

"Oh, there's plenty more. Aim is the 'crazy fire lady,' and to be honest, she scares me sometimes too. Agares, the draekis, is well behaved. The other woman is Allocer, and she's a damn firecracker, that one–"

"There was another one?"

Eyes widening slightly, Solomon realized at that moment that Edelein had never actually seen Allocer, stuck inside the walls of Fortress Black during their last bout. Gihon had stood alone atop the Fortress when he saw the clone, the other half of their group being the ones that fought her.

"Uh… no. Don't worry about it."

"How many homunculi have you made?"

"Seventy-two," Solomon admitted with an awkward chuckle. "Before I had the Verutian Order, I had to make my own followers. Most of them are either useless or dead. I kept my most loyal ones by my side. I even made one that looks like… no, never mind. I shouldn't tell you that story. That one goes to the grave with me."

"What are you talking about?"

"It's nothing. He's gone, anyway. Doesn't matter." Solomon looked away, eager to change the subject. "So, this void is really… empty, huh?"

"How long do you think it's been?" Edelein asked, looking around.

"It's impossible to tell. Time flows differently within reality bubbles such as this. A minute in here could be an hour outside. When weaponized, reality spheres can be highly dangerous… and efficient."

"We've been in here for at least twenty minutes, right? Does that mean it's really been upwards of a full day back home?"

"Quite possibly, though nothing is guaranteed. Could be longer, could be shorter. I told you, no one is coming for us. We're stuck in an invisible, untraceable bubble within an ever-changing labyrinth."

"It beats being alone, I guess," Edelein admitted.

Solomon hesitated, looking up. "Yeah, I guess it does beat being alone."

Silence fell between the two once more for a long moment.

"You know," Solomon started, looking over at her. "It's corny to say, but I wasn't always like this. I wasn't always Solomon."

"What do you mean?" Edelein asked.

"Solomon. It's… not my name. I changed my identity when I left the Athenaeum. I wanted to remove that stain from myself. My name, the one Arvien gave me, is Pishon."

"Why are you telling me this?"

"I don't know, honestly. No one has called me Pishon in years. It feels a bit foreign on my tongue now, but it's nice knowing that there's someone who knows who I used to be. Gihon hasn't called me Pishon since Othalgar. Actually, a little bit before Othalgar. Hiddekel and Perath aren't around to call me that, either. The four Marleogne siblings, all varying degrees of dead or useless."

"Do you want me to call you Pishon?"

"Nah, it's too weird at this point. I just… enjoy talking to you, almost. If we ever got out of here, I think we wouldn't be half bad as a team."

"Teaming up with you? I don't think so," Edelein chuckled.

"Think about it, Eddie," Solomon eagerly turned fully so he could face her head-on. "If you and Gihon stopped trying to get in my way, we could find a way to open the Gates and ensure everyone's safety. It's a compromise. Don't good guys make compromises?"

"There's too many risks to your plan, Solomon," Edelein sighed. "Helping you would make us accomplices. All I can do is try to convince you to not open the Gates."

"There wouldn't be as many risks if I didn't have to constantly work around you two getting in my way. We could do it. If you think about it, Gihon is to blame for the dangers, not me."

"I mean, diplomacy is my strong suit, as a Queen," Edelein admitted. "I would much rather find a solution that doesn't involve killing you, or anyone for that matter. However, my strong suit is in fact also very much *not* alchemy, so I would not be able to find said solutions. I'd need to talk to Gihon about it."

"Gihon's going to be a hard sell. He's pretty passionate about blindly hating me, if you haven't noticed. He doesn't exactly see me the way you do."

"And how is it that I see you?"

"Like a person," Solomon stated, his golden eyes meeting hers intensely. "I mean, I'm definitely a bit of a monster. He's honestly right for hating me. But it's nice to have someone believe in me without being programmed to do so. It's… nice."

"I think you're capable of doing good, Pishon."

"Good is a long shot," Solomon laughed. "I really do only care about myself, so doing good for others isn't exactly my goal."

"But you see it, though," Edelein nodded. "You see that you're selfish, which is the first step in growing and changing."

"Let's stick with mediocre at best, okay?" The homunculus sighed, looking forward into the void. "I'm not sure I'm ready to–"

A loud crash resonated around the void, interrupting Solomon as broken shards began to fall between and around the two. Turning towards the noise, Solomon's inquisitive gold eyes looked up to meet the burning glare of Gihon's, his face twisted in rage as he crashed down through the edge of the reality sphere. Shards of the sphere's casing scattered around them as Gihon landed on the ground in front of Solomon, golden eyes ablaze in an anger never before seen from the man. The Dirigent's skin was stained with red blotches, blood-soaked bandages around his chest that were visible through a loose white shirt.

Fuelled by wrath, Gihon gritted his teeth, launching himself at his brother with fists ready, letting a raging scream rip from his throat. "*SOLOMON!*"

Gihon's eyes burned mercilessly as he launched himself at his brother. Solomon, taken aback by Gihon's emotional outburst, leapt to his feet, narrowly dodging Gihon's grab.

"I have had enough of your *bullshit*, Solomon," Gihon spat, gritting his teeth as he went in for a heavy punch. "Enough games, enough toying around. I'm ending you. Right. Now."

"Gihon, wait!" Edelein cried out, running towards them.

Her words fell on deaf ears as Zander grabbed onto her shoulders, stopping her. He turned Edelein around to face him, hands clasped tightly onto her as he looked her over.

"My Queen, are you hurt? Did he hurt you?" Zander asked, checking her for injuries.

Edelein struggled against his grasp. “Zander, let go. Gihon’s going to kill Solomon.”

Confused, Zander looked behind her, where Gihon and Solomon were exchanging blows. Gihon’s attacks were forceful and filled with hatred, while Solomon found himself dodging more than usual and only returning hits in defense. “Yes, Your Majesty… that’s the point.”

“No, you don’t understand!” Edelein cried out, pushing Zander off of her. “Solomon didn’t do this! He was stuck in here with me, by accident!”

“With all due respect, Your Majesty, you did not witness what we have seen. There was a bit of an… *incident* back at the camp. All of this was a setup. Solomon planned for this to happen, that is for certain.”

“I… what? No way. He didn’t,” Edelein shook her head, confused. Turning to face the battle in front of them, her eyes met Solomon’s. He had a look of panic on his face as he dodged blows from Gihon, his eyes briefly flashing to meet hers.

“Edelein, get your pet bird off of me!” Solomon yelled over to her, frustrated. “Tell him that I didn’t do this!”

“I don’t care what you did or didn’t do. All I know is that I’m done messing around. If you hurt a single hair on her head, I swear to God–” Gihon growled, lunging at him.

Solomon backed away from Gihon’s lunge, summoning a cloudstep array underneath his feet as he stepped up into the air to avoid the attack. As Solomon stepped higher, a pressure tightened around his ankle. Looking down, Solomon noticed the cold glint of metal as a manacle fastened to his leg, a chain running down to an array on Gihon’s hand. Gihon held tight to the other end of the chain, a cold smirk on his lips as he pulled Solomon down into the ground.

Shards of the reality sphere cracked and flung upwards

from the momentum of Solomon's landing, breaking the ground underneath him and revealing the wet, muddy swampland once more as the reality sphere began to break down all around them. Looking around, Solomon's usual demeanor returned once more.

"Fine, Gihon. You want to fight? We can fight."

A large array glowed underneath their feet, heat rising from below them. Steam rose and clouded the area as water from the swamp bubbled and evaporated, temperatures rising rapidly around them.

Taking in the damage, Zander acted quickly, scooping his Queen up into his arms and ignoring her protests. He winced as the ground burned his feet, hot vapor singeing his skin as it seeped through his shoes and uniform.

"Zander, stop it! We have to stop them. Put me down!" Edelein protested. "That's an order!"

"I must act in the best interests of my Queen. I'm sorry, Edelein, but it's too dangerous to stay here. I'm bringing you back to camp. Gihon will figure this out. The ground is hot, so I will carry you until it is safe," Zander stated, nodding briefly to Gihon before dashing out of the battle, Queen in his arms.

Gihon cursed under his breath as the temperature rose, dropping the chain array on Solomon in favor of his bulwark, protecting his body from the boiling steam surrounding him.

Frustrated, Gihon darted out of the steaming area, dropping his bulwark. Reaching back to initiate another array on his cloak, the fabric split in two as it formed black wings, lifting the dirigent into the air. His eyes narrowed as he searched through the white steam for Solomon.

On the opposite side of the area, a puff of steam shot out from one end, following the momentum of the homunculus as Solomon darted away.

"There you are, little rat," Gihon growled, using his

wings to propel him quickly into the ground. He landed on top of Solomon, who quickly turned to face him in time to be pinned with his back to the ground.

Gihon grabbed Solomon's throat, crushing his windpipe for a moment as Solomon's hands clawed for a grip on Gihon's wrist. Connecting with his forearm, Solomon summoned another fire array, heating up his hands to scald the skin of his brother.

The dirigent sucked air through his teeth, wincing from the pain and diverting his body's energy to protect the skin of his arms. Sensing the grip loosen as his energy was diverted, Solomon wriggled free of Gihon's grasp and leapt to his feet.

"You know, we could talk this out!" Solomon rubbed his neck, coughing.

"I'm done talking," Gihon stood, his aura cold and menacing.

"Man, what's gotten into you?" Solomon asked, backing up. His back met a pillar behind him, which he recognized as one of the walls of Fortress Black. The brief distraction was all Gihon needed to strike, grabbing Solomon's arm and wrapping it in his cloak. Gihon held tightly to the other side of the cloak, wrapped around his own arm as an array began to glow. The soft fabric grew stiff and heavy as metal, locking both men's arms together, their faces and bodies uncomfortably close. The smell of his brother's seething hatred burned Solomon's nostrils.

"Fight like a man, Solomon," Gihon demanded, his legs sinking slightly into the ground as he locked himself in place.

Solomon tugged against him, but Gihon stood strong, refusing to budge.

"No more running," Gihon growled, throwing a punch with his free hand.

The punch connected solidly with Solomon's jaw, a sick crack resonating as Solomon recoiled. Gihon punched heavily into

Solomon's midsection before throwing an elbow into his nose. Taking the hits, Solomon coughed, spitting some blood from a split lip.

"Just leave me alone!" Solomon spat as Gihon pulled back another punch. An array began to glow from the ground beneath them, Solomon forcing a small geyser to shoot up between them. As the water caught Gihon's free arm, Solomon froze it, locking Gihon in place.

Wasting no time as Gihon began to struggle against the ice, Solomon placed his free hand on the cloak binding their arms, muttering to himself as he began to undo the transmutation.

"Come on, come on, come on…" Solomon muttered under his breath as the heavy, solid metal cage began to form back into fabric.

A sudden force lurched as Solomon was yanked forward, face crashing directly into the ice. Gihon had stepped back with a swift tug, eyes as cold as the ice encasing his arm. Cracks webbed through the ice from the collision, weakening it enough for Gihon to pull backwards and free himself.

Gihon slammed his fist down into Solomon's head with enough force to break the partially-transmuted cloak between them. The powerful hit sent the homunculus tumbling far backwards into the mud, winded.

Never more grateful to be punched, Solomon realized the distance between himself and Gihon and quickly scrambled to his feet, battered and bruised as he darted off into the darkness.

"Get back here, Solomon!" Gihon started to run forward, but a hand on his shoulder made him pause. He turned to see Zander, who had returned after escorting Edelein back to camp. Zander shook his head.

"It's no use chasing him through this land. I can feel it moving… he is long gone by now. Right now, Edelein needs you.

She's a bit shaken up."

"Of course she is, she was trapped in a reality sphere with Solomon."

"No, Gihon," Zander closed his eyes, processing. "She's shaken up by *you*."

CHAPTER 4

RAGE

A calm silence soothed the nighttime air around the camp, amphibian croaking and the chirping of crickets were all too familiar to Dirigent Gihon as he settled into the cot in his tent. The quiet gentleman was still dressed in a loose white shirt and black pants, knowing that he would eventually be awoken for his turn on watch. Propped up with an old book in hand, Gihon allowed himself the luxury of relaxing slightly, eyes wandering across the pages in the dim glow of an oil lamp as one gloved finger absentmindedly traced the leather binding.

Losing himself within the pages of yet another alchemical study, the Dirigent ignored the ticking hands of his pocket watch as time continued to slip away, the night growing deeper around him.

A quiet rustling of fabric alerted Gihon, snapping himself out of his trance and turning towards the noise. In front of him, he could barely make out Edelein's silhouette at the entrance of the tent, illuminated by the gentle, flickering light of his lantern.

Oh, the hours must have escaped me, Gihon thought to himself before addressing her.

"Good evening, Your Majesty. Would you like me to take the next watch?"

"Yes, it's your turn. Thank goodness you were… already awake," Edelein smiled a little bit, looking him over.

"That I am. I had planned to read a little before getting some sleep, but I suppose the time passed a bit faster than I expected," Gihon held the book up, signaling sheepishly to her his usual favorite pastime.

"I'm glad you were, actually," As Edelein stepped closer to him, he noticed that she was already in her nightgown, her curves partially visible through it against the low light behind her. The lioness approached quietly, sitting down on his cot.

Gihon looked at her curiously, setting his book down. "Is there something you'd like to discuss with me?"

"There is, and I figure now would be as good of a time as ever, since we have a moment… *alone,* if you know what I mean," she replied, honey dripping from her words as she turned to face him, her eyes exploring his body curiously.

Climbing closer to him, Edelein placed one hand on his chest, tracing idle patterns into his clothes. Moving her hand slowly, she slid one hand under his open collar, fingers grazing his collarbone and moving down to reach his chest. Edelein pulled herself closer to him, Gihon's eyes darting downwards briefly towards her cleavage that revealed itself from underneath the loose nightgown. His breath caught in his chest, blood rushing to his face and tinting his cheeks red as he looked up to meet her eyes, an inch away from his.

Edelein was straddling his hips, tail swishing eagerly as she caressed his face in her hand, one thumb rubbing his cheek gently as she toyed with the feathers behind his ear. Gihon found his hands wandering to her waist as she pressed her chest to his, their bated breath electrifying the air around them.

The moment Gihon leaned forward to meet her lips, she pulled away with a sly smirk.

"Do you know how badly I've wanted this?" Edelein asked, one thumb on his chin.

Gihon's breath was shallow and eager, though he tried to contain it. His chest was burning and aching in a way he had come to find familiar, almost as if there was something inside of him fighting to be freed.

"I should have told you this sooner, Edelein, I–"

"Edelein?" She laughed, sliding her hand from his chin to the back of his head, playing with his hair.

"Sorry, Eddie, I wasn't sure if you wanted me to call you that. This is all quite, ah, new to me. Forgive me."

"Try again."

Her other hand slid to her thigh, pulling up the hem of her nightgown. He tried to look down as his eyes followed her hand, traveling up her thigh, but she playfully pulled on his hair, keeping his gaze locked on her own.

"Ah-ah, no peeking," Edelein tutted softly, holding his focus. "It'll ruin the surprise. Now try my name again."

"Darling," Gihon whispered, the word feeling foreign on his lips as the hand on her thigh began to trace up his back.

"Good boy. I like that one more than Edelein," she chuckled, leaning into his ear as she whispered, "My name is Allocer, by the way. You should remember it next time, handsome."

Gihon's eyes widened in alarm, but the girl on his lap was fast, digging her blade into his upper back with a cruel laugh. The knife sliced upwards to the nape of his neck as he shoved her away. Gihon grunted in pain, his blood spilling down onto his cot and the ground underneath.

Allocer laughed, laying on the ground. Gihon approached her with a burning anger, his array glowing from his hand for a moment before it faltered and sputtered out, more blood pouring from the wound on his back.

"Good luck with that. You know you can't use your energy with a wound like that. Or a wound like this," Allocer replied. She waved a hand, and an array appeared on his chest where she had been tracing her finger earlier.

She was tracing an array onto me? Gihon realized, looking down. *I didn't even notice. What's wrong with me?*

His thoughts were cut short by a sudden stabbing pain in his chest, doubling him over. On his chest, black veins began to spread from the array over his heart.

Allocer stood to her feet casually as Gihon keeled over in pain.

"You're not immune to poison, silly boy. They told me it would take a lot to bring someone like you down, with how… *solid* you are. Yet, I don't think it took much at all."

She's going for my heart, which means she doesn't know about the contract. Still, this is a problem.

Thinking quickly, Gihon activated a bulwark on himself, feeling his body grow solid as bioalchemy reinforced his fibers and slowed the poison. Allocer's face dropped, noticing as the bleeding stopped behind him. Straightening up and cracking his neck, he stepped towards his enemy.

"You're a disgrace to her name, you know that?" He growled.

"Aw, did I upset you? I thought we were just playing," Allocer teased, backing up to maintain distance between them. As she stepped back, the light of Gihon's lantern illuminated her face more clearly, revealing to him that although she was a near-perfect replica of Edelein, she lacked the Queen's iconic highlights down the right side of her hair.

"You are wearing her clothing. Tell me where Edelein is, and I'll make your death quick and painless."

Laughing, Allocer shrugged, darting out of his tent and into the thickets surrounding the camp. Gihon pursued her, dropping his bulwark to summon a wall of the Fortress, trapping her in. As he did, the bleeding resumed on his back and the burning pain of Allocer's venom returned on its journey through his veins.

Cursing, Gihon dropped the wall and returned to his bulwark.

I suppose I will have to maintain the bulwark array to stop the poison for now, until I can undo her array, Gihon thought.

The wall, though for a moment, slowed Allocer enough for Gihon to catch up. She turned to flee as the wall crumbled down, but Gihon grabbed onto her tail as she let out a pained yelp. He spun her around, grabbing her by the neck.

"Where is Edelein?" he repeated.

"Don't… know!" Allocer choked out against his grip, clawing feebly at his tough skin. "Probably… dead… Solomon… found her."

"What do you mean Solomon found her? Where is she?!" Gihon screamed in her face as she flinched.

"Gihon, what the hell is going on?! Who is that?"

Gihon turned his head to the voice as Zander approached in a hurry, weapons at the ready. He stopped to quickly eye Allocer up and down for a moment Thorne and Everett followed after. The Ehret seemed hesitant to attack, his eyes betraying his senses, though his stance remained low and his eyes narrow.

"That's Edelein's clothing, I can smell her. But that's not Edelein."

"Long story, but you're right. I'll explain later."

Taking advantage of the distraction, Allocer planted a knee

into Gihon's groin, loosening his grip enough for her to break free. The bulwark reduced any severe damage, but the shock was enough for her to slip away from his grasp.

"Chase after me all you want, but the longer you spend with me, the more likely Solomon finishes the job and takes out your girlfriend. Her life, or mine?" A maniacal cackle sounded from the clone as she vanished into the trees, silence falling over the swamp once more.

The moment Allocer disappeared, Gihon dropped to his knees, weakened from the poison. Zander knelt down next to him in concern.

"Zander, get… Jana. There is a lot of poison in my body that I'm slowing, and a wound on my back that needs to be bandaged before I bleed out."

Looking up, Gihon realized Zander was already gone.

I'm going to assume he went to get Jana and isn't leaving me to die so he can find Edelein. Actually, it's very possible it's the latter of those choices. I'm done for.

"So… Edelein's gone crazy and is stabbing people now?" Thorne asked flatly.

"That's the lady I told you about from the other day," Everett replied, concerned as he crouched down by Gihon. "She stabbed Alett, too."

Gihon looked up with a glance that said *not now, you two*.

"Go after her, Thorne. Take Mandus. He has a medallion. Everett, stay here and keep watch with Jana," the Dirigent ordered.

Thorne nodded, backtracking to the camp to retrieve his ally and set out.

Slowing his breathing, Gihon focused on maintaining his bulwark until footsteps brought his mind back to his surroundings. Zander had returned, Jana following behind him with a full bag in her arms. Gasping in horror, she dropped the bag by Gihon and sat next to him, rummaging through it.

"Jana, there's a venom array on my chest right now. The bulwark is slowing the poison and stopping my bleeding, so I cannot drop it to undo the array. Please undo the array first and then provide an antidote, if you have one," Gihon instructed with a wince.

Jana nodded, pulling Gihon's shirt off. Exposing his heaving chest, she grimaced at the black veins blooming out across his torso. Gihon breathed heavily and slowly, eyebrows furrowed. Jana looked near tears as she placed her hands on his chest, touching the array. Shakily, she reversed the array and the black veins began to slowly fade.

"Fortunately, it's a common venom array, so I can fix it," Jana sighed, reaching into her bag for an antidote. "The chemical composition of a venom array is nearly identical to a cottonmouth's venom, so I have those on hand already, considering our location."

Producing a vial from her bag, she popped the cork open and held it to Gihon's lips, her master gladly taking the antidote. When the vial was emptied, she began to rummage through the bag again hastily.

"I have health potions and bandages for your back. Master Gihon, what happened to you? This isn't like you, taking so many hits like this."

"I was… distracted," Gihon coughed, cheeks flushing a bit as he recalled the events of the night.

Jana eyed her teacher curiously, though the man seemed to have no interest in elaborating.

"She told me her name is Allocer," Gihon winced. "Everett said she's the one who attacked you at the house and hurt Alett."

Jana handed him a health potion, sitting behind him to bandage up his back. She looked horrified by the state of his body, eyeing the wound.

"The cut is really deep. If you hadn't bulwarked yourself, you would have bled out by now," Jana commented, Gihon nodding in agreement as he drank the potion.

It wouldn't have killed me, but damn, it hurt worse than anything I've felt in years.

"I let my guard down. It won't happen again," Gihon sighed, frustrated. "There's a more important issue at hand, though. Something's happened to Edelein. Solomon's homunculus was here wearing her clothing, and mentioned that Solomon 'found' Edelein. It's likely she had a run-in with him during her patrol."

"She was patrolling alone?" Zander hissed. "Why did you let her go alone, you idiot? In this cursed land, of all places?"

"She has the medallion, so the swamp is safe to her. I didn't realize Solomon would be following us here, too. We're supposed to be the ones chasing him down."

"I… cannot get into this with you right now," Zander turned, crouching down to investigate the area around him. Turning to Gihon in alarm, he continued, "There's no sign of her anywhere."

"What do you mean?" Gihon challenged. "She said you have the best Seventh Sense of anyone in history. How can you not find your own Queen?"

Snapping in anger, Zander snarled, "Were we within the Deepwood, she would be home by now. This land does not speak to me, it closes me out. The leyline is suffocated by your master's work. She is outside of my current range, which means she is either *incredibly* far away, or has vanished entirely."

"Vanished? That's impossible. Unless… no, Solomon isn't stupid enough to… actually, he very well could be. Zander, do you know if your Seventh Sense could reach into other planes if you were to focus it enough?"

"You mean to tell me my Queen is not currently on Tevus?"

"Possibly. If she is still alive, she may be trapped within

a reality sphere. If anyone is stupid enough to weaponize a reality sphere, it would be Solomon."

"She is alive, of that I am certain," Zander crossed his arms.

"How do you know?" Gihon asked.

"I know," Zander stated bluntly. "If she died, I would feel it."

Not willing to argue, Gihon relented silently.

Sitting down, Zander pressed his hands into the ground, eyes closed. His ears swiveled around in every direction, drinking in his surroundings in silence.

Quietly, Gihon turned to Jana. "Jana, let me borrow your medallion. Zander and I will go search for the Queen. I need you back at camp in case she comes back on her own, to explain to her what happened if the rest of us are not present. Everett will stay with you. Even without your medallion, you should be fine at the campsite. You have enough know-how to ward Ravencroft's protections off."

"Yes, sir," Jana nodded, pulling her medallion out of her pocket, handing it to Gihon.

"Hush," Zander commanded, one ear swiveling backwards towards the others.

Jana stood silently, bowing as she took her bag and turned around, heading back to the campsite.

As Zander continued to hone his Seventh Sense in on trying to locate Edelein, Gihon took a moment to process the situation at hand.

Solomon created that disgraceful homunculus clone of Edelein just to mess with us, to distract me long enough to sneak in so he could take the real one. But what does he want with her? If Zander's right, he hasn't killed her yet. He's either toying with her before killing her, or he needs her alive for some reason. Either way,

I need to find them. Fast.

Looking at Zander who sat facing away, Gihon continued in his thoughts.

A reality sphere… It's almost a brilliant concept. They're entirely untraceable. Because the swamp is constantly shifting and moving, it would be essentially impossible to locate. But why trap her in one rather than simply killing her? Does he need her alive?

Gihon clenched his fists, anger boiling up in his veins.

How dare he sully her image? Worse, sending her to my quarters like that… I feel disgusting, filthy. All of that just so he can take the real one from under my nose. He is dead the second I see him again. I'll kill that evil, soulless, good-for-nothing–!

Gihon was pulled out of his thoughts by Zander suddenly springing to his feet, ears twitching.

"Gihon, I see her!"

The Dirigent stood to his feet, feeling the seething hatred within him as his imagination raced ahead with thoughts of what Solomon's intentions would be.

"She is here, but not, like you said," Zander darted off into the swamp, Gihon chasing after him. "There is a faint trace of her presence this way, though it feels muffled, suppressed. Like an echo of her."

It must be a reality sphere, then. She's stuck in a different plane.

"Zander, when we find her, I need you to take her back to camp immediately. I don't want her to see what's coming."

"I can feel your intentions radiating from you. You'll kill your own brother for what he's done."

"I've wanted to for long enough, but yes. I won't let him get away with hurting her. This ends tonight, for good. I'm done."

"Good. You're understanding the hearts of the Zenluvians," Zander huffed.

Gihon stopped in his tracks, Zander noticing and following suit. In front of them, it appeared that the thicket continued on, but as Gihon approached and reached a hand out, his palm pressed against an invisible force.

"This is it. A reality sphere, as expected."

"I can feel her within it." Zander affirmed.

"She's alive, though, right?" Gihon asked. "Oftentimes a reality sphere contains energy from other planes, and the air within can be hard or even impossible to breathe in unless the original source is banished, but I'm not sure she would know to do that. Breaking it could cause a blight event, like a phantasm."

"She's alive," Zander repeated, drawing his weapons.

Feeling the shell, Gihon focused in on the energy.

"The energy inside of it feels like the material plane, so I think it's alright. Solomon planned for this, to keep her alive inside of it," Gihon realized. Balling his hand into a fist, Gihon gritted his teeth, angrily banging his fist into the shell.

"Zander, I'm going in first. That way, if it does blight, you will be spared. One of us has to stay alive to tell the others. Got it?"

Clearly displeased with the idea, Zander nodded silently, backing up into the woods behind them.

Facing the shell once more, Gihon growled, "Solomon, you're dead when I catch you."

"She's scared of you," Zander repeated, Gihon looking at him in bewilderment as his thoughts caught up to the present once more.

"Me?"

"I don't know what Solomon said or did to her, but she seems different. Not physically, but emotionally. Regardless, you let your emotions control you. I want to crush Solomon as well, but emotion will only interfere. Hatred is just as dangerous to you as any blade," Zander turned, walking back in the direction of the camp.

Following him, Gihon asked, "You are possibly the angriest person I have met. Some hypocrisy, I may say, is it not?"

Glancing over his shoulder briefly, Zander's bright green eyes locked with Gihon as he huffed, "I am not *that* enraged, not like you. I also know how to contain my emotions within the battlefield."

Sighing, Gihon shook his head. "Perhaps you are right. Solomon has been in my head lately. I am not thinking clearly. That Allocer girl is a truly wretched creation of his. A new low."

"Is it Solomon that plagues your mind?" Zander questioned flatly. "Or Allocer?"

"It's both. They're one in the same. I just want them dead," Gihon clenched his teeth, frustrated. "We need to stop Solomon from opening the Gates."

"I will quite enjoy bringing my blade to their throats." Zander agreed, before turning forward again and continuing on in silence.

As the firelight of the camp ahead came into view, Gihon found the Queen wrapped in a blanket by the fire, trembling as she stared directly into the flames. Mandus was sitting with her, his bright smile an indicator that he was trying to take her mind off of the events. Everett and Jana were still awake, seeming a bit on edge as they cautiously inspected the woods around them. Thorne was not outside with the others, but Mandus' presence showed Gihon that the Fuuntet would likely be in his tent.

Gihon's feet began to move faster than his mind, carrying

him quickly towards the fire. He dropped down to where Edelein was sitting, pulling her into his arms and holding her tight. She tensed up, caught off guard by his actions. After a moment, the Dirigent pulled away, looking over her. In his mind, he found himself suddenly acutely aware of her body, chest and curves illuminated by the warm firelight. He sat back, one hand clasped on her shoulder as a blush tinged his cheeks.

"Are you hurt?" Gihon asked, glancing over her. "Did Solomon hurt you?"

"Solomon didn't touch me," Edelein stated, casting a harsh look at Gihon as he repeated the concerns Zander had already long-since fretted over. "But what the hell were you thinking, attacking him so brutally like that?"

"He's our enemy, Edelein. We've been trying to stop him this entire time," Gihon defended.

"He wasn't even fighting you back!" Edelein yelled, upset.

"He's been doing nothing but fighting us for the last week!" Gihon replied, frustration bubbling in his chest once more.

"Solomon isn't who you think he is."

"Of course he is. Did you forget what happened to Everett? He almost killed your own Zengarde. Would you still forgive him if Everett died?"

"I–" Edelein stopped, unable to deny Gihon's claim. She looked away, staring into the fire again.

"Solomon trapped you in a reality sphere. If it weren't for Zander's Seventh Sense, you'd still be there. Don't you understand that?"

"That's what I'm trying to tell you, Gihon!" Edelein hissed in frustration. "Solomon didn't do that! He was stuck too!"

"Of course he did. He sent one of his homunculi to attack the camp at the same time."

"You don't get it. It wasn't Solomon. It was his

homunculus, Kimaris! The lancer!"

"Ah, of course," Gihon sighed sarcastically, "it wasn't Solomon, just the creature he created to blindly obey him, acting out on its own."

"Yes!" Edelein snapped, ignoring his tone. "Kimaris acted out on his own. He almost killed Solomon. Solomon ordered him not to kill me, but Kimaris summoned a phantasm and tried to blight it to kill us both. Solomon is the one who stopped the blight from happening."

"Homunculi don't act out on their own." Gihon stated.

"Solomon did, the first time he tried to summon the Gates. Othalgar. Maybe he gives his homunculi free will, to make them feel more human."

This time, Gihon paused, drinking in what she said.

"When Kimaris broke the reality shell, Solomon covered the hole and told me to run, but I couldn't. The phantasm imploded and pulled us both into the reality sphere. He wanted me to escape. He saved me."

Gihon remained silent, looking at her. After a beat, he clarified, "He saved you?"

"Yeah, I suppose it runs in your family, huh?"

A tense silence fell between them as they stared at each other. Gihon's eyes wavered, his mind racing.

Breaking the silence, Edelein continued. "Anyways, we didn't think we'd be able to get out, so we… talked."

"You *talked*? With Solomon?"

"Yes, when you think you're doomed to eternity with someone, the least we could do is be amicable with each other, you know? He told me about Arvien, and about you."

"Don't listen to a word he says about Arvien. He's blinded by his hatred, and sees her differently than she ever was. I'll also encourage you to forget anything he said about me."

Edelein laughed dryly. “I thought it was kind of cute, the way he described you.”

“He hates me.”

“Hatred and love are two sides of the same coin. The fact that his feelings are so strong for you is a good thing. You know, I think you and Solomon are more similar than either of you realize.”

Gihon sighed, defeated. “Please don’t say that. I’m nothing like him.”

“You did nearly beat him to death with your bare hands earlier, need I remind you. You looked like a villain for a moment, there.”

“I apologize, Edelein,” Gihon’s gaze softened. “I didn’t want you to see that.”

“Are you sorry for being so ruthless, or for the fact that I witnessed it?”

“Because you witnessed it, to be honest,” Gihon admitted.

“Gihon!” Mandus shot him a warning glance. The student’s eyes screamed ‘*wrong answer!*’ as he put an assuring hand on Edelein’s shoulder.

Letting out a tense exhale, Gihon corrected himself. “Perhaps I could have been less… brutal… with my actions. I’m sorry.”

Am I really apologizing for trying to kill someone that’s been trying to kill us? I don’t understand this at all, Gihon thought, glancing at Mandus. Mandus looked back with an affirming nod and a warm smile, giving him a silent thumbs-up behind Edelein’s back.

Zander approached and sat down next to Edelein. She leaned on him, comforted by the familiar scent of her old friend.

“You need to sleep,” he advised, taking her gloved hands and helping her to her feet. “There’s not long until morning, and once the sun rises our hunt resumes. You’ve been up all night, and your exhaustion is palpable.”

Edelein nodded, fatigue beginning to collapse in on her mind and consume her body. Zander helped her to her tent, leaning in to murmur to her once they were out of earshot.

"I don't know what happened to you, but Solomon is our enemy. He has our leyline crystals, and plans to use them for evil. If Nalo finds out, we may lose the favor of the Deepwood. There's a lot more at stake than your feelings, Edelein."

"I know," Edelein sighed. "I just cannot help but think that perhaps the situation is not entirely black and white. He's still wrong, but not… not evil."

"He's evil, Edelein. Gihon has not shared what we witnessed during your absence, and I believe that he should be the one to tell you. When he's realized it, he will tell you, and you will understand. Hopefully that time comes before you find out for yourself."

"Find out what? What did you see?"

Zander shook his head, stopping in front of her tent. "Rest, Your Majesty. Gihon will tell you tomorrow."

As golden rays of sunshine lit up the clear sky above, the camp was already alive with quiet chatter as the Zengarde prepared their bags to continue on their journey. Edelein's tent was among the few that remained upright, a weary-looking Zander sitting outside of its entrance, eyes closed. Gihon approached quietly, but his light footsteps were still enough to rouse the Ehret, who stared up at him silently.

"Have you been out here all night?" Gihon asked, and Zander nodded.

"Have you slept?" he continued, as Zander shook his head.

"I let my guard down and almost lost her," Zander stood to face Gihon, addressing him with an exhausted salute. "Not again. I shall remain vigilant."

"You're being too hard on yourself," Gihon put a hand on Zander's shoulder, affirming him. "You're the reason we were able to find her. She'd still be out there, if not for you."

"Your flattery means nothing to me. I need to be on my guard."

"Yes, but you need to rest, too. Try to sleep tonight, okay?" Gihon smiled, trying to show kindness to the cold guardsman. Zander huffed, turning away and vanishing into Edelein's tent.

He's a dutiful one, that's for sure, Gihon thought, waiting outside the tent for Zander to arouse the Queen from her restless slumber.

A quick moment later, Edelein emerged from her tent, Zander following behind her. Edelein was fully dressed, despite just waking up.

"Edelein, good morning, I–"

"Gihon, where is my nightgown? Have you seen it?" Edelein interrupted him, seeming to be lost in thought and not listening to him. "Zander said you might know where it is. I can't find it."

Dammit, Zander, Gihon thought, sparing a glance at the sphynx. Zander stared back expectantly from behind Edelein, not speaking, though his eyes revealed exactly what he wished to say.

Visions of the incident from the night before flashed in Gihon's mind as he remembered Allocer in his tent, the glimpses of her figure in the dim light through Edelein's nightgown as she sat herself on his lap, pressing her chest to his. He pictured her soft lips an inch from his own, blue eyes piercing into his soul.

"Gihon," Edelein repeated, snapping him out of his

wandering thoughts. He felt the heat rise from his face as he looked down at Edelein, acutely aware of her figure. "My nightgown."

That wasn't her, Gihon reminded himself, trying to banish the thoughts. *She wouldn't do that. She doesn't see me like that. Allocer is not Edelein. Yet, why do I think so much about the possibility, with Edelein...?*

"I'm sorry Edelein, I haven't seen it," Gihon lied, looking away. "I will let you know if I find your nightgown. I'm sure it must be around here somewhere. Or perhaps it was forgotten back at the safehouse?"

"Everett did pack my bag, and he does have a tendency to forget things," Edelein sighed, satisfied with the plausibility of his answer as she walked off to greet the others and prepare to venture into the woods again.

Zander glared at Gihon with a knowing look. Gihon sighed, shaking his head. Ahead of them, Everett hoisted several bags over his shoulders with a silent nod to Zander, who turned to Gihon.

"Everyone's ready. Let's go," Zander stated, walking ahead into the swampland without another word. Thorne and Edelein followed behind Zander, Mandus tagging along behind them. Everett fell in line behind Gihon to bring up the rear as Jana approached her master to walk alongside him. Gihon was lost in thought, staring at the back of Edelein's head as she trudged through the mud ahead.

Thorne nudged Edelein's shoulder gently, his tone teasing yet warm and affectionate. "Not going into the trees again today, Ed?"

Edelein looked up at the canopy above her for a moment before shaking her head, remembering the pain in her back from the fall she took the night before. "Nope. I don't want to. I think I'll stick with mud for now."

Confused, Thorne shrugged.

Noticing her master as Gihon stared ahead, Jana spoke up softly.

"Master Gihon, you should talk to her."

"I know," Gihon pulled his gaze away from Edelein to meet Jana. "Yet, for the first time, it seems as though I have no idea what to say. I'm clueless."

Silence overcame Gihon as he pressed forward, his feet wading through murky waters and mud as the sun reached its peak in the sky.

"How is it that we continue to walk through endless terrain, only for it to feel like each step we take is the same one?" Everett asked, drawing Gihon's attention.

At the dirigent's puzzled look, Everett elaborated, "Normally I would see a change in scenery. The trees, stones, and so on. But all of this… it all just looks the same. As if we're traveling the same patch of land, just repeating endlessly."

"The swamp is meant to confuse and disorient, so it is likely that the leyline energy is messing with your mind as a defense mechanism."

"I thought you said we would be safe from all of that, because of the medallions?" Thorne asked, looking over his shoulder at Gihon curiously.

"We are. This is just a side effect of heavy exposure to leyline energy."

"You know we're all from the largest leyline region in the world, right? Leyline energy doesn't bother us. It may be worth taking Everett's concern into mind," Edelein added.

"No, I would trust Gihon's word over mine. This is his homeland. We don't know if this leyline is the same as ours," Everett looked at Gihon in agreement.

"I usually feel that way too, when I'm here," Mandus agreed, pulling his own medallion out for the others to see. "Even with mine, I usually feel a little wonky when I'm in the swamp. Granted, my senses don't come close to the legendary Zengarde, though."

"You have the heart of a Zengarde, Mandus," Edelein turned around, walking backwards as she smiled at him. "You'd fit in well as a Zenluvian."

Mandus' face glowed with pride as he beamed, turning to look at Gihon. "You hear that, Gihon? Queen Edelein thinks I should be a Zengarde! I think you and I should take a trip to Zenluve after all of this."

Gihon chuckled, his eyes flitting from Mandus to Edelein, who was laughing happily.

"I think I'd quite like that," Gihon agreed. "Perhaps we shall owe Her Majesty a visit one day, yes?"

"Please do visit Zenluve. You'll never want to leave, that's for sure. The Deepwood is truly magical. You'll feel alive, feel the zoa blood running through your veins," Edelein grinned, a tinge of wistfulness in her eyes, silently missing her homeland.

"I will," Gihon promised.

"If he goes, I'm going too!" Mandus agreed excitedly.

"You're both welcome. There's plenty of room for you at the castle. Jana, too."

Stars twinkled in Mandus' eyes, his mind filling with mental images. "We get to stay at the castle? The Luvestein Castle? Built by the hands of King Alderich himself?"

"Of course you do, Mandus!" Edelein laughed again. "I wouldn't put you anywhere else when my home has a guest suite bigger than any inn. Also, Great Ancestor Alderich did not… build the Luvestein, so you know. It was built during his reign, though. It is a thousand years old, like the rest of the kingdom. However, I am impressed by your knowledge of my people's history."

"Frankly, I am too," Gihon agreed, Jana nodding alongside

him.

"There aren't a lot of zoa in Caandemium," Mandus explained. "Of those, even fewer are born of zoa parents, most are transmuted. I'm one of the few with zoa parents, so I grew up with zoa bedtime stories. My mom used to tell me about Zenluve all the time. To be honest, I didn't think you guys were real until Gihon told us you were coming to Velkhamore. I had just… kind of assumed you were a children's tale. I never expected to meet the Lion Queen of Zenluve face-to-face, much less become friends with her."

"I understand. The story of King Alderich and the early tribes of humans that inhabited the Deepwood would seem quite magical to those unfamiliar with the territory."

"Not just that. You're pretty incredible too," Mandus admitted, looking away bashfully. "I mean, the way you fight so bravely with your bow, but also how you're willing to get down and dirty and fight with your bare hands if needed–"

"You flatter me," Edelein laughed.

Thorne fell back in step with Gihon, leaning over to him as he whispered. "Mandus is gonna steal your girl, Gihon."

"Mandus is just very passionate about legends and stories. He's meeting his hero. That is all. Also," Gihon responded, before stopping to take in what Thorne said, "'my girl'? You seem to be mistaken."

Thorne laughed, clapping a hand on Gihon's back. "Yeah, sure, buddy."

Ahead of them, a sudden exclamation from Mandus drew Gihon's attention.

"Your Majesty!"

Alarmed by his sudden outburst, Gihon ran forward, his eyes being pulled downward to Zander, who was kneeling on the ground with Edelein in his arms. It appeared that Zander had managed to catch her just before she hit the ground, the Queen laying fully unconscious in the arms of the Ehret.

Gihon knelt down across from Zander, worry and panic clouding his vision. Gently, he took one of Edelein's hands in his, pulling off her glove as the anxiety within him made time seem to freeze. As he removed her glove and pushed her sleeve back, color drained from his face as the haunting deep grey-black of blight corrosion climbed up to her elbow.

"Impossible. She was supposed to be cured. Even if the cure was fake, it has only been a few weeks… the blight should be at her knuckles, at most," Gihon evaluated, his long and slender fingers tracing the blight up her forearm.

"Uh, guys? I'm worried about Edelein too, but there's another problem," Thorne called out, pointing ahead.

Gihon turned to look at Thorne, and then in the direction he pointed. Ahead of them, the quiet town of Ravencroft stirred with its evening activities, a few onlookers noticing them, but not paying much mind.

"It's Ravencroft," Gihon confirmed, Jana and Mandus looking solemn as they realized what being returned to town meant. "The swamp turned us away from Solomon. We are not in the land's favor."

CHAPTER 5

RETURN

To my esteemed Court,

Hear your Queen, Edelein Alderhart von Luvemann. A few weeks have passed since we set foot in Caandemium, and the entourage has been doing well. The Society of Alchemists in Velkhamore, of whom I had previously corresponded with, introduced me to a zoa alchemist by the name of Gihon Marleogne; the Dirigent of Ravencroft. I only presume this must be the man that Alina recommended to us. I have come to understand that a Dirigent is the head of a town or city, and the highest position of power within said territory. It is quite refreshing to see a fellow zoa in a position of power, and comforts me in my consideration of opening trade up to the Midlands.

Gihon has done well to aid us, educating us in the basics of alchemy and teaching the 'banishment array' needed to rid us of the shadow beasts– which they call "phantasms." We have run into a few of them here, but Gihon and his students have been utterly phenomenal in banishing the creatures effortlessly. Truly impressive, that Gihon.

However, not all alchemists use their power for good. We have had some encounters with an alchemist by the name of Solomon Marleogne, a homunculus created by Gihon's former master. Unfortunately, he managed to steal both of our leyline crystals from under our noses, and we are hard at work trying to get them back. His army of followers includes more homunculi, and these artificial beings pack quite a punch.

In our search for the first crystal, our link has split up twice. I have kept Zander closely by my side, as per usual. I am unsure of the details regarding the other side's experience, but I was made aware that Solomon's forces attacked them and stole the second crystal from us. I know my Zengarde fought bravely. None have perished.

We are now traveling through Ravencroft, Gihon's hometown, in search of Solomon and our crystals. The town sits atop a leyline, similar to ours, and it infuses the nearby marshes with the same power that we can feel back home, though a bit less pleasant. We did get a bit turned-around by the swamp and ended up back in Ravencroft, but we are taking this opportunity to rest briefly before heading out tomorrow morning.

Finally, I will inform my dear Court that I have contracted an illness caused by the incident where we lost Tyrus and Cyzen. The monster's energy has infected me, and has been slowly draining my soul. However, please do not worry for me. Of all people, Solomon was the one who presented a cure to me, and I have been feeling better. I recently had a brief episode, but it surely was only a minor relapse. Gihon and his student Jana Hearts have been looking after me while Fiertet Lylia continues to venture with the others.

I hope all is well with my Kingdom, and I do miss my home dearly. I plan to invite the Dirigent for a visit sometime, once all of this has passed. I cannot help but wonder if Solomon is truly the cruel man he claims to be. We shall see, won't we?

Well wishes,
Queen Edelein Alderhart von Luvemann

Edelein sat alone at a desk in her room at the inn, eyes poring over a letter she had just written. The room was peaceful as morning bled into daytime, the town outside stirring with life. The innkeeper had recognized Gihon and offered several rooms for free to temporarily shelter the group, noticing the sickly Edelein in Gihon's arms. Her memory was a bit fuzzy of the event, but she could vaguely recall being brought up to the room and left alone to rest.

A few hours had passed since they arrived on accident back in Ravencroft, allowing the Zenluvians a moment's respite while Gihon, Mandus, and Jana returned to the Athenaeum for more supplies. Edelein looked down at her hands, remembering the panic in Gihon's eyes as she came to in his arms, being rushed towards the inn. She could vaguely recall a doctor in her room, confirming her blight once more, and then finally leaving her alone.

Edelein closed her eyes, drinking in the sounds and smells of the room around her. It was silent other than a ticking clock and some chatter from the town outside her window, and the room smelled strongly of old books and wood. Faint traces of Gihon's scent lingered in the room, warm and musky, while the earthy scent of Ehret Zander presented more prominently from outside the door.

I knew Zander would be out there, Edelein sighed. *So much for keeping a low profile.*

Standing to her feet, Edelein walked over to the window as

a slight sense of cabin fever began to bubble up within her. Pulling back the curtains, her blackened hand began to trace the windowsill, inching towards the latch.

"Absolutely not, Edelein. Alett's not here to let you get away with it this time," Zander spoke from outside the door.

Edelein moaned, turning around and pressing her back to the window as she responded, "Don't be a wallflower, Zander. We need to regroup and continue our pursuit."

"You need to rest. You are staying right there."

"And you need to stop standing outside my door. You're going to freak people out. We're supposed to be on a covert mission, and you're all but giving away my status."

Zander opened the door, stepping inside. His face was twisted in what looked to be anger, but Edelein knew him well enough to recognize his worried expression. He closed the door behind him and crossed his arms, guarding it from the inside.

"A wonderful idea, Your Majesty. Now I can keep a better eye on you, as well."

"Zander! We don't have time for this. Solomon is out there somewhere, and we need to find him."

"You heard what Gihon said. The swamp is not favoring us. It'll be impossible to traverse safely at this point."

"So that's it, then? We just let him go?"

"If it means keeping you safe, then yes."

Edelein let out a groan of frustration, stamping her foot in protest to the expected stubbornness of her guardian. The lioness could recognize what looked to be a glint of empathy in Zander's eyes, yet could only find feelings of frustration within her. She pushed away from the windowsill, sitting back down on her bed in defeat.

Zander was standing perfectly still, his eyes following her movements carefully.

Soulweaver

"Come on now, Zander," Edelein pleaded. "You cannot keep me here forever."

"We're staying here until Gihon returns from the Corvid Athenaeum, and then you can come out when I tell him that I'm bringing you back home to Zenluve."

"What?" Edelein exclaimed. "You cannot be serious. We're not going back to Zenluve when our leyline crystals are being used to threaten the safety of thousands of civilians."

"Caandemite civilians."

"It doesn't matter where they're from! They're people, Zander. They could die because of us."

Zander crossed his arms. "Is that what plagues you, then? You blame yourself for losing the crystals?"

"Solomon would not have them if we had never shown up to this godforsaken place. According to Gihon, Solomon can only power the Gates of Heaven with our condensed leyline energy. No matter how you look at it, this is our fault. I wasn't able to protect my people from the phantasm, and for all we know, more Zenluvians could be dying every day that we're here. Now, I'm risking the lives of thousands of Caandemites just by being too weak to fight back–"

"Cub," Zander assured, sitting down next to her. "Tyrus and Cyzen's deaths were not your fault. There was no way for you to know that the phantasm would react in such a way to physical damage. You are a fearsome warrior queen, and the consequence of fighting is that sometimes, you will lose. What matters is that you do not let your losses burden your future, or your victories will grow more scarce."

"Victories will also grow scarce if you run away at the first sign of struggle," Edelein added dryly.

"I am not running away, I am honoring my oath to your father by withdrawing you from danger when you are incapable of holding your own," Zander replied.

Edelein fell silent, staring out the window at the clear sky that taunted her through the glass prison that separated them.

"I don't want any more people to die, Zander," Edelein whispered, her voice trembling.

"I don't want *you* to die," Zander murmured in response to his old friend, twelve years of memories weighing heavily onto his voice.

The two zoa sat in silence for another long minute, both feeling the weight of each other's words on their hearts.

"Edelein, what will you do if one of the Zengarde dies here in Caandemium?" Zander asked. "Will you regret staying?"

"I…" Edelein faltered, at a loss for words.

Solomon isn't what they think he is, Edelein thought. *He wouldn't kill my allies. He's had the chance to before, but he's not the type to do so. Yet… I don't think Zander would understand if I explained that to him. No one seems to believe me, or see what I see in Solomon.*

"They would give their lives for my cause, as would you. I would understand that and be alright," Edelein lied, forcing strength into her voice.

Zander was able to clearly recognize her fib, but respected her bravery enough to not comment on it. "What happens to Zenluve if you die here, then? Are you willing to let Zenluve fall for the sake of saving Caandemium?"

Edelein sighed, thinking. "I cannot sacrifice Zenluve for Caandemium, but I can try to save both. If my life is at risk, I will fall back. Alright?"

"Your life is already at risk."

"Dire risk, then. I will retreat from battle if needed. Even if it means letting others die."

"Fine."

"You are incredibly lucky that I am kind enough to compromise with a mere guardsman," Edelein smirked. "I am the Queen. My will bends to no one. Yet, I care enough about you to heed your concerns."

"Your humble Ehret thanks you for your generosity, Your Majesty," Zander dipped his head in a delicate combination of respect and sarcasm.

"So, we can go?" Edelein queried.

"Yes," Zander agreed reluctantly, standing up and helping Edelein to her feet.

"I knew you'd never let me down!" she beamed, heading towards the door with a disgruntled Zander in tow. "Let's find Gihon and get a move on."

She certainly seems cheerier the moment she gets her way, Zander noticed. *Why do I have a feeling that she won't be backing out of any fights any time soon?*

Opening the door, Edelein was startled by the broad figure of Gihon, one hand lifted to knock.

"Oh, hello," they both greeted in unison.

Gihon placed a warm hand on Edelein's arm, concern written all over his normally stoic face. "Your illness…"

"I'm quite alright, Gihon, I assure you," Edelein lied again.

"The stress of our current predicament is worsening your condition. The vial Solomon gave you had alleviated your symptoms to prevent you from noticing it, so that you would avoid taking care of yourself. It was his infuriating way of destroying you right under our noses."

"I don't think Solomon did this on purpose. He thought it would work, but I was only the first test subject," Edelein denied, remembering how Solomon had acted around her during their most recent engagement. "If he wanted to kill me, he could have let that phantasm do the job. Solomon has saved me, helped me. This is just a misunderstanding."

Gihon sighed, withdrawing his hand from her arm and running it through his jet-black bangs in silent frustration. "Edelein, he converts all of his followers by healing–or attempting to heal–an illness. He was simply manipulating you so that you would side with him and not with us. The reality sphere was yet another related incident where he has attempted to fabricate trust and fondness between the two of you, and sow doubt in our cause. Let me guess, he then told you that I refuse to listen to him because I am too blinded by my love for Arvien, yes? Followed by a list of horrendous things he believes that she did?"

Edelein clenched her teeth. *He doesn't get it.*

Noticing her silence, Gihon's voice softened. "I understand that he can be very convincing. Just try to remember why we are here: he stole your leyline crystals, killed an alchemist, and attacked Dritet Jinn. Now he is threatening the safety of thousands of civilians with his ambitions, and we have to stop him from doing that by any means necessary. With all due respect, Your Majesty, this situation is much more significant than the feelings you have about him."

"I understand that," Edelein sighed. "Something just doesn't feel right about him. I wish I could explain myself better."

"You can withdraw from the fight, if it is a severe concern," Gihon suggested, but Zander shook his head from behind Edelein.

"I already tried that one, Gihon," Zander grumbled. "She isn't willing to leave."

"Correct," Edelein straightened up, forcing herself into a more regal aura. "We're doing things my way, and that involves getting a move on. We re-enter the swamp immediately."

"If you are feeling up to it, I may have a plan that will increase our chances at success," started Gihon.

"Tell me about it on the way," Edelein agreed, brushing

past him and heading outside of the inn.

Following her out, the three of them met up with Mandus and Jana, who were in a tense discussion at the edge of the town. Thorne was sitting on a ledge a little ways off, Everett leaning on a wall next to him. Thorne hopped down and jogged over to meet them as they approached, Everett in tow.

"Master Gihon, I'm not entirely sure this is a wise decision," Jana mumbled softly, Mandus clapping her back affectionately.

"It'll be fine! It'll only be open for a little while, and–"

"No, it will take some time to reignite the arrays afterwards," Gihon corrected him gently, as Edelein looked around in confusion.

Meeting her gaze, Gihon explained himself. "I know how to disable the landshift arrays that are under the swamp."

"What?!" Edelein's jaw dropped in disbelief. "Why didn't you do that sooner?!"

"The arrays are meant to protect my hometown, as well as the leyline, from intruders. They are not malicious to our–or at least *my*–cause. Until now, I had thought that they were working with us to help us reach Solomon, so I wanted to keep them active. Knowing now that Solomon has manipulated the marshlands to turn against me, I believe our only option is to disable them and risk opening Ravencroft up to the outside world."

"I understand," Zander nodded. "You have to choose between the greater good of Caandemium or the protection of your homeland. It is a dangerous choice, regardless of which you pick."

"Is there a possibility that Solomon means for this to happen?" Mandus asked. "That he wants us to disable the arrays to jeopardize Ravencroft?"

"It is a likelihood worth considering," Gihon admitted.

"What other plan is there, though?" Everett asked. "The

swamp threw us back out here even with your medallions. If we go in again as-is, it'll just be worse, right?"

Gihon shook his head. "I fear there is none. If Solomon intended for this to happen, he has us in a checkmate. All we can do is pray that this was not a part of his plan, and that he is too focused on the Gates of Heaven to care about destroying Ravencroft."

"He could send word anonymously to the Society, explaining that the marshland has opened itself up to visitors curious about the leyline," Jana theorized. "Once a few powerful Dirigents are here, he detonates the Gates of Heaven and blights the entire swamp, Ravencroft and all, taking out the big names of the Society of Alchemists with it."

"Thus forcing my hand to write a letter of my own, explaining to the Society that Ravencroft has been opened up, and fruitlessly asking them not to come," Gihon realized. "They would honor no such petition from me. The Society has hungered for Ravencroft's clandestine knowledge for years. A polite request would do absolutely nothing to stop them."

"Do we tell them it's a trap?" Mandus asked.

"If they understand that Solomon is the author of the original correspondence, they will send out alchemists to try to hunt him down. It would fail to deter them as well," Gihon replied in disdain.

"This is, of course, assuming that Solomon intends to destroy Ravencroft," Edelein muttered.

Gihon stared at Edelein in disbelief, trying hard to remind himself that Solomon had wriggled his way into her mind like a parasitic worm. "Edelein… he is setting up the Gates of Heaven somewhere in Blacktalon Thicket as we speak. That backlash will *absolutely* hit Ravencroft."

"Unless he does it right, isn't that so?"

"He is unable to do it properly. The point of the leyline

crystals is to force the Gates open with pure and unrestrained leyline energy. That type of alchemy results in severe backlashes," Gihon explained.

Something isn't right, Edelein thought, but was unwilling to argue her instincts further against Gihon's logic.

"The safest course of action is to assume that Solomon does not intend to lead the other alchemists here, and is hyperfixating on his Gates of Heaven instead. Any word from me would only cause the Society to come quicker, not slower," Gihon decided. "We shall dismantle the defense arrays for now and continue tracking Solomon more clearly."

"So getting rid of these arrays will let us track," Thorne confirmed with a nod. "Does it eliminate the, uh, other risks you mentioned?"

"Of course not. This will just allow us to move freely. The guardians of the land will still be active, just… easier to predict. It doesn't eliminate risk, but it does give us the upper hand."

"Great. I'll remember you when I'm pickled under the swamp."

"I have a few apprehensions about letting Edelein waltz into a monster-infested bog of horrors simply because she can detect them better now," Zander protested. "I would really rather she stay–"

Edelein interrupted her soldier with a curt grumble. "I'm a monster hunter, Zander. Anything in Blacktalon Thicket will be easy compared to the beasts I've hunted back in Zenluve. Plus, it's not infested. They live there. That's just their home."

"It's still too dangerous."

"I fear we may not have a choice if we want to get to Solomon," Gihon sighed. "Edelein would be a useful ally to have. Her archery skills are unmatched and offer a ranged coverage that we lack otherwise. As much as it conflicts me to admit this as a representative of the Society tasked with protecting you all, I believe that she should accompany us."

"I do not need permission from you," Edelein retorted. "I am going whether you'd like me to or not."

The rosy tint on her cheeks indicated that she appreciated Gihon's compliment nonetheless, though she made no attempt to show her gratitude.

Jana shifted from foot to foot, anxious. "Master Arvien worked really hard on these arrays. Is it really okay to just undo them?"

"She would understand. Arvien knows as well as I do the consequence of letting Solomon near the Gates of Heaven. When she came with me to Othalgar to help us stop him, she witnessed the same thing that I did."

Silently, Gihon crouched down and scooped away some mud, revealing a few faint lines of a decades-old array.

"All of the arrays here are connected to one another. I can overload one into a chain reaction that will fry the rest and disable them. It is a technique exclusive to mystic alchemy, only usable by myself and students of the Athenaeum. Though, I do believe that I have never taught this to anyone else. For obvious safety reasons."

Placing a hand into the mud, a turquoise light began to hum as it beamed upwards. A sudden pop echoed from the array, followed by a sequence of several popping noises from further and further into the swamp ahead until the sound was too far away to hear. Standing up, Gihon whispered under his breath, "Apologies, Master. I will set new ones as soon as I have finally vanquished the biggest stain on your legacy for good."

Facing the others, Gihon addressed them sternly.

"We cannot afford to waste any time. Every second these arrays are disabled is a second a wandering eye could find Ravencroft. Time to move."

"Arvien must have been really protective of this place," Edelein noted curiously as she stepped into the murky wilderness once more, the others following behind. "You seem to really love her."

"Oh, Arvien? Yes, I suppose so. She provided for me a life of unimaginable adventure, far beyond anything I could have known. I owe her my gratitude."

"You and Solomon appear to have quite different impressions of her," Edelein lowered her voice as she continued, to keep the conversation between the two of them. "When I was trapped in that reality sphere with Solomon, he told me a bit about Arvien. From how he described her, she seemed pretty… cruel."

"I would strongly urge you to banish any thoughts of her that he's given you. Solomon's memories are skewed, at best."

"You mean he misremembers?"

"That's all I can assume of him. We lived the same childhood, he and I. Yet, his heart is hardened towards any memories of the Athenaeum. I never supported his dreams of grandeur, nor his paranoia."

Edelein stared silently up at Gihon, listening intently.

"Arvien was a master of alchemy," Gihon continued. "Revered by alchemists all around Caandemium, and the founder of Ravencroft. In fact, she built the town herself to protect the leyline that sits underneath the swamp. It is her own energy that keeps the leyline contained in this location."

"I don't think the leyline wishes to be contained," Edelein mumbled under her breath.

"Nonsense, we are protecting it from outsiders. It is safe when it is kept here."

"It's being suffocated."

Gihon cast a sharp glance down at Edelein, eyes narrow. Sheepishly, Edelein spared an apologetic glance for implying negativity towards his master before averting her eyes towards the ground.

"Ravencroft was made as Arvien's legacy; protecting the leyline and the townspeople within. Arvien was a gentle woman, earnest in nature. The only things she ever wished for were to protect this land and to have a family. She lost her first child, a genetic complication that took the infant's life almost instantly after he was born. Afraid and unable to conceive again, my master turned towards alchemy to create the family she was so desperate to love.

My eldest brother, Perath, was her first attempt at creating human life from alchemy; a rough first draft of a homunculus. Perath was unwell, eternally suffering, a failed experiment. He died not long after. Pishon–Solomon–came next, her first successful homunculus. Arvien loved Solomon dearly, despite his claims otherwise. She worked closely with him and taught him everything she knew, and the two of them often took trips to Othalgar to further his studies. He was a young boy at the time that I first met them.

I was a young chick when I met Arvien, barely hatched. I don't have concrete memories of who I was before my transmutation, just… feelings. I took to Arvien as a fledgeling, drawn to her kind heart and inquisitive nature."

"How long have you been a zoa?" Edelein asked.

"About fifteen years now, give or take. I journeyed with Arvien for five years before she put me under the transmutation. My avian age roughly translated to about fifteen in humanoid years. I consider myself to be thirty in zoa years now, but as you likely know; transmutations leave a little bit of guesswork on our exact ages."

Edelein smiled to herself, the mental image of a young Gihon softening her heart. His words stirred thoughts of Cari Beaumont in her mind, her best friend that had accidentally turned out younger than expected with a five-year age gap.

I hope she's doing alright with Luthro, Edelein thought.

"Once I was transmuted, Arvien treated me like a son. I took well to her teachings, fitting in naturally to the rhythm of the Marleogne family. Solomon and I were close friends, brothers, learning about the wonders of alchemy and the significance of our family's footprint. Arvien loved her sons, until Solomon decided to ruin what we had.

Not long after my transmutation, Arvien finally managed to conceive once more. Solomon began to see Arvien's miraculous feats as crazed, disagreeing with the choices she made to protect our family. Solomon begged me to turn against her, to join him, but I knew that his mind had been corrupted from his own hedonistic ideologies and selfish nature."

"What did she do that turned him away like that?" Edelein asked.

"One of Arvien's many artifacts was a cursed hourglass from Limbo. The sand within it fell not from time, but from experience. It traded her lifeforce for the universe's secrets. The more she adventured, the faster the sand trickled down. As the sand neared its end, Arvien had decided to cloister herself within the halls of the Athenaeum to preserve her lifespan, sending Solomon and I out in her stead to live the experiences she could not. Birthing a healthy child, true motherhood, was the final experience that spelled out her end."

"She was experiencing too many new memories by raising the baby, is that right?" Edelein clarified as Gihon nodded.

"She gave birth to our baby sister, Hiddekel. The experience drained her hourglass and took her life when Hidde was a few years old. Solomon believes that it was cruel of her to give up her ability to live longer and love us by dying in order to love our sister."

"Where is Hiddekel now?" Edelein asked as she looked at

the Dirigent's sad and distant eyes.

"I am unsure. She was handed off to the Church of Prima Luma after Arvien passed. She would be a young teenager at this point."

"So Solomon cut ties with you because he was jealous of your sister?"

"Essentially, yes. It is the catalyst that started his obsession with the Gates of Heaven. Arvien stopped at nothing to love her children, and he believed it was because we contained souls, unlike him. Solomon convinced himself that if he had a soul, too, that Arvien would love him. He fails to realize that she always did. Needless to say, Solomon did not handle the news of her death well."

"Did you?"

Gihon fell silent, lost in thought.

"I knew it was coming, and I knew that she had chosen that fate for herself, so I suppose I handled it better. I feel her presence, her legacy, everywhere I turn. The final pieces of knowledge she learned were the names of Luthro, Mandus, Jana, and Spira. Those four pioneered a new generation of alchemists at the Athenaeum, and she was at peace knowing that the future of her legacy would be preserved. I do miss her, though."

"You know, you and Zander are more similar than either of you realize."

A quiet hiss from behind them indicated that Zander was listening, and unappreciative of the Queen's mention.

"Do not utter a *single* word, Edelein," Zander warned.

Edelein laughed comfortably. "Alright, alright. I'm going to go up in the trees and scout ahead a bit."

Leaning up to whisper in Gihon's ear, Edelein murmured, "Zander has a similar story. Go ask him about it. I think it would do you both some good."

CHAPTER 6

EUPHRATES

As Edelein vanished into the treetops, Gihon looked over at Zander with a curious and expectant look.

"No," Zander replied before Gihon could ask anything.

"Is it that painful to recall?"

Zander paused, hesitating. His eyes seemed to get lost in memories for what seemed like eternity before he nodded quietly and finally spoke.

"I was transmuted, not a born zoa like most others in Zenluve. My master was an elderly woman, her transmutation request was approved by the Court because she had no family, no caretakers in her old age. All she had was this hairless kitten that reminded her of home."

"Tozepia, yes? Sphynx cats are native there," Gihon hypothesized.

Zander nodded. "Master Khepri was a Tozepian human. Something about all the sand, hot weather, and political unrest seemed to not agree with her old bones, so she ended up in Zenluve. She… didn't really talk about Tozepia a lot, but she had a lot of heirlooms and artifacts."

Even someone from as far as Tozepia could end up in Zenluve. I suppose it really could be seen as a haven of refuge, like the stories say. Gihon thought as Zander continued.

"I was a young teenager when I was transmuted, like you. Master Khepri was a frail but well-meaning woman, and taught me some basic schooling. In return, I would care for her. I cleaned her home, cooked her meals just the way she liked them, and I… held her as she passed."

Gihon's gaze softened, Zander turning his head away as he got lost in an anguished flashback.

"I mean, it is as you said before. She was old. I knew it was going to happen. But with limited education, I didn't really consider what I would do once she was gone. She died with nothing to her name, and I was… I was alone. Master Khepri was all I had. Hell, I could barely even read or write, and I was a child with no kin."

"I understand that feeling. If I did not have the Athenaeum to manage, I believe that I would have been lost once Arvien died."

Zander nodded. "Obviously, no one was going to hire a barely-literate fourteen-year-old with zero formal education, so I had to turn to petty crime to get by. I am not proud of who I used to be, but I believe it is important to accept and remember, as it keeps me humble. I took to thieving, but just small things. Food, wallets, things like that. I tattooed myself with Tozepian imagery to remember my master by, and left the rest in the past."

I recall noticing his tattoos when we first met, Gihon remembered.

"Your tattoos, they mean 'protector' and 'ward of evil' don't they?" Gihon asked.

"You know about Tozepian symbology?" Zander asked,

surprised. "Yes, my eye tattoos. I thought they would protect and guard me from the cruelty of the world, but that was not the case."

"You ended up being the protector, instead."

"Yeah. I ended up being the protector for that little brat," Zander gestured up towards the treetops, the lioness barely visible as Mandus talked loudly up at her.

Gihon chuckled in understanding, his eyes fixed on the back of Mandus' head. "I have been the guardian of that troublemaker next to her for the last few years. I understand the feeling. How did you end up going from a petty criminal to the King's right hand?"

Zander's ears flattened. "I got cocky. I ended up running with the wrong crowd, joining a reputable gang. Crime got easier, so it got more frequent. I went from pickpocketing to worse things. Breaking and entering. Eventually a few murders. In my defense, the only people I killed deserved to die. Convicted criminals and such. However, a murder is still a murder, to the judicial system."

"You were a teenager?" Gihon asked. "Quite young to have such a notorious reputation."

"I wasn't the youngest. That's the worst part." Zander sighed. "There was a boy eight years younger than me. He was only ten years old when I was arrested. He's… if he's still alive, he'd only be twenty-two now. Barely younger than Edelein. My biggest regret is not freeing that child from that life."

"How did you get arrested?"

"Like I said, I got cocky. The gang and I tried to steal from the castle. We were fed up with the idea of all those rich assholes sitting on their wealth while the rest of us suffered, and we thought we could take it for ourselves instead. It turns out that the castle is pretty heavily guarded, which surprised my eighteen-year-old idiot brain. I was the most nefarious gangster in Zenluve, but I was no match for all ten Zengarde. I took out a few of them, but the higher ranks got to me. One of them cut off my tail, and it was actually Lylia who patched me up after the fight, since I was bleeding a lot from where my tail had been."

"Lylia was one of those Zengarde?"

"Yeah. She was new to the team, and was a lot more soft-spoken. She was lower ranked than she is now, too pacifistic to really be a fighter, but she was still skilled enough to scrape the low ranks. The other name you'd know at all was Tyrus Abbisard. Everyone else is pretty new."

Tyrus, I remember that name vaguely. He was one of the two Zengarde that were killed by the phantasm.

"I was the only one arrested that night. I took the heat so the rest of my gang could flee," Zander explained, gritting his teeth.

"You have always been a guardian, then. Even as a kid, you would take the fall for your companions." Gihon clapped a hand gently onto Zander's shoulder. "It is rather noble."

"Nothing noble about protecting criminals."

"They were your friends."

"Anyways," Zander huffed, changing the subject. "They threw me into the dungeons, scheduling me to be executed for my *extensive* criminal history. It was King Alderis himself who pardoned me. That was also the night I met Edelein for the first time. Alderis approached me, this shy little cub hiding behind him."

Zander smiled softly, recalling the look of the once-shy, young Crown Princess Edelein.

"Alderis brought his twelve-year-old daughter to a dungeon, to meet a criminal?" Gihon exhaled in surprise. "He really was a… free-spirited man. I see where she gets it from."

"Edelein really does remind me of him. She sees the good in people, like her father did. King Alderis praised my combat prowess, for taking down his Zengarde. I thought they had come to mock me, but… no. He introduced me to Edelein, and said that one day, she would need a guardian. That when he passes on, she will have her own Zengarde to care for her, and that he knows that I could be one of them. I laughed, because I refused to believe he was serious. He said he would pardon my crimes if I participated in the Zengarde Tournament, which was coming up. That if I joined their ranks to serve and protect him and his daughter, I would be given everything. Food, shelter, enough money to afford to live comfortably. It wasn't until he opened my cell that I finally believed him."

He opened the cell with Edelein right there? Gihon thought in astonishment. *Knowing full well that Zander could have easily killed them both? I'm certainly no expert in parenting, but that seems incredibly unwise.*

"Edelein looked terrified. I could tell she was thinking exactly what you're thinking now," Zander sighed. "Alderis… had faith in me. He knew I wouldn't hurt them, that I was just a scared kid like Edelein was. He offered to let me leave. He said that if I appeared at the tournament, my crimes would be pardoned; but if the tournament came and went and I was not there, the guards would find me again. Needless to say, I did appear at the tournament."

"That is incredible," Gihon breathed, his mind racing.

"I joined the ranks afterwards, and I worked closely alongside my allies. Alderis kept me close to Edelein, which I believe was because of my age. She didn't have a lot of friends, being the Crown Princess, so Alderis tried to surround her with younger people. I had no choice as a Zengarde, and Cari was like a little sister to her. Jinn had… no interest in so much as looking in the Crown Princess' direction." Zander laughed heartily, a joyful sound that surprised Gihon. "Jinn completely snubbed her one time, and she then told me that it was the second time it had happened. The first time, they were both just little kids, only six years old."

"Did you just laugh?" Gihon asked, smiling. "You really do care for your allies, Ehret Khepri."

"What? No," Zander denied as his face fell back into a stoic scowl.

"Edelein mentioned to me previously that Cari was transmuted from a Deepwood-native fauna and was raised to be her friend, but how does she know Jinn?" Gihon asked Zander, curious.

"A rosufex, yes. It's similar to a fox, but small and pink and without a tail. Edelein loved them when she was younger. Madame Beaumont, Cari's adoptive mother, is the icon of Zenluve's fashion industry and the head seamstress for the royals. Jinn, though, is a nobleman by blood. The secondborn son of the Canis Clan. His family attends most social events. Actually, Nephvir and Thorne are the only ones who had never met Edelein before joining the Zengarde. Everyone else has some sort of connection to her already."

She did mention that Alett's parents are friends of hers. Gihon recalled. *I suppose knowing her strong character made it easier for people to decide to join her.*

"I had not realized that so many of you were nobles. King Alderis' death must have been hard, then. Edelein mentioned a wizard's foresight being the cause?"

Zander nodded solemnly. "His death was incredibly unexpected. Our former High Wizard was an insatiable old man with an endless pursuit of knowledge. He started seeking out the forbidden truths, his stagnancy driving him to madness. He'd read every book thrice over at that point in his life, and was out of things to learn, according to him.

Alderis pulled me aside one night, a few years after I had begun my service. The panicked look in his eyes haunts me to this day. He spoke of fire, a burning inferno that consumed the streets of Zenluve. The wizard foretold what many believe to be Edelein's death and the end of Zenluve as we know it. Monsters never before seen, hellish abominations rampaging. A black-winged man descending like a raven of death, the commander of this legion of creatures, capturing Edelein and taking the future of Zenluve away forever.

As the King described this omen to me, we both understood the consequence of foresight; that this future was now inevitable. Alderis was in agony, beyond himself with grief. He told me that our only chance at saving her would be to recruit Nebeher, the Keeper of Mist. He thought that if we had the power of a dragon by our side, we would be able to quell the fires and ward off the evil that was looming ahead. He wanted to ask Nebeher to move within the walls of Zenluve, to be ready for the oncoming plight."

"A dragon?" Gihon asked, feeling the weight of the word on his tongue.

"Yes, the Keeper of Mist is a dragon that resides further north, in deeper territories of the Deepwood, a place known as the Shrouded Realm. His name is Nebeher, and he was closely allied with the Great Ancestor Alderich."

What exactly is Alderich, if he was befriending dragons like that? Gihon wondered silently as Zander continued to explain. *It has been centuries since anyone has even seen a dragon. I thought they had died out.*

"Every Crown Prince of Zenluve makes a pilgrimage to the Shrouded Realm at their coming-of-age. They pay homage to Nebeher, fraternizing with him in Alderich's honor. It is known as the Draconic Trial."

"Trial?"

"The road to the Shrouded Realm is dangerous, winding through the deepest parts of our homeland. If a Crown Prince can make it there and back alive, they are seen as blessed by Nalo, gifted with the forest's approval and protection, and destined to be a leader. Every Crown Prince so far has survived the trial, for their souls were pure."

"Did King Alderis attempt to make another Draconic Trial, then?"

"Yes, an action never before seen. The King is not supposed to travel that road, only the Crown Prince. Alderis has succeeded in his Trial before, but no one knew what would happen if a King were to attempt it. He left that night to seek the aid of Nebeher, not bothering to wait for approval from the Court. That was the last time I saw him."

"Do you believe he failed the Trial?" Gihon asked.

"No. Most people believe that, but I cannot believe that Alderis would have lost Nalo's blessing. He was a good man and a benevolent leader. I have sworn to kill whoever killed Alderis. I just… have no lead on who or what killed him. We could never retrieve his body, because the unfavored would die trying."

"Has Edelein done this Draconic Trial, then?" Gihon asked.

"No, Alderis died before she had come of age. Once she was coronated, no one would let her attempt it, as she was already Queen. They were afraid of her repeating the same action that got her father killed. Even more so as she has still yet to bear a son to inherit the throne."

Zander paused for a moment, his eyes locked straight ahead as he got lost in his thoughts.

"She's under a lot of pressure, you know. Poor kid," Zander said after a beat.

"I imagine the hole Alderis left behind was hard for such a young woman to fill."

"She was sixteen when she became the Queen. They've been trying to force her to marry since the day she was of childbearing age."

"Edelein has mentioned that before. Can she not just

silence them, as Queen?"

"She could, but it would be met with backlash from our kingdom. Her authority is the only reason she hasn't married yet, but only a tyrant would rule according to their own desires and not what is best for their people. She allows the Court to speak their public opinions, and tries her best to listen to their grievances. She strongly despises the idea of transmuting a lion into a man just for the purpose of being her spouse. She has always dreamed of finding a spouse organically, and marrying for love."

"What do you think she should do?" Gihon asked.

Zander stopped to think for a moment.

"I want her to be happy. That was my promise to Alderis, that she would be happy and safe for as long as I live. However, if she dies young, the lineage of Alderich dies with her, and there is a possibility that Zenluve will lose Nalo's blessing, or the guardianship of Nebeher. That also does not mention the consequence of breaking a thousand years of tradition."

"What consequence is that?"

"When people have done something the same way for a thousand years, they are reluctant to change. Some believe that the Bestial Spirit will only pass on to the firstborn of two lion zoa. If she doesn't marry a lion zoa, there's a possibility that the lineage will still die anyway. Even if that doesn't happen, people are resistant to the idea of a half-blood King. Anything other than a tufted-tailed blond-haired nobleman, and the entirety of Zenluve gets divided into disagreements. Traditions are hard to break. Worst case, she could end up shunned off of the throne entirely, disgraced by the public."

"Where do you get the lions from, anyway?"

"You ask strange questions, raven," Zander tilted his head, wondering why Gihon had chosen to focus on the logistics of Edelein's predicament. "There is a species of lion that is native to the Deepwood, believed to be evolved from Alderich's species. They respond positively to Zenluvian nobility; sensing the reverence, I suppose. One is lured and brought back to Zenluve, where they are then transmuted and raised up into etiquette training to become highly agreeable and elegant nobles. It's… not the most idealistic outcome."

Taking a wild, free animal into captivity and grooming it to become a perfect spouse. I can see why Edelein is not fond of this old tradition. Gihon thought with a grimace as silence befell the two men once more.

Zander and Gihon continued to walk on, thinking about each other's words.

"What is her alternative, then?" Gihon asked. "To keep putting it off, she surely must have an idea of what to do instead."

"She doesn't have one," Zander admitted. "All she's done for the last few years is cross her fingers and hope that something–or someone–comes along that can free her from her fate."

"Have you ever wondered if maybe that someone was you?" Gihon replied thoughtlessly.

Zander's eyes widened as he turned to face Gihon, appalled. "Are you really asking if I think I could be the one who marries her and frees her from the fate of her family's tradition?"

Gihon looked away, embarrassed. "I-I mean, you spend a lot of time with her. You know everything about her, and you care about her happiness. You're probably closer to her than anyone else is."

"I'm an ex-convict who spent his reformative years *babysitting* her. Like you said, I'm closer to her than anyone else. That means I know her flaws and quirks, and I am certainly *less* than compatible with them."

"How do you feel about her, then?"

"The most daring I could ever be would be to see her as a

younger sister. I don't have any family, so it's… almost indulgent to imagine her that way. Alderis is how I imagined a father would be, thoughtful and forgiving. I will never dare to call myself his son, nor will I call myself Edelein's brother. Sometimes, though, it's nice to think about them like that. I would never dishonor King Alderis by fawning over the very girl I'm sworn to protect."

Gihon let out a soft exhale, feeling a strange sense of relief wash over him.

"She has grown into a wonderful young woman, though," Zander continued. "I'm proud to serve her. She can still be that bratty little cub at times, but when push comes to shove she always steps up to lead people with courage and determination. Do *not* tell her I said that."

Gihon laughed. "Your secret is safe with me. Though, I think she would stand to benefit from you telling her yourself."

"And inflate her ego in the process? Not happening."

The men continued to walk in a comfortable silence, before Zander spoke again.

"Why are you so curious about her, anyway?"

Gihon felt a blush creeping up his cheeks, forcing the feeling back down as he replied. "I mean, it is as Mandus said. Zenluve is a legend to zoa, so it is only natural for a zoa to be curious. Certainly he is up there asking her all the same questions as we speak."

"Are you sure you don't have impure intentions with her?"

"I-impure intentions?" Gihon choked. "Of course not. I simply have a duty to oversee her while you all are under my protection in Caandemium, and as a scholar I enjoy learning about new cultures, and–"

"Do you not feel captivated by her? Is my Queen not good enough for you?" Zander asked, the wrap above his eyes scrunching as an eyebrow muscle raised in bemusement.

Gihon stopped, waving his hands as he searched for words. "N-no, of course, she is incredible. I find myself captivated by her stories constantly, and I am certain she would make a wonderful wife to someone someday… wait, are you messing with me right now?"

Zander laughed again.

"You *are* messing with me!" Gihon shook his head in disbelief.

"You're a nobleman, Dirigent Gihon. Intelligent, with good leadership qualities. You're also a terrible liar, which is good for me, because I can keep an eye on you. Just be good to her," Zander turned to look ahead again, keeping his gaze respectfully off of Gihon's fluster. "And if it turns out that you're the corvid from the prophecy, I'll kill you with my own hands. Keep your friends close, and enemies closer."

"Am I a friend or an enemy to you?" Gihon asked.

"I don't know yet. If you choose to become my enemy, though, I'd prefer you do it right in front of me so I can stop you."

"Alright, deal. I'll stay a close ally to the Kingdom, so you can stop me if I bring harm to your people."

"I have one demand, though."

"Oh, do you?" Gihon cast a glance at the sphynx, curious.

"Edelein deserves to know about Allocer," Zander huffed.

"Nothing happened between that *thing* and myself," Gihon denied. "She is wretched."

"I never said anything happened between you two," Zander replied flatly. "Now you're acting suspicious."

"I am not."

"I just said that she deserves to know about her. Especially considering we will probably end up crossing paths with the homunculi again soon. A homunculus that appears exactly like Edelein was in your tent late at night. It's a bad look for you,

Dirigent Gihon."

"She was trying to kill me!"

"How then, Dirigent, did she get so close to accomplishing it?"

Gihon paused, lost for words.

"She sought to seduce you, didn't she? You were caught off guard because you thought Edelein was in your tent, trying to sleep with you. Who knows how far she would have gotten if she hadn't stabbed you."

"Zander, *please* do not tell her about what happened. It is humiliating to me beyond words that I can even begin to express."

"I won't, so long as you swear to explain it to her yourself. She should know."

"I will tell her eventually, I promise. I just have no idea of how to go about it. It is not exactly a simple task to go up to a woman you have affection towards and tell her that her evil clone seduced you."

"So you *do* have affection towards her. I knew it."

Gihon opened his mouth to shoot him a sharp reply, but was interrupted by a sudden ripple of energy between the Zengarde. Edelein jumped down suddenly from the trees, bristling with anxiety as she looked at Gihon with a shell-shocked face. Zander's ears perked up, the sphynx darting forwards and pulling Edelein behind him as the others clamored uneasily, ears and heads swiveling.

"What is it?" Gihon asked, uneasy.

"What's that thing you mentioned, about pickling bodies in the swamp?" Edelein asked, the fur on her tail raised in alarm.

Her question was met with a visual as chaos erupted in a single swift moment. The quick movements of an expert hunter darted from the trees towards Thorne, the Fuuntet's eyes wide with fear as he reached into his pocket to grab his dagger. Zander launched himself from Edelein's side, drawing both blades and intercepting the monster's attack as his swords caught large claws in an x-shaped parry. Thorne stumbled to the ground, trembling as he fumbled for his knives. Another flash appeared as Mandus shot forward, planting a firm kick and sending the creature back a few steps.

As the moment passed, the nightmarish beast planted itself firmly into the mud, prepared to attack again. Its quadrupedal form was horrific to look at; fleshy skin of a greyish-brown color, with chartreuse streaks around its ribs. A large flower-like mouth filled with teeth opened to reveal a lifeless humanoid face fused inside of it as it let out a screeching roar.

The Zengarde unsheathed their weapons, Edelein brandished her bow, Jana and Mandus prepared their arrays for battle as Gihon pulled the Queen behind him, his answer to her question sending a chill through their bones.

"Euphrates, the Dweller."

The Dweller let out an uncanny chittering noise, petals of flesh rippling around the lifeless face in the center of its gaping maw. Long, slender limbs stretched out wide before swiping forward in a cross motion. Swirls of colorful energy in a sea of nebulous indigo surrounded the monster as a tear in reality formed from its arms, hues dancing like seafoam breaking against rocks.

As quickly as the beast appeared, it vanished, the vibrant hole closing behind it as it left. The alchemists sprung into action, seeming to understand the Dweller's intentions. Mandus and Jana produced small pieces of chalk from their pockets, meticulously drawing arrays onto nearby tree trunks.

Strength reinforced the fibers of each fighter, the link growing sturdier as Gihon's bulwark array flowed through his allies. The Zengarde were on high alert in a circular formation as they tried to locate the monster, though no amount of Seventh Sense could guide them to a creature that no longer existed.

"Gihon, this is the part where you tell us everything you know about this thing, immediately," Zander commanded. "It'll return, yes?"

"I do not have the time to tell you everything about its backstory, but its name is Euphrates. The Dweller. The final executioner of these lands."

"You've said that already and seem to have no concept of what information is critical to relay in battle. The name matters not," Zander huffed urgently. "Where did the thing go?"

"And what were those silver wires around it? It looked like a net," Edelein added.

"Wires?" Gihon furrowed his brow. "To answer Zander's question, Euphrates can shift into the Sea of Miracles to divert extraplanar entities that would end up as phantasms in Ravencroft. It is meant to thwart unwanted visitors."

"Are we unwanted visitors?" Thorne asked.

"We should not be, but it seems we are," Gihon confirmed. "It will return, so stay alert. It can appear from the Sea of Miracles and attack at any time, from any angle. This includes the ground and the air above, as well."

"Why is it attacking us, though?" Jana asked, looking over her shoulder from where she had just finished drawing an array. "We have the medallions!"

"Solomon likely did something to it. It refuses to trust medallion-holders anymore," Gihon theorized.

"The arrays are complete, Master Gihon," Jana added, motioning for the others to come closer.

"Mine looks rough, but I promise it'll work," Mandus assured.

Together, the students placed one hand each on the chalk markings, careful to avoid smudging them. The arrays began to illuminate as warm wind pulsed through the thicket, a silvery image of the Dweller circling the group.

Sensing that it had been located, the monster lunged out from another rip in space, splashing shimmering deep blue water around the area as it re-entered the material plane. It swung a claw at Zander, who dodged and returned a deep slash through the Dweller's tail. The severed tail dropped into the murky water of the swamp as the Dweller dove back into the sea of miracles, its glimmering, silver silhouette regrowing the very same tail.

"What gives?!" Thorne cried out, clutching his knives as he tried to align his trajectory to the beast's afterimage. "Is it regenerating?"

"The Sea of Miracles is formulated to your own beliefs," Jana explained. "When it retreats, it can imagine itself healthy, and so it will be."

"Why don't we go in there, then, and imagine it dead?" Thorne suggested.

"Oh, so you're suddenly a plane-shifting expert?" Mandus retorted. "Be my guest, then. I'll cheer you on!"

"There are dangers to plane-shifting," Gihon added. "It would be safest for us to attack it from the material plane. As long as Mandus and Jana keep their arrays active so we can see it, there should be no issue. My bulwark array will protect you, as well."

"Above!" Edelein called suddenly, as more starry water poured from a rip in the sky.

The Dweller crashed down, fire spilling out from its flowery head. Wasting no time, Gihon leapt up to grab the petals of its mouth, attempting to wrestle it away from the others as flames singed his clothes and skin slightly through his bulwark array.

Gunshots reverberated as Jana landed a few clean bullets into the monster's chest. Brandishing his swords, Zander darted forward to mercilessly strike at the Dweller's neck, but the creature dissipated into the ground as another plane shift whisked it back into the Sea of Miracles. Gihon let go of its head as it sank down, understanding the consequences of being pulled into the rift.

The Dweller darted through the trees once more, a silvery shadow waiting to strike. Heads on a swivel, the team prepared themselves for the next attack.

"The threads!" Edelein repeated, this time with more fervor. "Gihon, do you really not see them? Does no one see the wires all around it?"

Is this a Zenluvian thing? Gihon wondered. *What threads?*

Lunging out from another rift, Euphrates turned its attention towards Edelein.

Whatever those wires may be, it seems to dislike that Edelein can see them. It is targeting her now...!

Gihon stepped in front of Edelein, activating a rampart array to block the hit from the Dweller's extended claws. A sudden crack alerted Gihon as Euphrates continued to push forward into him, its strength growing until the array shattered under the pressure.

"Gihon!" Edelein called out as the Dirigent tumbled backwards, a bleeding wound slashed across his chest.

"It's not deep," Gihon assured her as he sat up. "Fall back, quickly!"

Edelein turned to face the Dweller, eyeing the silver cords that enveloped the creature. She reached forward, grabbing a bundle of threads with both hands.

"Edelein, what the hell are you doing? I said fall back!" Gihon repeated, watching Edelein hold onto nothing with her hands extended. "Zander, stop her–"

"Ahead of you," grunted the sphynx zoa, already in a full sprint to intercept the unfolding scene.

The threads wrapped around Edelein's wrists. The

lioness looked down curiously as the silver cords connected her to Euphrates, almost seeming to share a powerful moment with the monster. In a flash, the rift opened beneath the Dweller again and the beast dropped down into the Sea of Miracles once more. Edelein slipped to the ground as her arms were yanked downwards, causing Zander's desperate leap to miss her as she hit the mud below.

Edelein let out a quick yelp as the threads tugged her arms forward, twisting her feline body helplessly to share a desperate glance towards her allies as the Dweller pulled her into the Sea of Miracles, closing the rift behind her and leaving nothing but silence where she had stood only a moment before.

CHAPTER 7

TRAGEDY

"There's a storm rolling in. It's going to snow."

Spira's sudden comment drew Luthro's attention from his seat beside Cari at the campfire. The team had just settled down for the evening, pitching tents and preparing rations. Lylia was tending to the flame, engaged in quiet conversation with Jinn.. Alett's hands were deep into his satchel, seeming to scrounge around for his tools. Nora sat cross-legged, dividing up portions of dried meat. The lightbound alchemist was staring up into the sky as she spoke, unblinking.

"It does feel a bit cold. The tents are weatherproof, though, so it should be fine," Luthro offered as he rose to his feet. "I'll go fetch Nephvir and let him know he needs to come back before the storm hits."

"Something's off about it. I can see the energies mixing with each other up there. There was no sign of inclement weather even ten minutes ago. Isn't that strange?" Spira continued as Luthro disappeared into the swamp.

"The thicket around us feels concerningly still, more so than usual," Cari added.

"There's no animals, either. Until now, there's been frogs and birdsong. The forest holds its breath," Jinn stated. "It awaits… something."

"What is it waiting for?" Nora asked, far from familiar with the Zengarde's abstract concepts of nature.

"Nothing good, I'm sure," Lylia replied with a tense sigh.

Luthro returned a moment later, dejected. "Nephvir insists on being alone, and claims that he will simply shadow-step out of the storm if it gets bad."

Lylia sighed. "That's our Neph, alright. I suppose we cannot stop him. He really should stop running off alone, though. His solitary nature isn't great for team morale."

Luthro sat back down beside Nora, picking up a stick with his left hand to tend to the campfire. "I've come to learn that this is normal behavior for him, so we have to trust his judgement. He would return to us if something went wrong."

Nora handed Luthro a piece of dried meat. The alchemist passed the meat to Jinn, who tossed an apple back to Luthro from his own bag in return. Luthro effortlessly caught the apple with his free hand, still idly tending to the fire with his other one.

"Thank you, Dritet Jinn," Luthro smiled gently.

"Excellent reflexes, Luthro," Jinn replied. "Your right-hand dexterity has improved. If I were more unfamiliar with you, I'd wonder if you were ambidextrous."

"I am most definitely left-handed, like Master Gihon, but I find it important to train both hands to be prepared for anything. I care about competence, not just pure academics."

"Maybe spending time with real warriors has opened Luthro up to real combat training," Spira chuckled.

Nora looked up, extending her palm as snow began to fall. Gentle flakes landed on the tips of her grey feline ears, cold and unwelcome.

"It's a bit early for snowfall," Nora wondered aloud. "Like Spira said, this weather is a little strange. We don't usually get the first snow for another month."

"The leaves have been changing color for some time now, though, so I suppose it's not entirely unconventional," Luthro assured. "I quite enjoy the break from the heat, and the brilliance of the foliage this time of year is refreshing."

Spira and Nora stared blankly at Luthro. After a long moment, Spira asked, "What's your favorite color, Luthro?"

Luthro glanced back at Spira, his expression deadpan. "Really? Look at me and tell me what you think it is. I don't just dye my hair green for fun."

Lylia and Alett picked up on the lightbound alchemist's mannerisms, tensing up as they realized what Spira was implying. Still wary, Alett gently asked, "Luthro, I thought your favorite color was that deep fuschia shade of Cari's hair, not the green of yours."

"Don't get me wrong, it suits her wonderfully. She looks like a rose," Luthro admitted with a quick glance at the zoa he spoke of. "I would still say that I prefer green, though."

"I knew something was off about you!" Cari sprung to her feet, pointing at the alchemist. "You told me you thought my hair was purple when we first met. Luthro can't see pink!"

"Cari's right. Reds are too dull for Luthro to make out clearly, so mixed colors tend to lean more blue. You're the fae from the dungeon, aren't you?" Spira spat, drawing a hardlight spear and pointing it at her friend. "Luthro's pretty bad at using his right hand, too. The way you caught that apple wasn't something he'd do."

"I'm color-deficient, not colorblind," Luthro retorted. "I thought Cari's hair was purple, but she explained to me that it's more of a magenta color. I learned, that's all."

"You said it suits her, even though you don't know what the color really looks like. Luthro isn't the type for empty flattery. Plus, you commented on the changing leaves earlier, as well as the green of your own hair. Reveal yourself, puca," Lylia thumped her staff against the ground, vines springing up and grabbing Luthro's wrists.

"Something's wrong," Jinn stressed, standing.

"You mean something *else*?" Lylia asked. "We've got a handful to deal with already. Can it wait?"

"Where the hell is Luthro?" Cari asked, shoving him down with one boot on his chest, lips curled into a feral snarl. "What did you do to him?"

"It's Nephvir," Jinn continued urgently. "I sense danger nearby."

"Seriously?" Spira groaned. "Luthro is missing and Neph is in danger at the same time? Alright, look. We don't have time for this. Tell us where Luthro is, admit to being a fae, and we will let you go. If not, we torture the information out of you. Your choice."

"Spira, stop! I'm your friend, Luthro, I swear. You wouldn't hurt me."

Spira laughed, pressing her spear forward to touch Luthro's neck. "You severely underestimate how badly I've wanted to shove that little nerd around. Go ahead, give me the chance."

"Can we do this later?" Luthro pleaded. "Let's go find Nephvir first, and then you can interrogate me until you decide that I am the real one. Deal?"

"Don't say anything, Spira," Lylia warned. "He is trying to bind you into a fae contract. If you agree to his deal, we cannot be sure what hidden meaning there may have been within it."

"I've got Neph's location," Jinn opened his eyes, Seventh Sense guiding him towards his fellborn ally. "It's bad, Lylia. We have to go."

The color drained from Lylia's face, the elf understanding the meaning of her partner's words. Her druidic magic faltered as fear consumed her, allowing Luthro to wriggle free and push Cari off of him. Putting a few paces of distance between himself and the others, a cold laugh bellowed from the alchemist's chest.

"You were so focused on keeping the wolf zoa in your sights, it was all-too easy to replace your friend Luthro. You should have trusted your prior instincts, elf," the puca sneered, running a hand through Luthro's black hair. "Small frame, dark hair. You should have kept an eye on Luthro instead."

With a flash, the creature ahead of them turned into a perfect replica of Jinn Canis, the only difference being the cold and wicked grin across his lips.

"This form doesn't suit me as much, don't you think?" Kow extended its arms wide, flexing Jinn's muscular body. "It is far too high-maintenance. Anyhow, your Luthro is long-gone. I've been here much longer than you fools realize. But don't worry, I've put in a good word about Nephvir to my supervisor. He'll be in good hands."

Almost as if on cue, a voice called out from behind. "What's going on, you all? Is something happening?"

The group turned around, relieved to see an unscathed Luthro. When they looked back at Kow, there was nothing standing where the puca had stood a moment before, only faint footprints to indicate that Kow had been there at all.

Cari ran forward and embraced Luthro tightly, comforted by the knowledge that he was unharmed. The alchemist blushed deeply, grabbing Cari's shoulders and gently removing her.

"Cari, we're wasting time. We have to go," Jinn huffed, taking off into the frigid swampland.

"We have to get him out of there," Lylia explained in a panic as she hurried after Jinn. "I-I don't know what to do. We can't fight, and if we flee, they will just follow–"

"Who will follow? Lylia, why are you so spooked? What's going on?" Luthro reiterated, begging for an explanation as he chased the others.

Rime and frost began to coat the leaves and bark as the group sprinted forward, hot breaths visible as small puffs of desperation to find their missing ally.

"Neph stole his scythe, Crescent Shadow, from the Winter Court," Alett explained. "The puca mentioned a supervisor. I think it told the Unseelie where to find Neph after our first interaction, and they've finally come for him."

"Pissing them off is a certain death sentence. He's only escaped his fate for so long because the Deepwood is the Summer Court's territory," Jinn added.

Alett continued, "The Summer fae are allies of Zenluve. They thought it was funny that he stole from the Winter fae, so they've been offering him protection by giving him the position as a Zengarde."

"Wait, the puca came back?" Luthro exclaimed in disbelief.

"As you, yes!" Cari replied. "We thought something had happened to you!"

"I-I apologize, I couldn't find Nephvir, so I was looking for him. Nothing was amiss, I promise," Luthro assured. "I shouldn't have left. All of this served as a distraction to inhibit us from reaching Nephvir before the fae did."

"Nephvir!" Lylia called out, trembling as she slowed her pace to take in the clearing ahead.

"Don't come any closer, Lylia!" Nephvir warned in response, hearing the sound of his allies approaching. "Stay away!"

Sleet froze the ground underfoot, overcast cloud cover dispelling any shadows for the fellborn to hide himself within. Nephvir was engaged in battle with a single fae, as a hunting pack surrounded the two to prevent him from fleeing.

The icy fae warrior was large, with silvery armor coated in frost. His helmet bore large antlers and obscured his face, but menacing blue eyes glowed from the shadows beneath. Taking in the sight of such a fearsome foe sank the hearts of Nephvir's allies into despair, almost as if their blood was frozen just from looking at him.

The hunting pack around them was composed of several different races: the approaching team were able to recognize dwarves, elves, and humans alike mounted on ghastly white horses. A few ghost-like hounds stood at attention behind the one attacking Nephvir, drooling in anticipation as they awaited commands from their master.

Lylia brushed against an unusual texture underfoot as she stopped running. Looking down, a familiar violet notebook was lying open on the ground, scrawled onto by the familiar handwriting of the Zengarde's Noentet. Picking it up, the elven warrior began to read the hastily-written warning from her friend:

Lose your head while obliged to fae

Gallop by night, grieve by day

Return the blade back to the source

Lest you suffer from the one on horse

Nephvir Nyxveil, he comes to collect

Dullahan beckons

Dullahan beckons

The Pale King comes to collect

The Pale King is here

Dullahan beckons!

Beyond the cryptic poem, Nephvir had scribbled his full name repeatedly onto every other page. Old sketches were covered in the same prophetic words, each one signed more desperately by the same name: Nephvir Nyxveil.

"A situation involving the fae and someone's full name is never going to end well," Lylia muttered under her breath, dropping the book.

"Dullahan," Cari whispered, glancing down at the page for a moment before looking ahead. "The headless hunter. That guy has his head, though. He's not on a horse, either."

"Neph isn't fighting against Dullahan," Lylia realized. "He *is* Dullahan. This writing isn't a poem, it's a prophecy."

Alett shuddered, adding, "If we're to believe the frantic scribbles Neph wrote, it would mean the one he's up against is the

Pale King."

"We have to do something!" Luthro insisted, confused by the stillness of each Zengarde.

Hearing their debate, Nephvir spared a quick glance to the side as he continued to exchange blows from his scythe with the Pale King's broadsword. As the fae struck at Nephvir's neck repeatedly, the fellborn retaliated with defensive blocks to create distance.

He's going for the neck. Decapitating Nephvir, fulfilling this prophecy of the headless hunter, Lylia thought.

"Get out of here, you guys!" Nephvir demanded. "You're just putting yourselves in danger!"

Noticing the distraction, the Pale King made a short gesture towards the team. One of the hounds lunged forward, baring its fangs. Luthro wasted no time in retaliating, enhancing the mass of his pocketwatch and hurling it forward by the chain.

The golden watch passed cleanly through the dog's spectral form. Narrowly dodging the beast's bite, Luthro darted to the side and began to think quickly.

The stories say that fae can only be affected by iron, Luthro recalled as he set up another array.

"Spira, use your hardlight to create a shadow for him!" Luthro commanded.

"Luthro, don't–!" Lylia warned a moment too late.

Luthro's watch faded from a brilliant gold to polished iron with only a moment to spare as he struck at the hound. The dog yelped, tumbling backwards.

Bright light surrounded Spira as she summoned a large shield of hardlight. Raising it upwards to cast a harsh shadow, the shield dissipated as bone-chilling fog immediately obscured the area in response.

"It's not going to work in the Unseelie domain," Lylia

warned, "and hurting the fae is the last thing we want to do right now. We'll all die if we do anything."

"So what, we let them kill Nephvir, then?" Spira retorted.

"You don't get it!" Lylia yelled.

"Explain it, then!" Spira countered.

"Nephvir was a mercenary before joining us. He had taken on a mission to retrieve a scythe, Crescent Shadow, and reunite it with its owner: a fae named Dullahan, the headless hunter."

"Neph was never able to find Dullahan, is the thing," Cari added. "He kept the scythe and joined the Zengarde so that the Winter Court would never be able to hunt him down for failing the mission."

"And as we are learning now, the fae he took the deal with was none other than the Unseelie's Pale King himself. Erlking Eochaid," Lylia concluded. "The reason why I told you to stop is because the fae operate with hidden rules that us onlookers are wholly unaware of. The frost indicates that we are in Eochaid's domain right now. If we don't follow his rules, we die."

In the battle ahead, Nephvir took a wide swing towards the Pale King. His scythe stopped suddenly, lodged onto conjured icicles from the ground as Erlking Eochaid planted a firm kick into Nephvir's solar plexus. The fellborn tumbled backwards, slamming into a tree and buying the Erlking time to turn towards the new arrivals.

The Pale King slowly approached the group. Luthro stepped forward to meet him, raising his head and declaring, "I would like to make a bargain with the fae."

"What are you doing?!" Lylia hissed under her breath. "That'll be a death sentence!"

"It's the only chance to save Nephvir," Luthro whispered. "I'm the reason this happened. I should be the one to take responsibility for it."

"Don't tell him thank you, please, or that you're sorry," Lylia hurried through her warnings as the Pale King approached them. "And don't–"

The Erlking looked down at Luthro, his words cold as ice as he asked, "Who am I addressing?"

Lylia coughed, throwing in a warning, "Don't give your full name."

"My friends refer to me as Luthro," the alchemist answered.

"How am I, who is not your friend, to refer to you?"

"You may refer to me as Luthro as well."

"So we are friends, then?" Erlking Eochaid queried.

"If you so wish," Luthro replied. "As friends, how may I refer to you?"

"The Pale King." The wind picked up as the name is uttered, almost as if even the atmosphere itself bows to the title. "You attacked my hound. Unbecoming of a friend, wouldn't you say?"

"I'm—" Luthro stopped himself as he remembered Lylia's words.

I shouldn't admit fault. If I say yes, would that mean I am no longer a friend, but an enemy?

"That action was to prevent further harm between the two involved parties," Luthro pivoted.

"How very kind of you, Luthro. Though I do not find your method of using iron a kindness. My hound is injured, limiting his propensity to hunt foxes."

Sweat dropped down Luthro's brow. He could feel the trail it left behind as the cold air brushed past, reminding him of the dangerous game he was playing. Behind him, Lylia was frozen still.

Should I intervene? I know more about the fae than he does, but even I am not confident in my ability to speak to one, Lylia wondered. *No, I need to trust him.*

Luthro reached into his pocket and unhooked his pocket watch from its chain. The alchemist nervously and slowly approached the Erlking, the hoar frost crunching underneath his shoes ringing loudly in his ears.

"My pocketwatch, Pale King. I offer it to you."

The Pale King extended his armored hand towards Luthro. "Luthro, my friend, lend me a hand and help me receive your gift."

As Luthro started to move again, Lylia chimed in, "Pale King! Your friend, Luthro, needs both of his hands. His profession requires it."

"And who is this who speaks for my friend, Luthro?"

Trying to suppress her fear, Lylia stepped in front of Luthro to address the fae.

"Pale King, I can tell you my name, though you cannot have it. I am Lylia, a humble elf. The watch is sentimental to our friend Luthro. He cares for it as I am sure you care for your subjects."

The watch flew out of Luthro's hand as it zoomed into the clutches of the Pale King. He turned it over, admiring the polished gold before opening it. "Lylia, the humble elf, I wish to hear from my friend Luthro."

"What do I say?" Luthro whispered to Lylia.

"The truth. He will kill you if you lie. But be careful, as he will use anything you reveal against you if you don't take precautions," the elf warned quietly.

Addressing the Erlking, Luthro stood firm. "Over time, your hound will heal, ready to hunt foxes once more, my friend. The watch is important to me, and I ask that it be important to you, Pale King."

Eochaid remained silent as he pocketed the watch. The archfae stared deeply at Luthro for a long moment before addressing him once more. "Luthro, my friend, you wish to bargain with me. May I have ten minutes of your time?"

Lylia's eyes widened as she turned over to Luthro, the alchemist responding with a resounding, "Yes, of course."

"The conditions of your bargain. Speak it," demanded the Pale King.

"You wish to behead Nephvir, subjecting him to become Dullahan. I ask that you spare Nephvir of that fate, so that he may keep his head and not live as the headless hunter Dullahan," Luthro requested slowly, trying to place each word intentionally.

Lylia's face dropped as if she noticed an error in Luthro's request, but did not intervene in understanding that doing so would further anger the archfae. The Pale King had already made it clear that he wanted to speak with Luthro alone, and Lylia knew more lives would be endangered if she spoke up again.

Eochaid paused and turned to look at Nephvir. The fellborn was leaning heavily on his scythe, clearly damaged from the fight. Returning his icy gaze to Luthro, the Erkling replied, "Very well. I will not behead Nephvir Nyxveil, and he shall not live as Dullahan. The scythe, however, will return to its master, the one known as Dullahan."

Relief washed over the party silently as Eochaid mounted his white steed.

"Pale King, you have not stated your terms. What do you want from me in return?" Luthro asked.

Looking down from his horse, the Pale King replied simply, "Friend Luthro, you have already given it."

"I have not given anything," Luthro responded, eyebrows furrowed in confusion.

"You gave him ten minutes of your time," Lylia explained. "I wish I could tell you what he plans to do with it."

"Hello? Where did you all go?" Nephvir's sudden question

struck a sickening fear into his allies' hearts.

"Can he not see us?" Nora asked.

"No, it's–" Lylia's attempt at an explanation was cut off by an airless gasp as her body slowed until it was frozen in place.

Luthro and Cari began to run forward towards Nephvir, only making it a single step before their bodies froze beside each other.

Nora, Spira, Alett, and Jinn became immobilized on the backline, suspended in time. The Pale King leaned down from his horse, opening the pocket watch and extending it towards Luthro. The alchemist could barely make out the time on its open face as Nephvir continued to stumble around, searching for his allies.

"Oh, my. To think I would be so lucky," spoke a giddy and unwelcomed voice.

A familiar tenebrous mount charged forward, hooves like thunder as Kimaris extended his lance. With no shadows to step into, Nephvir was powerless to escape the speed of the homunculus' horse as the lancer struck, driving his weapon through the fellborn's chest and pinning him to a tree.

Dismounting, Kimaris let out a joyful laugh, approaching the tree to admire his work as the lance impaled into Nephvir's sternum fixed him helplessly in place. Looking around for the other Zengarde, Kimaris shrugged.

"I don't know what happened to you, but you look like you got the shit kicked out of you. All alone, too! Usually you bastards are crawling around each other like roaches. When there's one, there's more. And yet, here we are!"

Kimaris chuckled as Nephvir's blood welled around the large lance, spilling out and staining the grass a dark indigo color. The homunculus withdrew his weapon, watching as the Zengarde crumpled into the grass, his body soaked in a pool of his own blood.

Time held its breath as Nephvir Nyxveil bled out into the

ground, his allies powerless to do anything but watch helplessly as the Noentet let out a single, lonesome cry, dying as lonely as he lived.

As the life faded from Nephvir's eyes, the Erlking's fog lifted. Noticing the scythe laying alone in the mud, Kimaris approached and lifted it into the air, relishing in his trophy.

"This'll make things easier," Kimaris said with a grin as he vanished into the shadows.

"Two minutes and thirty-seven seconds," the Pale King stated, closing the pocket watch.

Time resumed as the watch's face was obscured once more, the warriors feeling warmth and movement returning to their bodies. A desperate wail ripped from Cari's throat, the zoa stumbling forward towards her fallen friend.

"The agreement has been honored," continued the Pale King. "Nephvir Nyxveil will keep his head and he will not live as the next Dullahan. As he suffers from the one on horse, so too the prophecy has been fulfilled. Friend Luthro, I will meet you again to claim my remaining seven minutes and twenty-three seconds. Perhaps then, my hound will have returned to hunting foxes."

Eochaid put away Luthro's watch. Satisfied with the tragedy he delighted in witnessing, he turned his horse and disappeared into the woods, followed after by his hunting party.

The swamp's silence was broken by Cari's racking sobs. Frost began to melt as the Pale King exited, the clearing beginning to warm up, though the scene ahead was colder than ever. Cari knelt over Nephvir's body, grieving loudly and ignoring the gruesome hole in his chest.

"I-I don't understand," Luthro trembled, approaching beside Lylia. "He agreed to spare Nephvir from his fate–"

"You weren't clear enough," Lylia mumbled, her voice broken. "You didn't ask to spare his life, only to change his fate.

Neph didn't become Dullahan, which is what you requested. He did honor the agreement, and now he has seven more minutes to do that to us again. We could all die, one by one, while you're left alive and forced to watch. This is why I warned you to not interact with the fae. Those cunning, good-for-nothing, heartless–"

"Lylia!" Alett called out, his voice shaking and filled with panic.

The owl zoa's face was stained with tears. Beside him, the young alchemist Nora was crying into Spira's embrace, and Jinn was crouched down, facing away. In his gloved hands, Alett was holding onto the relay stone as it glowed and buzzed.

"Eddie's in trouble," Alett whimpered.

Luthro's eyes widened at the sight of the stone, realizing another life was in danger. Another life that, if the alchemist stepped out of line a single time, would be another death by his hands.

CHAPTER 8

ANGUISH

Edelein's piercing blue eyes opened as she felt her body grow weightless. The Queen was floating in space, an ocean of stars enveloping her and soaking her skin with realities never before seen. Fragments of other planes hung suspended in the distance, revealing slivers of every possibility contained within their universe. Looking down, Edelein eyed the silver cord around her wrist. She followed the trail it left until her eyes met an unfamiliar pair of sad gold ones.

The man in front of her was frail, nothing more than a skeleton wrapped in skin. His hair was dark and disheveled, shaggy and unkempt like a prisoner. He was restrained by a netting of silver threads, his eyes pleading for escape.

A sense of cosmic understanding began to overflow from Edelein's heart. Reaching forward, the Queen began to undo the tangled web that imprisoned the distraught man.

On the material plane, tensions rose as Gihon and the others followed the afterimages of Edelein and the Dweller as they floated high off the ground.

"What is it doing?" Zander asked.

"I am… not sure," Gihon admitted, "I have never seen it be so stationary."

"Zander!" Alett's voice called out from the treeline behind.

"Oh thank God, they got our relay," Mandus sighed in relief. "Luthro, can you take over this array for me? I need a break."

"Are you hurt?" Luthro asked his friend as he approached, placing a hand onto the array and relieving Mandus from his duty.

"No, I'm good. We lost Edelein, though."

"What the hell do you mean you lost Edelein?!" Cari bellowed, fighting tears again. "Zander, you were supposed to protect her! I can't go through this again!"

"No, she is not dead, she is–" Gihon began to explain, but stopped suddenly. "Again?"

"The homunculus, Kimaris. It's a long story," Spira started, her voice burdened. "Neph… didn't make it. He's gone."

A beat of silence swept through the group like a cold wind, sending chills through each fighter.

"I… wish the circumstances were better for this. We need to move right now if we want to save Edelein," Gihon said, seeming to be at a loss for words. "Spira, swap places with Jana. I will need Jana's help with this."

Refusing to waste any more time, Gihon activated a groundshift array in the center of the clearing. A large indent pressed downwards, forming a pool of murky water at his feet just large enough for the broad-shouldered Dirigent to fit into.

"What's your plan, raven?" Zander asked, watching as Gihon began to purify the water inside.

"Edelein kept commenting on some silver threads that none of us could see. Euphrates may have been trying to lure her with illusions and could have some sort of plan, so I need to get her out of there before she gets hurt."

"Mandus," Luthro commented, "either you hold this array or you get to draw the new one."

Mandus whined, trying to follow along with the other alchemists' quick thinking.

"It's a planar anchor. We can keep it here once it comes back. Hold the visibility array, or make the anchor. Your choice," Spira explained.

"I'll… hold it," Mandus decided, swapping places with Luthro again and freeing his ally to start drawing a large array into the mud.

"I'm going after her," Gihon clarified as he carefully lowered himself into the tub. "I'll dive into the Sea of Miracles. Once I have her, Jana will pull us both out."

"Pull you– you're not using a projection?!" Jana realized. "Master Gihon, you can't–"

"I know the risks, but it's our best bet right now, and we don't have a second to spare. The longer Edelein is in there, the less likely she is to be able to return fully. She may be permanently changed. I need you to guide me, my star student. Be my eyes."

Jana trembled, nodding obediently.

"Lock the Dweller onto our plane as soon as you see it. The Zengarde will be able to kill it easily once it cannot dive again," Gihon instructed, laying back and submerging himself fully into the water.

The Sea of Miracles continued to swirl around Edelein as her body pressed closer to the anguished man before her. Freeing him of the threads, the man reached out and touched Edelein's temple gently.

The Queen's vision shifted from the endless Sea in front of her to a new sight. A young woman's shoulders shook as she clutched onto her baby, golden eyes brimming with tears as long black hair fell to cover her face. The baby was barely moving, barely breathing as the mother wept, mourning what she knew would soon be the loss of her son.

Edelein blinked and the scene before her jumped once more. This time, the tormented mother ached as she bent over a creature's body, fastening it onto an alchemical array. Wisps of energy congregated around her and into the creature, and Edelein quickly understood the vision.

The creature she's creating is the Dweller. Euphrates. That means this woman is Arvien, Gihon's mother.

The scene changed again before Edelein could think further, this time showing Solomon and his crew pulling Euphrates out of the Sea of Miracles with a silvery net. Impaling the Dweller with his Divine Sword, Kether, Solomon imbued the monster's blood and the primordial waters of the Sea into his weapon.

For a brief moment, Edelein could see the present: a ruined city lost within time, a man in red barking orders at his lackeys.

I understand, Edelein thought, her heart full of sorrow and grief. *I know who you are.*

A sudden grip around Edelein's waist startled the lioness, firm arms interlocking around her. Pulling her against his body with one arm, Gihon freed his second hand to tug on a silvery chain that was attached to his own waist.

On the other side of the chain, Jana tugged back in response. "Go, Mandus!"

Luthro had taken over the concentration array after completing the anchor. The alchemists, ever the type to use their intelligence for clever solutions, had fastened the furthest end to the chain to Mandus after looping it through a hastily-made pulley up on a tree.

"Don't you fail on me, pulley thing," Mandus muttered to himself as he broke into a sprint.

The chain spilled out from the pool, whittling away at the ground and causing friction to resist Mandus' pull. The Zengarde waited, bated breaths held and weapons ready as they silently pleaded for the safe return of their Queen.

Primordial water rushed forth from the pool, Gihon holding tightly onto Edelein as they were pulled out of the Sea of Miracles. Not a single moment later, the tub exploded from force as the Dweller breached after them, sending mud and water spewing in every direction.

Spira activated the anchor array, locking the Dweller into their material existence. Mandus doubled back as Gihon threw his end of the chain to Luthro, the alchemy student gripping tightly until Mandus could wrap enough of the chain around the Dweller. The Dweller screeched as Luthro increased the mass of the chain, now webbed to imprison the monster as silver threads did just a moment earlier.

"Now!" Luthro called.

The Zengarde lurched forward, striking to kill. The seven warriors stopped, however, when they noticed that the creature was not resisting. The flowery petals surrounding its humanoid face had spilled open as it laid on its side, tears forming in Euphrates' empty eyes.

Gihon shook water from his limbs as he approached the Dweller. His adamantine sword conjured itself from the flowing fabric of his cloak, resting comfortably in his hand as the Dirigent gripped it tightly. Slowly, the Zengarde backed away as they noticed a shift in the energy around Gihon, allowing him space as he knelt down and put one hand on the creature's head.

Gihon closed his eyes as he ran his sword through Euphrates' heart, ending the decades of suffering that the Dweller had endured.

"Wounded, to me," Lylia commanded, drawing the

attention of the other Zengarde.

Gihon rose to his feet. Chest heaving as blood stained his clothes and hair, he withdrew his adamantine blade from the creature's body and dispelled it into a wisp of shadow. Shaking his head to clear his thoughts, the Dirigent turned to face his allies.

Edelein was breathing with short and panicked breaths from the shade of a black willow tree, laying flat on her back with her head propped up in Zander's lap. The sphynx stroked Edelein's hair gently with sympathetic eyes, ignoring everyone around them as he attempted to soothe her.

"What's happening to her, Gihon?" Alett asked, eyes wavering.

"Petrification is how Euphrates takes its victims," Gihon started, chest tightening as he recalled the anguished expression on the Dweller's face. "By dipping them into the Sea of Miracles, it effectively stuns them with an onslaught of cosmic knowledge, immobilizing them to then be buried alive."

"You can… fix it, though, right?" Alett pressed. "A-and why didn't you get petrified, too, then?"

"I bulwarked myself before I dove in after her, and I was only there for a moment," Gihon explained. "Edelein was far more exposed than I was."

Gihon approached Edelein and knelt down beside her. The Dirigent gently took her body from Zander's lap, propping her upright against the willow tree.

"Seeing every reality of every plane all at once, it is too much for one brain to comprehend. She's been exposed to the cosmic horrors and truths of our universe," Gihon explained further, removing his gloves and placing his bare hand on her cheek.

"You don't need your alchemists' gloves?" Alett asked, crouching next to Gihon and placing a warm hand on Edelein's shoulder.

The Queen's eyes were wavering, holding an emotion that no material being could understand. Gihon shook his head, rubbing a thumb along her cheek gently.

"Alchemy cannot cure petrification. In fact, the opposite is necessary. She needs to be grounded to our reality, so touching my skin to hers directly would help her more," Gihon continued as he pressed his forehead to Edelein's, looking into her eyes and taking deep breaths.

"I am here, Edelein," Gihon spoke softly. "Look at me. Focus on me and nothing else. I am with you. Everything will be alright. Breathe with me."

Edelein's eyes met his, tears forming and staining her cheeks as she began to shake.

"I… cannot move," Edelein whimpered, voice barely audible through her frozen jaw.

"I know. You are doing wonderful, though. You're coming back to us. You can be scared and you can cry," Gihon encouraged her gently, knowing that catharsis would only ground her even more. "Deep breaths, my Edelein. Just focus on me, here and now. I am here, and I will not leave you."

After a long moment, Edelein's breaths began to slow, her eyes still locked on Gihon as their foreheads remained pressed together.

"Do you see me, Edelein?" Gihon asked. "Only me?"

Edelein choked out what sounded to be an affirmation, unable to nod.

"Are you here with me on the material plane?"

Another grunt of acknowledgement.

"Excellent. I'm so proud of you for coming back."

Gihon withdrew himself, eyes softening with empathy for what was to come. Placing one hand on her thigh and the other on her calf, Gihon began to slowly lift and bend her leg upwards.

Edelein let out a sudden yowl, causing the Zengarde to stir with action. Alett leapt between Zander and Gihon with hands extended, having anticipated the sphynx's reaction. A short ways away, the other five members bristled and tensed, though they remained in place as Lylia continued to work her healing magic on her allies.

"Zander, stop! Don't interfere!" Alett warned. "Gihon knows what he's doing. This is the only way to help Eddie."

"My deepest apologies, Ehret Zander, but Alett is correct," Gihon said with a soft sigh. "Edelein needs a bit of help to be able to move on her own. I have to reintroduce the overexposed brain to her material body by moving her joints for her and forcing a neurological connection. The process, so I have heard, is incredibly overstimulating as the nerves become quickly flooded with stimuli. Edelein, are you alright?"

Edelein grunted again, managing a slight nod. Gihon set her leg down slowly and offered his bare hand to the lioness, holding it in front of her mouth.

"You can bite my hand if you feel pain, alright? I do not mind. Brave lioness, we are almost done. One more leg."

Shifting his position to where his free hand was placed under her other knee, Gihon began to lift it in the same gentle manner as before. Edelein gasped in pain before biting down on Gihon's hand, whimpering into his skin and shutting her eyes tightly as her nervous system began to awaken her body, rooting it to the material plane once more.

Edelein loosened her clamped jaws from Gihon's hand as he set her leg down. She began to roll her ankles and move her legs gingerly, testing out her body as Gihon pulled away.

"Do you still feel stiff anywhere else?" Gihon asked, discreetly wiping blood from a new puncture wound in his hand and putting his gloves back on.

Edelein shook her head, massaging her wrists. "What

you did to my legs seems to have restored the rest of my body, somehow."

"Your feet are the farthest part from your brain. If I can connect the neurological pathway back to your legs, it will fill in the rest for me. You need to take it easy for now, though. Rest for a few more minutes before we continue onwards."

I don't know if I should tell them that Edelein handled the petrification almost concerningly well. Exposure to the Sea of Miracles could be permanent at worst, or take weeks to recover from in a better scenario. How was she able to work herself out of the petrification so easily? This, alongside her natural affinity towards the Plane of Light... what exactly is Edelein's ancestry? Gihon wondered.

"Gihon," Edelein started suddenly, "I saw something in the Sea of Miracles."

"I mean, did you not see… everything?" Gihon asked. "Something is a bit of an understatement."

The lioness locked her gaze on Gihon's golden eyes for a long moment, reading his expression.

"So you do know. You found out too."

Gihon froze.

Does she mean...

"Euphrates, the Dweller, is your brother. Perath. The one that Arvien told you was dead. Alive, living as that… thing. That tortured creature."

Alchemists and Zengarde alike stirred at Edelein's reveal, concerned. Gihon paused, and nodded warily.

"I saw what he showed you when I touched you. What you say is true. I first thought that she turned his corpse into Euphrates to protect the leyline, except… I saw just now that my brother wasn't dead at all. Perath has been alive this whole time, living in agony. I-I don't understand why Arvien would do that to her own son," Gihon stuttered, a rare sight as his steady foundation showed its first crack. "Surely, there was a reason. She told me he was sickly. That he died."

"He provoked us because he yearned for his release, and thought we would be the ones capable of doing it," Edelein confirmed.

"It has been nearly thirty years since Arvien first created Perath. This was before any of the rest of us. When I got close to the Dweller earlier, his face looked so… mournful. He was in pain. I recognized him as my own kin."

"Perath also wanted to show me something else," Edelein struggled to her feet, leaning on Zander. "Solomon isn't here. The trail we're following is a fake."

"Solomon isn't here? Aren't you and Thorne tracking him?" Luthro countered. "How could he not be here?"

"I believe that we have explained how Solomon lacks scent. We can really only trace the empty pocket where there is no scent… the issue I've realized is that all of the homunculi are like that. He may have left a homunculus in the swamp as a decoy, leaving us to trace it instead of him," Edelein huffed.

"Well, we know which homunculus he left behind," Jinn muttered.

"Oh, did you see one?" Edelein asked.

"We had a run-in with the Unseelie Court," Lylia started, her voice cracking as her throat tightened. "They came for Crescent Shadow. Luthro tried to barter, but Kimaris showed up, and the fae had frozen the rest of us…"

Edelein fell silent as she realized the weight of Lylia's words, noticing her fellborn warrior's absence.

"Nephvir. He's… gone, isn't he?" Edelein asked with wide eyes, her voice barely audible. "The fae killed him?"

"Kimaris did it while the fae were occupied with us," Lylia

confirmed. "It was the Pale King. He froze time, isolating us from him. Your Majesty, I am so–"

Edelein buried her face into Zander's chest. The Ehret held onto his Queen as she let out mournful, anguished sobs. Zander's face was stern, any emotion deeply hidden by his sense of duty.

Edelein, what will you do if one of the Zengarde dies here in Caandemium? Will you regret staying? Zander's words echoed in the Queen's mind as she cried, grateful that Zander had offered enough empathy to console her from the exact thing he had forewarned her of.

"We have to go back for him. He deserves to be buried," Edelein choked out softly. "I was never able to bury Tyrus and Cyzen. I've lost too many of you already."

Gihon nodded, knowing better than to challenge her priorities during a time of grieving. "We will go back for Nephvir and bury him. When you feel ready, we can go after Solomon again."

Edelein blinked, grateful for his understanding as she wiped her tears. The team, now united, began to head back in the direction where they had met the archfae.

"As I was saying," Edelein shakily forced herself to speak after a long moment of silence, trying to push through her despair for the sake of the mission. "Perath showed me where Solomon was. A fallen city where time does not flow."

"Othalgar," Gihon realized aloud. "It makes sense. His plan is clever."

The Sea of Miracles is a total overload of information, and nearly impossible to discern our reality from others, yet she was able to identify and recognize powerful intel. Is this related to why the Dweller seemed so eager to target her? Did Perath know she could do that?

"He has already ruined Othalgar once, so he would not

percieve it as problematic if he repeated the events once more. The only issue with this is that Othalgar is a day or two journey by autowagon, and the entrances are swarming with Inquisitors of the Church. The Church has a warrant out for Solomon, so he could never make it past them without being caught–" Gihon stopped suddenly, his face dropping.

"What is it?" Edelein pressed, grabbing his arm as her eyebrows furrowed, trying to read his expression.

"I think that I may be the most foolish person in the Marleogne family."

"What are you talking about?"

Gihon reached a gloved hand upwards to cover his mouth, his mind racing as his eyes darted around as a sea of thoughts crashed over him.

"I am an absolute *simpleton*. I cannot believe I have never realized this."

"I could have told you that you're an idiot, but I'll hear you out anyway," Zander huffed with his arms crossed.

"When I was younger, Arvien used to take Solomon to Othalgar for his studies. Somehow, I had never considered asking *how* they were traveling there in such short periods of time. I figured that Arvien always told me the things that mattered to me, so I never thought to ask her how they got there. This entire time, my entire life, there's been an index to Othalgar inside of the Athenaeum, and I had no idea until this moment."

"Mandus, translate the man's spiral into madness, please," Thorne instructed.

"You know the little chess piece Gihon has? It's called an index. Gihon uses the rook piece to summon the big Fortress Black out of the limbus plane, kind of like teleportation but more science-y. Gihon's saying that there's an item somewhere in the Athenaeum that could teleport its wielder to Othalgar, similar to how the rook teleports the Fortress to our plane. You caught up yet?" Mandus replied without missing a beat.

"Could technology like that be used to teleport people across the world? Would something like that make it easier to get from here to Zenluve?" Edelein wondered aloud, but Gihon shook his head.

"Not quite, it's a bit more nuanced than that. The further away a target, the less accurate the index becomes. A distance like that would likely thrust the user into the middle of the Deepwood, and you know what would happen to someone in that situation."

Luthro's eyes flashed briefly as he looked up. "I wonder if we were to combine index alchemy with something similar to Mandus' speed arrays, we could circumvent that."

"The user would explode," Mandus denied. "There'd be no way to guarantee they wouldn't impact any object in that long distance. At a speed like that, everything in their path would get obliterated. You know that's why I can only use speed arrays for very short, straight, and unobstructed distances."

"We're wasting time," Zander growled, seeming to be eager to change the subject away from the idea of connecting Zenluve to the Caandemites.

"I actually agree with Zander, for now," Gihon nodded. "I don't know what item the index will be, so we will have to scour every corner of the Athenaeum until it's found. But, for now…"

The trees opened up to a clearing stained with the death of a friend. The sight made Edelein's knees buckle, caught by Zander as he held onto her to keep her upright. Nora looked away, grimacing, afraid to relive the memories of just a short while earlier.

Nephvir's body was still and cold. He was slumped onto the ground by the tree where Kimaris had impaled him, exactly where the others had left him to pursue Edelein and her team. The gaping hole in his chest was horrific to look at, grotesque and bloody.

"Gihon, can you…" Edelein stopped herself as she felt anguish begin to close her throat.

The Dirigent clasped his hand on her shoulder gently. Nodding, he turned to the clearing and activated another groundshift array, opening up a grave for the Zengarde's Noentet.

"Neph, I'm so sorry," Edelein whispered as Gihon lowered his corpse down. "You lost your life serving me. I'll never forget your courage and your spirit. I couldn't be there to save you."

"Your Majesty," Zander consoled, his voice gentle. "Us Zengarde… we swear to serve you at the cost of our lives if necessary. Nephvir made that promise to you, just like the rest of us. Hold your head high, for it will honor him."

"I don't want to lose any more of you, alright?" Edelein sniffed. "That's an order."

"We'll kill that Kimaris guy, too," Thorne added. "Whether you order us to or not. We're going to avenge Neph. It's what he would want."

"For once, I agree with Thorne," Jinn confirmed.

Edelein nodded, pulling away from Zander and wiping her face. "Neph, I'm sorry that we can't spend more time together. You deserve better than this. But for now, we're going to go after that bastard, okay? We'll kill him, and… and we'll give you a good Zenluvian sendoff when we're back home."

This is so unfair, Edelein thought in dismay. *I want to lay down and give up. I want to mourn. But if I do, more will die. Thus the Queen must press onwards. I'm sorry, Neph.*

A cold silence overcame the group as they turned back towards the town, the sounds of their footsteps heavy and uneasy.

The sun began to sink lower in the sky as the group pressed on through the town of Ravencroft, each member of the large team lost in their own thoughts and focused on maintaining their pace with the others.

An index to Othalgar, right under my nose this entire time. Gihon thought silently to himself. *I cannot believe that I never asked Arvien how she was taking him there so quickly. Why did she keep this from me? She always told me everything. Why did Arvien not want me to know about this? I would consider the idea of this theory being incorrect in favor of believing that I would have known by now, but this is the only logical solution with any plausibility. Arvien must… she must have had a reason to hide this from me. Though, admittedly, nothing comes to mind if I try to think of one.*

Gihon shook his head, ridding himself of the clouded thoughts. *Solomon is wrong about her. Arvien was kind and benevolent. Certainly there was a perfectly normal reason for her to not tell me about the index. She doesn't keep secrets. She never kept secrets. Did she?*

Ahead of him, a familiar library silhouetted itself against the setting sun as the Corvid Athenaeum loomed overhead.

"We're here. Honorable Zenluvians, this is my true home; the Corvid Athenaeum. It's a large library of collected works from my master and her master before her; with study halls to educate my students, a few guest rooms, as well as my own master suite as the current keeper. Maintaining it is my pride and honor, so please make yourselves comfortable."

"We promise not to destroy it this time," Everett joked as Jana sighed beside him.

Ignoring the comment, Gihon continued as he opened the large and ornate wooden doors.

"We need to find the index as quickly as possible, but everyone needs to rest up as well. If everything goes according to plan, tomorrow will be the day we finally put an end to my family's greatest stain. Instead of a normal watch, everyone will rotate time spent sifting through items to see if any of them are indexed."

"How are we supposed to know if they are an index?" Jinn asked.

"Yeah, we're not exactly experienced alchemists, like you," Thorne added.

"Each shift will have one alchemist and two Zenluvians. Divide yourselves however you'd like. For now, I will be getting Her Majesty situated for the evening to rest."

"I'll take the last shift, earliest in the morning." Edelein agreed, feeling the weariness of the day beginning to catch up to her. "Zander, you will join Gihon and me for that."

Zander bowed his head obediently.

"We can take the first shift. I have some ideas of things to check," Jana offered. "Nora and Everett can join me."

Gihon nodded, turning to Edelein to confirm. "Is everything in order?"

"Yes," Edelein agreed, turning towards an elegant wooden staircase. "Though, if you do not mind, I am genuinely quite exhausted. I'll be off now."

"Would you like for me to see you up to a room?"

"No, it's fine. Work out the details with the others. I can find a place to sleep by myself."

I know this mood of hers... Edelein wants to be left alone. She's been a bit shaky for the last hour or so, so I believe it is not a ploy to sneak out. I can tell from her body language that she has aflare-up coming on and needs to sleep it off. Plus, with the death of her soldier weighing on her, it would be best to give her what she wants, so she can grieve.

Gihon nodded in understanding, leaving her alone and turning towards a set of hand-carved wooden doors beside the staircase. The large room inside boasted high ceilings, with wooden shelves reaching up to the very top of the walls. A perfect dream of any man with an affection for reading, the heart of the Athenaeum:

its main study hall.

In the center of the room stood a few antique desks, commonly used for his students' studies. One difference stood out to the Dirigent, however, as his eyes met those of an unexpected visitor.

Justice Vensworth sat expectantly at one of the desks, rising to greet Gihon as he entered the room. Justice was a dark-skinned woman with sharp features, around the same age as Gihon. She donned a black and gold uniform, capelet resting over her left shoulder. The uniform bore a golden crest, familiar to the Dirigent as the emblem of the Church of Prima Luma.

"Inquisitor Vensworth," Gihon greeted her with a firm handshake as he masked his confusion. "If you seek Spira, she's–"

"I'll speak with Spira later. I'm here for you, actually. Official business," Justice interrupted. "Dirigent, I've been in contact with the Society of Alchemists."

Why on Tevus would the Society be reaching out to the Church? Gihon wondered.

"Forgive my blunt approach, but consider this a courtesy for my sister's teacher. I have intel about the proposed removal from your position of Dirigent."

"What?!" Gihon shook his head in disbelief, pondering the source of her words. "Is it…"

"Rovanda Fairgraves is spearheading the movement, yes. The Dirigent of Lulgirm."

Gihon's face darkened with understanding, clenching his teeth.

"She's bringing personal business to work, is she?" Gihon asked after a long moment.

"According to Rovanda, you killed her son. She has a good reason to call for your removal as Dirigent."

"Tristan's blood is on my hands," Gihon muttered in

agreement, grief filling his voice. "It's been *years*, Justice. I do not deserve nor do I seek her forgiveness, but I've atoned for my sins. Tristan's death haunts me every single day, and I tried to shut down the Athenaeum as penance until Arvien commanded that I reopen it. I've never let another student die under my care since, and yet I am still eternally the enemy of Lulgirm."

Justice nodded, idly tucking a dreadlock behind her ear as she explained the situation further.

"To be frank, the other Dirigents don't like you, and you haven't given them a reason to feel otherwise. Your teaching methods not only resulted in Tristan's death, but also blinded Spira, for Ethereus' sake. Everyone up the chain of command knows that you've been off cavorting with the Queen of Zenluve, yet you have chosen to abstain from relinquishing any insider information about the Zenluvians."

"The Zenluvians do not wish for private information to be given to the Society. Not yet, at least," Gihon argued, "I am not withholding intentionally, nor am I here for espionage on behalf of the Society. Those were not my orders. This is absurd, Justice. This is just Rovanda allowing personal feelings to impact our workplace."

"This is a habit of yours, though," Justice countered. "No one in Caandemium knows a thing about Ravencroft, either."

Gihon's mind raced, anxiety setting in.

Arvien wished for Ravencroft to stay hidden, to protect the leyline. I cannot divulge that information to the Society under any circumstances.

At Gihon's silence, Justice continued.

"Dirigent, you understand that if you are removed from office, the Society will plant someone more favorable to their agenda. Whatever you've been hiding here is going to become accessible to every alchemist in Caandemium."

Gihon shut his eyes tightly, thinking.

"What do I have to do?" Gihon asked.

"Ravencroft or Zenluve. I need you to tell me everything you know about either your land or theirs. I'm on your side, Gihon, but you have to give me something to bring to the Society. If I can show them that you are gathering intel about the Zenluvians, I can get the other Dirigents to side with you over Rovanda and dismiss the case. You won't be considered as obstructing the flow of knowledge anymore," Justice pressed, looking at Gihon sympathetically. "I'm sorry it's come to this, but you have to choose."

Tense silence hung in the air as Gihon weighed his options, his hand forced by the very people who had placed him into this position. Justice stared at him expectantly, awaiting his answer.

"Very well. I'll tell you everything I know about the Zenluvians."

CHAPTER 9

THE CONTRACT

Passing by an open door obscured in shadow, Edelein hesitated for a brief moment as she felt a strange energy pass through her. In a swift moment, the lioness' eyes widened in alarm as two large hands darted out from the shadows, grabbing onto her and covering her mouth as they pulled her from the hallway and into the darkness.

Edelein clawed at the hands that pulled her in, the white gloves that hid her blackened skin straining to keep her sharp nails from breaking through. The room was dim, with nothing but gentle moonlight from an open window illuminating the space within. The stranger's hands turned her around, one hand still clasped firmly over her mouth as her face stopped an inch from Solomon's.

"I'm not wasting any time, Edelein. This is important. You know the drill," Solomon barked impatiently, his voice a quiet hiss. "I'm a mimic, don't break my figure. I'm not here, because I'm not stupid. I will let go of you and we can talk like adults, just you and me. This is *incredibly* important right now. Got it?"

Edelein nodded slowly, eyes narrow. Solomon gently removed his hand from her mouth and stepped backwards, towards the cold moonlight.

"I'm really not in the mood for this right now, Solomon," Edelein spat with a heavy heart.

"Ever since I was stuck with you in that reality sphere, I've been thinking. I've had this suspicion for a while, but seeing the way that Gihon reacts around you… seeing the way he handled that entire event, it has confirmed my theory."

"Your homunculus killed one of my men. Leave now. I have no interest in hearing you out anymore, and I shouldn't have trusted you back in the reality sphere."

Solomon hesitated for a moment.

"I'm sorry, Edelein. I really am. Kimaris has a tendency to do his own things, if you don't recall from the time he got me stuck with you in the aforementioned reality sphere. I made him stay behind to lure you guys away because I didn't trust him enough to keep him close. I'm sorry that it got your shadowstepper killed."

"How did you know that it was Nephvir?"

"I know everything. You should have figured that out by now. Are you going to accept my condolences or not?"

"What are you here for, homunculus?" Edelein hissed.

"There's something you need to know about Gihon. You can help him, I think." Solomon started, sitting on the windowsill and letting the evening breeze blow through his thick white hair.

Edelein crossed her arms warily, tail flicking. "Gihon has told me about his upbringing already. Mind you, his belief of what happened is surprisingly different from yours. I'm beginning to question if you were telling the truth back then."

"I'm telling the truth!" the homunculus whinged. "He doesn't see it the way that I do. He's blinded by his admiration for our mother. Come on, Edelein, you need to hear me out. I don't have time for debating whose idea of our tragic childhood is reality, and why mine is the correct answer. That's not what this is about."

"I have no reason to trust you."

"Get the raven out of your head for a moment. I didn't fight back when Gihon found us in the reality sphere, out of respect for you. You said that you saw some good in me, and here I am now, doing good. I have an idea on how to help Gihon with something that he needs, but for obvious reasons, he would not be open to hearing it from me."

"Why help him?"

"Because this particular issue doesn't affect my plans to obtain a soul, and the problem I am trying to fix is something that has annoyed me about him for a long time. Has he told you about his contract?"

Edelein paused, confused. "Not in much detail, only that Arvien traded something with some entity from Limbo to obtain Fortress Black for him."

"What did she trade?"

"Gihon doesn't know."

Solomon sucked air through his teeth, wincing at her words.

"I don't know how to say this nicely, so I'm going to be blunt. Gihon lied to you," Solomon stated.

A long beat of silence fell between the two, Edelein hanging on the words in confusion as she thought about the implication of Solomon's point.

"You're telling me that he *does* know what was traded? That doesn't make any sense. He'd have no reason to not tell us, and he knows that lying to me is a fast way to get me to stop trusting him."

"You know that he's lied to you before, so why is this any

different?"

"I'm… not sure," Edelein admitted. "I was hoping it was because he's learned his lesson from the previous mistakes."

"Lying is a defense mechanism of weak-minded men who are afraid of themselves. It's why I don't lie. I do not fear the truth."

"Or its consequences," Edelein huffed.

"Correct. See? You're getting it now. All of that means nothing to me, which is why I always tell the truth, in one way or another. Gihon, on the other hand, is a coward who hides from himself because he fears that his choices will bring pain onto others."

"That isn't cowardice."

"So you've accepted him as a liar?"

"I-I don't like it, but… I guess he has his reasons."

"That tells me everything I need to know about you two," Solomon stood up from the windowsill, approaching her. "The rosy tint you see his world in makes you the perfect one to save him."

"Save him from what?" She asked.

"From Limbo, and from himself," Solomon earnestly clasped her shoulders, his eyes alight and swimming with thoughts. "He never told you what that bastard Arvien traded for the Fortress."

Edelein paused, her eyes locked on his.

"She gave them Gihon's heart."

The lioness laughed, bewildered as she pushed him away.

"You've lost it, Solomon. That doesn't make any sense. You're telling me that Gihon doesn't have a heart? He wouldn't be alive."

"Your naïveté knows no bounds, Your Majesty. Alchemy is a bit more complicated than you have come to understand, and that's not even mentioning the mystic alchemy that the Athenaeum practices. Extraplanar contracts don't necessarily adhere to Tevus logic." Solomon sighed. "There is a connection of limbus energy that binds his heart to Limbo. A thick layer of limbus energy coats his heart, impenetrable, forever muffling his emotions. The forces of Limbo hold his life in their wretched claws, and he gets unfathomable strength in return: Fortress Black, straight from the Curator's Collection itself."

"That makes no sense," Edelein denied, shaking her head in confusion. "No mother would trade their son's heart for power."

If that's true, why wouldn't he tell me? Edelein wondered in a silent addition.

"Now you see Arvien's true colors. She was pretty messed up in that head of hers, desperate to protect her favorite son. As for why Gihon didn't tell you, I can only theorize that to be because he was afraid of you seeing him as heartless," Solomon answered, seeming to read her thoughts. "He sees himself as a monster."

"I… don't understand," Edelein admitted. "Why his heart? Why any of this? What does that mean for him?"

"Trading his heart was meant to keep him safe, at the cost of his joy. Allowing Limbo to keep your heart is a contract that enforces one's physical resilience in exchange for emotion. Gihon is near impossible to kill, but he doesn't feel emotions the way the rest of us do. His entire life is a monotonous slog through academics and alchemy. Nothing means anything to him, not since he was given the Fortress."

"That's not true," Edelein replied, recalling all of Gihon's fierce anger and flustered stutters. "I've seen him express emotions before."

"That's *exactly* what I'm getting at. Ever since my brother took on a part of the Black Armament, he stopped feeling anything. His smiles were courteous, and nothing more." Solomon clutched one hand to his chest, the way Edelein had seen Gihon do countless times before. "He had no joy, no anger, it was like everything was trapped under a wet blanket. Seeing him with you is… fascinating. You're forcing his body to slowly weaken its contract."

"What happens if the contract breaks?"

"He'll finally be able to be in love with you."

Edelein's ears flattened, a blush rising to her cheeks as she shifted from foot-to-foot in embarrassment, searching for words.

"I'm sure you meant beyond that. Gihon's contract has a clause in it that forbids him from taking a lover, because it would be a recipe for disaster for the poor soul he chooses. He can void his contract at any time by choosing to be in love with someone. That choice will unshackle his heart, freeing him to experience the wide range of emotions that people are designed to feel. You see, contracts with the Bookkeeper aren't like contracts with a devil. They're meant to be equally beneficial, no corrupted fine-print, and fully reversible."

"But then he would be vulnerable."

"Vulnerability is one of the beautiful things about being human."

"You'd be able to kill him! That's what this is about, isn't it? You want to murder even more people that I care about!"

Solomon sighed, pressing a hand to his temple. "This isn't some ploy to take his life, I assure you. My hatred for Arvien far exceeds my hatred for Gihon. Gihon is a sad, brainwashed little fledgeling who doesn't know any better. Undoing the contract is my magnum opus of a middle finger to Arvien, and frees my poor brother up to finally get a girlfriend. Everyone benefits from this except for Arvien, but she's dead. It's fine, though, because she sucks anyway."

Edelein hesitated, thinking it over before shaking her head. "This can't be true. You must have some sort of ulterior motive. Gihon would… he would have told me about this."

"You still don't believe me?" Solomon groaned, gesturing

towards the door behind her with one exasperated arm. "Ask him yourself, then."

Edelein turned around in the direction he pointed, eyes widening as she took in the familiar silhouette of Gihon standing in the entryway, illuminated by the hallway light behind him. His posture was tense, and it was clear that he had overheard enough of the conversation to know exactly what they were talking about.

As Gihon stepped through the door, the Queen's eyes adjusted to drink in his familiar features, cold in the dimly lit room. His eyes were conflicted, eyebrows furrowed. His clothes were still tattered from the fight against Euphrates, and yet it seemed to be the least of his worries.

"Forgive me for not telling you sooner," Gihon spoke quietly, his voice cracking. "Solomon is correct about the contract. I had a similar theory that I didn't take seriously until recently."

"Did you?" Solomon asked, bemused and curious.

Gihon nodded, touching his chest. "My chest… hurts when I'm around her. Sometimes she has these warm glances, or speaks in that warm and gentle way, and I feel this tug. It feels like the limbus energy is loosening within me."

"The fiery rage that Gihon had when he thought I had taken you, that was the most dangerous he's ever been. For any of us," Solomon mused. "Here's the issue, though. Gihon has to choose between his strength as a protector or his desire to be in love, and I can tell that he's hesitating. If he chooses you, he loses his power, and he isn't ready to let go of that yet."

"Is that true, Gihon?" Edelein asked, turning to face him.

Gihon looked down, his eyes studying the old hardwood under his feet. After a moment of consideration, he turned away.

"Solomon, leave now before I smash your clay doll to pieces. I am going to go get cleaned up from that fight earlier. You should get some rest, too, Edelein."

Tension was palpable in the air as Gihon turned away, exiting the room.

"See? He's hesitating," Solomon insisted.

"I think you should leave," Edelein glanced over her shoulder at the clay homunculus, her eyes lost in a thousand thoughts.

"I'm just trying to help," Solomon shrugged. "It's really got nothing to do with my plans. I just want Gihon to get a girlfriend so he won't be so miserable and empty all the time. You can fix him, you know."

"Right, I'm certain that losing the Fortress has nothing to do with us trying to stop you, right?" Edelein snapped from the doorway.

Silence met her words. Turning around, Edelein realized that the figure of Solomon was gone. Only a pile of clay remained in the empty room where they had spoken, and yet his words still hung heavy in her mind.

What if he's right? Edelein thought to herself as she made her way upstairs to the third floor of the Athenaeum. *For some reason, I can't shake it. I need to talk to Gihon about this more. I need to hear it from him.*

A large set of ornate wooden double-doors greeted the Queen atop the final flight of stairs, clearly indicative of the Athenaeum's master suite. Placing a hand on the brass doorknob, Edelein opened the door and stepped inside as her mind continued to race.

"Gihon, I need to talk to you," Edelein announced, closing the door behind her.

The Dirigent was standing on the opposite side of the room, by a large window and facing a beautifully-carved wardrobe. His mud-stained shirt and vest had been tossed onto a plush bed, fresh white button-down in his hands.

Edelein paused, her eyes wandering across the tight muscles of his upper back and landing on a large scar that cut through his otherwise flawless and pale skin. The scar started at the nape of his neck and scraped downwards between his shoulderblades, appearing to be a rather recent knife wound.

The frozen moment of time shattered as Gihon turned around suddenly from the sound of her voice, presenting his defined torso for a brief moment as he hurriedly pulled his shirt on to cover himself. Edelein noticed his physique as he fervently buttoned up, with large pectoral muscles befitting of his broad-shouldered build garnering her attention, drawing her gaze upwards from the toned abdomen beneath it.

"Edelein!" Gihon's eyes widened as he buttoned the bottom half of his shirt. "You should knock before you enter a room. I-I apologize for my indecency."

"Your scar," Edelein started softly, approaching him and placing a gentle hand on his upper back. "It looks recent. What happened?"

She felt Gihon's back tense at her touch, or perhaps her words, as his mind began to recall unpleasant memories.

"No more lies, Gihon," Edelein whispered, looking up at him.

"No more lies," Gihon closed his eyes tightly. "I should have told you about this sooner. You had a right to know, for a lot of reasons. It happened on the night that you were trapped in the reality sphere."

"Who did this to you?" she asked.

"Solomon has a homunculus named Allocer. On the night that he took you, he had sent Allocer to infiltrate our camp with the intention of killing me."

"I don't get it. You could easily take on a homunculus. Solomon's not stupid enough to send a single one into our entire camp–"

"She is a clone of you."

"What?"

Silence hung in the air, Edelein finding herself in disbelief and confusion for the umpteenth time since meeting the Marleogne brothers.

"Solomon made her after he first crossed us, back at the roadside on our way to my personal estate. She is, physically speaking, almost entirely identical to you. The only difference between you two is that she lacks that white streak you have in your hair. I think her pupils are not diamond-shaped, either, but I was not able to get a close enough look–"

"So she was able to infiltrate the camp because you thought she was me?"

"She stole your nightgown while you were out. I thought you had returned from your patrol and were coming in to fetch me for mine. She had, ah…" Gihon cleared his throat awkwardly, tugging on his collar as heat began to rise to his face. "She had very convincing methods of distraction. She was able to get one blow on me before I stopped her."

"She's dead now, right?"

Gihon hesitated with a disappointed sigh.

"Gihon?" Edelein pressed.

"I let her go. I was weakened and she told me that Solomon had taken you. Saving your life was more valuable to me than ending hers."

"That would explain why you were so angry that night," Edelein nodded, gently understanding his position.

"I thought Solomon was going to kill you. That, plus seeing that disgraceful, *promiscuous* woman parading around pretending to be you... it was too much to bear."

Gihon stopped, turning to face the window with another

sigh.

"Edelein, I have been thinking. You should stay here tomorrow."

"What?" Edelein asked, surprised. "Absolutely not. I would never force my men to fight somewhere that I myself am not willing to go."

"This is neither a matter of pride nor glory. Othalgar is a necropolis of my own doing. I was unable to stop Solomon the first time, and everyone there is trapped in a zombified eternity because of my own shortcomings. I do not wish for you to set foot in such a place of shame and despair. If I fail to stop him again, you and your men will be doomed to the same fate. I would rather you not be near, just in case."

"If you were unable to stop him before, why would going in alone make you any more likely to succeed? You need Zenluve's aid," Edelein paused, thinking. "Is this because of what Solomon said? That I weaken you, and that you don't want to give up your strength?"

"No! No, it's not that," Gihon turned around to face her, taking her hands in his. "It is precisely the opposite. I *want* to be with you, and if you die tomorrow, I will never have the opportunity to choose you."

"So what if you go in alone, and you die? What then?" Edelein asked.

"I will not die. I cannot. What Solomon said about me is correct, Edelein. The contract I hold with Limbo traded my emotion, my love, for a hyper-durable body alongside Fortress Black. I can survive anything and come back from it, but you cannot. Your illness is worsening, and I fear that I would be worried about–"

"Worry not about my blight," Edelein interrupted, "I'll be fine. No Luvemann would ever turn away from a battle like this. I do not fear for what tomorrow brings, but instead I face it with courage and nobility. That is what makes me the Lion Queen of Zenluve. My Kingdom stands with you, Dirigent Gihon."

Gihon looked down at her hands as he held them, and then up to her eyes gently.

"You are quite stubborn, you know," he mused.

"As many have claimed," Edelein smiled wryly at him.

"I vow to protect you, then."

Gihon's words were interrupted as Edelein pressed her lips against his suddenly, her sweet scent complimenting the softness of her delicate lips as she kissed him passionately. Her hands reached up to grab the lapel of his shirt, pulling him into her as the kiss deepened. Wordlessly, the lioness desperately poured her heart out to him, her lips meeting his in a gentle but earnest rhythm.

Gihon placed a hand on her waist, his touch soft as if afraid of breaking the fragile woman underneath him. She pulled away slightly, her lips only a hair's breadth away from his as their breaths mingled. He could feel the familiar ache and tug of the limbus energy trapped inside of him as it loosened more within his chest, feeling the connection weaken as his bond grew with the woman in front of him. His mind raced for the right thing to say, but the raven quickly realized that no words could express the yearning that his heart desperately wanted to feel.

Edelein remained frozen as her face stayed close to his, as Gihon closed the distance to lock lips with her once more. He kissed her with the fervor of a man willing to risk everything for a single moment, one hand creeping up to caress her face gently as he leaned down into her.

I will keep you safe, Gihon thought as he pulled away, looking down at Edelein softly.

"I-I should probably get some rest," Edelein stuttered, cheeks flushed red. "My knees are feeling a bit weak, which I assume is from the blight and from nothing else."

"You are precious to me," Gihon said suddenly as Edelein began to head for the door. "I cherish you, you know. As much as a man like me could ever hope to feel."

The Queen stopped, turning around to smile and laugh softly. "I'll see you tomorrow morning, Gihon."

CHAPTER 10

INDEX

A soft touch flicked across Gihon's leg, rousing him from his thoughts as Edelein passed by him early the next morning. He was seated in a large leather armchair in the main library, buried deep in a book as usual. Her tail grazed his trouser leg as she walked, flicking upwards to draw his gaze up towards her face. The Queen was looking over her shoulder with a coy smile as she gestured for him to follow with a slight nod of her head.

"It's almost morning now, Dirigent. I've relieved the others of their duty, so we should resume the search for the Othalgar index. In fact, I have an idea of where to look."

She seems bright and alert, despite the hour, Gihon thought, setting his book down and rising to follow after her.

"The others have been searching through Arvien's belongings in her old study, and the storage rooms of her belongings. I believe we were missing a crucial detail about this, though," Edelein explained, stopping in front of an old door.

The door appeared to be identical in appearance to the others inside of the Athenaeum, but a painful nostalgia hit Gihon as they stopped, recognizing the pattern that Edelein was alluding to.

"This is Solomon's room," Gihon murmured. "You think the index was in his possession, and not Arvien's."

"Maybe Arvien made it for him, and they used it together, but something tells me that Solomon was keeping it. My instincts led me here, and then I realized something," Edelein started, opening the door with a soft creak.

The room beyond the door appeared untouched by time, other than a thick layer of dust coating every surface. A bed was tucked into the corner of the room, perfectly made but cold and musty. Bookshelves lined the walls, filled with a combination of ancient leather-bound books and bizarre trinkets from across the continent. A few old vials were knocked over, remnants of fluids caked onto the inside of each glass. The rising sun illuminated through an east-facing window, only serving to highlight the particles of dust that swam around the stale air.

"It's been years since I've last set foot into this room. After he left, we just… closed it off and forgot about it," Gihon reminisced, lost in thought.

"You told us about Othalgar and what Solomon did to it. You explained that Arvien and yourself had to pursue Solomon to stop him, but you were too late. If the index was in Arvien's possession, that would not have happened. It is much more likely that he had access to it independently."

"He could have also stolen it, but I see where you are coming from with this. It would be wise to look in here, considering that the others have been sifting through everything of Arvien's."

"Do you think Solomon could steal from Arvien?" Edelein asked, looking at him.

Gihon paused, thinking.

"I cannot say for certain. He is quite the slippery bastard, but Arvien was very protective of her belongings."

"She built an entire labyrinth of arrays to stop people from accessing the leyline. You think she'd be any less diligent with items in her physical possession?"

"True," Gihon replied, flipping through the pages of one of the old books and relishing the scent that the pages and leather carried.

Footsteps caught the attention of the two, both heads turning to greet Zander and he bowed to Edelein.

"I apologize for my delay, Your Majesty. Alett was briefing me on his team's findings, and… well, you know how it is to have Alett tell you about things. I am here to assist in the search."

Edelein laughed, dismissing his bow. "Yeah, he does tend to overshare, doesn't he? Did he find anything of value?"

"Not for our mission, though I am fearing that he might become a notable alchemist if we let him near any more of Arvien's belongings. He's learning too much."

Gihon sighed with a warm chuckle, setting down the book. "I would do anything for a student like him. He'd be welcome to stay and study with me."

"Don't poach my warriors, Dirigent!" Edelein scoffed, laughing as she brushed her tail against him again, leaning in to poke a finger against his chest in a playfully scolding manner. "I need Alett in Zenluve! You have plenty of intellectuals here. I've only got one."

Gihon laughed, placing his hands on her shoulders to stand her up straight again. "Alright, you can keep him, I suppose."

Zander's eyes darted between the two of them, narrowed as he noticed the affectionate shift in energy between them.

"You seem more… *energized* than yesterday. Both of you," Zander commented.

Gihon and Edelein's eyes widened in realization, blushing and turning away from each other awkwardly as they faced Zander, hands firmly by their sides.

"Anyways, the index. Do you have a lead?" Zander continued, allowing the two the luxury of privacy by not prying further.

"I theorize that Solomon had it in his possession. This is his old room, so it would be in here, if anything."

"Great. The room is full of a thousand trinkets; of course it's the room where a single one of these things might be an index," Zander grumbled, picking an old pocketwatch off of the shelf to inspect it.

Picking up a second book, Gihon began to skim the pages of it once more as Edelein and Zander sifted through each shelf.

"Master Marleogne, are you in here?" A soft voice spoke up from the hallway, Jana's light lavender-grey hand rapping on the door. "May we come in?"

"Of course, Jana." Gihon confirmed, looking up curiously from the book in his hand as Jana entered the room, Luthro following closely behind.

"We'd like to help, if you don't mind," Jana explained, gesturing to the student behind her. "We couldn't sleep, knowing you were working. Plus, it's pretty much morning anyway."

"I appreciate the support. You two can start on the other side of the room." Gihon nodded, returning to the shelf and retrieving another antique tome.

Opening the cover of the book, an old paper slid out from inside and landed on the floor. Gihon's eyes widened as he recognized the paper's contents, an old pen sketch of his younger self standing next to a wide-smiled teenage Solomon.

I drew this years ago. He... kept it? We're so young in this portrait. Gihon thought, eyes wide as he bent down to gently pick up and admire the page.

A sudden wooshing noise drew the attention of the rest of the group, the noise subsiding as quickly as it started. Turning to face the sound, the five all laid eyes on a single piece of paper as it fluttered to the ground again, Gihon nowhere in sight.

"Gihon!" Edelein cried out in alarm, running towards the spot where he stood.

"No!" Jana exclaimed.

"Stop!" Luthro commanded.

As Edelein lunged for the paper on the floor, Zander grabbed her firmly, pulling her back as she struggled against him.

"Let me go, Zander! Gihon just *disappeared.* He needs help!" Edelein protested, squirming against his firm arms across her chest.

"It's the index," Luthro explained. "Don't touch it, Your Majesty."

"What are you talking about? If that's the index, it means that Gihon is facing off against Solomon alone right now. We have to help him immediately!" Edelein barked in frustration, still trying to wriggle free from Zander's grasp. "Gihon's alone in Othalgar, with no backup. We can't leave him there!"

"If we rush in alone, we're of no help to Master Marleogne," Luthro explained. "The best course of action is to gather the others quickly and work out a plan."

Zander's grip loosened on the Queen as Edelein regained her composure, clearing her throat and nodding in understanding.

"There are minor considerations regarding index travel. As Master Marleogne mentioned back in the swamp, they are not perfectly accurate. The farther one travels, the wider range the point of arrival can fall. Between here and Othalgar, it puts the range at about the size of the city itself. Meaning, Gihon could be anywhere in the city, and each time one of us travels, we will end up in different coordinates within Othalgar," Luthro continued.

"So we fetch everyone and travel together," Edelein assumed.

"Not quite, Your Majesty," Jana offered politely. "There are a lot of risks associated with index travel, and the more shadow mass that gets relocated, the higher the chances of the index placing you into an object, like a wall, killing you instantly."

Edelein and Zander's faces dropped in unison at Jana's grim warning.

"The safest use of an index is limited to groups of two," Luthro stated.

"We'd be split into far too many groups that way," Edelein denied. "Groups of four would be a better option."

"Four would be too many for a dense cityscape. The total mass of four people would inevitably hit a building's shadow," Luthro explained.

"True. Three, then."

Luthro hesitated, considering the option.

"Three could work. It's a bit risky, but I think it's a low enough chance at failure that we could make it."

"Three leaves an odd one out. Two groups will have to be only two people anyway, since four isn't an option," Jana realized aloud.

"I'll go," Zander and Edelein offered in unison.

The rest of the team unwilling to waste their breath on denying Zander and Edelein, murmurs of agreement spread across the room.

"Maintain the same groups as we held overnight," Edelein commanded with a quick glance at Luthro. "For ease, and to keep the division of alchemists amongst my men. Put Spira and Jinn together for the second group of two. I theorize that they'd work well together."

Luthro nodded as he procured an old map, laying it out across a vintage desk by the room's only window. The others huddled around it curiously, silently assessing each stroke of ink across the parchment.

The map detailed a city, formed with a wheel-and-spoke layout that boasted a large central hub with major streets extending from it in every direction. In the corner, a single word was scrawled on by hand: Othalgar.

"The most likely outcome is that Solomon intends to be here, at the heart of the city. We will end up placed all over and far apart, so our rendezvous point will have to be there. Parties that encounter him first are free to engage if needed, though I would recommend staying back until we find ourselves together once more," Luthro explained, tapping the center of the map.

"Why would Solomon be in the most obvious location, though?" Edelein asked.

"The Gates of Heaven are large. He needs a place big enough to hold them. Solomon would likely also find the heart of Othalgar to be poetic in nature, as that is where he first struck. I cannot imagine that man would end up anywhere else, frankly," Luthro shrugged. "If your senses take you elsewhere, well, that is why we intend to split our links between Zenluvians and alchemists. If there's a change, you'll all notice."

Edelein nodded, satisfied. "We shall waste not a second more, then. Zander, fetch the Zengarde at once. Jana, bring me the alchemists."

Zander bowed deeply at his Queen before hurrying out of the room, Jana in tow, leaving just Edelein and Luthro together.

"Your Majesty, should I also gather–" Luthro started, but Edelein interrupted with a raise of her hand.

"Luthro. Gihon is alive, right?"

Luthro stared at Edelein in befuddlement, nodding slowly.

"Y-yes, Your Majesty. I'm certain that this is an index array, and nothing nefarious."

Luthro gently turned over the sketch with a single gloved finger, careful to avoid touching the array drawn onto the back.

"You see here, this is what a standard index array looks like. I believe Master Marleogne activated the array unintentionally by touching it when he picked up the page, since he didn't realize it was there on the back of the page. I promise, he's alive, just alone in Othalgar."

Edelein's shoulders relaxed slightly, and Luthro noticed for the first time that her stiff demeanor was from nothing more than anxiety and fear rather than obligation and duty. Luthro's gaze softened sympathetically.

"Gihon is the most powerful alchemist of our time. He's gone up against Solomon alone before. He is a fearless leader, like you."

"I'm far from fearless," Edelein laughed dryly.

"Yet your fear never stops you, does it?" Luthro asked. "Master Marleogne is the same way. He will be alright on his own until we find him."

"Thank you, Luthro," Edelein smiled, grateful for his kind words.

"Do you have enough stamina elixirs to get you through this?" Luthro queried after a quiet moment. "I can make you one before we go. Gihon keeps panax oil in his study–"

"I'll be alright," Edelein denied gently as she pulled a small vial from her pocket. "I have one. I'll use it."

"Use it right before we engage Solomon," Luthro advised. "You have a habit of not backing out of fights long enough to restore your stamina."

He noticed? Edelein thought.

With a laugh and a nod, Edelein pocketed the vial once

more.

"Will do."

"Oh, and one more thing. I'll inform the others, but you and Zander can't go alone."

"You're in no place to deny me, alchemist," Edelein countered in irritation.

"Othalgar is infected with limbus energy, and the only way to survive it without being dragged into the necropolis is to utilize an array that fills your own bodies with the essence of Limbo. You can move the limbus energy inside of you to nullify the effect of the area. It is complex alchemy, and–"

"I can do it."

Luthro stopped, unsure if Edelein was simply being overconfident or stubborn, wondering if it was perhaps both.

"Can you draw the array for me? I can activate arrays well enough from Gihon's teaching. I just… I do not know how to draw them."

Luthro pondered her words silently and nodded in agreement.

"I have a solution for you. Please allow me to step out for a moment."

Towards the door, footsteps approached as a crowd of allies began to fill out the small bedroom, passing Luthro as he exited the room. Alchemists and Zenluvians were positioned from wall to wall, awaiting orders from the Queen. Wasting no time, Edelein began to gesture and split the groups apart.

"Nora, Everett, Jana together. Spira and Jinn. Mandus and Thorne with Alett. Luthro will be with Cari and Lylia. Finally, Zander and I shall travel together. There will be no objections to this."

Edelein's authority rang out as she spoke her commands, each group gathering together silently at her word.

Raising one hand, Everett broke the silence.

"We'll go first, if that's alright," Everett offered, Jana nodding in agreement as she approached the index. "Sentinels should be on the front line."

"More like you need the head-start," Thorne snickered.

"Brag all you want, but I could carry a dozen Thornes without breaking a sweat," Everett countered.

"Thorne does make a point. Faster teams should go last." Edelein's demands pulled attention once more. "Everett, thank you for offering. We have no time to waste."

"One more thing, quickly," Luthro added as he returned, holding on to a piece of parchment. "To prevent our bodies succumbing to the same fate as Othalgar's civilians, we need to utilize limbus energy. Alchemists, please prepare to maintain such an array until we reunite with Master Gihon."

"I'm on it," Jana nodded, Spira crossing her arms with a huff of confirmation.

A whine from the other side of the room drew everyone's attention as Mandus whimpered.

"More constitution arrays," Mandus complained. "I'll… do my best, though. For Gihon."

Everett grunted, picking up Nora with one arm and grabbing onto Jana's waist with his other. As the fellborn's petite lavender hand touched the index, the three vanished in a single wooshing noise, the same way Gihon had just a few minutes earlier.

"That… they just vanished. Are we sure that's safe?" Thorne asked.

"It seems similar to Neph's shadowstepping," Jinn noted, approaching the page with Spira following closely. "Nothing to fear, Thorne. See you around."

As Jinn spoke, Spira laid a firm hand onto the array and the two disappeared.

"I do *not* like this, man," Thorne groaned as Mandus pushed the human closer. "This is weird. Don't make me do this."

"Relax, fae-boy!" Mandus laughed. "It's just an index that will whisk us to the other side of the continent and into a frozen necropolis of death with only minimal chances of being obliterated immediately. We'll be fine!"

"Mandus, I think you're making it worse..." Alett warned, approaching and clasping a hand onto Thorne's shoulder assuringly.

Mandus shrugged as Alett picked up the index page, assessing its details while carefully avoiding the array scrawled onto the backside of it.

"We'll see you in a bit, Eddie!" Alett smiled, activating the array and whisking the fox and human off with him.

"Alett had no issue activating the array himself. I'm impressed with how quickly that boy has learned the basics of alchemy," Luthro mused as he stepped forward.

"Yeah, well, that's kind of his thing," Cari replied, "being the smartest kid in any room."

Luthro handed Edelein a piece of parchment that he had been holding onto and pointed down at it.

"I ran into Master Gihon late last night as he was working on this. It's a signature alchemist's array for you. I took the liberty of quickly drawing the limbus array into it as well, on this outer ring here," Luthro explained. "From my evaluation, he has drawn your hardlight arrow array here in the center. Above it is the banishment array, and beneath lies a fleetfoot array for speed and a stamina haste array. Depending on which part you touch, different techniques will activate. This is your own signature array, like what the rest of us have. Welcome to the Corvid Athenaeum, Your Majesty."

Edelein's curious gaze flickered over each line, taking in Luthro's words with a slight blush as she remembered her last interaction with Gihon that evening, recalling the fervor of his lips on hers and the firm and yearning touch of his hands on her waist. A kiss that had kept the heartless yet diligent alchemist awake all night, inventing a new signature array to protect the woman he had come to desire.

"Right, that makes sense," Edelein spoke after a moment. "Thank you, Luthro."

Luthro bowed deeply, kissing the Queen's gloved hand.

"Your Majesty, I will take care of Cari and Lylia in your absence. I look forward to reuniting swiftly."

Ever the proper one, isn't he? Edelein thought to herself warmly as the young alchemist approached both female Zengarde. *We'll see who ends up taking care of whom.*

"Would one of you like to attempt activating the index array?" Luthro asked, following in his master's footsteps as he sought to provide a learning opportunity.

The women both nodded curiously and Lylia crouched down to gently pick up the index from where it had fallen after the previous group departed.

"Carefully, now. Don't touch the array until we are all together," Luthro instructed as he took Cari's hand, placing it on Lylia's forearm.

Taking Cari's other hand, Luthro held it tightly and rested his second hand on Lylia's upper back as she studied the page.

"Whenever you're ready now, try to activate the arr–" Luthro's direction was cut off by a sharp whoosh as he vanished alongside both girls, leaving only Edelein and Zander in the now-silent room.

"Are you sure this is wise, Edelein?" Zander asked. "I'd prefer if you would stay–"

"I'm not staying here. I have stamina potions as well as this new array, and you're all going to be there to back me up. We have to go get Gihon," Edelein denied, her regal demeanor wavering slightly as soon as she was alone with her old friend once more. "I am not opening up this discussion again. There's no time. Let's just go, alright?"

Zander nodded sharply, understanding her stance as he brought Edelein over to the index. The old page fluttered onto the floor, array facing downwards so the sketch of Gihon and Solomon greeted them.

"Very well. Hold onto me," Zander instructed, reaching down to pick up the index.

Edelein grabbed onto the Ehret's tanned arm and the world suddenly vanished around her, fading quickly into black as her body became enveloped in dark and heavy shadows.

CHAPTER 11

OTHALGAR

A shudder ran up Everett's spine as his feet touched the cold cobblestone of Othalgar, a haunting and foreign energy sending his instincts alight as his Seventh Sense repeated the same two words in his mind: *Wrong. Leave.*

"This is Othalgar, right? We made it?" Everett turned to Jana and Nora as he spoke.

Jana nodded solemnly, a violet array glowing in her hand. Nora and Everett looked around, curiously taking in the environment.

Huge buildings reached desperately for the reddish sky above, as tall as the Deepwood's lush ironwood trees. The clouds had seemed to absorb the reds and browns of the brick and left the buildings void of any color other than a cold indigo hue that stained the entire city. A few buildings had begun to topple, large chunks tumbling from their once-proud stance only to remain suspended in space as the debris floated timelessly in midair.

"I've never been here, either," Nora admitted. "I see why the Church doesn't let anyone near this place."

The three had been placed by the index onto a busy street a ways south of the central plaza Luthro had mentioned. At first glance, the area seemed to be bustling with life. A few dozen civilians dotted either side of the road as they engaged with one another at outdoor cafes and restaurants.

The longer they spent evaluating the scene, however, the more uncanny it became. The people were colorless and shadowy specters of what once was, ghostly and gaunt in appearance. A stale odor filled the air that would remind an onlooker of a musty attic, a scent of decay lost within time itself. The civilians were only barely moving as they continued with their routines.

"Are these people… alive?" Nora asked. "I can't tell."

Everett approached a bench where a couple was sitting, a young woman leaning affectionately on her lover. Both of them held the same empty gaze, frozen. Everett's heart began to ache for the two, empathy filling his chest with grief. The man began to look up at Everett at an agonizingly slow pace as his lifeless gaze met the bovine warrior.

"They aren't alive," Everett realized after evaluating them closer, keen Zenluvian senses leading his hypothesis. "They aren't dead, though, either. I don't know how to describe it. It gives me chills."

"Me too," Nora shuddered.

"This is what Solomon is capable of. We need to go find Master Marleogne at once," Jana interrupted. "Everett, can you tell where the plaza is from here?"

"North of us," Everett confirmed. "We're a ways off."

"Let's go, then."

Everett nodded, leading the way as both girls fell into step behind his large frame.

"Jana, will you be able to maintain that Limbo thing?" Everett asked.

"I can manage it, but I won't be very useful if we run into any opposition. It's possible to use a limbus array as a battery for our movement while activating a second one, but that's an advanced technique, beyond what most alchemists are capable of. Dirigents are generally the only ones who can do two arrays at once, and even then it's only on occasion. I… don't think I've even seen Master Gihon do it, either. If anyone finds us here, I won't be able to fight."

"You won't have to worry about that. I'll protect you if anything tries to attack us," Everett beamed assuringly. "You're both so tiny. Leave it to me, okay?"

Jana blushed, looking at her feet as she walked.

"Everett, are you taking the limbus energy alright?" Nora asked.

"Oh, is that what I'm feeling?" Everett replied. "My body's been feeling really weird since we got here. I think I'm doing fine, though."

Wrong. Leave.

That must be my Seventh Sense's reaction to having limbus energy inside of me, Everett realized.

"We're rather far from the city center, but I don't sense any alarms," Everett continued. "My senses are telling me that everything here is wrong, but there hasn't been any warning of danger."

Jana and Nora seemed to relax a bit at the Zengarde's assurance, trusting his instincts.

Silence fell over the group for a few minutes, all three fighters lost in their own thoughts and memories. Everett could feel the empty gaze of the man on the bench burning into his mind, his heart heavy as he mourned for that couple once more.

"Have you guys ever been in love?" Everett started

suddenly, never one for concealing his thoughts.

A shock jolted through Jana's body, her array flickering for a split-second as the ox's words surprised her.

"Nah," Nora replied first as Jana searched for words. "Being at the Athenaeum isn't much of a way to find love. Not a lot of people my age, there, and I'm too busy with Master Gihon's assignments to have much of a social life."

"Jana?" Everett pressed.

"I-I-I… I suppose not," Jana admitted. "Similarly to Nora, there's not much time for fraternizing when we're at the Athenaeum. Luthro and Mandus are my only classmates, and they're not really my type, and I'm so busy with the tasks that Master Marleogne has entrusted us with, and–"

"You're rambling, Jana," Nora laughed.

"You have a type, then?" Everett asked.

Jana froze, the array flickering again.

"I don't think I do. Maybe it's just because Mandus and Luthro are like brothers to me. I guess I would just like someone that's different. Unique."

"You're not one of those weirdos who gets crushes on their teachers, right?" Everett continued with a hearty laugh. "You crushing on Gihon?"

"N-not at all!" Jana waved her free hand desperately to banish the thought. "Master Marleogne is an inspiration to me, nothing more. I'm not that type of girl. I don't think I'd be suited with another alchemist at all. They're all the same… it's kind of boring."

Nora looked at Jana and Everett, grinning as she made a sudden connection.

"What about you, Everett?" Nora said, turning the question back onto him. "Have you been in love?"

"Sure, I guess so. I thought everyone had an experience

or two with some young schoolkid crush. At the same time, I kind of also struggled with the whole time-management issue like you two did, so I've never had anything truly meaningful. My dad is the Zengarde's blacksmith and the head of the smithing guild, so I spent a lot of time in his smithy, learning his trade after school most days. Once I retire from the Zengarde, I'm supposed to take up his mantle. When are people ever supposed to get girlfriends?"

That's why his surname is Smith, the fellborn realized.

"How busy are your days as a Zengarde?" Jana asked.

"Pretty filled up, but it's fun work. We start really early in the morning with combat training every day, and then our tasks are divided up by Queen Edelein's plans. Either we're escorting her, posted outside her suite, or patrolling the castle grounds. Sometimes we go out on patrol audits, supervising the patrolmen units. That's the best gig, because we get to fight monsters. Oftentimes, Queen Edelein will throw a huge dinner event that we act as security for, but she always lets us eat the leftovers. Those parties are fun. There's live music and entertainment, and she rotates her guest list with a variety of noblefolk or esteemed guests. Getting invited to dinner in the castle is the biggest honor a Zenluvian can receive. Not to mention the lavish balls she throws–"

"Wow, that's a lot," Nora interrupted Everett's maundering. "Probably not a lot of time for a girlfriend, then."

"Well, I guess I've never tried. We get time off and great benefits. I'm usually hanging out with Thorne most of the time, but if I met the right girl I'm sure I could..." Everett trailed off, suddenly remembering the teasing comment Mandus had made back at Gihon's estate.

"Jana definitely likes you," Mandus' words echoed in Everett's mind.

The ox zoa turned to look over his shoulder, down at the petite fellborn as she trailed behind him. Her pale complexion was flushed with a deep violet on her cheeks, her eyes looking anywhere but at Everett.

Nora peered up at Everett's shocked expression, tilting her head to the side.

Did Everett... just now realize it?

"Be careful!" warned an irate man as he supervised his subordinates.

The man, clothed in the elegant black and white robes of a Veruthian vicar, stood in the middle of a large pedestrian street as cultists milled around him. Othalgar's Main Street was once the pinnacle of shopping and entertainment, cutting straight through the city. Scattered along the length of the street, lower members of the Veruthian Order carried metal plates engraved with a familiar array to each corner of the area.

A metal clang reverberated through the street. Letting out a frustrated groan, the vicar turned towards the noise. A follower, in his attempt to hoist one of the metal plates onto a streetlamp, had bashed it into the post.

"I just said to be careful," the vicar repeated, irritated. "Break one of those plates and this entire area gets swallowed up! Do you want to end up like them?"

Following the exasperated gesture of the vicar, the cultist grimaced under his mask as he laid eyes on the shadowy specters of Othalgar's former residents as they slowly moved past.

Grunting an apology, the man gently hung the plate. The glowing limbic array illuminated in the same way as the others, surrounding the area in a barrier that protected the visitors from succumbing to the static fate of the necropolis.

The wind swelled and converged in the middle of the street, swinging the plates and threatening to knock them down. A shadowy substance spilled out from a rip in space as Jinn and Spira leapt out, boots thudding against the stone pavement.

The Veruthians froze. They eyed the two newcomers, befuddled by their sudden appearance. The warriors regained their balance and looked around, trying to orient themselves to their new surroundings as quickly as possible.

"They've got limbic arrays up for us. Nice," Spira realized, dropping her own in favor of a hardlight throwing knife.

"Keep the one closest to us active while disengaging the others. I'm with you," Jinn affirmed, his Seventh Sense technique attuning him to his ally's intentions.

Jinn pulled his arm back. Whipping forward as Spira's conjured dagger appeared in his extended hand, the wolf zoa launched the knife down the street, cleanly knocking the furthest plate off of its post. The cultists underneath it began to scramble, racing towards Spira and Jinn, but began to slow as Othalgar's curse consumed them.

The volley of daggers continued as Jinn trusted Spira, keeping his throwing motion at full velocity while Spira summoned blade after blade into his hands.

"Take over for me," Jinn instructed, sprinting towards the nearest streetlight.

The wolf zoa dodged panicked blasts from the cultists' gauntlets, weaving effortlessly between them. Planting a firm foot onto the pole, the zoa darted up the vertical length of the streetlight. With a flash of his sword, Jinn severed the plate's rope attachment to the lamp, flipping down as he caught the metal slab by the cord and swung it into the face of the cultist that had fired at him.

Two cultists, spooked by being on the edge of the rapidly-shrinking permitted area, ran towards Spira with electrically-charged gauntlets raised. The alchemist stopped them in their tracks as she conjured her spear and extended it outwards, warding them off. The cultists could tell that they didn't have the range to contest her, and in their moment of hesitation, Spira lunged forward to swiftly dispose of them.

Jinn returned to his position beside Spira, dented plate in hand. Energy was humming through the metal plate, the array glowing with a complex alchemical power.

"This one is still functional," Jinn stated, tying the severed rope around Spira's waist. "If we keep it, you won't need your limbus array and there's no concern of being lost to the time-curse as more plates go down."

"What about you?" Spira asked.

"I'll stay close by your side, fellow warrior," Jinn huffed.

"Good. It seems like these guys aren't giving up without a fight. You ready, Dritet Jinn?"

The zoa turned his head to take in what Spira had observed. Five ornately-dressed knights were approaching, limbic arrays carved into the breastplate of each defender. The ceremonial garbs of each knight had their own color: red, violet, green, pink, and yellow, making them stand out against the black-and-white-clad cultists that were frozen mid-run beside them. They walked towards the two warriors with a gait unimpeded by the limbic environment surrounding everyone, prepared for battle with longswords and heater shields.

"Intruders, as Master Solomon has foretold. Destroyers of salvation!" the red-clad knight shouted, standing his ground.

"The Knights of Pentagoth have decided your fate. You shall travel no further!" added the green knight, her powerful voice reverberating off of the suspended stones.

"They're like a group of children pretending to be heroes,"

Jinn muttered to Spira in annoyance. The wolf zoa briefly recalled his younger days as an adolescent pup, dressed up in green and waving a wooden sword as he fantasized about being a Zengarde warrior.

"It's like I'm watching a play," Spira laughed. "We should take them out before they start striking poses."

The knights raised their weapons, clearly unappreciative of the duo's comments. Spira sighed, raising her arms diplomatically.

"If you lose your arrays, you'll be forced into the abyss," Spira explained. "This isn't a cause worth dying for. If you stand down and let us through, you'll live."

"Master Solomon has positioned us here to protect him. That alone is worth dying for," the yellow knight replied.

These five are too far gone. Solomon has corrupted their minds, Jinn thought.

Jinn kept his eyes on the knights as he asked Spira, "All it takes is a scratch or dent to disrupt an array, right?"

"Yes, that is correct. We don't need to harm them, we just need—"

"To hit them really hard," finished Jinn.

"Stand down, or face the fury of salvation!" the red knight warned, raising his shield up to approach with the others in formation behind him.

"Are you good with anything other than that sword of yours?" Spira asked.

Jinn looked at this sheathed sword and back at the plated armor.

Spira brings up a good point. Armor like that would deflect my sword effortlessly, Jinn thought to himself. *I could brute force it, but that is extra energy I could be saving for the final battle that awaits us*.

After a quick moment, Jinn replied, "Zengarde train with

each other's weapons. Anything you've seen them do, I can do as well."

Spira smiled and conjured two weapons: a flail and a whip.

"Really? You could have chosen any of them, and you gave me *Cari's* weapon?" Jinn complained, taking the whip.

"Look at the end of it," Spira added.

Glancing down into his hands, Jinn noticed a rounded metal tip slightly smaller than his palm. The meteor hammer ending offered a blunt solution to their need to dent armor, but maintained the form of a familiar weapon, proficient in the hands of Zenluve's weapon master.

"This one is straight out of Luthro's books," Spira said as the two charged forward.

They probably should have engraved the array on a smaller, more unassuming spot. They make for easy targets, Spira thought as her lightbound eyes fixed on the limbus energy radiating from their arrays.

The knights responded with their own charge, keeping in formation to protect their angles. Jinn made the first swing with the whip towards the pink knight, who countered by bringing her shield up to block.

Jinn continued to press the attack, striking again as his hardlight whip met the edge of the knight's heater shield. The whip wrapped around the shield as the hammer end landed square in the knight's chest, disrupting her array and slowing her down as she succumbed to Limbo.

That's one.

The knights backpedaled to keep Spira's flail from coming around their shields, making extra efforts to block the swinging end. They moved to a more defensive position, thrusting with their longswords at the two warriors.

Spira adapted in a moment of quick thinking befitting of the lightbound alchemist. A backstep created distance as she conjured a halberd, hooking the yellow knight's shield open. In the same moment, she dispelled Jinn's whip and replaced it with an axe. Noticing the opportunity, Jinn tossed the axe through the gap in the knight's defense as it hit his array, denting the knight's armor with a loud thunk.

The green knight swung at Jinn in retaliation, taking her opportunity to strike at the weaponless zoa that had just discarded the hardlight axe. Anything but unprepared, Spira summoned a staff into Jinn's hands, the zoa warrior already in motion to parry the knight's sword as if he had been armed the entire time. As the knight recoiled back from the parry, Jinn struck at her chest with the staff's blunt tip, leaving another solid dent.

With wide swings in an arc, Spira forced the remaining two knights to move back. The purple and red knights hesitated, knowing they couldn't afford for the halberd to hook their shields. Sensing the opening, Spira used the chance to toss Jinn a battle scythe.

A scythe, really? Jinn thought in dismay.

"Go high!" Spira commanded as she swept low with the halberd, forcing the knights to bring their shields lower.

The red knight blocked the oncoming halberd strike, but the threat was enough for the violet knight to reactively bring his shield down. Spira's attack exposed the breastplates of the remaining knights once the shields dropped lower, allowing Jinn to strike from above. The scythe's hooked blade landed on the purple knight, dismantling the array on his chest.

"All bark, no bite," Spira laughed. "These guys aren't real knights. Not seasoned ones, at least."

"I *implore* you to not make a canine comment right now," Jinn pleaded.

"Oh, are you a dog zoa? I didn't realize," Spira apologized.

"I can't see you well, I can really only make out the pointed ears. I assumed you were a cat, like a lynx or Zander. My bad."

"A wolf zoa," Jinn corrected, eyebrow twitching as he readied his stance against the remaining knight.

"Mithril means nothing against a foe that can create weaponry for any situation," the red knight admitted, realizing his position as the last remaining member of the Pentagoth.

"It's not too late to surrender," Spira offered. "You don't have to end up like the others."

"With glory I shall fall," decreed the knight, "in the name of truth and salvation!"

"No, it's definitely too late for him," Jinn denied, gripping the sheath of his sword.

"What weapon would you like for the final blow?" Spira asked, ready to conjure at his command.

Shaking his head, Jinn thrust his ironwood scabbard forward, denting the red knight's array and sentencing him to a fate of eternal limbo. "My own."

"Mandus, buddy, are you good?"

Thorne's concerned voice was the first sound to ring out in the silent streets of Othalgar as Alett, Mandus, and Thorne touched down on lifeless cobblestone. Mandus' eyebrows were furrowed as an orange array illuminated his palm.

"Y-yeah, I'm good," Mandus lied through gritted teeth. "I'm just kind of bad at holding concentration arrays, that's all. I think maybe no one should talk to me until we get there."

"What happens if you drop the array?" Thorne asked.

"That," Alett stated, gesturing to a colorless figure as it slowly walked. The specter was barely moving at all and not acknowledging the three new visitors.

"I'm not gonna drop it," Mandus affirmed, though it seemed the words were more to assure himself than Thorne. "Can you guys tell where we need to go? Use your Zenluvian powers or something? I don't want to do this any longer than I have to."

Alett nodded, scanning around the area.

"The three of us are pretty fast. We're a little ways off from the city center and nowhere close to our other allies, but we could make it to the plaza Luthro mentioned quickly. We landed east of it, so we need to head straight west for about a mile."

"Good. Onwards, then. Make haste," Mandus insisted.

The fox zoa started westward, wasting no time as Thorne and Alett followed suit.

"Alett, do you have enough spell bombs to get through this? You don't need to stop and craft, right?" Thorne queried in a moment of surprising diligence.

"I'm good. Gihon is letting me borrow another satchel since that mimic lady took mine. It's not a bag of holding, but it has enough space," Alett beamed, patting the new leather bag resting at his hip. "I stayed up all night crafting extras."

"Wait, what is a spell bomb?" Mandus turned to look over his shoulder, curiosity getting the best of him. "Is that what those things you fight with are? How do they work?"

"My bombs are a unification between several types of arts. I weave magic into innovative artificer techniques and essentially create a super-condensed version of a spell that anyone can use, regardless of arcane ability," Alett explained eagerly.

"Are you a wizard? How are you weaving magic, and how are you alive? All the wizards died during the Great Disappearance decades ago. I have so many questions."

"Zenluve still practices wizardry," Alett explained. "I'm not a wizard, though. I just borrow some of their techniques."

"The Court Wizard is a dude in his mid-forties named Jax," Thorne added. "Cool guy, but he can be a bit much. Alett spends a lot of time learning what Jax does, so that way he can replicate it without needing to cast spells in battle. The two of them are practically inseparable, which makes sense when you consider–Mandus!"

Thorne cried out in disdain as he felt his body begin to slow, feeling as if cement was filling his veins.

"Mandus, the array!" Alett yelped.

"I-I'm sorry!" Mandus pleaded, recentering his focus.

As quickly as the moment began, it ended, the three regaining their speed and balance.

"I got distracted by the wizard thing. That's so cool. I'm so sorry," Mandus apologized, tensing up as he began to focus once more on the array.

"Yeah, okay, maybe we shouldn't talk to Mandus," Thorne sighed.

"You can talk to me! Please, it'll get so boring if you don't. Just… don't tell me anything really cool like that Alett is secretly a wizard and that Zenluve is the coolest place in the world. I want to go there so badly. I've been thinking about moving my family there, actually. Better life for zoa families, you know?" Mandus stopped speaking suddenly, focusing again on the array as he felt it begin to waver.

You were the one who said we shouldn't talk. Did you get that bored already? Thorne wondered silently.

"Can we talk about how freaky this place is, then?" Thorne asked.

"No. That's just going to bum me out," Mandus denied.

"So we can't talk about where we are, where we come

from, or what we do," Thorne confirmed. "We're not allowed to be silent, either."

"Yes. You get it," Mandus replied with a forced smile.

A long beat of silence hung over the three as they continued to close the distance to their final destination, searching for a topic just interesting enough to stimulate Mandus' hyperactive mind without distracting him too heavily from his concentration array.

"Do you think Edelein has feelings for Gihon?" Thorne suggested after a minute.

"Oh, definitely!" Alett laughed. "I noticed it the day they first met. I think Gihon feels the same, but he's a little harder to figure out. It feels like there's something in between him and his feelings, which is why he hasn't confessed it yet."

"It would beat out forcing her into an arranged marriage. I just know that she's gonna make that our problem once we go back home," Thorne rolled his eyes. "It would be nice to see her find love, I guess. They could call it a strategic political marriage."

"There has to be something in the air, though. It's not just them. When we were at the safehouse awhile ago, Jana and Everett were so flirty. I mean, they were both kind of bad at it, but they get all flustered around each other," Alett added.

"Something about the potential threat of our world's safety makes everyone want to pair up, I guess," Thorne shrugged. "I noticed Jana and Everett back when she started talking about his dense muscles and whatnot. I hope her feelings don't change when she realizes that Everett's stupidity isn't a joke or anything. I love the guy, but he is *definitely* dumb as rocks. If she turns on him when she realizes it, I'll have to kill her."

"Luthro has a crush on Cari," Mandus blurted out, his array faltering for a single excitable moment.

"Oh my God, what?" Thorne let out a hearty laugh. "He's going to need a lot of help with that. We've gotta wingman *hard* for him, if he wants a shot with Cari Beaumont."

"What's wrong with it?" Mandus asked. "I mean, I know Luthro's a big dweeb, but maybe Cari's into that."

"Cari is a total man-eater," Thorne answered, stifling his laughter.

"Thorne is being a bit blunt, but isn't entirely wrong. Cari is a noblewoman of very high status. She's the talk of Zenluve's entire fashion industry, the admiration of stylists across the entire Kingdom. Cari is kind of a celebrity," Alett added, "as is her adoptive mother, Madame Beaumont. Luthro's a smart guy, though. He's classy. It could work."

"Aren't you all pretty much celebrities?" Mandus pressed.

"The Zengarde have really high acclaim, yeah, but Cari is a step above the rest of us when it comes to popularity. There are people who know and respect us as warriors, and there are people who are into culture and fashion. Cari gets the love and affection from both sides. Plus, being nobility puts her even higher than a regular guy like Thorne. It's why she rejected him," Alett explained with a cheeky laugh. "They call her the Crown's Rose. The delicate flower of the people."

"Every rose needs its Thorne, but fine," Thorne huffed under his breath. "Go for the little tiny nerd man. Your loss, Cari Beaumont."

"Cari is far from delicate, though," Mandus continued. "She's pretty spunky, like Edelein. Actually, all the Zenluvian women are pretty strong. Is that a Zenluvian thing?"

"Her and Eddie are long-time best friends. She gets that attitude from the Queen. It's nice seeing Ed have a friend to banter with, since being royalty seems to be pretty lonely from what she's told me," Alett replied, reflecting fondly on the affection that Edelein and Cari share.

"Should we help him? Do you think Luthro's got a

chance?" Mandus asked.

"A better chance than Thorne has with Lylia," Alett snickered. "But yeah, I like Luthro. I'll put in a good word for him."

Emerging from the shadows, Luthro Apocathra took point as his two Zengarde allies fell into step behind him. Lylia and Cari, Zenluve's fiercest femmes, quickly noticed a meticulously-carved statue of a woman in scholarly robes, holding onto a snake that was eating its own tail. The group had emerged in the middle of a once-lively park made dreary by the colorless curse of Othalgar.

Luthro checked over his shoulder at the two Zengarde warriors as they admired the figure. The alchemist continued to maintain his limbus array, allowing the three to move freely as they took in their surroundings.

"Who is she?" Cari asked Luthro, gesturing to the statue. "I'm kind of obsessed with her, I think."

"Cleopatra. One of the four women who discovered how to create the philosopher's stone. A pillar of ancient alchemy, revered by alchemists all across Tevus," Luthro explained proudly, happy to educate Cari on his favorite subjects. "The place we touched down in is her namesake: Othalgar's Cleopatra Park."

Cari looked like she wanted to ask more questions about the women of alchemy, but a loud crash interrupted their conversation. Turning towards the sound, the three warily moved closer towards a commercial street.

Three men, donning the recognizable black and white robes of the Verutian Order, peered over a crater in the middle of the road. With pavement in disarray and smoke rising from the blast, a curious sight played out as the smoke froze in midair once it cleared above the heads of the cultists. In the hands of one of these men, a glowing limbic array allowed them freedom of movement.

"Did we get it?" One of the men asked.

"I don't know. I don't see a body," replied the second.

They don't seem like an attack force, Luthro thought. *Perhaps a recon link. If Solomon knew we were here, he would have sent more.*

"You know," Cari started, her eyes wandering down the streets. "I think this is the first time I'm seeing Caandemite fashion. These clothing shops are fascinating."

"Now is hardly the time for window shopping, Zentet Cari," Lylia griped, "though very much expected of you."

"What? I don't really care what those guys are doing. There's a mannequin in that store behind them, though, that's–wait!" Cari stopped herself, eyes wide as she gestured towards the shop.

In the reflection of the glass, the three could barely make out the figure of a humanoid creature as it stalked the three men, who seemed to not notice.

"It's an invisible monster," Cari realized. "Only visible in reflections."

A scream ripped from the throat of the middle cultist. An obscured claw had pierced through the man, hoisting him into the air. The two remaining cultists blasted their gauntlets at the beast, trying unsuccessfully to pinpoint its location. The creature dropped the first man and slashed at the other two, growling as it tore through each Verutian cultist with a quick barrage of slashes.

Satisfied with its kill, the monster stood upright. The creature was slightly taller than the average human, and had long claws on gnarled hands. Its skin was an inky black color, with violet eyes that glowed with rage.

"You were quite close, Cari," Luthro corrected, "it's a phantasm. Reflective shell type, to be precise. It is not exactly invisible, but it is capable of traveling through reflections."

"That sounds like a terrible time," Lylia grumbled, clutching her staff.

The phantasm approached the edge of the glass of the clothing store. It stepped through the reflection and into the street, almost stumbling as it readjusted itself. Cari glanced at the window again and noticed that the phantasm, now on the material plane, had no reflection in the window anymore; opposite of its planar orientation a moment ago.

"This is the last thing we need to go up against. I need to maintain my limbus array, so I won't be able to banish it. Cultists would have been one thing, but this is out of my wheelhouse," Luthro explained in dismay.

"We should move around it and try to find the others," Cari suggested.

"We might end up running into it anyways if we don't handle it now," Lylia countered. "It's currently positioned between us and the center of the city. We don't want it to ambush the others later on, knowing we could have stopped it now."

"I hate to admit it, but Lylia is right," Luthro sighed. "Can one of you banish it?"

"You do it, alchemy boy!" Cari retorted. "That's your whole job!"

Gesturing with his free hand to the limbus array in his left, Luthro clarified, "I can't if you want me to keep us out of the necropolis. I'd have to activate a second array at the same time, which is impossible for an alchemist of my caliber. Only incredibly powerful Dirigents can do two at once. Not even Gihon can consistently keep two arrays active."

"Figure it out, then," Cari snapped. "Also, not to alarm you, but where did the phantasm go?"

"Shit, we lost it," Lylia muttered.

"As long as we don't show up in a reflection, we won't be exposed to any attacks from the phantasm when it's in the windows," Luthro instructed.

The alchemist peered out from the underbrush of the park to plot a path ahead. Everywhere Luthro looked, there was a reflective surface: polished metal handrails, bodies of water, or suspended pieces of broken glass hovering in the air.

"It's impossible to move without being in a reflection–" Luthro started, gasping as Cari pulled him back suddenly.

The bush Luthro was hiding in was torn apart in seconds by an invisible force. Turning around, Luthro followed Cari's gesture as she motioned to a copper monument a notable distance away, realizing that he had shown up on the reflection from quite far off.

"Thank you, Cari," Luthro dipped his head gratefully. "I must have missed that one."

"New plan. We make a run for it," Cari suggested.

Luthro nodded and the three took off. As they ran, they could see the phantasm moving from reflection to reflection, jumping from windows to statues to puddles. Grumbling under his breath, the alchemist picked up a rock and hurled it at a window where he had seen the monster, shattering the glass. Almost instantly, the phantasm appeared in the window next to it.

"I saw the jump," Cari noted. "The moment the window broke, it leapt into the next one. I saw it move."

"Does the phantasm take damage if we damage the reflections?" Lylia asked, slamming her staff into the ground. Vines rose from the cracks in the sidewalk, puncturing the window and forcing the phantasm to jump again.

"It wouldn't hurt us to try," Luthro agreed. "Keep hitting the reflections. At the very least, it'll keep the phantasm in a defensive stance, to minimize attacks it makes against us."

Cari let out a pained yelp, tumbling to the ground as an invisible claw struck her back. Lylia turned around, spotting the phantasm in the reflection of an autowagon's polished door where Cari's reflection had collapsed.

"Cari!" Lylia cried out, acting quickly as she summoned vines to surround the three and protect them from any reflections.

"There are simply far too many reflections to account for," Luthro realized. "We can't keep this up. Cari, how badly does it hurt?"

A bulwark array would do wonders for us here. The phantasm's attacks are swift, but not powerful. I doubt it would be able to break through a bulwark at all. If only I were stronger, Luthro cursed at himself silently.

"I'm alright," Cari insisted as Lylia expended a bit of healing magic to stabilize the wound. "We can't use too much energy on this, or we'll be useless against Solomon."

"There's no reflections in here, so we're safe for the time being," Lylia stated. "If it wants to strike at us, it needs to strike on the material plane."

Looking down at Cari in the enclosed space of Lylia's vines, the alchemist found himself peering closely at his ally's face as she strained against the sting of Lylia's healing magic. His sigh of relief was cut short abruptly as he caught a glare from Cari's large, round glasses.

Luthro could see the reflection of his own glasses in the light of Cari's. In the echoing light of their spectacles, a certain phantasm had poised to strike at the reflection of Cari.

"Cari!" Luthro screamed, lunging forward.

The alchemist pulled the Zengarde forward into his arms, throwing his glasses to the ground with his other hand to disrupt the phantasm's motion.

"Lylia, cover the top! Don't let any light in!" Luthro commanded.

The elf slammed her staff and willed the vines to grow taller. They interlocked at the top of the wall, cutting off the light from above. As the reflections faded to darkness, the phantasm was expelled from Luthro's glasses, tumbling out into the close confines of the vine pod.

Cari grabbed her whip and let her instincts guide her. Through complete darkness, the zoa trusted her Seventh Sense and planted a knee into its midsection, tying her whip around its neck. The zoa flipped the phantasm over onto its back and Lylia jabbed it in the gut with the base of her staff. The creature squealed in the lightless enclosure, struggling to break free from the two Zengarde women.

"Luthro, come on!" Lylia yelled.

"Banish it!" Cari barked. "We can't hold it forever!"

"T-the limbic array!" Luthro insisted. "I can't do both!"

"You have to, and I know you can!" Cari pleaded. "You're going to be a great Dirigent one day, I know it. Now send this thing back home!"

Luthro let out a yell of exertion, pushing his body's energy past its limit as a banishment array flickered in his free hand.

"I'm losing my grip," Cari panicked, feeling the whip begin to slide from her grasp. "It's struggling… too much… Luthro!"

As the phantasm broke free from Cari's hold, it turned to strike at the rose-colored fox zoa.

The banishment array in Luthro's hand sputtered to life for just a split second. Needing only a moment with it, Luthro lunged forward and slammed his palm into the phantasm. The array connected with the creature, absorbing it and whisking it away into the Sea of Miracles.

"You did it, Luthro," Cari panted as the vines dispelled

around them. "I knew you could. And… thank you for saving me back there."

"Yeah," Luthro blushed, trying to maintain a casual demeanor as he realized how close he was to the stunning, powerful zoa. "Can you, uh, hand me my glasses?"

Cari laughed, picking them up and handing them to the alchemist. "They cracked when you threw them. Hopefully they still work."

Luthro squinted, looking at the thin webbing of cracks on the glass.

"Not to worry, I can fix them. Let's go."

CHAPTER 12

THE GATES

As quickly as the overwhelming darkness appeared, it then vanished, leaving the Queen with one arm wrapped tightly around Zander's. The Ehret steadied her as light filled their eyes and their feet found themselves touching the cold streets of Othalgar. Edelein looked around in morbid fascination at the necropolis around her, shattered buildings suspended in time as they hovered overhead.

Lethargy immediately began to seep into her skin. Wasting no time, Edelein laid a hand on the page that Luthro had given her, deep cobalt light shimmering upwards to meet her curious eyes. The aching slowness faded as Edelein's array imbued limbus energy into the air, protecting her and the Ehret from the necrotic space around.

"I thought Ravencroft felt dead," Zander huffed, crossing his arms in disgust. "This place makes the Blacktalon Thicket seem as lively as the Deepwood."

"I can feel my fur standing on end," Edelein mumbled, touching a wall with her free hand. "I don't like it at all. Zander, can you tell where we landed?"

The Ehret closed his eyes, focusing on the area around him.

"Close to the center, I believe," Zander replied after a moment. "I can feel Solomon's presence directly in the center of the city as Luthro predicted, a plaza that's about a half-mile west of us. Much closer than the others landed. The presence of the other Zengarde feels much further."

"Let us not waste a single moment."

Zander nodded in agreement as Edelein set off at a quick pace, following closely behind her. He kept his head on a swivel, cautious towards any perceived danger in the unsettling area around them.

After a beat of silence as the two walked, Zander spoke.

"Why did you not tell us about the blight returning?"

Edelein stopped in her tracks, her shoulders tensing.

"I failed to realize that the effectiveness of the cure had waned. I was focused on the mission, that's all."

"I am the Ehret of the Zengarde, and more importantly, I have known you since you were a child. What I cannot tell about you just from being beside you for all these years, my Seventh Sense will–"

"Do not say I'm lying."

"You're lying, Edelein."

The Queen tensed at his words, displeased.

"Fine. My condition did improve, that part was true. I think the vial Solomon gave me worked to alleviate the symptoms, just not the disease itself. I noticed a few days ago that the darkness was spreading once more."

"Why would you not tell me?" Zander pressed, concerned. "Tell Gihon, even? Anyone?"

"We have bigger issues to worry about right now, Zander," Edelein turned around to face him, her eyes lost in a sea of wild thoughts as her mind raced. "We need to find our crystals and stop Solomon before more people get hurt. My body is not a priority right now."

"Your life is, and always will be, a priority to all of us. Not only are you our Queen, but you're our future right now. You aren't married, you have no son to lead should you–"

"I know, I know. I hear it all the time. I am well into my twenties and have borne no heir because I simply *refuse* to marry. I just… don't like the idea of alchemically transmuting a lion zoa specifically for breeding an heir. I don't want an arranged marriage. You know that better than anyone, Zander."

"I understand, but time is running out. You're the last remaining true blood of Alderich. Your uncle, Vang, isn't a purebred."

"Vang also couldn't run the Court, much less the Kingdom, even if he was crowned as the new King the very moment I left," Edelein countered, desperate to change the subject.

Vang was another lion zoa, related distantly through Alderich's youngest son, who had no need to carry out the leonine traditions of the firstborn. A sycophantic and underhanded man in his forties, Vang and Edelein constantly found themselves at odds with one another, though both parties were too proper to dispose of the other. Vang was a valued member of the Royal Court through his bloodline, but was often the head of the Court's movements against Edelein.

Undeterred, Zander continued to speak his mind. "When you're gone like this, people have nowhere to turn but to him. Without an heir, that tailless mixed blood is all the Zenluvians have left of Alderich."

"Ehret Zander, we are a proper folk, beyond the need to use slurs," Edelein warned. "Plus, as a tailless yourself, you're in no place to talk in such a manner."

"My tail was cut off for my sins against your family. I'm a transmuted full-blood. And as you recall, I do *not* enjoy that subject," Zander spoke in short, gruff sentences as the sensitive topic was thrown back in his face.

"Maybe being mixed isn't so bad, though," Edelein wondered, looking off towards the horizon. "Certainly less cruel than bringing an animal into all the laws and regulations of our society. It is something Tyrus always believed in, and I understand why. Whatever lion is out there deserves to remain a lion, remain free. He doesn't deserve to be transmuted into a zoa just to take on the burden of ruling a Kingdom." Returning her focus to Zander, she went on, "I mean, look at what being transmuted did to you. You lost everything. You became a thug on the streets."

"I met you, though."

After a beat of silence, Zander continued.

"I wish you had a choice in the matter, Edelein, especially with your illness returning. However, think of how much King Alderis loved your mother, Sola. Your father loved Sola so deeply that he refused the Court's pressure to remarry and create a male heir. They were arranged the way the Court will do for you, and yet he loved her with everything he had."

"And because of it," she noted dolefully, "his mantle has become my prison."

"My point is," Zander added with unusual tenderness, "you will prevail."

Realization dawning on her, Edelein chuckled, "Are you trying to comfort me by using my dead parents as consolation for my inevitably loveless and desolate future?"

Zander's eyes widened slightly, ears flattening against his head in embarrassment.

Smiling, Edelein punched his chest affectionately. "Thank you. I'm still conflicted about transmutation, but I know I must consider it."

"Edelein, I do wish there were another way. If you insist on marrying for love, you would be breaking a thousand years of tradition and, worst of all, risk losing the crown."

"Maybe that is for the best," Edelein sighed, turning around to face the streets and stare anywhere other than at his piercing green eyes. "I lack the spirit that makes for a viable queen."

"Don't say that. I have no interest in serving as Vang's Ehret. He's a slimy bastard. You're an excellent queen, despite being so free-spirited."

Edelein laughed, and noticed Zander growing quiet and pensive. Tilting her head, she encouraged him silently to speak his mind.

"You want to be with Gihon, don't you?"

"E-excuse me?" Edelein stammered, caught off guard by his sudden comment.

"I know you, cub. You're in love with him."

"That is absolutely *none* of your business–"

"It's quite alright, Edelein. He's a good protector. If anyone could tolerate a life by your side with the pressures of a king, it would be Gihon. It won't be easy, but I'm sure you can convince the Royal Court to grant a marriage to a powerful Caandemite Dirigent. We could call it a strategic political arrangement."

"If you have forgotten, Gihon is not quite leonine."

"He's a zoa and an influential figurehead; a compromise that the Court will have to accept. Dirigents are the closest thing the new world has to kings or queens. You marry for love, but that doesn't negate the political benefit of allyship. It's not a bad idea."

"Gihon doesn't want to marry me," Edelein laughed dryly, to Zander's confusion.

"Why not?"

Edelein paused, recalling the conversation she had with the

Solomon clayman.

I don't think I can tell Zander about Gihon's power, and the Limbo contract. Gihon isn't ready to give that up for me.

"No man wants to marry a woman he just met. I have only had the pleasure of knowing the man for a few weeks. He hasn't courted me at all, so naturally he would be opposed to a sudden marriage."

"For the right woman, perhaps he would. When all of this blows over, you should talk to him about it."

"You sound even crazier than I do. I guess I'll… I'll think about it."

"You deserve to be happy. It's the promise I made to your father."

Zander's eyes softened as he knelt down before her. She turned around, looking down at him curiously as he bowed his head.

"Your Majesty, in honoring the spirit of your late father, my King, I will fully support your decisions. Where you go, I will follow, and what you speak, I will echo. This was my promise to you on the day of your coronation, and I will stand by you until I draw my last breath."

Touched, Edelein's mind raced back several years to the day they called off the search for her father, rushing the teenage Crown Princess into an emergency coronation ceremony. She recalled the faces of her father's Zengarde as each one bowed before her, repeating those same words.

Where you go, I will follow. What you speak, I will echo. As your Zengarde, I will stand by Your Majesty until I draw my last breath.

The Zengarde Vow echoed in her mind, tears forming in her eyes as Zander rose to his feet. She hugged him suddenly, biting back grateful tears as he put a hand on her head.

"You'll be okay, Eddie. You're a brave girl," Zander

whispered, his own mind slipping away as he recalled more silent promises in his memory.

After a long moment, Edelein pulled away, wiping tears from her eyes. Turning around to face the streets ahead once more, she stated, “I can sense that Gihon is close by. We should focus on that for now.”

“Yes, Your Majesty,” Zander nodded, as Edelein pressed onwards.

“And thank you, my Ehret,” she added quietly without turning around.

“You won’t know or see it now. One day in the distant future, you are going to have to give your heart to someone. It will be a choice that won’t feel like a choice. They will have it, and eventually you won’t be able to distinguish yourself from them.”

The words echoed in Gihon’s mind as his golden eyes wavered, brimming with grief. In front of him, the specter of a tan-skinned older gentleman stared lifelessly ahead, unresponsive to the presence of the Dirigent of Ravencroft.

For a moment, Gihon felt young and naive once more. Hardly even twenty years old when Ruther was lost to the timelessness of Othalgar, the young raven zoa ached as Arvien cried, holding his mother close in a frail moment of comfort.

The ghost in front of the Dirigent was that of Ruther Hilmatesh.

Colorless, neither living nor dead.

Ruther was an old father figure to Gihon in his youth, a close ally from Arvien’s adventuring link. Well over the retiring age of thirty-five for adventurers, Ruther continued onwards with Arvien regardless for reasons it took Gihon a decade to finally understand.

He had no choice. Ruther stayed with Arvien because he loved her. She had his heart, and it cost him his life.

Anguish swelled as Gihon remembered the wails of his mother as Limbo consumed her lover, recalling the rage in his chest as Solomon turned his back on his family for the final time.

Gihon reached forward towards Ruther's body, wishing that he could seek wisdom from Ruther just once more. His hand passed through the image of his old mentor, a lonesome ghost trapped between planes.

"I see it now, Ruther," Gihon spoke into the empty air, silently hoping that the man could somehow hear him. "She is captivating my heart. If I give it to her, though, I lose the ability to protect her. Yet, I don't have a choice, do I? You had no choice, either. This is what you warned me of."

After a moment, Gihon felt realization wash over his mind.

"It wasn't a warning at all, was it? You would have chosen this fate a thousand times over just to have another moment with Arvien. Giving her my heart is what it means to be free. Even if we die, we die together. That is… love, is it not?"

At his word, a stabbing pain brought the Dirigent to his knees. His chest throbbed as the limbus coating loosened its grip, its power waning. Gihon could feel his heart pounding desperately, palpitating off-beat as it tried to steady itself, gritting his teeth in pain as limbus coating ripped itself off of his heart.

It feels like my heart is being torn to pieces, the Dirigent thought as he endured the pain. *The contract is being undone..!*

"No," Gihon denied, clutching his chest, "not yet. I need to keep her safe a little longer. I need the Fortress! Please!"

The shade of Ruther slowly looked down towards Gihon as

he begged against invisible entities of Limbo, feeling the weight of unfettered emotions fill his heart for the first time in twelve years.

I cannot defeat Solomon without Fortress Black! I need to contain my heart until he has been–

Sharp pains prevented his thoughts from completing, the Dirigent pressing his palms into the pavement desperately as tears began to form in his eyes.

"I love her. I love her, I love her, I love her," Gihon repeated desperately, trying not to cry out every new emotion that consumed him. "I just need a little more time. Bookkeeper, please! Grant me Fortress Black for just one more day!"

Silence met Gihon's fervent plea. The Dirigent struggled to his feet, defeated, as he fetched the rook from his pocket. In his hand, the chess piece began to melt into shadow until nothing remained of Fortress Black.

"No, no, no!" Gihon trembled, hands shaking as the black rook vanished. "I need to protect her!"

Giddy laughter echoed from behind Gihon. Recognizing the voice of his brother, the Dirigent's heart filled with newfound feelings of desperation and rage.

"I knew she was going to ruin you," Solomon sneered.

Gihon turned around, clenching his fists as identical gold eyes interlocked.

"You're pretty close to finding me, you know," the clay mimic hopped down from a ledge as it approached Gihon. "It's unfortunate that you won't be able to stop me now that you don't have the Fortress."

"I'll fight you without it, to my last breath," Gihon countered, setting off towards the plaza as the clone jogged after him.

"You'll lose. If you leave now, you and Edelein can escape with your lives. You can have a future with her."

"If we die, we die together."

"Romantic. Is that what you told Ruther?"

"How can you make light of this, Solomon?" Gihon spat, enraged. "Ruther was like a father to us. You saw the way Arvien mourned! Does that not mean anything to you?"

"I didn't want Ruther to die, okay? Sometimes, people have to die for the greater good. He died doing what he loved. It's been ten years, Gihon. Get over it," Solomon retorted, turning away.

"You toy with peoples' lives in such a cruel manner," Gihon growled.

"You're not so different from your dear older brother, though. As we speak, your allies are being attacked by my forces. Yet, you're willing to let them die in order to stop me. People have to die for the greater good, am I incorrect? Isn't it worth losing a Zengarde or two for the greater good of destroying me?"

Gihon froze, anxious.

"Who is being attacked?" the raven zoa pressed.

"Oh, would that help you decide if they're worth the sacrifice or not?" Solomon laughed. "You'll let the Zengarde die, but you do realize that each group contains an alchemist. Your students are there. No matter which group, you'll lose a student. Unless you're implying that some students are worth saving over others? Little Luthro's life matters more to you than, say, Tristan Fairgraves?"

Gihon's blood boiled at the name coming from Solomon's mouth, feeling the anguish of losing his student stronger than ever before.

"What if I told you that Edelein is the one being attacked? Would you let me walk free to save her life?"

A million worst-case scenarios plagued Gihon's mind at Solomon's suggestion, overwhelming him.

"Gihon!" A new voice filled the Dirigent with relief as

an arrow pierced through the Solomon mimic's head, the figure crumbling into clay and vanishing.

Turning, Gihon laid eyes on Edelein von Luvemann. The lioness lowered her bow, eventually slinging it over her shoulder as she approached. Zander followed closely behind, head on a swivel, ever vigilant.

"Edelein, you're alright," Gihon sighed as he pulled her close into a firm embrace. "I was worried that–"

"There is nothing amiss. I had Zander with me. You, on the other hand, were all alone. I was terrified that something would happen to you."

"How did you two make it here without suffering from the effects of Othalgar's necropolis? You do not have an alchemist with you to utilize a limbus array," Gihon realized, trying to quell his fretting heart.

"Luthro gave me this array that you made," Edelein replied, pulling out the meticulously drawn alchemy circle. "He added a limbus array onto it and showed me how to use it. I got us here."

Gihon blushed, realizing that his efforts had been revealed at the hand of his top student. After a moment, the Dirigent began to beam with pride.

"Incredible, Edelein. You picked it up so quickly, clever girl. You maintained a limbus array with concentration until you got to me?"

Edelein felt her cheeks heat up in return, Zander grumbling under his breath as he took the lead of the group to allow the two a moment of privacy.

"Y-yes, I did. Gihon, are you alright? You seem different."

"Never better. I am so delighted to see you, Edelein. It is such a relief that you made it here safely."

"That's a lot of emotions, Gihon. Did you…"

"I did."

"So you don't have..."

Gihon hesitated, nodding.

"It is finished," he confirmed. "I will be alright, though. You will be protected by my own hand. If I need to rely on someone or something else's power, then I deserve to be neither a sentinel nor a dirigent."

"It is strange though," Edelein added, "I dropped my limbus array to shoot at the Solomon mimic when I felt your presence. Enough limbus energy emanates from your body to cover a fifty-foot radius, I think. Even now."

"I suppose the energy still remains within me, although it no longer shackles my heart. I have traveled to Limbo enough times, not to mention the limbus energy in my cloak techniques, to where I surely have residual energy inside of me. A relief, knowing I can fight Solomon without worrying about the rest of you succumbing to the necropolis."

"Succumbing to the necropolis is unfortunately going to be the least of our worries," Edelein replied, looking down at her feet.

Underfoot, the three stepped across delicately engraved lines in the pavement of Othalgar's main plaza, each perfectly straight line connecting into a pattern that Gihon wished he didn't recognize.

"The Gates of Heaven."

Solomon's true form stood atop a tower, peering down at his brother from above. The building, known to alchemists as the Warded Tower, had once been Othalgar's bastion of scholars: countless shelves with an endless sea of books filled the interior with knowledge for those who sought it. In the distance, Solomon could barely make out Ruther's shade, the specter unmoving as it watched Gihon and Edelein unwaveringly enter their fate together, Zander now covering their flank.

"It's time for the final act to begin, now that our audience has arrived," Solomon mused to the white-scaled draekis that stood by his side.

"Are you sure?" Agares asked, fiddling with the sleeve of his tunic.

"Agares, old friend, if there's anything in the world that deserves your full faith, it would be this," Solomon replied.

Placing a syringe filled with dark red liquid into Agares' draconic hand, Solomon closed his ally's fingers around it.

"You need to have confidence. If in nothing else, in this. In my cause," the man in red encouraged. "You know what to do if things go south."

Agares nodded. He was clearly uneasy, but not bold enough to challenge his master's beliefs. Satisfied, Solomon summoned the Divine Sword, the blade called Kether. In his other hand, the homunculus drew a glowing blue stone from his pocket, dropping it onto the rooftop underfoot. The crystal landed atop a small, intricate array, an ignition array meant to spark the Gates of Heaven below.

Kether began to hum with life as the blade heated, hungry for its next target. Solomon plunged the blade down into the leyline crystal, piercing and imbuing it with the energies he had spent the last few weeks collecting.

Limbus energy, primordial water, and Kether's natural divine energy mixed together, pouring into the leyline energy that flowed from the broken crystal. The full spectrum of reality merged into one, bowing to the will of the man that wielded it. The array began to glow, slowly pouring the provided energies into the larger circle taking up the width of the plaza.

"It'll take time to transfer to an array of that size, especially one in another plane, but it is self-sustaining and cannot be disrupted by the oncoming battle," Solomon instructed Agares. "Stay up here and protect the material connection while I greet our visitors."

Beneath the man in red on the ground below, his foes sprung into sudden action.

"Behind!" Edelein called out to Gihon suddenly.

Moving quickly, Edelein pressed her bow outwards, catching a familiar shadowy scythe before it could strike the Dirigent. Behind the black blade, Kimaris chucked, and then vanished again as he disappeared into Zander's shadow the moment the sphynx had leapt to strike.

"Crescent Shadow," Edelein realized in disgust. "I cannot find the words to describe that thieving murderer."

"It's more of an advantage to us than he realizes," Zander muttered to her under his breath, spotting Kimaris as he showed up in a shadow across the plaza. "He lacks proficiency in using the blade, and shadowsteps like an amateur. We, on the other hand, have sparred against Nephvir for years. I know every move that Kimaris could possibly make."

"We'll leave him to you, then," Edelein commanded in a cold voice. "Kill him, my Ehret."

A sudden rampart array from Gihon returned the favor to Edelein as he countered a stream of flames aimed at the three, his large array forming a barrier to protect them from the oncoming inferno. Kimaris mounted his horse while the three were surrounded by Aim's pyre, charging towards his enemies with a gleeful smile.

Edelein dove low to the ground, taking a risky low-angle shot at Kimaris with a hardlight arrow from under Gihon's rampart array. Kimaris dropped off of his steed, vanishing into the horse's shadow and reappearing from Zander's. The sphynx swung down at him, rage fueling his strikes towards Kimaris and his stolen technique. Kimaris dipped back into the darkness, emerging in the shadow of the plaza's main fountain.

"As expected," Zander repeated to his allies, "uncreative. He cannot shadowstep well. This should be easy."

Clay golems started to emerge from the pavement as Aim's fire dispelled. They began to surround the area, moving in towards the trio of intruders. Kimaris summoned his lance and thrusted it into the fountain, shattering stone and sending bursts of water forth to fill the plaza.

"Perfectly distracted," Solomon said under his breath as he knelt down, placing a hand on the Gates array to speed up the process.

"Incoming!"

An orange blur kicked up the fountain's water as it skidded across the plaza, tackling Solomon and interrupting his action.

"Sorry, but I think we're supposed to be preventing you from doing that!" Mandus exclaimed as he stood back up, taking off before Solomon could stop him.

Mandus circled over to Aim and used his momentum to spray the fountain water over her, dousing her flames. The fire witch let out a frustrated yell as her flames sizzled and steamed, puttering out.

"Sorry to make you wait, Your Majesty!" Thorne called as a sharp whistle of air carried his dagger into the head of a larger golem. Two more knives followed suit, striking the clay figure's center of gravity and causing it to crumble.

With a loud crack of electricity, three more golems fell as blue lightning jumped between each one. Alett's head poked out from the rubble, goggles protecting his wide orange eyes. The owl zoa lobbed a second bomb into the air, which exploded into a rain of acid that dissolved a handful of golems nearby.

"You were supposed to wait for us!" Alett complained as he pelted another chain lightning spell-bomb into a few more figures. "Not to worry, though. Can someone make it up top to get to the caster?"

"I can do it if you clear me a path," Mandus offered,

glancing up to where Alett had gestured.

Loosing a hardlight arrow at Solomon's feet to disrupt his focus, Edelein began to call out her orders over the cacophony. "Zander, focus on Kimaris! Mandus, get up to the golem summoner and Alett will clear his path. Thorne, throw projectiles at Solomon to prevent him from speeding up the array!"

Edelein turned to Gihon, continuing, "Gihon, can you keep the fire witch busy?"

Gihon grunted in agreement, looking ahead at his target. "She doesn't have her hat anymore, after Luthro disposed of it in the last skirmish. I presume she has some sort of plan to fuel her flames beyond the wild sputters, so I want you to be careful regardless. I'll keep her away from you as best as I can."

For a moment, Edelein recalled the last time they had engaged with Aim, and the look of rage on the witch's face when Luthro's mass-manipulation alchemy reduced her enchanted hat to be featherlight, the wind carrying it off into oblivion.

Aim's face twisted with concentration as she focused on her next move. Condensing her energy, the mage shoved her hands downward into the ground. A large array formed beside her, recognizable to Edelein not as Aim's array, but Agares'.

A towering golem rose from the plaza's shattered stones. The figure was ignited in flame, a pyre of death pouring heat towards the flame witch.

"I knew she'd have a plan," Gihon muttered, readying himself for a counter.

"Good luck with that," Zander stated as he dashed forwards to take on Kimaris.

Kimaris stepped into the shadow of the fountain to dodge Zander's attack. Reappearing in Zander's shadow as he had done before, the new owner of Crescent Shadow met a rude awakening as the Ehret of the Zengarde had long since anticipated the move.

Leaping up into the air, the sudden shift in his shadow's positioning flung Kimaris backwards. Zander laughed, a rare sound, though dripping with hatred.

"You know, I used to get Neph with that move all the time," Zander growled, lowering his stance and darting forward to strike at Kimaris while the lancer was still staggering back to his feet.

The sphynx zoa ducked as he ran, dodging a hardlight arrow from Edelein that whizzed towards Solomon. The man in red ramparted himself, blocking the arrow, but not without an irritated huff.

"Can you stop? I'm busy," Solomon snapped, trying to focus on his array.

"He's not fighting back," Edelein commented quietly to Thorne. "I may be able to handle this job myself if you want to help Mandus, my fae-blessed warrior."

"Oh, keep sweet-talking me," Thorne smirked, eyes following Mandus' incredible speed as the fox programmed a path that took him vertically up the side of the tower.

Landing on the rooftop, Mandus stopped for a quick moment to catch his breath and orient himself to his new location. He noticed Kether piercing the leyline crystal on top of an array beside the draekis summoner.

"There's no point," Agares said, "I'm just another clay mimic. The real Agares is hidden, as he was last time."

Mandus' brow furrowed, pausing to consider Agares' words.

No, Solomon wouldn't leave his weapon and the leyline crystal in the protection of a mere mimic. If this guy is a fake, the real one is still on this rooftop. I'm sure of it.

"Well, if you're not real, then I don't have to feel bad about destroying you!" Mandus replied brightly.

Programming his path, Mandus readied his array and

lowered his stance. The fox darted towards the sword and stopped on a quick pivot, diverting to punch Agares in the face. Agares stumbled, clutching his dragon-like snout.

"That didn't feel like clay to me!" Mandus beamed.

The hyperactive student of alchemy glanced over his shoulder, noticing several razor-sharp stalagmites that had erupted from the ground surrounding the sword.

As I hoped, my feint triggered any hidden traps they had around the target. But man, that could have killed me! Mandus thought.

"That was a clever trick, fox," Agares taunted as he wiped blood from his nostril. "Do you, perhaps, struggle at focusing on several things at once?"

"What's that got to do with–" Mandus' reply was cut off by a yelp as an arm reached from the floor and grabbed his foot.

The whole roof is coated in clay, but I was too caught up on trying to figure out how to get to the sword! Mandus thought in a panic as a second arm grabbed his other foot, locking him in place, powerless to do anything as clay began to creep up his legs.

CHAPTER 13

INFERNO

Gihon activated a groundshift array on the plaza floor, moving the fire golem between himself and Aim to obscure her vision. The water from the broken fountain sloshed around with the sudden shuffle of shattered cobblestones, temporarily dousing the flames around the golem's feet. As Alett lobbed a smoke bomb to provide cover between the two, he fell back to assist the Dirigent.

"The fire golem is inauthentic, and not a fire elemental either," Gihon explained to the owl zoa. "It is a standard clay golem, set alight to be used as supplemental fuel for the homunculus, Aim. Do you have anything in your bag that could increase the temperature of the flames? I have an idea."

Alett paused in a brief moment of confusion before quickly understanding Gihon's stance. "I've got magnesium, but that would probably kill everyone here."

"Magnesium would *definitely* kill everyone here," Gihon confirmed. "Nothing else?"

Alett shook his head. Gihon gave an affirming smile, unbuttoning his vest. The owl looked puzzled at his ally's sudden decision to disrobe, but remained silent in trust of the Dirigent's knowledge, assuming there was a plan behind the action.

"Not to worry. I was merely hoping there was an outcome that would not require me destroying my favorite vest," Gihon chuckled dryly, creating an array that enveloped the fabric in light, leaving a sheet of iron in its place. "Alchemy comes at a cost, you know."

The Dirigent knelt down, soaking the iron vest in fountain water. On an elevated pile of rubble, Gihon selected a flat and intact stone to begin chalking a new array into.

"I'm following. You're oxidizing the iron, right?" Alett asked.

"Correct. Well done," Gihon affirmed, laying the wet iron on top of the array. Rust began to form at a highly excelled rate until the vest was fully coated in reddish-brown flakes.

"A smoke bomb, please," Gihon requested, holding out a hand to Alett.

Alett reached into his satchel without hesitation, handing one over. Sparing a quick glance at the battle ahead, he noticed that Thorne and Edelein had picked up on the plan and were taking out any golems that wandered past the smoke screen to buy time for the two men to work.

"You use saltpeter in these bombs. I saw you working on one before," Gihon explained as he gently cracked open the casing. "Potassium nitrate will oxidize the flames, but I need it to burn hotter. It won't be easy to transmute the saltpeter into aluminum powder in a rushed setting such as this, but it will have to suffice."

"And Eddie calls *me* a nerd," Alett laughed, impressed.

A quick flash of light enveloped the saltpeter, leaving a tiny but deadly pile of grey dust: aluminum powder.

Gihon ran through the smoke and spotted Aim. The homunculus made eye contact with him, immediately shifting her position to draw flame from the golem and launch it in his direction.

"This is far from my best work, but it'll have to do," Gihon said to himself, wrapping the smoke bomb in the rusted vest.

Tossing the bomb high into the air, Gihon activated a bulwark array onto himself with just a moment to spare as his concoction connected with the golem's body. The oncoming blast exploded the golem into a brilliant light and flung both Aim and Gihon away from its intense heat. Ally and enemy alike stopped for a brief moment, witnessing the impressive pyrotechnic display of blinding sparks.

"I wasn't sure it would work, but you really did just make thermite in under a minute," Alett admired, his goggles keeping his eyes from burning out.

Gihon nodded weakly, winded from the collision.

As Aim struggled to her feet, she formed an array to draw flames from the golem, only to have it burst out of control in front of her. The golem lumbered about, chaotic and agonized as the fire burned hotter.

Everyone around could feel the intense heat in the plaza before the flames finally died down, a blackened ceramic figure now frozen near Aim. Aim looked up, astonished, before glancing around and seeing other clay golems too close to the flames had also been fired into ceramic. The pyromancer could feel a sting on her arms as she realized her array's reaction had singed her skin.

"I figured that Aim might not account for the oxidizer in her array. She just sped up the pottery firing process," Gihon explained to Alett. "Her ignorance towards her own alchemical technique just turned this entire plaza into a giant kiln."

Agares looked down at his fire golem, now a ceramic art installation.

The Dirigent was able to improvise several transmutations in such a short amount of time. He's serious about his studies. I can see why Master Solomon would despise such a man, Agares thought.

"C-can you stop the clay now, please?" Mandus begged on the other side of the rooftop, clawing at the alchemically-enhanced clay as it crept up his legs and encased his torso.

"The clay won't kill you, but if you keep struggling against it, that could change," Agares explained. "I really don't want to do that. I'd rather turn you into a golem and make your allies kill you by accident instead. But hey, maybe they'll recognize you from within the coating and choose to break you out of it. Either way, that's way more interesting, isn't it?"

"I think the most interesting play would be the one where I get out of here alive!" Mandus exclaimed as he continued to fight back against the hardening mud.

"You don't think it's interesting? I thought my plan would be fun," Agares paused, doubting himself.

A sharply-dressed man swung himself up over the ledge of the rooftop, landing between the two alchemists. He appeared to be as light as a feather as he touched down, adjusting his glasses and readying a long golden watch chain between two gloved hands.

"Luthro!" Mandus cried in relief, never more grateful for the assistance of his best friend.

"How unfair, little fox!" Agares claimed as he eyed his new foe. "If you can have more, then so too can I, right?"

Three more golems began to rise from the clay layer on the rooftop. Luthro swung his chain, striking at the golems and disrupting their creation.

"Luthro, jump!" Mandus warned. The alchemist heeded his ally's command, leaping into the air and avoiding an arm that reached from the ground to grab him. "The rooftop's all covered in clay. If they grab you, it's game over!"

Luthro reached down, digging his hand into the clay.

"N-no, Luthro, that's not what I told you to do!" Mandus yelped, helpless only to watch as clay began to crawl up his partner's arm. "That's kind of the opposite, actually!"

"It's all connected, isn't it?" Luthro realized aloud as the clay sank back down from his arm and reassimilated onto the roof.

Mandus felt his legs grow impossibly heavy, his bones screaming under the pressure of Luthro's alchemy. The clay's mass increased further, sliding down his body as Agares struggled to weave the weighted clay into his will. The three golems dissipated, Agares instead focusing his energy to keep anything he could through the weight.

"Alright, alright!" Agares admitted. "You were right, fox. Three was unfair. How about we have an even fight, with one warrior each? Your friend versus a single golem."

Just one golem? That should be easy, Luthro and Mandus both thought.

"I'm… I'm going to take your silence as agreement," Agares decided.

A sudden blur of motion alerted the students. Mandus was hardly able to call out to Luthro in time as a golem shot forward at an alarming speed, dagger extended. Luthro twisted his body aside just in time for the knife to only graze his side, tearing through his vest and a thin layer of flesh, and disrupting his mass manipulation array.

Luthro put distance between himself and the golem. He found himself surprised at the proficient stance of his new foe, the clay figure holding a low center of gravity and wielding twin daggers that were poised to strike at any instant. Taking advantage of the distraction as Agares focused his energy on controlling the golem, Mandus struggled free of the remaining clay around his ankles.

Mandus looked down at the clay flooring, glanced at Agares, and then at the Divine Sword Kether. Noticing the fox's shifting eyes, Agares extended a hand and started to make spikes out of clay to surround the sword, keeping Mandus from dashing over to it. Mandus sprinted over to Agares at blinding speeds, and after throwing a quick punch, the fox zoa dashed backwards towards the clay golem fighting Luthro. Agares tried to keep up with his quick movements, dismissing the spikes around the sword to replace them around Luthro's opponent instead. The speedster alchemist turned on a dime, heading to the sword, and pivoted back towards the golem as Agares returned to maintaining the stalagmites around the blade.

Completing his triple-feint and successfully overwhelming Agares, Mandus planted a kick into the golem's midsection. It didn't crumble as expected, but stumbled back a few steps.

"You're breaking the rules!" Agares whined. "This isn't fair. Should I summon another golem for you to fight?"

"Good luck with that," Mandus retorted, "you're barely keeping this one up as well as the spikes. Not to mention, you're in charge of all the ones down below, too, aren't you?"

"Mandus," Luthro whispered under his breath as the battlefield reset between himself and the golem. "Something is unusual about this one. It's not like his other golems."

"I had the same thought," Mandus replied quietly, readying another speed array. "Earlier, he was trying to turn me into a golem to force me to attack you. That could be one of our allies in there, being subjected to the same thing."

"Several of us are still unaccounted for," Luthro agreed, though his face was twisted in disgust. "But who uses twin daggers? I don't think any of us do."

"Unless the daggers are meant to throw us off," Mandus

suggested, dodging a swipe from the golem. "Zander has those dual swords, which is close, but I saw him down below earlier."

"I doubt Zander would be incompetent enough to be trapped," Luthro denied with a shake of his head. "There's also a possibility that there's an enemy inside. One of Solomon's cultists or another homunculus. There's too many theories for us to draw any conclusion without finding a way to expel whoever's in there non-lethally."

Luthro wrapped his chain around the golem's left hand and sent the other end over to Mandus. The fox zoa ran and caught it effortlessly, ducking down to avoid a powerful roundhouse kick from the golem.

"The chain's mass is near-zero!" Luthro called out to his ally.

Understanding Luthro's idea, Mandus flicked the chain. A wave of kinetic energy traveled down the chain and into the golem's body, sending it flying towards the edge of the roof.

Agares quickly moved his hands to draw an array. The golem melted down, spitting out a familiar leonine figure onto the clay roof, just in time as Mandus yanked the chain at superspeed to rip the arm off of the golem as its shell tumbled down fifteen stories.

The lump of lifeless clay splattered onto the ground next to Cari and Lylia, both girls paying it no mind as they leapt over it and skidded to a stop in front of Edelein. They formed a protective barrier alongside Thorne, Gihon, and Alett to cover the Queen; the six allies coming together to assess the state of the battlefield.

Ahead of them, Zander was interlocked in a fierce fight against Kimaris and his horse. The steed charged at Zander, who flipped out of the way. Kimaris took the opportunity of Zander's distraction to shadow step behind the sphynx cat, delivering a solid blow to Zander's right leg. Zander feinted towards Kimaris and threw one of his swords towards the sign post behind him as

Kimaris vanished into the shadows once more. The sword struck Kimaris right in the shoulder the moment the homunculus emerged, his movement having been predicted by the skillful Ehret.

An agitated voice called out from across the battlefield as Solomon dodged more projectiles from Thorne and Edelein, drawing the lancer's attention.

"Get a little more serious, Kimaris!" Solomon yelled. "Now!"

"Of course, Master," Kimaris said with a smirk.

The homunculus drew his lance, stabbing it into the ground. A small compartment on the handle flipped open and Kimaris reached inside, pulling out a small black object. Gihon's face fell, recognizing the chess piece in Kimaris' hand. In the homunculus' grasp, a delicately-carved black knight piece hummed with limbic energy.

"Zander, fall back!" Gihon commanded. "He's got–"

"Cavalier Black!" Kimaris finished gleefully, channeling his energy into the chess piece.

Zander sprinted backwards, noticing the shift. Limbus energy erupted, surrounding Kimaris in a void of purplish darkness. As the beam faded, a new foe was standing in Kimaris' place.

The creature was fearsome, with the body of a shadowy horse. An armored knight rose from the torso of the stallion, Kimaris' face barely visible under its black helmet. Large dark wings stretched from between the horse's shoulders. The winged centaur wielded his lance in one hand, Crescent Shadow in the other.

"Oh, come on!" Thorne cried out. "Gihon, do yours!"

"I… cannot," Gihon admitted. "I lost it."

"You *lost* it?!" Thorne screamed.

"Fortress Black would be inefficient against a pegataur anyway. The Black Armament is meant to be used together, not against each other," Gihon explained hastily as he watched the Cavalier launch into the air.

Cari readied her whip, dashing forward to provide backup to the Ehret. Kimaris dove down, charging at Zander, but met nothing but pavement as the sphynx zoa dodged. The pegataur took off into the air again, circling the plaza as he planned his next strike.

"The energy from that tower is still flowing," Edelein realized as she scanned the battlefield. "We've been trying to slow down Solomon, but we need to take out the power source up there. Mandus and Luthro might need help."

Dread filled Gihon's veins, fearful of the possibilities that could be hampering his students. "The array down here has not been affected by my groundshifting, which means the array up there is powering it via extraplanar travel. Fighting down here is useless if we mean to stop Solomon."

As Kimaris took another dive down at the plaza, Cari threw her whip up to wrap around the lancer's front hoof. The Cavalier soared into the sky, pulling the dangling Zentet Cari into the air with him. He began to drop down, the momentum raising Cari into a better angle for him to slash at her with the scythe. A quick pivot from the pegataur avoided collision with Zander's blade, and Cari used the sudden shift to find her footing, kicking off of a streetlamp to avoid Kimaris' swipe.

"Thorne, help Cari and try to slow down Kimaris," Edelein ordered. "Lylia, Alett, go after Aim!"

A blood-red array activated from Solomon's palm. The leader of the Verutian Order began to step up into thin air, his cloudstep array lifting him up towards the top of the tower. Gihon summoned his cloak around his shoulders, transmuting it into black wings as he grabbed onto Edelein's waist.

"Hold onto me," Gihon instructed, his grip tightening as Edelein looked up at him. "I will get us both up to the tower, and–"

The Dirigent stopped suddenly, wings furling back into a fabric cloak that draped from his wide shoulders. His eyes were locked on something behind Edelein, causing the lioness to turn and follow his gaze.

As Lylia and Alett approached, Aim pulled out a ball of silvery-white material from a container, her burned hands trembling. Recognizing the action, Alett grabbed onto Lylia to stop her from going any further.

An array ignited the ball in Aim's hands. Intense white light burned, its energy assimilating into the array as she prepared it to blast forward.

"Magnesium fire!" Alett and Gihon exclaimed in unison.

Gihon ran forwards, Alett sprinting backwards with Lylia in tow.

"Stay behind me!" Gihon screamed, heart sinking as he realized he wouldn't be able to make it to the others before the white-hot flames overtook them.

Aim let out a blast of impossibly bright white fire in Lylia and Alett's direction. The flames skirted across the water that had coated the ground, the brief touch of moisture being enough to cause a powerful explosion to envelop the area, consuming the two Zengarde.

"Lylia! Alett!" Edelein screamed as the pyre took her warriors.

Explosions rang out from the magnesium fire, shaking the tower that held the skirmish between Luthro, Mandus, and Agares' creations.

"Agares, what the hell!" Allocer cried out, lifting herself up from the rooftop where she had landed unceremoniously after he had ejected her from the golem. "I was having fun!"

"Y-you would have died!" Agares argued, gesturing to the fifteen-story drop where the clay figure had been reduced to a pile of rubble.

"What was that sound?" Luthro asked, gesturing for Mandus to quickly check as he put his guard up against the two homunculi.

Mandus darted to the edge of the rooftop, peering down below before returning to Luthro with a sour grimace. "It's bad."

"What is it?"

"A magnesium fire. I think it got Lylia and Alett."

"*Magnesium?* Master Gihon is the only alchemist down there, too," Luthro realized in dismay. "Even if he managed to bulwark or rampart every Zenluvian in the area, I am unsure if it would be enough to stop them from being instantly incinerated. A flame like that is over half the temperature of the sun's surface. Nearly thirty-five hundred degrees centigrade."

I wasn't able to save Nephvir from the Pale King. I won't forgive myself if more Zenluvians fall today, Luthro thought, his heart sinking to the floor. *I have to trust that Master Gihon had a plan and was able to get to them in time.*

"What's the matter, boys?" Allocer taunted. "Can't handle the heat? Let's just keep playing up here, then!"

Allocer closed in on both alchemists, taking quick swipes at each of them while expertly dodging their retaliative attacks. A second golem began to rise up from behind her as Agares leveled the field to make it a fair fight once more.

"We need a better plan," Mandus huffed, dashing behind Allocer to kick her in the back of the knees. The lioness stumbled but righted herself quickly, twisting her body to slash Mandus' forearm. The fox zoa yelped, jumping backwards and narrowly evading a punch from the golem.

Mandus ripped his tie from his neck, wrapping it around his arm tightly to stop the bleeding as best as he could while Luthro pulled the enemies' attention.

"Mandus, remember that thing you've always wanted to try?" Luthro asked, backstepping closer to his ally. "I think it's time."

Mandus' face lit up at the idea. "But you said you'd never do it!"

"You're going to have to bulwark us both, though. I have a plan."

"Are you sure it'll work?" Mandus asked, clutching his wrist and applying pressure.

"I'm going to do what Master Gihon would do and take the most direct path down," Luthro explained vaguely, hoping Mandus would understand the plan without Allocer picking up on it. "Trust me. Please."

After a moment, Mandus nodded. Luthro activated his array beneath his feet, feeling his body lighten to near-weightlessness as his mass reduced. Mandus reached back and crouched, allowing his friend to climb onto his back.

Allocer cackled loudly, mocking the two students. "What the hell are you two doing? Is this a joke?"

"They're going for the sword!" Agares realized, summoning stalagmites to impede the pre-programmed path that the fox zoa carried his ally through.

Mandus crashed into each spike as he ran, fragments of shattered clay flying and slicing Luthro's skin. After igniting his speed array, Mandus had swapped to holding a bulwark, though it seemed to favor Mandus' body more as the fox found himself protected from the brunt of the damage.

The path of the two boys brought them to Kether. Luthro's arm extended outwards, reaching for the hilt of the blade. Instead of grabbing it, however, the alchemist barely grazed the handle with a loud crackling noise as Mandus stumbled briefly, before the fox's path continued onwards, running over the ledge and down the side of the tower.

"He… missed?" Allocer tilted her head, sheathing her knives.

"The sword is deeply lodged into the clay, so they wouldn't be able to pull it out so easily. Master Solomon also imbued a counter onto it, so it will provide a hefty shock to anyone that touches it without disabling the array first," Agares explained. "I think they fled to provide backup to their allies below. Or die with them, I suppose."

Agares stopped talking as the sword shifted in the clay and suddenly dropped through the roof. Several crashes echoed further and further away as the sword barreled through each floor of the tower, careening towards the ground with an incredible force.

"The mass alchemist transferred his manipulation array to the sword, and made it so heavy that the roof couldn't hold it!" Allocer realized, running towards the hole where the sword once stood. "I love a smart man. I'm going after him."

Luthro and Mandus continued their path down the side of the building. Solomon, in the middle of his cloudstep, watched them pass by with a curious look before reaching the top where Agares stood alone.

"I'd say you did your best, but I'm not sure you really did," Solomon snapped as he eyed the hole in the center of the tower rooftop.

Agares bowed his head in apology.

"You know what I'm about to say, don't you?" Solomon added, narrowing his eyes.

Agared nodded silently, producing the syringe of reddish-black liquid from his pocket.

"Great," Solomon turned around and peered over the edge, preparing to jump back down. "I'll leave you to it, then."

On the ground below, Solomon could barely make out

the figures of Gihon and Edelein as they scrambled away from the magnesium fire. Edelein was running in front of Gihon as they retreated, the duo trying to put as much distance between themselves and the water as possible.

"It is going to get worse," Gihon explained in a hurry to Edelein, taking her wrist and willing his feet to run faster. "Every time the magnesium fire spreads to another puddle of water, it creates a very flammable hydrogen gas. I need to get you out of here before the whole plaza blows."

"But Alett and Lylia–!" Edelein choked out.

"Your life is my priority. There is nothing we can do to help them but pray they found a way to survive," Gihon mustered, knowing his response was a cold but honest truth, and that surviving a burn from such an intense heat was impossible by any logic.

Edelein screamed in anguish as the flames faded and revealed where Alett and Lylia had stood, nothing but cinders and ash remaining as everything the fire touched was instantly incinerated.

"I can't lose any more of them!" Edelein wailed. "Gihon, do something. Anything!"

Gihon felt his heart shatter as the woman he loved mourned her allies, the once-fierce lioness sinking to her knees in defeat.

Behind the couple, the stones of the plaza began to shift. Roots protruded from the ground, opening up the space for a large tangle of ironwood branches to emerge from below. The roots dispersed and returned to the dirt, expelling a heavily-burned elf that clutched onto a smaller figure in her arms.

"Lylia! Alett!" Edelein cried, crawling over to her charred allies.

Between the two, it looked as if Lylia had taken the brunt of the damage, putting her body between Alett and the inferno. They had been protected by the sturdy ironwood, only barely making it out alive as Lylia tunneled under the plaza with roots.

Alett let out a hacking cough, struggling to sit up. His left arm had been torched with several burns, but was mostly unscathed otherwise. Lylia remained curled up on the ground, coughing and barely moving.

"Lylia poured healing magic into the ironwood to keep it from getting instantly incinerated," Alett explained, knowing the others would be curious. "She's alive, barely, but has used up a lot of her energy. She was facing the fire head-on. It was remarkable."

Lylia mumbled something, weakly sitting up with Alett's assistance. Her hands were badly burned from holding onto the ironwood, her face and arms scorched as well.

"I'll be alright. I have enough left to heal the major burns, but not much else," Lylia said weakly, holding her hands together as a green glow began to emanate from her palms. "I don't think I'll be much help beyond this. Alett, I'm sorry about your arm. I won't be able to prevent it from scarring."

"This is nothing!" Alett assured, turning his body to hide the burns from Lylia's concerned gaze. "Take care of yourself. You saved my life back there."

"While I'm relieved to see that you're alive," Zander called out from the other side of the battlefield, "I do believe we're losing the main objective."

Gihon looked up towards the sky. Following Zander's gesture, he noticed a formation that seemed to be coalescing as clouds swirled together. Glyphs of a forgotten tongue surrounded the portal on shifting metal rings, illuminated with divine energy. A gate, the Gate, had begun to descend upon them.

"Get to the sword!" Gihon commanded. "I believe Mandus and Luthro brought it down inside the Warded Tower. Fighting inside will nullify Kimaris' aerial advantage. Everyone, go!"

Alett, Gihon, Edelein, and Zander turned heel and sprinted

towards the tower as Lylia continued to heal herself. Kimaris, noticing their plan, dove down to intercept them, but let out a screech as the pink fox on his back refused to give in. Cari wrapped her whip around the pegataur's neck, diverting his plummet away and into the cinders of the magnesium fire. Thorne vaulted himself over to land on Kimaris' back, digging his knife in between the plates of his armor.

Mandus and Luthro touched down at the bottom of the tower as Gihon and the Zenluvians arrived. Setting Luthro down, Mandus evaluated the student's shredded uniform, offering an apologetic glance.

"Your bulwark sucks," Luthro complained, adjusting his glasses.

"I know, but we're both alive. More importantly, the sword is down here. And *most* importantly, that was cool as hell," Mandus smiled, trying to cheer his friend up.

"If things go wrong, back out," Gihon instructed his students. "Lylia cannot heal anymore. She's barely even alive after that magnesium fire. I will not be permitting any of my students to die by Solomon's hand."

"Nor my Zengarde," Edelein added. "The same applies to you. Mandus, Zander, go help Cari and Thorne with Kimaris. We'll handle the sword."

Zander and Mandus nodded, taking off towards the battle. The sphynx cut at Kimaris as he stomped a hoof onto Cari's whip, yanking it out of her hands. The pegataur twisted, a large armored glove grabbing Thorne and throwing him off.

Now rid of the fae-blessed Fuuntet, Kimaris turned his attention to stab at Zander with his lance. The sphynx backstepped, raising his swords as his Seventh Sense led him to block a tenebrescent slash sent from the scythe. Zander slid back into the rubble as Kimaris then swung at Cari, who had pre-emptively vaulted backwards.

"Roaches. You're like roaches," growled Kimaris with a booming, reverberating voice. The Cavalier swung at Thorne, who sent a gust of wind to hydroplane himself on top of the water. Thorne's smile faded as Kimaris had expected his maneuver, the pegataur turning to deliver a deadly back kick with his hooves.

The kick met the glow of a hardlight shield, held firm by the strength of the lightbound alchemist behind it. The force of the blow sent Spira into a skid, colliding into Thorne and causing them both to tumble backwards. An orange blur caught the two, stopping their momentum as Mandus appeared behind them.

Kimaris let out a pained screech as Jinn sliced through his right wing, landing effortlessly in front of Zander and Cari with his sword raised and stance low.

"You two are alive!" Cari breathed in relief. "Thank the heavens. We needed the backup."

At the same moment, an ear-splitting roar echoed from the rooftop of the Warded Tower. The team flinched at the sudden loud noise, turning towards the horrific and unfamiliar sound.

"Great," Zander growled, "it seems they have provided reinforcements as well."

CHAPTER 14

TURNED TIDES

Luthro scanned the first floor of the Warded Tower. A once-warm lobby that had long ago greeted alchemists to a gateway of endless knowledge, now reduced to shadowy rubble with debris surrounding the receptionist's front desk. Luthro's eyes locked on the source of the chaos, the Divine Sword Kether now impaled deep into the ground, as the others filed in after him. Approaching the artifact warily, the student quickly scanned around the blade to find a small array carved into the rain guard of the sword.

"By God, is nothing sacred? I can't believe they etched onto a holy relic like this," Luthro complained aloud as he looked around for any material he could use to disrupt the array.

"Solomon was never one to respect the Church of Prima Luma," Gihon commented flatly.

A loud thud from behind alerted the student. Luthro glanced over his shoulder to see that more wreckage from the ceiling had crashed down upon his allies. Alett had narrowly avoided being crushed, but Gihon and Edelein were trapped beneath the stones. On top of the pile, a nefarious man in red rose to his feet.

"Master Gihon!" Luthro called out.

"Eddie!" Alett cried at the same moment.

"Oh, don't tell me you're worried about those two. They're fine. A couple rocks can't take out that sturdy raven," Solomon sneered, hopping down from the rubble. "I'm going to need you two to step away from the sword now."

"I'll cover you, Luthro," Alett offered. Standing his ground, the owl zoa slowly reached into his satchel. "Just keep doing your thing."

The rocks behind Solomon shifted, parting as Gihon pushed himself up from the ground. Edelein was underneath him, protected by the Dirigent's rampart array. Gihon helped her to her feet, and the couple both drew their weapons as they laid eyes on Solomon.

Effectively surrounded, Solomon seemed anything but bothered by his predicament. The homunculus lifted a large cinderblock by its protruding rebar and activated an array on its base with a coy smile towards his brother. The stone's form shifted slightly to become a proper hammer, and Solomon raised it up to rest on his shoulder.

Gihon spared a quick and fervent look at his student over Solomon's shoulder, his eyes silently commanding, *continue dismantling the sword while the rest of us distract Solomon. I believe in you.*

Luthro nodded, turning his attention back to the holy sword lodged in stone and getting lost in thought as he tried to ponder his next course of action.

I could sand it. No... I don't know how deep the etching goes, so that could take a while. Should I just etch my own array on top of it? Shit, Spira's going to kill me. I'm going to have to damage this ancient artifact of the Church even further, Luthro concluded.

He started by transmuting a sharp spike from the concrete, but was interrupted by a loud roar coming from the top of the tower that made him flinch and drop the stone.

What the hell was that? Luthro wondered, reaching for the stone again. *It didn't sound like the pegataur.*

With no time to waste, the young alchemist returned his focus to the etched-on array that scarred the sacred blade. Luthro began scratching at the array, only to reel back from a sudden jolt of electricity on his fingertips. Looking closer at the Divine Sword's ornate details, an unfamiliar array had been etched onto the fuller of the blade.

It appears to be some sort of safeguard. That would explain the shock I felt when I touched it up on the rooftop, Luthro realized.

The sudden rush of heeled bootsteps alerted the young alchemist. Luthro placed his hands onto his torso, transmuting the remains of his tattered vest to adamantine as Allocer's blade struck. The dagger repelled unsuccessfully, and the lioness let out an annoyed huff as her cover was now blown for nothing.

"Having some trouble with the sword, little boy?" Allocer taunted.

Not interested in engaging with her in conversation, Luthro drew his watch chain and touched one end of it. Dropping it to the ground with a loud thud, Luthro kicked the chain towards Allocer. The homunculus dove out of the way, rolling to avoid the strike, and brandished both of her daggers in a low and catlike crouch.

"You ready for round two?" the huntress sneered with a wicked smile.

Behind Luthro, his three allies had pulled Solomon outside of the Warded Tower, effectively distracting him from the student's work. Alett tossed a wire bomb at Solomon, who anticipated the attack and thrust his hammer into the ground to send up a pillar of water which froze at his command, crackling and crumbling as the ice took Alett's entanglement trap.

Gihon rushed his disgraced brother at the opportunity. Adamantine sword in hand, the Dirigent struck at Solomon, who countered with his stolen rampart technique.

"I do not enjoy your lack of creativity," Gihon growled under his breath as he recoiled.

"Perhaps you'll enjoy the fireworks, then," Solomon retorted, activating a cloudstep array and leaping into the air.

As Solomon fled, Gihon could make out Aim's figure in the distance, bundling more magnesium strips in her hand.

She still has magnesium left over?! Gihon realized, rushing forward to stop her.

"I can starve the exothermic reaction with a frost bomb to lower the temperature," Alett suggested, keeping up with Gihon's pace.

Gihon was startled, not having realized that the owl had followed him, but grateful nonetheless.

"Get the flames cool enough for my arrows to pierce through without incinerating instantly," Edelein commanded from Gihon's other side.

"Edelein, you should be back… you know what, never mind. I won't try to stop you," Gihon agreed in defeat, knowing better than to challenge the stubborn lioness.

Aim ignited the magnesium in her hands as Gihon sprinted ahead. The Dirigent planted his feet and summoned a rampart array, willing the energies of his bulwark to reinforce the rampart. The array increased in size and durability as two techniques merged into one, creating a new and improved dual-array.

"Bastion!" Gihon shouted, exerting his energy into the two simultaneously-cast arrays. Aim's inferno roared, white fire made more powerful by hydrogen explosions from the surrounding puddles of water.

Alett looked up at the Warded Tower, and back at Gihon. "I have an idea on how to stop the fire."

Drawing two bombs from his satchel, Alett weighed both in his hands for a brief moment before chucking one of them up at the side of the building. The owl zoa tossed the second one a moment after the first, planning his trajectory to hit the same spot on the wall overhead.

The first bomb detonated as it hit a window ledge, leaving a mimic of Alett clutching onto the side of the tower. The second bomb sailed up and the owl's copy reached out to catch it, gloved hand extended. He caught the bomb and planted his feet onto the side of the tower, pushing off and launching himself into the air. The second Alett threw the bomb down over the flames to land in front of Aim before dissipating into thin air.

The bomb connected with the pavement, bursting out into a cone of ice that shoved Aim back a step. The ice quickly melted into water by the heat of her pyre, the magnesium flames drawing out hydrogen and creating a gas that exploded in the witch's face.

Aim ceased her magnesium fire as she attempted to control the flames from Alett's explosion, barely sparing herself from an instant fiery death.

Taking advantage of her distraction, a light arrow soared through the flames as it lodged into Aim's chest. The homunculus stumbled and fell backwards with an agonizing scream, her flames extinguished.

"Gihon, Alett, go help the others with Kimaris," Edelein ordered. "I'm going to check on Lylia, and then head up for aerial support."

Not waiting to hear an answer, Edelein backpedaled to the elf's hiding spot, nestled behind more stone ruins. She seemed stable, but looked exhausted.

"You're going to pull through, right?" Edelein asked with a

soft voice.

Lylia nodded, grunting as she sat up. “I just need a few minutes. Are you all doing alright out there?”

“Aim is dead, Kimaris will be soon after. The golems disappeared a moment ago, so something happened to Agares. Solomon… we’ll get him,” Edelein recounted.

Producing a shimmering golden vial, Edelein extended it towards her soldier. Lylia shook her head, pushing it away.

“Your Majesty, those are for your blight. You were supposed to take that earlier, weren’t you?” Lylia gasped in disbelief. “I am *not* taking my Queen’s medicine!”

“Fine,” Edelein huffed, popping open the cork and taking a hefty swig. “I took it. There’s some leftovers, though, and I can’t finish it, so I’m leaving it here.”

Eyeing the vial as Edelein set it down, Lylia noticed the liquid was still over half-full.

Queen Edelein really means it.

“Thank you, Your Majesty,” Lylia conceded, taking the vial.

Running out to join the others in their fight against the pegataur, Edelein was met by Solomon once more. He seemed relatively uninterested in countering her, instead taking a defensive stance in support of Kimaris.

“Just stall a little bit more,” Edelein could barely make out Solomon’s command to Kimaris as a loud explosion resonated from the top of the tower.

Dust and rubble cascaded down into the plaza below. A pearlescent dragon with scales like stones took flight from the top, soaring into the air. Solomon let out a bellowing laugh of excitement, triumphantly extending his arms.

“And thus, Master Solomon of the Verutian Order becomes the first alchemist to successfully transmute a full-fledged dragon!”

Solomon gloated.

"They have a *dragon?!*" Thorne cried out in dismay.

"Get down!" Gihon yelled as the dragon breathed down on the plaza, a scorching breath of silt and clay. His allies dodged the attack and the dragon soared high into the air, circling around the plaza's airspace.

"Thanks to the blood of Euphrates, my new pet is invulnerable to the curse of this forsaken land," Solomon explained with glee. "He exists within all planes, subject to all and yet none."

It appears to be a stone dragon. That clay breath... did he transmute his own ally into a dragon? The draekis summoner? Gihon realized, noticing that the golems had all disappeared.

Zander ran forward to engage Solomon. The man in red conjured a blade of ice from the water underfoot, blocking a right hook swing from the sphynx. Zander's sword cut partly into the ice, lodging into place. Solomon twisted his sword to try to disarm Zander, but was met by Zander's quick anticipation as his Seventh Sense unclenched his hand from the hilt, striking at Solomon's stomach. Solomon was forced to block again, giving Zander the chance to yank his curved sword free from its frozen prison.

Kimaris, grounded by Jinn's previous wing strike, caught Zander's attention with a fierce swing of his stolen scythe. Eager for a rematch, Jinn lunged at Solomon as the man in red reshaped his ice sword into a two-pronged bident.

Solomon caught the zoa's blade and brought it down into the water. Angered, the man in red attempted to stomp on Jinn's sword to snap it out of his grip, but found himself shoulder-checked by Jinn as the wolf zoa dislodged his weapon.

Jinn struck with several feints, looking to exploit gaps in Solomon's defense. Solomon hesitated to throw out attacks, expecting Jinn to bait him into overcommitting as he began to adjust to the Zengarde's new dueling strategy.

"It's nice that you've improved," Solomon taunted. "It would have been awfully boring to have to fight you again, considering how badly you lost last time."

Irritated by Solomon's words, Jinn lost his rhythm. The man in red thrusted his blade forward, slicing across Jinn's face in the same manner as the wolf zoa had once done to him. Jinn staggered backwards, wiping the blood from his cheek as he reset his balance.

Gihon willed the bastion array into existence a second time, shielding his allies from another draconic spray. As the dragon soared off again, Gihon was able to get a clear look at the near-completed Gate.

"Mandus, Spira, get to Luthro!" Gihon commanded. "If he hasn't stopped it yet, there's likely a reason. Go!"

The dragon form of Agares landed on top of a nearby building. The structure remained unscathed by his landing, almost as if the dragon was weightless upon it. Charging up another breath, Agares was interrupted by several well-placed bullets to the face.

Jana lowered her smoking gun, Nora letting out a triumphant whoop at her ally's clean shots as she enlarged her hammer and prepared to strike.

"Sorry we're late!" Everett apologized, blocking a blow from Kimaris with his shield as he ran to take his place on the frontline.

"That's everyone accounted for," Edelein sighed in relief. "The battle's far from over, but everyone made it here safe."

In the lobby of the Warded Tower, Gihon's top student was engaged in a fast-paced battle against Solomon's newest and fiercest homunculus creation.

Luthro swung his chain rapidly to create a net of attacks that kept Allocer away. Allocer dodged each strike at a distance, circling her opponent as she looked for a way to get in close.

"Luthro!" Mandus called, arriving with Spira and rushing Allocer from behind.

The leonine warrior flipped out of the way of Spira's hardlight spear, backing into the shadows of the ruined tower.

"She might strike from any angle," Spira warned, trying to locate Allocer's lithe body with her lightbound eyes. "Luthro, keep working at the sword. Mandus and I will cover you."

Luthro nodded appreciatively and knelt down by the blade, continuing to examine the array on the sword to figure out how to get rid of its protection without shocking himself.

A loud boom resounded from outside, followed by a draconic roar. Nora grabbed another one of Jana's bullets, touching it to her bright pink array and handing it over to the petite fellborn. Jana loaded her revolver, firing a bullet that expanded to the size of a missile as it exploded into Agares' side.

"Dragonslayer bullets!" Nora beamed as she reached down, preparing a third strike.

Agares launched himself into the air. Jana aimed carefully at the quickly-moving target and fired, the projectile barely missing as it soared past him and through a group of frozen pigeons. Her missile collided with the pigeons, shifting them a few feet before passing through, the small shades remaining intact. Agares continued his ascent, trying to avoid the spectral birds consumed by limbo, but crashed into the displaced ones and tumbled down a few dozen feet before righting himself.

"He isn't affected by the cursed zones, but he also cannot affect them," Jana realized. "Anything affected by the curse becomes a tangible yet immovable object to him."

"That's why he was able to land on the building earlier as if he didn't weigh anything," Nora concluded from her ally's observation. "He isn't weightless; he can't impact limbic terrain."

Beside the sniping fellborn, Zander was engaged in fast-paced combat with Kimaris. The Cavalier's moves were predictable to the sphynx, his moveset limited by the simultaneous use of both the lance and scythe.

Kimaris swiped low at Zander with his scythe. The Ehret of the Zengarde leapt over the blade effortlessly, sliding in under Cavalier Black's horse-like body to jab upwards with his curved sword and strike the beast's heart. The pegataur squealed with a dissonant screech, limbus energy seeping out of the wound, and stumbled backwards.

Darkness spilled out from the beast, the Cavalier shrinking down in size and leaving a familiar homunculus in its place as Kimaris' time ran out with his piece of the Black Armament.

He's just a damn zoa, Kimaris thought, leaning on his lance and catching his breath. *I shouldn't be losing to a cat!*

With a sudden firing of Zander's Seventh Sense, the sphynx zoa stepped out of the way as Jinn tumbled past.

"Still not good enough," Solomon sneered at Jinn, turning his attention to Zander. "How about you, cat boy? You want a turn?"

Solomon looked up at the Gates of Heaven as they hung overhead, near completion.

Not long now, Solomon thought. *Any moment. They're strong, but not enough to stop my plans. Between Agares' and Kimaris' transformations, these little zoa never stood a chance.*

Enraged, Zander flipped both swords in his hands, preparing to strike at Solomon.

"Kimaris is injured. I'll keep Solomon busy. The rest of you, focus on the dragon," Zander instructed.

"Kimaris is *leaving*," Kimaris added snarkily, fleeing into the shadows to recover.

"Yeah?" Solomon taunted, turning Zander's attention back onto him. "You tired of hitting mimics, kittycat? You finally want a taste of the real thing?"

Zander leapt forward, narrowly dodging a blast from Agares as he ran at Solomon. Behind him, his allies tried to plan out a course of action to slay a dragon.

"I think we can utilize the environment," Jana suggested, explaining her earlier observation.

Alett nodded, following, "We could drop a building onto him and encase him in rubble. He can't move the debris, so he'd be pinned there permanently."

Nora pocketed her now-miniature hammer, thinking out loud, "Jana shot some birds and they moved for a second before freezing again. It's possible that we could topple a building from inside the safe zone, get it to fall outside, and freeze on top of him."

"It is possible, but a risky plan," Gihon explained. "There are far too many variables. We have no evidence of how long the building will fall for before the limbic curse overtakes it."

"It's better than nothing," Edelein added. "If it fails, we pivot."

"It'll work!" Everett assured. "Jana came up with it, and she's the smartest."

Jana blushed, looking down as she began to load more alchemical bullets into her revolver.

Another strike from the dragon's silt breath scattered the team. Edelein and Jana let loose a volley of bullets and arrows aimed at the creature's wings, piercing through and slowing down its flight. Alett dove under the safety of another half-demolished building, planting force bombs onto its supports.

Gihon activated a groundshift array underneath the building, trying to dislodge it from its place. Everett pushed from the other side to help guide the fall as the supports detonated and the building began to topple.

Agares looked up at the source of the groaning sound. Noticing the building, the dragon took flight, flapping helplessly before tumbling to the ground as its punctured wings struggled to catch the current of the air.

Just inches above the dragon's head, the rubble froze in place as the curse took hold too soon. Crawling carefully out from underneath it, Agares spewed more of his clay-breath into Gihon's bastion array.

From behind the heat of battle, an exhausted elf struggled to her feet. Lylia made eye contact with a foe once thought to be defeated as Aim removed her hand from her chest, wound cauterized and eyes blazing with rage.

"It's not working!" Everett realized. "Everything's going wrong. Jana, give me one of those strength potions you have!"

Jana nodded, tossing a scarlet vial to her ally. Beside her, Cari rolled out from under Gihon's protection to crack her whip into Agares' eye, blinding his right side. The zoa tried to fall back after succeeding in her attack, but found herself slowed by the thick layer of muddy clay surrounding the area.

Everett ran forward, his muscles reinforced and strength enhanced by Jana's potion. The ox zoa leapt up, grabbing onto the maw of the dragon and slamming it down into the pavement. Letting out a grunt of exertion, Everett began to slowly push Agares back underneath the frozen building, trying to pin him between the shards of debris.

A knife zipped through the air, nailing Agares' left eye with perfect precision guided by the wind. The dragon roared, spitting out slivers of stone shards towards Thorne. The fragments pierced through the Fuuntet's body in several places, sending him reeling backwards. Everett screamed, enraged, as he clamped the beast's jaws shut with his own two hands. Agares continued to thrash about, but Everett refused to relent.

"Luthro, I don't mean to alarm you, but the others are struggling out there," Mandus relayed as he observed the fight against Agares. "The Edelein clone is nowhere to be found. We're out of time. Any last-minute bright ideas?"

Luthro gritted his teeth, thinking.

"I had an idea for a sink-or-swim moment. It's risky," Luthro started.

"We're definitely sinking now, so go for it," Spira confirmed.

Reaching down to the ground surrounding the sword, Luthro began to draw a banishment array.

"W-wait, you're going to banish the sword?!" Spira yelled. "That's a terrible idea. Don't do that!"

"Kether is imbued with the energies of several planes right now. There are several possibilities as to where it could end up after this; but if it's not here, Solomon can't use it, and that's what matters."

Spira's face dropped, watching in horror as the priceless artifact of the Church of Prima Luma vanished into nothing.

The three alchemists, with their goal in some roundabout way accomplished, ran out to rejoin the others. Agares was clawing blindly at Everett, slashing his chest. The ox contained his agonizing screams as he held his position, pushing the dragon closer to the edge of the limbic zone with blood pouring from his chest.

Agares slammed his tail down, sending shards of stone towards Jana. Everett watched as the fellborn activated a bulwark array to protect herself, reducing the fatal blow to a few deep scratches instead.

There's no time for this, Everett realized. *The dragon can't move anything that's inside of the cursed area, right?*

The potion of strength surged through Everett's veins, fueling him into his final attack as he let out a forceful yell. With the roar of a berserker, Everett tightened his grip on Agares' head and flipped the dragon with a powerful suplex, throwing both himself and the beast into the limbic zone.

Jana screamed in horror as the curse began to overtake Everett, slowing his body to a stop as the color faded from his figure. Agares thrashed about, trying to free himself from Everett's frozen grasp, but unable to affect the lifeless ghost of the Zengarde warrior that willed himself to an eternity spent containing the dragon.

CHAPTER 15

LOSS

Thorne dropped to his knees, clutching his bleeding shoulder on the edge of the plaza as he stared at Everett's spectral form, eternally cursed to hold the struggling dragon in place. Cari sat down next to him, trying unsuccessfully to bite back an ocean of tears as she leaned on him.

"We can't give up now, Thorne," Cari mustered. "Can you stand?"

"Right," Thorne sniffed, wiping his eyes. "If we lose, it means that Everett sacrificed himself for nothing. There's still a lot more fighting to do, isn't there?"

Surprisingly, of all the remaining allies, Luthro placed a warm hand on Thorne's shoulder. Thorne looked up and struggled to his feet, warily eyeing the alchemist.

"Everett… he's not dead, right?" Thorne asked. "If you alchemists were to undo the curse that plagues this city, he'd come back?"

Luthro shook his head as he offered a health potion to the Fuuntet. "The shades of Othalgar are neither living nor dead. In ten years, no one has ever come close to cracking the curse. Hypothetically, though… if someone did, it's possible that the specters would live again. Maybe not fully the same, but they'd exist in real time, and that may be all we can ask for."

Thorne looked like he wanted to reply, but his face drained of color as he saw the scene unfolding over the alchemist's shoulder. On the other side of the battlefield, Lylia was leaning heavily on her staff in a face-off against Aim, fearless.

"Lylia!" Thorne screamed, pushing past Luthro and sprinting forward. "I'm not losing you, too!"

Thorne's cries were drowned out by the clashing of blades as Zander used his rage to push harder into Solomon. While seemingly flashy, the sphynx kept his blades flying to control as much space as possible between himself and the alchemist responsible for ending the life of yet another Zengarde. Solomon backpedaled, blocking with his frosted sword. The ice slowly got more and more chipped, forcing the man in red to draw up an array to replenish it. Seeing the array being formed, Zander moved in closer, almost pressing his body through Solomon's space of influence to catch him off of his footing.

A sudden thrust from a second assailant's sword caught Solomon's attention. The homunculus dodged, immediately turning to parry and shove Jinn back a few steps.

"It seems your backup has arrived. How unfortunate for you," Solomon laughed.

Zander noticed the change in Solomon's direction. The man in red had all but forgotten Zander entirely, pushing into a flurry of attacks against Jinn instead.

The wolf zoa was struggling to keep up with the speed of Solomon's blows, proficient but outmatched against the bane of alchemy himself.

As long as I don't give him any breathing room, I can win this, Zander thought as he feinted with a left swing into a leg swipe.

Solomon tripped, but stopped in midair as he used a cloudstep array to catch himself. Zander let out an annoyed hiss and sliced upwards, his blade recoiling off of the homunculus' weapon as it was parried.

The momentum of Zander's attack propelled the suspended homunculus into a flip. Solomon reached down and slashed the water to bring up a barrage of icicles towards his opponent. Zander began to pivot away from the attack, but stopped suddenly as his Seventh Sense triggered a warning. A jetstream of water pierced Zander's shoulder, painful but not fatal. Behind him, Jinn righted himself, clutching his sword as he realized that Zander had taken the hit to the shoulder to prevent the attack from striking Jinn's heart.

"That was a dirty trick, homunculus," Zander spat.

"Oh, I'm wounded, kittycat," Solomon mocked with a playful pout. "A scrappy street-cat like yourself should appreciate a bit of misdirection in a fight!"

Zander fell back a step, ripping a piece of fabric from his pant leg and tying it around his bleeding shoulder. Solomon allowed the action without pressing an attack, grateful for a brief moment to catch his breath.

"Jinn, fall back," Zander demanded. "He only pulls out tricks when he's outnumbered; targeting you to force me into a defensive position. It'll be easier if I fight alone. Go back and help the others round up the remaining enemies."

"You're smarter than you look, cat," Solomon replied. "We both know that the better warrior is the one who does whatever it takes to win the battle. Run along now, pup."

Jinn growled, ears flat, but nodded at the command of his superior.

Looking up at the sky, Solomon beamed as he laid eyes on the fully-realized Gates of Heaven overhead. The man in red glanced around the battlefield, seeming to be looking for something, before gazing confidently at Gihon with his head held high.

Gihon summoned the shortsword out of his cloak, motioning for his allies to fall behind him as he stood facing his brother.

"I want you to see it this time, *brother*," Solomon gloated. "It'll work, and you'll be wrong. Oh, how I've longed to see you be wrong for once, perfect son of Ariven."

"Your extra precautions won't save you from the backlash that'll come with it," Gihon warned, pointing his sword at his elder brother in a warning motion.

"How about one more duel, then, for old times' sake?" Solomon offered.

Edelein paused, something unusual clicking in her mind. Stepping forward to stand beside Gihon, she boldly commanded the homunculus, "Open the Gates, Solomon."

Gihon froze, looking down at the lion zoa with eyes that begged, *don't!*

Solomon's eyes darted around the arena again before landing back on Edelein.

"That would be no fun," Solomon denied. "I think I'd rather play a bit longer."

Edelein laughed. "I knew it. You aren't able to open them."

What on Tevus is she trying to do?! Gihon thought.

Under her breath, Edelein whispered, "Whatever he needs as a key for the Gates, he doesn't have it. Keep him busy while I figure out what it is."

Gihon kicked up stones from the pavement, sending them careening towards Solomon. The man in red swatted away the bricks and shot a jetstream of water towards his brother, who transmuted his sword back into loose fabric and quickly hardened at an angle to deflect the attack.

Transmuting his cloak into a sword once more, the Dirigent ran forward to engage with Solomon's ice blade. The man in red stepped back, melting his sword into an aqueous orb, and pulled fire from a smoldering pile of clay to create an explosion of steam in front of Gihon.

"Is there any way to dispel the Gates while Solomon is distracted?" Alett asked, turning towards the alchemy students.

Nora, Spira, and Mandus turned to Luthro for an answer. The top-ranked student shook his head, unsure. Jana was tuned out of the conversation entirely, eyes locked on Everett's strong form as he held relentlessly, lifelessly, onto Agares.

"Edelein thinks that Solomon is missing a key to open the Gates. Do you think it was the sword?" Zander asked. "What did you do to it, anyway?"

"I banished it," Luthro admitted.

"Like a phantasm?"

"I had no other choice! We were out of time. However, I don't think the sword was his key. More of an igniter, or battery," Luthro hypothesized.

"The second leyline crystal," Edelein thought aloud. "We haven't seen it. The fact that Solomon came back for it meant he needed it."

At that moment, a silver-haired figure leapt up from Cari's shadow. Sensing his movement with only a heartbeat to spare, Zander shoved the zoa out of the way, moving her shadow and flinging Kimaris out of it.

"Ow!" Cari whined. "Zander!"

"You would have been dead otherwise," Zander replied in his own unconventional way of apologizing. "That's the second time I've gotten him with that move. Pathetic."

"I've got an idea, but I need to confirm it," Edelein realized suddenly, scaling a nearby building to get an aerial advantage as she fired down at Solomon.

The arrows missed, but distracted Solomon enough to allow Gihon to land a solid kick into his side. As the homunculus staggered back, Edelein lowered her bow and called out with the same bold demeanor that had drawn him to her in the first place.

"I know what you need to open the Gates of Heaven," Edelein declared, crossing her arms. "I know exactly where you're hiding it, as well."

Solomon's eyes darted towards Kimaris as the lancer exchanged blows with an enraged Zander once more. The moment only lasted a split second, but it was all Edelein needed to confirm her suspicion.

"Get his lance!" Edelein ordered, gesturing towards Kimaris.

Mandus crouched down, programming a path to attack the homunculus. As his sprint started, a wall of flames roared out of seemingly nowhere, intercepting his movement. The fox zoa was unable to stop mid-dash and crashed through the fire, though his speed prevented any severe damage.

"That fire…" Edelein realized. "The flame witch lives!"

Turning her gaze to the source, Edelein spotted Lylia and Thorne engulfed in Aim's inferno. The wall had separated Gihon and Solomon from the others as well, and the rest of the team were in pursuit of Kimaris as he jumped from shadow to shadow.

Solomon's head had also turned at the sudden burst of action, his eyes following Kimaris and his lance. Gihon pressed forward at an advantage, striking while the homunculus was distracted.

Solomon looked past Gihon's shoulder up at the lioness, noticing that her gaze had also been diverted to the blast of fire, facing away from Gihon and Solomon. The man in red extended a hand towards Gihon, palm first as his blood-red array began to form.

"Sorry," Solomon muttered under his breath as he twitched his hand ever-so-slightly to the side, missing Gihon and firing at Edelein instead.

A blast of lightning struck the lioness from behind. Edelein let out a sharp yelp of pain, shocked, as her body tumbled off the ledge of the rooftop and plummeted to the ground below.

"Edelein!" Gihon exclaimed, turning his head to follow Solomon's diverted attack.

Turning his back on his enemy entirely in an unwise moment of heated emotion, Gihon sprinted towards the lioness. The Dirigent slammed his sword against his back, willing it to unfurl into dark wings as he launched himself into the air with a powerful beat. Arms extended, Gihon caught Edelein in a tight grasp, touching down lightly onto the ground a moment later.

Edelein's eyes were wide and she shook her head quickly to center herself. Gihon set her down, firm hands clamped around her arms to steady her.

"I need to get you out of here," Gihon pleaded. "We've been at this for too long. At this rate, the blight is going to flare up and make everything worse than it already is. Where's your stamina potion?"

"I gave Lylia the rest of it," Edelein explained. "I took half. She needed it more than I did."

Gihon's eyebrow twitched, both impressed by her devotion and annoyed by her lack of self-preservation. Presenting a second vial, the raven zoa placed a gentle thumb on Edelein's chin and tilted her head back, helping her take a swig of the golden liquid inside.

"I thought you might do something foolish, so I kept an

extra one," Gihon replied with a sigh. "Stay on the ground and provide cover for me, alright? If you keep Solomon focused on blocking you, I should have no issue finishing him. It will be easier for me to protect you if you're close to me."

It's so much harder to shoot from the ground, but fine, Edelein thought with a huff.

Gihon's eyes softened empathetically. Reaching back to touch his wings, the feathers furled and dislodged from his shoulders to create a sword once again. The Dirigent turned heel and took off towards his brother, grateful for the volley of hardlight arrows behind him preventing Solomon from striking at range.

Gihon struck at Solomon with his adamantine blade. The man in red countered with a quick parry, followed by a wall of ice to block Edelein's line of sight the moment she tried to reposition herself to his right side.

Solomon turned to dodge another thrust of Gihon's sword and cloudstepped overhead. He pulled his hand to bring water out of the ice wall in an attempt to freeze it around Gihon, which the Dirigent blocked by transmuting his sword into an adamantine fabric wall to interrupt the ice formation. Gihon reversed the transmutation and stomped his back foot to send a groundshift towards Edelein, extending a platform of stone up so the lioness could shoot over the towering wall of ice.

Platforms of air lifted the man in red upwards towards Edelein, dodging her arrows. As Edelein leapt from the pillar to avoid Solomon's approach, Gihon caught her with a ramp that slid her back onto the ground. Solomon pressed his hands down onto the platform and transmuted a familiar pyroclastic blade, spewing magma out from the fissures down to the two, buying himself time to leap down as Gihon ramparted the blast.

Gihon compressed his cloak into an arrow and tossed it to Edelein as he rushed Solomon. The man in red fired off several ice shards at his brother as Gihon bulwarked through, the ice shattering weakly against his toughened frame.

Edelein glanced down at the black arrow in her hand, curiously trying to understand Gihon's plan.

I have the hardlight arrows. Why did he fashion his sword into an arrow for me? Edelein wondered. *I suppose that's his way of romancing me.*

Gihon deflected another spray of lava as Edelein fired the black arrow at Solomon's back. Gihon sparked the delayed activation of his array, expanding the arrow back into a cloak and hardening it as it wrapped around the befuddled homunculus. Gihon approached quickly and started pummeling Solomon like a boxing bag, landing a few hits as solid as the man who threw them before Solomon finally burned through the cloak.

The wispy, burning fabric slowly drifted down into the water. Solomon wiped blood off of his mouth, eyes alight with hatred.

"I always thought that fighting you was frustrating," Solomon snarled, "but seeing the two of you together makes my blood boil."

"Stand down, then, and you will not have to bear witness to another moment of it," Gihon retorted.

"You don't get it! You never will," Solomon spat. "You'll never change, even without your stupid Fortress Black. This dream of mine is all I have left. If that's an issue with you, you should have considered that before you took my entire life away from me. You and that godforsaken mother of ours are the only reason I'm doing *any* of this!"

A roaring flame scorched the plaza and drew everyone's attention as Aim let loose. From within the inferno, Lylia brought up her fists to cover her face as druidic magic covered her skin with ironwood from a barkskin spell. The elf advanced towards Aim, enduring through the flames, as Aim pulled more over to her hands from nearby, forming searing claws over her fingers to swipe away the throwing knives that Thorne pelted her with relentlessly from his position beside his elven ally.

Both Lylia and Aim began to weave in and out of each other's space, testing their opponent. Aim made the first attack, swinging pyro claws at Lylia. The druid blocked the attack with barkskin and countered with a jab, barely missing Aim's head by a hair's breadth.

The homunculus retaliated with an attack on Lylia's ribs. Her fiery hand met sturdy flame-resistant ironwood, dealing very little damage to Lylia as the elf took advantage of the opening to punch Aim with a left hook.

"I didn't expect a druid to be proficient in melee," Aim mused, stepping back to put some distance between them as she tried to ignore the ache in her jaw.

"Most people don't. I'm not just a druid, you know," Lylia replied flatly with fists still raised.

A monk? Aim wondered, sending flames out from a further range.

Lylia stayed low to the ground, arms covering her face to block the quick bursts of fire.

Her attacks are weakening, Lylia realized as she weaved through to close the distance. *Possibly conserving fuel. She doesn't have that enchanted hat like last time, and the others destroyed the golem earlier.*

Aim dipped under Lylia's right cross punch, rolling to the side to grab a handful of clay from the ground. Her vermillion array sparked for a quick moment, transmuting remnants of magnesium oxide into silicon powder.

The homunculus threw the powder forward at her opponents, igniting a clouded pyre between Thorne and Lylia.

The fae-blessed Fuuntet leapt out of the way, summoning a gale to splash water up between himself and the flames. Sparks and heat exploded out as the water combined with the silicon fire, sending Thorne tumbling backwards at high speeds with a loud exclamation of pain as the flames licked his skin and his body thumped against the pavement.

Lylia ran in front of her wounded ally, raising several ironwood barriers to reduce the brunt of the attack. Aim's fire scorched through the first few walls but slowed down with each one, petering out before it could reach the Zengarde.

"Lylia, you can't keep going like this," Thorne said, his voice low. "You don't have any magic left. I can tell."

The elven Zengarde helped her ally to his feet. "You're right. If you can help me, I've got a little something that I was saving as a last resort."

"Don't say that. I don't want to be at a last resort," Thorne whimpered, glancing down at her closed fist.

Lylia chuckled, raising an eyebrow as she took his hand in hers. "It's *her* last resort, not ours. I'll make an opening, and you finish the job."

Thorne nodded, understanding the elf's intentions. Tilting his head from side to side and cracking his neck, the human awaited his perfect opportunity to strike.

Noticing their delay and defensive reactions, Aim tossed forward another puff of silicon powder. Aim remained unassuming of the audacious human carefully eyeing her every move and ignited the spark of her array to send the flame bursting forth into the silicon. Anticipating her attack, Thorne used that exact moment to send a gust of wind, his zephyr blowing the silicon towards Aim as it connected with her kindling and detonated in her face.

The pyromaniac stumbled backwards with a painful scream as her skin burned, allowing Lylia the chance to strike with a flurry of blows. Aim feebly tried to defend herself, getting lucky enough to manage a single slash across Lylia's left arm with a heated claw attack. The druid paid no mind to the blow, landing a clean punch into the cauterized wound on Aim's chest. The gash from Edelein's arrow reopened, and Aim let out a hiss of pain as she stepped back.

"Now, Thorne!" Lylia commanded, ducking down to the ground.

The Fuuntet extended his hand, a powerful gust of wind plowing directly into Aim's body and stinging the reopened wound. Aim took another backstep, wincing, before laughing maniacally.

"That was your grand plan?!" Aim taunted. "To, what, show me a nice summer breeze?"

"No," Lylia denied, backing up to stand beside Thorne and giving herself ample distance from the homunculus. "This was."

The elf felt a surge of power as she willed the forces of nature to bend to her command. With a yell of exertion, Lylia poured the scraps of her remaining druidic magic into the green glow of her hands, closing her eyes as flowers began to bloom from the wound in Aim's chest.

Mere moments before, the hand Lylia had offered to her ally contained several tiny chrysanthemum seeds. Feeling the tiny life-bearing beads in his palm, Thorne understood Lylia's silent suggestion and held tightly onto them until Lylia could reopen Aim's wound and expose her flesh for a gruesome final strike.

The gust he had summoned was not just composed of air, but decorated with a pocketful of flower seeds that buried themselves under Aim's skin upon contacting her open wound. With the will of nature itself in the palm of her hand, Lylia overflowed the seeds with life, blossoming an array of scarlet and white chrysanthemums out of her foe's chest.

With an agonizing scream as the flowers' roots dug into her veins and tissue, blooms desperately reaching inwards to search for vital nutrients, Aim collapsed for the final time, lifeless. A corpse turned garden bed, the cycle completed as the death of one became the life of many.

Edelein drew her bow, trying to aim a shot at Solomon. The hardlight array whirred under her thumb, raring to let loose another luminous arrow, but the man in red continued to weave behind the broad shoulders of Dirigent Gihon.

Gihon reached down into the clay, scooping up a mass of it to be transmuted into a rocky blade. As he crouched, Solomon dipped as well for a low strike, making it effectively impossible for Edelein to take a shot.

"Ugh!" Edelein cried out in frustration, lowering her gilded warbow. "Gihon, this is pointless. Get me to higher ground!"

"Absolutely not. If he shoots at you again—" Gihon started.

"Then place me above and *behind* him, so he'd have to turn his back to you to reach me, and that would let you punch his lights out!" Edelein interrupted.

She makes a convincing argument, Gihon admitted to himself.

Placing a hand down onto the stones, the Dirigent sparked a groundshift array under Edelein's feet. The lioness lowered her center of gravity to keep her balance as the pillar began to rise and convey behind Solomon, drawing back her bow to line up a clear shot.

Solomon faced his brother ahead, paying no mind to Edelein. An array illuminated under his palm before fading out as he continued to swing his pyroclastic blade relentlessly at Gihon.

What did that array do? Edelein wondered, senses on high alert. *Was it a feint?*

Sudden movement in the air raised the fur on Edelein's tail. Swinging her bow just in time to intercept her assailant's dagger, Edelein felt her legs give out as the new opponent swept low, knocking her to the ground.

Edelein acted fast as the woman pinned her down, catching her wrists as she attempted to plunge a second knife down into the Queen's throat. Locked in a stalemate, Edelein looked up to see her own eyes gazing back down at her, the wild and fanged grin of her own face uncanny and unnerving.

"Surprise," purred Allocer as she straddled Edelein with powerful legs, unrelenting on the blade as she continued to push down.

Edelein jolted with a sharp twist of her arms. Allocer's dagger dipped to the side, freeing the Queen to jam an elbow into the homunculus' face. Allocer fell back with a yelp, allowing Edelein to squirm free and distance herself.

"Edelein, are you alright?" Gihon called from below, barely able to make out the sounds of the two lions scrapping with each other over the noise of everyone else as they tried to stop the shadow-stepping Kimaris and round up the remaining cultists.

Solomon laughed, pressing his advantage. Gihon fought defensively, stepping backwards as his mind and heart grew occupied with the well-being of his woman.

The Dirigent raised his sword to meet Solomon's, the stones searing as they met a blade of magma. Solomon brought up his guard hand, grabbing Gihon's sword and beginning to superheat it further. Noticing his plan, Gihon expedited the process by scorching his blade into lava and swinging it forward, attempting to splash the viscous liquid at his brother.

The attack was met with a flaming parry, Solomon raising

his pyroclastic blade to absorb the lava. Gihon stepped back again, trying to get another look at the pillar above.

"Edelein, do you need help?" Gihon fretted as he called up to her for the second time.

"I'm fine, Gihon!" Allocer responded sweetly.

Edelein opened her mouth to yell down to Gihon, but stopped to conserve energy and swing her bow to catch another one of Allocer's relentless, never-ending attacks. Allocer locked the warbow between her daggers, sliding them down to cut at Edelein's fingers. The Queen yelped in pain, dropping her bow and kicking Allocer away as she clutched at her bleeding fingers.

She'd have cut my fingers off if I didn't let go, Edelein thought with a distressed whimper. *She's not exceptionally skilled in combat, but she's ruthless. Keeping me on the defensive so I can't call for help while also forcing me to be mindful of her off-hand weapon, it's like she was made to counter me. I need to be smarter about this.*

Keeping a wary eye on the homunculus, Edelein dove down to grab her bow again. Allocer swiped, aiming to stab the Queen in the neck, but stood no chance against Edelein's reflexes. Edelein ducked under the knife, grabbing the bow and catching Allocer's second hand between the string and the main body. She twisted the weapon quickly, forcing Allocer to drop her dagger as the bowstring bit into her wrist with a force that the homunculus hadn't expected. Edelein quickly pushed the disarmed knife away, sending it skidding off the edge of the pillar.

Allocer jabbed her dominant-hand blade down and sliced Edelein's shoulder. Edelein let out a sharp cry as the knife tasted her blood, her grip weakening on her bow as the overwhelming weight of fatigue and blight began to settle in.

No, not now! Edelein pleaded silently as Allocer disarmed her, pinning her down again.

Allocer laughed, pressing her blade against Edelein's throat and leaning in close as she sensed her impending victory. Wishing to revel in her own superiority, Allocer drew the dagger at an agonizingly slow pace across the Queen's neck to admire beads of blood as they slowly welled up.

"I want to hear you scream, you pathetic worm," Allocer gloated. "I want you to feel *agony*. Tell me how much it hurts, little kitty."

With a flick of her ear, Edelein narrowed her eyes. "You desire to know pain?"

A strong hand grabbed the back of Allocer's neck, long nails digging into her flesh as she was hoisted into the air. Allocer's gaze met the bloodthirsty, malicious green eyes of the Ehret of the Zengarde. Zander Khepri grabbed Allocer's wrist, snapping the bone with a single crushing grip and forcing her to drop her second dagger.

"Tell me how much *this* hurts, then," Edelein retorted as she rose weakly to her feet.

Fearful of the murderous aura radiating from the Ehret, Allocer raised her voice to let out her last anguished impression of Edelein von Luvemann.

"Somebody, please help me!" Allocer screamed with a sickening gurgle as Zander's curved sword impaled her chest and filled her lungs with hot blood.

The battlefield seemed to silence itself for a moment as the Queen's voice begged to be saved. Gihon looked up, his heart sinking at the sound. Even Solomon hesitated for a second, trying to figure out which one of the lionesses had won the battle.

Zander dropped the homunculus' corpse, wiping her blood from his skin with disgust. He approached his Queen, fiery anger giving way to relief as the adrenaline settled.

"Next time you try to get yourself killed, can you do it

anywhere other than a perfectly smooth, vertical pillar?" Zander pleaded wearily.

"I thought you'd admonish me for continuing to fight," Edelein replied. "I broke my promise to you."

"I never expected you to keep it. I know you better than to try to stop you when you get foolish ideas in your head," Zander huffed.

The ground began to tremble suddenly, lowering as Gihon brought the pillar back onto his level. He had run past Solomon ignorantly, which proved to be no issue as the homunculus curiously followed behind his brother, also eager to identify the source of the cry.

As the pillar returned underground, the Marleogne brothers laid eyes on Queen Edelein as she leaned on Zander, exhausted but alive. A sigh of relief seemed to pass through both of them, even Solomon pleased to know that he had eluded a berserk and shattered Gihon while ridding himself of the obnoxious asset he once called Allocer.

Gihon stepped forward slowly, happy to see Edelein standing. His shaky exhale was cut off abruptly by an excruciating rush, glancing down to see a large metal lance gleaming with scarlet blood.

Edelein let out a bloodcurdling scream, one that put the death throes of Allocer to shame. Behind Gihon, protruding from his shadow, stood the wildcard homunculus Kimaris. Kimaris withdrew his lance from Gihon's chest, leaving a gaping wound identical to the fallen Zengarde Nephvir.

So this is love, Gihon thought as he collapsed.

CHAPTER 16

LIMBO

"No!" Edelein cried, the noble Lion Queen of Zenluve pushing away from Zander and stumbling towards her lover. Gihon sank to his knees, blood staining the ground as a fountain of death poured from his heart. In a moment where the world seemed to hold its breath, the Dirigent of Ravencroft crumpled to the ground, only affording a quick and mournful glance towards Edelein as his sight faded into the dark and lifeless void that loomed beyond him.

Edelein trembled greatly as she dropped down next to him, touching his face and letting painful sobs wrack her body.

He's not breathing, Edelein realized in anguish. *Not even Lylia can cure death.*

Burying her face into his neck, the Queen silently willed for a miracle as she breathed in his fading scent, begging any force of nature or divine authority to bring back the Dirigent she had come to love.

This can't happen. I didn't tell him how I felt. I didn't get to say goodbye. My Gihon.

"Kimaris, you idiot!" An angry yowl echoed from ahead, drawing Edelein's attention.

Solomon was exchanging blows with his own creation, fuming as Kimaris used his lance to parry the attacks.

"You should be thanking me!" Kimaris countered with a laugh. "You couldn't do it, so I did it for you!"

"I told you to leave the Dirigent alone!" Solomon screeched, his swipes becoming more aggressive as rage filled his veins. "He wasn't supposed to die!"

Not supposed to die, Edelein thought, turning her attention downwards to Gihon's still body. *If he were still connected into Limbo, he would be alive. This is my fault. He lost his contract because he fell in love with me.*

A quick beat passed as realization hit Edelein.

Contracts. A force of nature and authority. Sounds like the perfect task for the Lion Queen of Zenluve.

"Luthro!" Edelein cried out, rising to her feet. "Send me to Limbo!"

"What?!" Luthro denied, appalled. "Now?!"

"Yes! I don't have much time. I need to speak with the Bookkeeper!"

"Y-you've never even met the Bookkeeper. It's dangerous!"

"Then I'll go too," countered a certain sphynx as he stood at the side of his Queen.

Luthro looked briefly at the pool of blood that drenched his master, before nodding solemnly and producing a small piece of chalk from his pocket. He crouched down and began to swiftly draw perfectly precise lines into an array.

"I don't know what you're planning, but if there's even the slightest chance that you can help, I am not one to pass up that opportunity. Limbo is not for the weak-willed, but I have come to know that facing adversity is your greatest strength, Your Majesty. As long as you know exactly what you want, you will not succumb."

Edelein turned, watching her allies defend their position against Solomon's forces on the front line. Behind Solomon's cultists, the man in red himself continued to spit insults at Kimaris while their weapons clashed.

Their infighting is an advantage to us. Aim and Allocer are dead already. I don't have much time, but I cannot waste this opportunity.

"Stand here, you two," Luthro instructed.

Zander took Edelein's arm and guided her with a firm grip onto the array. Luthro placed his hands onto the outer ring. As it began to glow bright green, an obnoxiously cocky voice let out a squeal of glee. Kimaris had pushed Solomon back, activating a dark violet array on his own body.

"Go find him, then!" Kimaris laughed giddily, Edelein straining to make out what he was saying over the cacophony of fighting throughout the plaza. "So I will be rid of both of you!"

Kimaris hit Solomon with a swift shoulder to the chest and the array flashed. Solomon flew backwards, skidding towards Edelein as the kinetic array transferred and amplified his momentum.

"No, no, no, no!" Luthro warned, a second too late.

The array reached completion, a bright light consuming the Queen before reducing to nothingness.

Opening her eyes, Edelein took in the unnerving sights of

a vast emptiness ahead of her. The world around was hues of black and violet, speckled with obsidian ruins. The sky was like a cloud of purplish darkness, while the atmosphere felt still and suffocating.

The Queen turned to look for Zander, instead meeting the unexpected gaze of a bipedal phantasm. The creature was a bit taller than Edelein, but much shorter than the other phantasms she had encountered. It held a much more humanoid form, with long pointed ears atop a hooded head.

Edelein let out a yelp of fear, stumbling backwards and scrambling to pull her bow from off her shoulder. The creature put out its hands reassuringly, seeming to be wary of her as well. As the lioness struggled to grab her bow, she looked down at her hands to discover illuminated violet claws.

"Edelein?" The phantasm spoke.

Edelein stopped moving, tilting her head as she recognized the voice.

"Zander?"

The phantasm nodded.

"Congratulations, you've discovered phantasmal forms," a third voice groaned from the ground below.

A third humanoid phantasm was laying flat, long flowing hair spilling out from around it. It seemed uninterested in getting up or speaking further.

Zander bristled. "Solomon!"

"Look, I'm not jazzed about it either, big guy. Stupid Kimaris betrayed me, and now I'm stranded in Limbo with no way back. He's going to open the Gates of Heaven without me and get a soul for himself while I'm stuck here for all eternity."

"What do you mean, no way back?" Edelein asked, extending a clawed hand to help Solomon up.

Solomon stared at her hand for a moment, before taking it and rising to his feet.

"Luthro is going to bring you two back. He has no reason to bring me with you. I'm more useful to your agenda if I am eternally imprisoned down here, as I'm barred from traveling to and from Limbo myself. Frankly, I'm not even sure how I was able to get in with you two. I've tried this before. It never worked."

From my understanding, Limbo is a space of in-between that feeds on uncertainty. Perhaps Solomon was able to pass through because for the first time in his life, he feels uneasy about his choices. The weight of his consequences, the death of his brother, is making him feel guilt, Edelein theorized.

"There are things you should know. First of all, time passes differently here. Luthro will bring you back after a few minutes on the material plane, though it may be hours here. Cozy up with each other until then," Solomon explained.

"No time to do such things," Edelein countered. "I need to speak with the Bookkeeper immediately."

"I just explained that you have plenty of time. Were you not listening?"

"You didn't want Gihon to die, either. I believe I can negotiate with the Bookkeeper to bring him back. I won't waste a second on that."

"Yeah, good luck with that," Solomon huffed, sitting back down.

"You're coming too."

"Like hell I am!" Solomon laughed.

Zander growled, grabbing the phantasm's flowing hair and yanking him to his feet. Solomon whined in pain and irritation, but remained standing once Zander let go.

"If the Queen says you come, you come," Zander stated.

Solomon paused for a moment, considering something silently. After a beat, he shrugged nonchalantly.

"Yeah, sure, I'll help," Solomon answered, suppressing a

coy smile from underneath the phantasmal shell.

"Excellent," Edelein nodded in satisfaction, turning around to face the vast expanse of nothingness. "Now, where is the Bookkeeper? Show me the way, Pishon Marleogne."

Rolling his eyes, Solomon crossed his arms.

"You think *I* know where the hell we're supposed to go? If you haven't forgotten, I'm public enemy number one of Limbo. They don't allow me to come here. I'm just as unfamiliar with this place as you are, which means we are totally and completely lost in Limbo. Was this part of your plan, O Great Lion Queen?"

Edelein let out a long groan of irritation. Whipping around to look in every direction, the Queen found nothing but open expanses of empty land stretching ahead.

These phantasmal forms dull my senses. Either that, or the stillness of Limbo makes it impossible to orient myself. Everything is the same, and yet everything is nothing.

"Are you sure you want me to stay with you?" Solomon asked. "As I mentioned, I am a huge target in a place like this. It's more than likely that keeping me around will get you both killed."

"You got us into this mess, so you're going to get us out of it," Edelein hissed. "All of this happened because *you* tried to steal my leyline crystals."

"I didn't try. I succeeded."

Through the masks of their phantasmal forms, Solomon could feel the burning gaze of Edelein's irate stare. He dipped his head in what seemed to be a rare moment of apology.

"Gihon was killed because of my own creation. I know. I'm upset about it too. It's just… I really think I'd be more useful to you both if I was far away. Before anyone else gets hurt, you know?"

Is Solomon finally softening up? Edelein wondered. *Or is this some sort of ulterior motive?*

"If you want to atone for getting Gihon killed, stay with us and help us find the Bookkeeper," Edelein answered.

The Solomon-shaped phantasm turned to Zander, pleading.

"Come on, kittycat, you don't want me near your Edelein! Right? What if I turn on you and kill her?" Solomon pressed.

Zander shook his head, brushing past Solomon as he and Edelein set off in an indeterminate direction. "Queen's orders. Come on."

The homunculus whinged under his breath, following after the two feline zoa.

"I really think that something is going to try to kill me," Solomon insisted.

"Then we shall fight back," Edelein stated simply. "You're one of us, for now."

"I never agreed to this."

"I never agreed to your pet homunculus killing Gihon."

"That's… fair. I never agreed to that either."

"Truce?"

Solomon hesitated.

"Yeah, truce."

A beat of silence fell over the group, before the signature Marleogne curiosity took over Solomon's thoughts. "How did you get him to break his contract?"

Edelein's pace faltered for a brief moment, her heart aching as she recalled her fond memories of the Dirigent.

"I don't suppose I really did anything. It just kind of… happened. I wasn't even present when he lost it. Your clay mimic saw him before I did. I only knew because his demeanor had changed. He was… warmer."

The Queen bit back tears as Zander placed a gentle hand on her upper back.

"We will get him back," Zander assured.

"Speaking of, what exactly is your plan?" Solomon

continued.

"I am going to renegotiate his contract for him," Edelein explained. "I deal with legislation and legal paperwork every day back in Zenluve. If I can just get my hands on Gihon's contract, I might be able to find some sort of way to bring him back. There must be a loophole or weak point that I can exploit."

Solomon considered Edelein's words carefully, thinking.

"I believe that could be possible. Limbo is the space where souls go to await judgement after their death, so Gihon himself could actually even be around here. The forces of Limbo have access to his soul, so there is a chance they could replace his soul into his body. As for exploiting his contract… as cute as it is to see you think you can outwit the Bookkeeper itself, that one's going to be tough. From what I know, the Bookkeeper is pretty strict on its contracts, so it's more than likely that all the phrasing is going to be watertight."

"The Bookkeeper will listen to me," Edelein insisted stubbornly. "It has no choice. I'm not leaving here until it agrees to give me my Gihon back."

"I don't think your dominion applies to Limbo, but I like your spirit, kitten."

"I see my dominion seems to not work on you either," Edelein spat. "I thought I made it clear to you that I do not wish to be patronized in such a way."

"Yeah, yeah. When you talk, the world listens."

Edelein paused, stopping in her tracks.

"You're right," Edelein realized. "The world listens when I speak. The Bookkeeper only shows itself to the worthy and the strong-hearted."

Planting her feet firmly into the ground, Edelein raised her voice to bellow into the empty air that pressed heavily against their phantasmal shells.

"Bookkeeper!" Edelein yelled with an authoritative tone. "I am Her Majesty Queen Edelein Alderhart von Luvemann, the noble and sovereign Lion Queen of the Kingdom of Zenluve. Show yourself to me at once!"

Solomon's face dropped in disbelief. In front of the group, air began to fizzle and melt as a large obsidian museum began to take form. The front doors, large and ornate with black trim, presented themselves in front of Edelein as they swung open to lead into the amaranthine halls within.

"See?" Edelein beamed, starting forward again. "Every world bows to me."

"Edelein," Solomon warned. "Stop."

The Queen's laughter echoed against the obsidian walls ahead of her. "What, are you intimidated now?"

"This is the Curator's Collection. This isn't where contracts are made and kept. This is where the Curator guards its lost treasures."

"How do you know?" Edelein asked.

Solomon gestured ahead. "Because the Curator is coming to greet us. By greet, I hope you understand I mean that it plans to kill us for trespassing."

Crawling out of the shadows of the open museum doors was an otherworldly beast of ruin. A draconic eight-eyed head protruded from a spider-like body with webbing between each of its eight legs, a large spindle on each of its two front limbs.

"If the Bookkeeper is the brain, this is the brawn," Solomon explained in a hurry. "The Curator protects the lost artifacts of Limbo, while the Bookkeeper negotiates the use of them. They work together, but this thing doesn't listen to reason."

"I thought you weren't ever allowed in here," Edelein retorted.

"I wasn't! Don't act like you don't know how much Gihon

loves to prattle on about these things. I lived with that man for long enough to get the gist," Solomon snapped. "I figured I would offer a bit of advice, since this guy is most definitely *not* going to 'listen when you speak,' as you so claim the world must do!"

The Curator shot a torrent of webbing out from its mouth. Zander barreled into Edelein, pulling her out of the way of the attack as Solomon leapt in the other direction. Solomon extended a hand, trying to ignite his alchemical array, and grunting in frustration as it fizzled into nothing.

"What the hell was that?" Edelein hissed.

"I can't use alchemy!" Solomon complained. "I can't pull any energy from Limbo, and my connection to Tevus is completely severed right now."

Drawing his dual swords, Zander muttered under his breath, "Typical whining alchemist. Fight like a warrior for once."

The swords, in the hands of Zander's phantasm, began to assimilate into the arms of his shell. Zander darted forward, blades protruding backwards from his forearms, and took a swipe at the Curator's neck.

Zander's attack grazed the arachnid monster briefly before the Curator smacked him away with a swift slap of its limb.

Edelein pressed a clawed thumb against the array etched into her bow, silently pleading for a reaction. Nothing happened, and in dismay, Edelein realized that she wouldn't be able to summon any arrows to help Zander fight.

In a final desperate attempt, Solomon held out his hand. This time, instead of his array, the Divine Sword Kether appeared into his palm.

"Yes!" Solomon triumphed, running forward to swing at the beast.

The Curator's scaly head turned to face Solomon. As its eyes locked onto Kether, the blade disappeared from Solomon's hand. The man in red pivoted from attack to defense as he rolled out of the way of the Curator's webs, now weaponless again.

"Give that back!" Solomon demanded. "That's not yours!"

"How did you do that?" Edelein ran over to aid Solomon, helping him up as Zander pulled the creature's attention. "Kether. How did you summon it?"

"I don't know. I needed a weapon, and it was the first one I thought of. The damn bastard stole it, though, so it's gone now. It'll be a part of his collection," Solomon admitted.

He willed for it to happen. Though uncertainty is the passageway to enter, the key to surviving in Limbo is a strong will, Edelein concluded.

"Got it," Edelein said, drawing her bow as a dark arrow formed in her hand. "Speak and the world will listen—"

Solomon tensed anxiously as Edelein vanished mid-sentence, her bow and arrow clattering to the ground.

"Shit!" Luthro screamed, pounding his fist into the ground. "I need to pull them back, I have to—"

"We have to trust them," Cari assured, though she was shaking as she helped him to his feet. "Solomon was furious when Gihon died. Maybe he'll help them. Right now, we have to try to stop Kimaris."

Kimaris pointed his lance upwards towards the gate, relishing in the feeling of victory as energy from the second leyline crystal that was hidden in his weapon hummed and flowed.

"Take cover, now!" Spira warned as a wave of energy cascaded out from the sky and slammed into the plaza.

Each student of alchemy activated an emergency rampart array to block the blast from hitting the Zengarde. The wave slammed into Kimaris, sending him careening into what remained of the plaza's central fountain. He groaned, flat on his back atop the stone rubble, as time suddenly began to slow to a stop.

Debris that had been kicked up from Kimaris' impact hung suspended in the air as an ominous chill fell across the arena. Cold settled into the bones of ally and enemy alike, freezing everyone in place, only able to watch helplessly as frost began to creep across the stones.

He's here, Luthro realized, his heart dropping to his stomach.

An otherworldly figure brushed past the alchemists, his footfall echoing like crunching snow on a silent winter day. He seemed to ignore them entirely as he approached Kimaris, greatsword in hand.

"The Pale King collects," spoke the icy cold voice of the winter archfae as he raised his sword. "Pay your dues."

Unable to turn away, the Zengarde and alchemists stared ahead in horror as Eochaid brought down his sword onto Kimaris' neck, lopping his head off with a wet thud as it hit the cold stone beneath his altar of sacrifice.

"Rise, my Dullahan," Eochaid commanded.

Kimaris' headless body trembled. It stood upright, Crescent Shadow in hand. The bleeding wound of his decapitated neck froze over as it followed the orders of the Erlking, leaving just the head itself to spill polluted blood onto the streets of Othalgar.

The Pale King turned to face Luthro with several slow steps. Luthro tried to move, but was frozen in place as he held his rampart array in front of his allies. Presenting a familiar pocket watch, Eochaid spoke again.

"Friend Luthro, the Pale King thanks you for the time

you have given. I have taken another one minute and twenty-three seconds, leaving exactly six minutes remaining. I look forward to collecting the rest of your time in the future."

A freezing wind picked up, an endless storm of snowflakes obscuring the Pale King from view. As the blizzard faded, time resumed, and another cascade of divine energy crashed down onto the plaza.

"Is everyone alright?" Luthro asked, turning around.

"What the hell *was* that?!" Thorne cried out with a shudder. "A fae?"

Luthro nodded solemnly. In a silent beat of understanding, the rest of the group realized that they had just witnessed the one who pursued Nephvir.

"Not important right now!" Mandus cried out as he felt the divine energy reverse, pulling everyone closer to the center.

"Oh, shit!" Spira exclaimed. "Luthro! Jana!"

The Gates of Heaven started rotating counter-clockwise as it pulled the energy back. The energy began to form a concentrated sphere of brilliant white light, a backlash only a mere second from detonating.

"Jana, bulwark!" Luthro commanded, sprinting to her side and grabbing her arm.

Pouring every ounce of his body's energy into his alchemy, Luthro activated a rampart array. He pulled the energy of Jana's bulwark, borrowing her strength to form a bastion array large enough to cover the group from the impending backlash.

The sphere imploded, pure and total brightness consuming the plaza and leaving a single entity standing atop the shattered fountain.

The entity was humanoid, clad in a white chitinous shell. Gold metal fragments floated behind its head like a crown of sunshine, framing the holy creature with light. Its face was vaguely human with an amorphous nature to it; the face contorting and shifting, almost like it yearned to display every human emotion all at once yet lacked the ability to do so.

Luthro dismissed the bastion array, feeling his body ache and scream from the divine energy as it burned through the shield. Everything in front of them had been wiped out, including the remnants of clay golems and the corpses of the fallen homunculi. The backlash seemed to remain contained within the free space of the plaza, unable to pass through the barrier of frozen energy that surrounded the area.

"What kind of phantasm is that?" Jana whispered. "I've never seen anything like it."

"Well, if that was truly a rift to Ethereus, it's likely that this is its guardian," Spira replied under her breath. "The Angel of Death."

"Its target is dead, so now it's going to turn to us," Luthro sighed. "Fan out and surround it. We need to engage safely and intentionally to gather information on what it does. Zengarde, allow us to run point first and follow our lead once it's safer."

Nora peeled off with Cari and Jinn to flank the phantasm, Mandus leading Thorne and Lylia to the left side. Alett followed Spira and Jana to the right, leaving Luthro alone to ready his attack.

The Angel of Death looked down at the fountain where Kimaris' head had been a moment before. The head of the guardian twisted to take on the homunculus' appearance, scanning the plaza with Kimaris' lifeless eyes. The face changed each time it made eye contact with the warriors surrounding it from past and present alike; grotesque and uncanny as it changed from Kimaris to Aim. It stared through the living warriors to the corpse of Gihon that was laying still and cold behind them, turning to his beloved student Mandus, and then looking out into the sea of shades as it morphed into what remained of Everett's frozen specter. Turning from Everett to the motionless warrior's best friend as it laid eyes on Thorne, Mandus crouched to strike.

"This thing is creepy," Mandus shuddered, picking up a rock.

The speedster zoa dashed forward. Slamming the stone into the phantasm's face and skidding to a stop on the other side, Mandus noticed a trail of shimmering golden afterimages that recreated his steps.

The guardian swung at one of the echoes with a sturdy gut punch. Mandus watched in horror as the following copies of himself changed one-by-one to keel over and spit blood until the action caught up to him. The punch hit impossibly hard even through Jana's bulwark, causing a pained cough as Mandus doubled over and grabbed his stomach, weakly spilling his blood onto the stones.

"Did you guys… see that?!" Mandus hacked. "You all see the afterimages, right?"

The images faded and the Angel of Death examined its fist curiously, seeming to only be interested in retaliating when provoked.

"This being exists in the fourth dimension, which is how it could see Aim and Kimaris even though their bodies were obliterated," Luthro realized. "How do we fight something like that?"

Ahead of the others, Alett tossed a few smoke bombs to provide cover as everyone regrouped to strategize.

"There's an ancient alchemist named Moebius who was known for studying higher dimensions," Luthro explained, "are any of you familiar with the Moebius strip?"

"Back up. What does it even mean to be fourth-dimensional?" Thorne asked, exhausted.

"The fourth dimension exists outside of our understanding of time," Alett explained. "This thing, the Angel of Death as Spira called it, can appear at any point in time and affect us."

"Time travel?"

"Not entirely. Think of a drawing on paper. If the drawing were alive, it would only be able to perceive us if we are touching the paper, but we can simply remove our hand at any moment and disappear from its reality."

"So we're the paper-man?"

Alett smiled warmly and replied, "Now you've got it!"

"When it's on the material plane, it seems locked into our third-dimensional space," Luthro added.

"Jana, bulwark me," Jinn commanded as he drew his sword.

"What the hell do you think you're doing?" Luthro snapped.

"You need information, don't you?" Jinn retorted. "The alchemists should stand back and evaluate while a Zengarde strikes. I have the fewest injuries, fastest speed, and the strongest Seventh Sense of anyone here. I'm your best bet."

"That's the most I've ever heard Jinn talk," Thorne whispered.

Luthro was silent for a moment, before nodding in agreement. "I know to trust your senses. We'll see if we can figure anything out. Stay safe, and fall back if you're injured."

Without waiting another second, Jinn took off towards the phantasm at an impressive speed. Afterimages of each step began to fizzle into existence as he approached.

"The temporal echoes start fifteen feet out from the Angel's body," Luthro noted aloud.

The Angel of Death raised its hands to counter a slash from Jinn's sword. The white wolf backstepped, creating an afterimage in front of himself, and darting forward again to block the anticipated strike. The phantasm took the bait, swinging at Jinn, but being intercepted by his sword instead.

The phantasm backed up and lunged at one of Jinn's echoes behind him, attacking it with an overhead chop on the shoulder. Jinn took the hit and rushed up against the phantasm again, ignoring the remnants of pain that stung through Jana's bulwark. The Angel, being next to more of Jinn's afterimages, started to attack all of them with several quick swipes.

Jinn gritted his teeth as he got close enough to land a slash on the phantasm. The Angel of Death swung at the afterimage right next to Jinn, swatting the echo of his sword strike away. In dismay, Jinn watched the bleeding wound fade as it was wiped from their reality, having never existed at all.

"Blitz it!" Alett commanded with the authority of the highest-ranked Zengarde present. "Anyone who is able-bodied, go!"

Jana unloaded bullets at the phantasm as Spira, Alett, Cari and Luthro rushed in. The fellborn extended her bulwark to the others, weakening Jinn's, but providing wider protection. Mandus tried to slowly rise to his feet, still weakened from the earlier punch, before stumbling down again in defeat.

"Lylia, do you… do you have anything left?" Mandus pleaded.

The elf shook her head weakly, her eyes apologetic and exhausted.

"Mandus, can you buff my bulwark array?" Jana requested, noticing Mandus' disdain at being unable to fight.

The fox zoa grunted. Sitting by Jana's feet and grabbing onto her leg, Mandus channeled his energy into Jana's bulwark array, amplifying its strength to empower the remaining fighters.

The battle ahead raged on, Alett taking point as he tossed out two more bombs. As they detonated, copies of himself emerged from the smoke, darting left and right to create a net of false afterimages to cover Alett's true movement.

The Angel of Death turned to face Jinn again. It let out a blast of energy from its mouth, aimed at one of Jinn's echoes. Spira intercepted the beam with a large shield of light, deflecting the attack with a groan of exertion. The phantasm darted in to punch Spira, but stopped as Cari's whip wrapped around its arm and pulled it off track. A giant hammer blocked its second hand from swinging forward, resulting from Nora's quick thinking.

Spira converted the shield into a spear and rammed it into the creature's side. The Angel let out a squeal, trying to navigate around the oversized hammer to strike at Spira's afterimage and remove the spear. Taking advantage of the distraction, Luthro slammed its back with a banishment array.

"Don't tell me a two-dimensional banishment array doesn't work!" Luthro exclaimed, leaping backwards. "Two-dimensional arrays work on three-dimensional phantasms. Do I need a third-dimensional array? I don't think that's even possible!"

"Her Majesty Queen Edelein Alderhart von Luvemann, the noble and sovereign Lion Queen of the Kingdom of Zenluve," spoke a new voice as Edelein suddenly found herself alone in an unfamiliar room.

A man was sitting across from her behind a large desk, hands clasped. At first glance, he seemed to be a sharply-dressed gentleman in a three-piece suit and top hat. Dread settled in the pit of Edelein's stomach as she took in his uncanny appearance: the hat was fused onto his head, and the suit appeared to be made of an organic tissue-like material.

Gesturing towards the seat across from his desk, he spoke.

"Sit, please."

"You're the Bookkeeper?" Edelein asked, sitting down.

The man nodded.

"You're the one who brought the bane of alchemy into my realm," replied the Bookkeeper.

"And you're the one trying to kill my friends," Edelein countered boldly.

The man chuckled.

"The Curator will not take their lives."

Edelein remained silent, waiting for the Bookkeeper to explain further. Seeming content with his response, he spoke not another word as silence hung heavy between them.

"I'm here representing Gihon Marleogne. Allow me to read his contract."

The Bookkeeper nodded in understanding, producing a scroll from thin air and handing it to the Queen.

That was easy. He's just going to hand over private documents?

"I am neither a force of good nor of evil, and thus are my contracts a representation of true neutrality," he explained, as if he could read Edelein's thoughts. "If you believe there to be an error, it is in my best interest to correct it. I understand that Gihon Marleogne was killed by a homunculus after forfeiting his contract. While I do send my condolences to you and your allies, nothing is amiss about his death in regards to his contract. If I am wrong, I encourage you to challenge me to restore the balance of Limbo."

The Bookkeeper's words were void of any emotion, truly neutral. Edelein listened intently to him as she scanned through the small text scrawled onto the scroll. A pang echoed in her heart as she saw the name *Arvien Marleogne* elegantly signed on the bottom, remembering that Gihon was never even given the chance to consent to his contract to begin with.

Maybe he doesn't want his contract. He deserves freedom. Maybe everything that happened was for the best. And yet... I find myself unable to let go. Maybe it's selfish of me, but I want him back.

Looking up from the contract, Edelein addressed the Bookkeeper.

"Why was the contract not voided after Arvien's death? She was the one who signed."

"Section 2A: Death of Signee," he answered without missing a beat. "In the event of an untimely death before the Signee can void her contract on her own, the contract will be inherited fully by the Recipient. The Recipient is Gihon Marleogne, as he received the contract's benefits that his master signed on his behalf."

"Why was Arvien allowed to sign for Gihon? At the time of signing, he would have been a legal adult and able to bear full responsibilities."

"Section 4B: Definition of Humanity. All creatures and species created through artificial feats of alchemy, including but not limited to homunculi and zoa, will be considered as subhumans and must be spoken for by their master. Natural-born zoa who have no master are to be excluded. Gihon Marleogne is a transmuted zoa, student and heir to Arvien Marleogne."

Edelein tensed unhappily at his words, scouring the text further.

"The contract can only be voided with the consent from its holder, yes?" Edelein queried. "Are there any other instances in which the contract can be terminated, without consent from the recipient?"

"You are correct. The contract can only be removed when Gihon Marleogne falls in love, and accepts this desire over his possession of Fortress Black. At that time, he will lose both the Fortress and his invulnerability, but will regain his heart."

"What do you consider to be falling in love? Is this not subjective?"

The Bookkeeper's stone-faced demeanor seemed to falter for a split second, his answer unprepared for the first time.

"Love is what he feels when he sees you, Edelein von Luvemann."

"Where is your evidence?" Edelein grilled. "Has he ever said that? Has Gihon admitted that he loves me? He's certainly never told me such a thing."

"I urge you to leave personal feelings out of this."

"I do not inquire about this due to personal feelings, Bookkeeper. A verbal contract is legally binding and can be upheld. Dirigent Gihon has not verbally spoken to admit his love for me. He did not choose his love, yet, and did not agree to sacrificing his power. You took it from him without his consent."

The Bookkeeper nodded, still emotionless. "Admittedly, Gihon Marleogne did exude conflicting signs upon the removal of his contract."

Tears welled up in Edelein's eyes as the Bookkeeper opened his mouth again, this time the voice of the man she loved meeting her ears.

"Giving her my heart is what it means to be free. Even if we die, we die together. That's... love, isn't it?"

Voice returning to normal, the Bookkeeper continued.

"These were Gihon Marleogne's final words under contract, which were interpreted to imply his consent in the nullification. He gave you his heart. However, upon the contract's removal, he began to beg for it to be reinstated. Ultimately, I decided that he would not be able to balance both his power and his feelings for you. It would have destroyed him."

"Because you voided his contract prior to his expectations, Gihon was made vulnerable and ultimately killed in battle because of it. You did not adhere to the contract in an attempt to save him, as you say, but that is how he…" Edelein's voice trailed off as her throat closed in anguish.

The Bookkeeper remained silent.

"His death was due to negligence on your part. I demand that you restore his soul into his body and let him remain free of your contract."

"I cannot just reanimate someone for free. Everything has a price, Edelein von Luvemann. Are you prepared to pay?"

Edelein nodded, setting Gihon's contract down on the desk.

"If you seek to grant him a new life without the involvement of his limbus contract, that means that the contract will fall on you instead. Edelein von Luvemann, I will restore him if you offer me the thing you value most."

"What do you want, then?" Edelein asked. "My crown?"

"Your freedom."

CHAPTER 17

GIHON

"They need you, Mandus."

Mandus looked up at Jana, noticing the glimmering red potion in her hands as she extended it to him.

"It's my last one," Jana admitted, "so make it count."

Mandus took the health potion with a grateful smile, realizing the situation at hand.

If the phantasm is using ranged attacks and can target those afterimages, Spira can't be fast enough to deflect its attacks and dodging is completely useless. I need to borrow her shield and play on the defensive to keep everyone safe.

"Nora, swap with me!" Mandus called, programming his path forward. "Help Jana with the bulwark. Spira, give me a shield!"

"On it!" the girls replied.

Mandus sparked his array, feeling his body carry him forward. He grabbed a hardlight shield from Spira's extended arm, his route landing him in front of the Angel of Death to intercept a blow towards Jinn's afterimage.

Jinn grunted in acknowledgement, the wolf's way of thanking his ally for the assist. His eyes were trained on the monster's movements, studying each step carefully. Feeling the familiar jolt of Seventh Sense in his veins directing him, Jinn readied his stance.

Alett watched curiously as echoes of Jinn began to move forward in time, showing all the possible attack angles he could choose. The Angel of Death struck at one of the future echoes, only for Jinn to slash its back from another direction. The phantasm whipped around and attacked the afterimage that cut him, nullifying the attack and sending Jinn flying backwards.

This creature has a limit to fourth-dimensional access while on the material plane, Alett noticed. *It can affect our pasts, but not our futures. With a strong enough Seventh Sense to direct us, we might be able to land a hit. Jinn could be onto something.*

"Cari!" Alett called. "Focus on your Seventh Sense to lead you! Alchemists, cover our afterimages so it can't retaliate against us!"

Alett ran in alongside Cari, the zoa letting their honed instincts take control of their bodies to mimic Jinn's strategy. Echoes of their potential futures fanned out and converged onto the Angel from different points, overwhelming and confusing the phantasm.

The phantasm's face twisted and turned as its movement seemed to stutter, confused by all the different possibilities it was seeing.

They're doing it, somehow, Luthro thought. *Now to figure out how the hell to make a three-dimensional banishment array.*

The Angel of Death's face stopped transforming as it settled onto Alett. Another version of the phantasm donning Cari's delicate face split off from the first, and the two began to attack the future echoes that Alett and Cari sent out. A third version of the phantasm with Jinn's face appeared, blocking Jinn's sword thrust to its face. All three versions of the phantasm seemed to occupy the same space, translucently layered on one another.

It's adapting to their strategy. Is it evolving? Luthro wondered as he backpedaled for a moment to distance himself and think. *We need more help. We need Zander and Edelein back.*

Luthro gritted his teeth, torn up by the decision of sacrificing their only shot at saving Gihon for the sake of more firepower. Bring them back now and his master remains gone forever, but wait longer and risk letting everyone die at the hands of Ethereus' guardian in a battle that they shouldn't even be fighting in the first place.

If we die here, Edelein and Zander stay stuck in Limbo, as well. I can't let more people die, Luthro realized to himself with a glance over his shoulder to the deceased body of his master. *I'm so sorry, Master Marleogne, but I know you would have chosen the same thing. Her life, our lives, over yours. The many over the few.*

Luthro returned to the planeshifting array he had drawn earlier. Placing his hands down onto the cold stone, he could feel the despair well up in his chest as the array began to illuminate. Air converged right above the array and expelled upwards, creating a thin line overhead.

"C'mon, you two. Find it. Find it…" muttered Luthro, searching for the connection of his lost allies. "Are they… not together right now?"

And you bet your ass I'm leaving Solomon down there. He can't travel between the realms, so he'll be stuck there for eternity. I should be hailed as a hero, Luthro added silently.

The rift opened up with a loud crack. Darkness spilled out, Zander leaping through with Edelein's bow in hand. Edelein followed a moment after, taking her bow from Zander.

"Where the hell have you been?!" Zander yelled as he grabbed Edelein's shoulders. "I've been–"

Zander's nagging was cut off as he ducked, pulling Edelein down with him. A blast from the phantasm cut through the air where they had been standing as one of the Angel's bodies attacked the new targets.

"What was that? What is going on?!" Zander spat. "What did you do while we were gone?!"

"Summoned an ancient fourth-dimensional guardian of Ethereus," Mandus panted, "no big deal, right?"

Sensing the new threats, the three overlayed phantasms simultaneously sprinted closer to put Zander and Edelein within its fifteen-foot radius. All three of them fired an energy blast towards Edelein, Zander and Luthro, each with its own target.

"Shit!" Mandus cursed as he and Spira ran desperately towards their allies to block the attacks, knowing they'd still be one shield short.

A large teal array formed in between the blasts and the newcomers. From behind, a chilling voice bellowed out his command.

"Bastion," said the Dirigent of Ravencroft as he stood bloodied, but alive.

The bastion array faded as the Dirigent stepped forward, taking in the scene in front of him. The three simultaneous phantasms had slowed down, seeming to curiously eye the new opponent.

"I apologize for the delay," Gihon stated. "What are we working with?"

I do not know what happened, but now is clearly not the time for that, Gihon thought.

"Spira called it the Angel of Death," Alett began.

"The guardian of Ethereus?" Gihon realized.

So he did it, then. Solomon opened the Gates of Heaven while I was out cold. As expected, a divine backlash has now unleashed horrors never before seen. Once again, I am left to pick up after him.

Looking around, Gihon realized that the only figures around were of his allies. Solomon and the other homunculi were nowhere to be found.

"It can attack us in the past by targeting the golden afterimages we leave within fifteen feet of it," Alett continued before Gihon could pry about his missing brother. "The banishment array didn't work, which we think is related to the array being two-dimensional."

"Master Marleogne, how do we make an array three-dimensional?" Luthro asked.

A third-dimension array? Gihon contemplated for a moment. "I do not believe that is possible."

The drop in everyone's morale was palpable as the reality of his words set in. Gihon ran forward to engage the monster, trying to study it as he attacked.

Edelein backed out of the Angel's radius, drawing her bow to let several hardlight arrows pelt the creature. One of the three versions of the phantasm blocked the volley of arrows while the second one punched Gihon, only to be met by the ultimate resistance as its fist stopped dead in its tracks.

The Angel of Death attacked Gihon with the other two versions of itself. Gihon grabbed the arms of one as it sent another echo out, which was met by a stone pillar to the face.

"He's not leaving any echoes," Nora realized aloud.

"Master Marleogne was entirely dead until about a minute ago. There's about a thousand possibilities that all result in Gihon's body being an undetermined entity of Limbo, meaning he exists neither in the past, nor future, making him impervious to the Angel's attacks. Either way, it's an advantage that we must not waste," Luthro commented.

The outer rims of the Gates of Heaven began to spin again, starting slow but picking up speed incrementally. Spira looked up at what her lightbound eyes could make out, before scowling and calling out to the others.

"We need to hurry! We're having a hard enough time with one of these things. If they send a second one down, we don't stand a chance!" Spira yelled.

Edelein dropped her bow, darting low to sweep up Kimaris' lance from the ground.

"This was the key, wasn't it?" Edelein asked. "If it opened the Gates, can it close them?"

As Gihon kept the angel pinned, the Zengarde launched themselves at it simultaneously. Even with the angel's three echoes, the barrage of strikes outpaced its ability to nullify the attacks.

Edelein looked at the phantasm, then up at the Gates of Heaven. Turning to Luthro, the Queen called out her commands.

"Luthro, make the phantasm as light as you can. If a banishment array doesn't work, let's just send the bastard home the way he came!"

That would be easier than trying to invent a three-dimensional banishment array on the spot, Gihon thought to himself. *A rare moment where brute force actually may be the most efficient answer.*

"Do it!" Gihon agreed, lifting the phantasm up the moment Luthro's hand touched it.

Jinn planted his knee into the Angel's face, sending it into the air. Thorne sent out a galeforce wind to boost Zander's jump, the sphynx planting both feet firmly into the creature's torso and drop kicking it upwards.

As Thorne's wind padded Zander's landing, the fighters watched as the Angel's momentum began to slow at the edge of the gate.

"It isn't enough!" Luthro exclaimed.

"Nora, boost me!" Edelein demanded, dropping the lance and grabbing her bow. Nora grabbed onto the gilded handle of her regal weapon. A pink array sparked, the warbow tripling in size.

Edelein eyed her target carefully, tracking its momentum.

"Take the shot, Edelein!" Gihon called out, recalling the previous times she had let her fear consume her. "You can do it!"

The Lion Queen of Zenluve placed one boot on the bow, feeling the familiar jolt of static pass through her body as the hardlight array ignited. Pulling backwards and twisting her body, Edelein used her perfectly-balanced body weight to nock the arrow and draw the enlarged bow fully.

As the arrow soared through the forgotten skies of Othalgar, everyone watched as it pierced the chest of the Angel of Death with a great momentum that sent it careening up through the Gates.

Gihon rushed over to the lance, drawing an initiation array to send the energy of the leyline crystal up into the gate. A bright blue light burned through the air, enveloping the gates with the power and authority of the leyline's converged planes. He drew another outer circle connecting to an intricate diamond array, activating it as the outer rims of the Gates of Heaven began to rotate counter-clockwise.

With a surge of divine energy, the Gates of Heaven closed and vanished, leaving nothing but a heavy silence hanging over the ruined plaza.

"Did we do it? Are we done?" Mandus asked, hands on his knees as he took a few deep breaths.

"Gihon," Edelein mumbled to herself, voice hoarse.

"I am here," Gihon assured as he approached.

The Dirigent of Ravencroft was hardly recognizable through the deep red stains that covered his body. The wound through his heart had closed and left his pale chest exposed, but blood still soaked what remained of his vest and shirt.

Tears welled in Edelein's eyes as she faced him, as if she were afraid to believe in his presence. Gihon clasped her shoulders, pulling the Queen into an overdue embrace as he gently kissed the top of her head.

"I thought I lost you. No… I did lose you," Edelein whimpered. "You were dead. I…"

Dead? Gihon realized.

As Edelein's weak voice trailed off, Gihon let go of her and addressed the rest of the group.

"Now that the presence of Limbo is fading from this plaza, we need to leave quickly. I don't want to risk any harm from overstaying our welcome in Othalgar–" Gihon's thought was interrupted as a warm body slammed into him. "Mandus!"

Mandus wrapped lanky arms around his master, the other students following suit. They clamored in relief, relishing their victory and the return of their teacher.

"R-really, I am fine," Gihon insisted, though he made no effort to pull away.

"How did you pull it off, Your Majesty?" Spira asked from beside Gihon. "I've got to admit, your plan was bold. I wasn't sure we'd be able to bring him back."

"You did this?" Gihon asked, turning to Edelein only to realize she had left his side.

Edelein was standing at the edge of the plaza, looking mournfully at Everett, the ox zoa doomed to an eternity of holding a monster's mouth closed. Agares was still alive, though it seemed he had given up the fight and was now laying pathetically on the ground, jaws stuck permanently between Everett's unmoving arms. Thorne was standing beside her, leaning on her shoulder as they grieved together.

"If we undid the curse, Everett would come back to life, right?" Thorne asked softly.

Edelein extended her hand outwards, touching the edge where freedom met eternity. Gihon grabbed her hand as her fingertips brushed against Limbo, the Dirigent offering a sympathetic look as he drew her hand back away from the curse.

"What Thorne says is hypothetically true," Gihon offered gently. "We have never been able to fix this place. But if we can find a way, we can bring Everett back. I swear to do everything in my power."

"Zenluve will sponsor Othalgarian research. We do not leave our men behind," Edelein stated. "Bring him back at any cost, Dirigent."

If it were that easy, I would have rescued Ruther from here long ago, Gihon thought. *I cannot find the courage to tell her that it is impossible.*

"Your Majesty, how am I alive right now?" Gihon asked, eager to change the subject.

"Luthro sent me into Limbo so I could negotiate with the Bookkeeper, and–"

"Luthro did what?" Gihon exclaimed, turning harshly towards Luthro. "Mr. Apocathra, you know how incredibly irresponsible and dangerous something like that can be. You should–"

"It was my idea, Gihon," Edelein continued. "Luthro was hesitant, but it was the only shot we had at getting you back. If I've learned anything from you, Dirigent, it's that I should always take the shot."

Silence passed between the group as a collective memory

formed of the mirror phantasm that threatened Mandus' life not long ago.

"Come, now," Gihon turned away to hide his fluster, starting towards the outskirts of the city. "I need to get you all out of here before anything else goes wrong. I will deal with you later, Luthro. But… thank you, for risking it."

They should not be messing with fate like that. Though... by doing so, they've allowed me a chance at a lifetime with her, Gihon thought, sparing a quick glance at the leonine woman by his side. *A second opportunity to find her cure, so we both may live for each other.*

"I think it's got something to do with leylines," Alett said suddenly, appearing at Gihon's other side as the group continued onwards. "The cure, I mean."

I don't know what I find more jarring, the sudden appearances or the fact that he seems to read my mind.

"When Edelein consumed the vial Solomon gave to us, she commented on its resemblance to leyline tea. The potion seemed to have some sort of leyline energy condensed into it," Gihon added.

Alett nodded in agreement. "Eddie only got sick after we lost her tea block on the ship. Whether it could be a cure, I'm not sure of, but leyline energy seems to dampen the symptoms of blight."

I can use Ravencroft's leyline to study the theory. It truly is a shame that Edelein cannot stay with me, though. For a few reasons.

A gentle, yet firm hand pulled Edelein away from Gihon and Alett's conversation, the Ehret of the Zengarde looking down at his Queen with a scowl.

"Your plan worked, cub, but what was the cost?" Zander muttered under his breath, barely loud enough for Edelein to hear.

"I don't know what you mean," Edelein lied.

"That Bookkeeper, he doesn't just give things away. Especially not lives. You traded something, didn't you? What did you give him?"

"Nothing," Edelein lied again.

Zander's frown deepened. "Are you safe?"

"Yes, Zander. I didn't do anything rash, I promise. No harm will come to me from it."

Narrowing his eyes, Zander sensed the lies written all over Edelein's body language.

Edelein means that literally. She didn't offer anything that would risk her own life. Whatever she bartered with that thing was an internal part of her essence, not her safety.

"Fine," Zander relinquished. "Tell me if you are in danger, though, cub."

"I will."

The party fell into silence, broken only by quiet chatter between friends. Most were continuing to avoid looking at the scene around them as they passed by more specters of lost citizens, uncomfortable as they walked through the throngs of those neither dead nor alive.

At the front of the group, Thorne turned around with a grimace.

"Gihon, you said this place is off-limits, right?"

"That is correct."

"There's a ton of people up ahead. By the city gate. Is that normal?"

"The Church of Prima Luma often has guards posted to ensure no one enters Othalgar," Gihon explained, "though we will certainly have some explaining to do on our way out. I would rather them not know what happened, frankly."

Up ahead, the Zengarde could sense a dozen warm bodies just beyond the gates. The still air of Othalgar began to fade as they neared the exit, bringing fresh breaths into everyone's lungs for the first time since their arrival.

A guard donning black armor and a large pike made eye contact with Gihon through the iron gates, his face dropping in shock.

"Survivors!" The man called out, alerting his allies as they hurried to open the gates. "A lot of them, too!"

"What the hell?!" A broad-shouldered half-elf exclaimed. "You lot. How are you alive? You aren't related to the Othalgar Incident from ten years ago, are you?"

"They're alive inside of the city walls. They must be," a tall human woman replied, lowering her pike warily. "What were you doing in there? Speak."

"Sorry, but I think the big guy there is the one in charge–" Thorne's retort was cut off as the woman planted a swift strike to the back of his knees, bringing him down and wringing his arms behind his back.

"I am in charge, actually. It would do you good to remember that," the woman spat.

The half-elf sighed, grabbing Edelein and pinning her arms back. The lioness let out a low growl, but did not retaliate in fear of worsening the situation. Alett grabbed Zander's arm tightly, shooting a warning glance upwards at his ally.

I know, Zander, but we don't want to be on these guys' bad side. He isn't hurting her. Let's play nice before we become fugitives, Alett's large eyes begged silently.

"Who are you?" the woman pressed.

"Release her and we'll tell you. Maybe," Zander hissed.

"You're not the one who gets to negotiate right now," the half-elf man warned. "We've been looking for leads on the Othalgar Incident for ten years, and you're our best bet. How the hell are you lot alive, if you're not related to the event?"

Gihon raised his hands in a peaceful manner, attempting to dispel the bubbling tensions. "My associates and I were here on official Society business involving the wanted homunculus Solomon, who has been eliminated. I am Dirigent Gihon Marleogne of Ravencroft. I kindly ask that you let my allies go. We can talk this out. Please."

"Dirigent Marleogne! There you are," a new voice called from behind the crowd of uneasy guards. "Move aside, everyone, please."

The black-clad guards parted as a lean, dark-skinned woman wove through them. She wore a familiar black-and-white uniform boasting a dazzling golden crest.

"Inquisitor Vensworth!" Gihon sighed in relief.

"Justice!" Spira beamed.

"'*Justice*?' Who are these people to you, Inquisitor?" The half-elf asked, letting go of Edelein.

"My younger sister, her classmates, and her teacher. Behold, the keepers of the Corvid Athenaeum."

Justice's tone seemed formal, yet affectionate, reflective of a fond older sister caught in the middle of her diligent work. The Inquisitor shook Gihon's hand firmly, smiling.

"The Society had sent Dirigent Marleogne and his link to Othalgar on a classified assignment far beyond your paygrade, supervisor Maliya. I have been working alongside them to oversee their tasks and to escort them safely out."

The woman, Maliya, dipped her head apologetically as she let go of Thorne. The Fuuntet cast a glance to take in Justice's composed demeanor, and Lylia quickly jabbed an elbow into his side.

Don't even think about it, Thorne, Lylia's cold eyes warned. *If you flirt with her right now, we might end up in jail. Don't say a word to anyone. This is serious.*

"Dirigent Marleogne, allow me to accompany you back to Velkhamore," Justice continued. "You can brief me on your experience along the way. I am very relieved to see you all made it out safely."

Gihon nodded, gently leading Edelein away from the half-elf guard and the woman named Maliya. Taking point with Gihon, Justice lowered her voice.

"My plan worked, Dirigent. The Society has rescinded your removal movement, thanks to what you provided. You've made the Society proud."

Gihon scowled. "At the cost of my own values."

"It's your values or your job. We've all seen what happens when you pick the former. You should be thanking me."

"Now isn't the time for this. I don't want anyone catching wind of what you made me do."

What's he talking about? Edelein wondered, feline ears drinking in every word of their private conversation.

"I put my own neck on the line to help you twice now. You and I both know full well that the Society didn't send me here to escort you. You were about to get yourselves arrested, you obtuse raven. I know you want to protect her identity, but being anonymous is only going to get you in jail if you're trying to break into Othalgar."

"Solomon has been subdued. That's what matters."

"You killed him?"

Gihon paused, shaking his head. "He is gone. I am a bit fuzzy on the details, admittedly. I was dead for a lot of it, but I know for certain that he is not on Tevus anymore. Most likely lost in the Sea of Miracles, or his own plan blighted him out of existence. Either way, we will never see him again. I have done Caandemium a service."

"You said you were dead."

"Alright. The Zenluvians did Caandemium a service by erasing him. Is that better? So please, for my sake and for theirs, do not let the Society abuse the information I provided. I desperately do not want any harm to befall her."

"I've heard they plan to use the intel to pursue trade, to get ahead of Shuxing."

"I must insist once more that they do not use the intel for anything other than learning."

"When has that ever been the case with you damn alchemists?"

"Fair."

Gihon let out a tense sigh, feeling the weight of the world fall onto his broad shoulders once more for the first time since his life was restored.

"Just… allow me the chance to share one more cup of tea with her before everything falls apart."

Nature greeted the senses of the Zenluvians as they approached Velkhamore Port. Salty air in the nose, crashing waves in the ear, and the sight of endlessly stretching ocean lay ahead of six homesick warriors and their fierce Lion Queen.

Edelein's steps faltered as her entourage escorted her closer to a large passenger ship, crowds bustling around as they hauled luggage towards their new beginnings. Slowing down, the lioness turned lonesome eyes upwards towards the Dirigent of Ravencroft as he walked beside her.

"Is something the matter, Edelein?" Gihon asked, his voice warm, though tinged with his own masked sadness as he tried to maintain a brave front to his students that watched from behind.

Edelein shook her head after a moment. “No. I wanted to tell you that I enjoyed my stay in Canademium, even though we ended up whisked off on some sort of heroic adventure to save your people. You’re welcome, by the way.”

A gentle laugh like wind chimes brought a smile to Gihon’s face, reveling in the sound of Edelein’s joy for the final time.

“Thank you for helping me put an end to Solomon’s rampage. And for saving my life,” Gihon replied with a slight blush. “And… all the other things.”

“You have the crystals back at the Athenaeum, yes?” Edelein queried.

Gihon nodded. “They have been slightly abused by Solomon, but it should be more than enough to fuel my research. In return, of course, I have imbued your weapons with banishment arrays. Should a phantasm show itself in Zenluve, you should have no issue dispersing it.”

Zander drew his dual blades at Gihon’s word, pressing his thumb against the hilt as each sword began to shimmer slightly. A ripple of uncertainty passed through nearby civilians at the sudden gleam of his weaponry. Noticing the change, Alett extended his hands assuringly and offered a bright smile to dispel the tension, waving and laughing.

“Don’t worry! We’re trained guards! Just doing an inspection, is all. Zander, can you please put your swords away when we’re in the middle of a crowd?”

“I extend gratitude towards you this one time, corvid,” Zander stated, sheathing his blades. “Your duties were satisfactory. Though I look forward to our paths never crossing again.”

“Actually, I was thinking that Gihon should visit Zenluve some time,” Edelein countered. “If the crystals prove insufficient in providing a cure, we have endless amounts of them back home.

You'd be welcome. Mandus and his family, too."

Mandus beamed, hugging Edelein tight.

"I'm going to talk to my mom and have them all on the next boat over," Mandus said excitedly. "I mean, if you're really okay with it."

"Of course. I will personally oversee their immigration process, as I mentioned. I will make sure the Tigalo family is well cared for. Jinn will get them residency in the Canis clan, and they will live as nobles. You have to promise me you'll come visit them, though." Edelein chuckled, peeling Mandus off of her.

"Gihon, can we?" Mandus begged.

"I will discuss it with the Society of Alchemists. Hopefully we can arrange an exchange program of some sort to allow zoa alchemists entry into Zenluve," Gihon replied. "I will be in touch, Queen Edelein."

"What do you have in store for the future of Zenluve, Your Majesty?" Luthro asked.

"Alett and Gihon exchanged notes on blight illness. He will continue to see what he can discover on his own. Aside from that, we have the Zengarde Tournament coming up next year. It is a several-day-long festival of fighting where the fae's Summer Court will determine who our new Zengarde will be. Now that there's four open spots, it will be… a memorable one," Edelein explained, looking down at the mention of her fallen allies. "It would be a great time to visit."

"Do you think you're going to open up Zenluve's walls to Caandemite communications and trade?" Luthro pressed not with malice, but curiosity.

Edelein paused, thinking, before shaking her head. "With Ravencroft, I am warm. However, Caandemium has shown me both the good and bad sides of technology and alchemy, which I am unsure if I would be comfortable hosting within my own kingdom just yet. I don't think Zenluve is ready for the industrialization of Velkhamore, or the Society. I'm sorry, Gihon."

"I understand your apprehension," Gihon assured. "Just be careful. The Society of Alchemists plans to deepen their trade routes throughout Avalstice, with your neighboring kingdoms. I fear it could bring harm to Zenluve if not handled well."

A loud call from a nearby crew member drew the attention of the entourage as the ship's large sails began to unfurl.

"Edelein, it is time," Zander warned. "Bid your farewells."

"Bring my belongings up to my suite, please," Edelein requested, turning to her soldiers.

"I'm not letting you out of my sight," Zander retorted. "The rest of you may go."

Beside him, Cari flicked a delicate finger across Luthro's chin, offering a quick wink as she brushed past. Luthro's face turned red as blush burned at his ears. Stumbling over himself for words, Cari spoke first.

"Talk less and smile more, Luthro," Cari laughed, heading towards the ramp without another word.

Lylia bowed politely towards Gihon, Jinn offering a small nod.

"You've helped our people tremendously, and we will remember such kindness," Lylia stated.

Thorne snickered and waved at the students as he followed Lylia and Cari up. "Bye, ladies. Dream of me. Stay cool, Mandus and nerd boy."

Jinn bumped the hilt of his sword to push the blade ever so slightly out from its sheath. Pressing his thumb down, the sliver of visible metal began to glimmer as Zander's did a moment before. "Thank you."

"Recreate the array on anything you need to. You know what it looks like. Though, make sure whoever draws it has an incredibly steady hand, or you'll end up with more phantasms," Gihon added.

As the Zengarde disappeared into the depths of the passenger ship, another call from the crewmate indicated that their time together had come to an end.

"This is where you kiss her, Master Gihon," Mandus whispered.

The crowds thinned, leaving just Edelein, Zander, and Alett in front of Gihon and his students.

Gihon placed a hand on Edelein's waist, his heart feeling almost fully unburdened for the first time in his life as it pounded freely in his chest. Ignoring the scowl from Zander, the Dirigent swept Edelein into a gentle kiss. His lips found hers even more naturally than they had the first time, reveling in the soft touch and warm breath on each others' lips.

A hitch in Gihon's throat caused him to release Edelein, turning his head and stifling a sudden cough. Edelein pulled back, tears in her eyes. Gihon wiped a tear with his thumb and furrowed his eyebrows as he tried to read her.

"I apologize. I may be dehydrated, is all. I will see you again, my dear," Gihon assured as Edelein stepped away and wiped at her face. "I will visit you."

"I have to go," Edelein replied, throat tight. "Goodbye, Gihon."

Placing a hand on her back, Zander pulled the Queen away. The sphynx cast a glance at Gihon that said *I'll let it slide this time*, before escorting the lioness inside.

Alett waved fondly, as bright as ever.

"Thank you, Gihon!" Alett beamed. "We won't forget you guys!"

Gihon waved back, the students of the Corvid Athenaeum offering the same courtesy to Alett as the final member of the entourage began to journey home. The boat's sails whipped in the coastal winds as the anchor began to hoist, wood groaning against the waves as the ship pushed off from the dock.

I should have never agreed to take this job, Gihon thought for a moment. *Now my entire life has been turned upside-down, and I have nothing to show for it but an overwhelming desire to see her again.*

CHAPTER 18

TIME

Dust settled throughout the Corvid Athenaeum as days bled into months. Gihon's tall, broad stature became a ghost that haunted lonesome hallways, rarely seen and never heard. A stale and anxious air stagnated the once-lively space, and the ticking of a clock grew louder with each passing day.

"You know, this is more of a peer study group than anything else at this point," Mandus groaned softly, leaning back in his chair.

Beside him sat Jana, Spira, and Nora. Luthro was nowhere to be found, yet each student knew exactly where he would be. They were sitting in one of the grand study halls of the Corvid Athenaeum, at a table surrounded by antique bookshelves. A gramophone stood in the corner of the room by a large window and churned out soft, brassy tunes underneath the chatter of anxious students.

"Both of them just locked themselves away, devoted to

research. I understand the sentiment, but it's not healthy," Jana sighed.

"Do you think Luthro's trial is too harsh?" Nora asked.

"Nah," Spira replied, "Gihon only asked him to improve upon the quartz relay stone technology we used. Luthro is the one taking it upon himself to go above and beyond, as always."

"It takes a lot to become a Dirigent. I think Luthro knows that Gihon is going easy on him, which is why he's being so ambitious about the project," Jana added.

After the magnificent blunder of Torphus, Clotho, Bex, and Rahzopa in managing the case of the Zenluvian entourage, the three remaining alchemists were removed from consideration as the new Dirigent of Velkhamore. The news shook the core of the Society of Alchemists, with prospective alchemists rising up from across the continent to seek out an endorsement to become the new Dirigent themselves.

To receive an endorsement, an alchemist must complete three trials from three different dirigents. These tests are meant to improve and innovate alchemical technologies, and tend to range from merely difficult to near-impossible, so the alchemist must choose their endorsing dirigents wisely.

Gihon's task was difficult, but vague: *improve quartz-relay technology*. These four words were uttered passively and one of the last things the students had ever heard him say. The ambiguity of what *improvement* means could lead Luthro's trial to become his easiest one, but the youngest son of the prestigious Apocathra family would accept no shortcuts.

"I'm going to bring him tea," Jana decided as she stood up.

"We aren't allowed to help Luthro with his trial," Spira countered.

"Tea doesn't count. We have to make sure he eats and drinks things. It's just the research that we can't assist with. It'll be fine!" Jana smiled assuringly.

"Can I come too? I want to make sure he's not dead," Mandus added.

Following Jana to the kitchen, the fox zoa shifted from foot-to-foot as he watched her diligently prepare a well-loved Caandemite black tea.

"Jana, don't you think this whole thing is just… weird?" Mandus asked in a hushed whisper. "Gihon cancelled classes, but he won't send us out on any external missions. We never see him or Luthro at all. I'm pretty sure they're both living and sleeping in their offices."

"Master Gihon's trying to find a cure for blight," Jana reminded her ally. "Widely regarded as an incurable disease, but he knows that Queen Edelein will die if he can't cure her in time. He owes her his life. There's a terrible amount of guilt weighing on him right now. Maybe I should make him some tea, too."

"He's also definitely hopelessly in love with her," Mandus added, recalling the way Gihon and Edelein had exchanged their goodbyes at the pier. "In love with a dying woman who lives on the other side of the ocean. A woman who isn't allowed to marry outside of her subspecies. Yeah, it's rough. Still, though, I just wish there was something we could do. He won't let us help."

"Tea it is, then," Jana pressed, handing Mandus the second teacup.

Passing through the cold hallways, the sound of quick footsteps caught their attention. Nora had followed behind them, waving a letter in her hand.

"If you're going to Master Marleogne, give him this!" Nora huffed.

"Gihon doesn't want the post. Luthro's been handling all of the administrative work lately–" Mandus stopped himself as Nora handed him the envelope, eyes widening as he took in the delicate handwriting on the outside.

Addressed to Dirigent Gihon Marleogne, an elegant cursive penmanship displayed a recognizable name on the return.

"Edelein Alderhart von Luvemann," Mandus gasped, "Queen Edelein sent a letter!"

"Take it with the tea to Master Gihon. I'll bring the other cup to Luthro," Jana instructed.

Mandus nodded eagerly, his pace increasing as much as he could without spilling tea on the hardwood floors underfoot. Knocking on the door to Gihon's office, Mandus chimed, "Gihon!"

Silence met the fox-boy, not uncommon as of the last few months.

Right.

"Yeah, I'm coming in anyway!" Mandus warned with a big smile, opening the door.

Gihon was facing away, hunched over a large desk filled with flasks and bottles as he fiddled with a syringe of blue liquid. One of the leyline crystals from Edelein was mounted carefully on a wire rack. Papers were scattered around the room, research scrawled onto them with messy handwriting. On the floor, a well of ink had been knocked over, spilling out onto an open leatherbound journal. A board was mounted onto the wall to his left, filled with just as much incomprehensible writing as the parchment surrounding the Dirigent.

Master Gihon is usually really meticulous about cleaning, but this is absolute disarray, worse than me. The whole Edelein situation must really be getting into Gihon's head. I've never seen anything like this before. I hope he's doing alright, Mandus furrowed his eyebrows sympathetically.

"Gihon," Mandus repeated, his voice a bit softer than before as his cheery demeanor faltered.

The Dirigent of Ravencroft turned slightly at the second

calling of his name, seeming to hear his student for the first time. "Not now, Mandus."

Gihon's voice was hoarse and fatigued as he dropped his head back down to his research, ignoring his student.

"It's important. I think you'll like it," Mandus encouraged as he stepped into the room.

The fox zoa set the steaming teacup down on Gihon's desk, shifting some papers to make room for it. Mandus noticed on one of the papers was a sketched portrait of Edelein, drawn more meticulously than any of the alchemy notes on the rest of the desk. She was looking over her shoulder, smiling, though her eyes looked sad.

"The tea is from Jana. And this letter, well, I'll let you see for yourself," Mandus forced a smile, trying to remain cheerful as the looming despair that enveloped the room tried to take him down with it.

"Give it to Luthro," Gihon replied with an empty voice, continuing to stare down at the syringe in his hand.

"Not this one, big guy," Mandus held the letter directly in front of his teacher's eyes, forcing him to look.

Gihon's eyes widened after a moment, snatching the letter from Mandus' hand. He turned to face his student for the first time, and Mandus could clearly see the dark circles accentuating his gaunt golden eyes.

He looks like he hasn't slept in weeks, Mandus noticed.

"It's from Edelein," Gihon realized aloud, cutting the wax seal and opening the envelope.

Time seemed to slow as Gihon pored over the letter, his eyes lighting up for the first time in months as he took in the handwriting of his muse. After what felt like an eternity, Gihon leaned back in his chair and covered his eyes, laughing.

"She is recovering," Gihon sighed. "She made it home

safe. Her symptoms worsened on the boat, but when she returned to Zenluve, her condition stagnated. Edelein believes my theory is correct, that a cure could be tied to leyline energy."

"She isn't healing, but she isn't getting worse when she's in Zenluve, either. The presence of their leyline must be helping her," Mandus realized.

Gihon picked up the tea, relishing in a long sip.

"I think I need more crystals. This one is nearly spent," Gihon concluded. "Mandus, how about a little trip to Zenluve?"

Mandus beamed for a moment, but his smile faltered as Gihon let out a sudden coughing fit.

"How about you take a nap, first?" Mandus countered. "You're working yourself to death. You can't write back to Edelein like this. She deserves you at your best."

"There's no time for that, Mandus," Gihon denied.

"There's no time for you dying again, Gihon!" Mandus retorted with a pout. "You just read that Edelein is doing better. The clock has stopped ticking. Let's get you to bed, freshen up, and then write a reply to Edelein and ask if you can go over to study their leyline."

Gihon sighed, nodding. "Fine. Is Luthro doing alright with his dirigent trial?"

"Uh, you know, I'm not too sure. I was going to check on him next. Not unlike you, he kind of locked himself away and doesn't talk to anyone."

"I'm sorry, Mandus. I know I've let you all down as your teacher. It's just… I really need to do this for Edelein. I promised I would cure her. I figured you would understand."

"We do," Mandus assured with a gentle hand on Gihon's shoulder. "We just want you to take care of yourself. Rest is important, too, you know."

A sudden exclamation echoed through the halls of the

Corvid Athenaeum, a voice that was befuddled and caught off guard.

"That was Luthro!" Mandus gasped, taking off down the hallway with Gihon following behind.

Rejoining the rest of the group in the main study, a curious scene was unfolding. Luthro was standing at the other entrance of the room across from Mandus and Gihon, hand clasped around a piece of quartz. Jana was holding the second piece as she stood by Spira and Nora, who were by the window next to the gramophone as it continued to drone out mellow jazz.

"No one say anything!" Luthro commanded.

Silence fell across the room as Luthro held his stone up higher. Music was echoing faintly through the quartz, tinny and muffled. Curiously, Jana raised the quartz in her hand to the gramophone, and the sound from Luthro's quartz began to transmit a bit more clearly.

"I've got it. I understand now," Luthro beamed as he deactivated the array on his stone. "I asked Jana to move the other piece so I could test the distance, but I suddenly started hearing the gramophone from my office. They aren't just emitting frequency, but recreating sounds entirely. If we connect quartz into the city grid through power lines, it can act as a receiver that transmits audio across the entire city. I'll have to improve the device itself, but this could lead to long-distance vocal communication. Successfully improving quartz-relay technology."

"How long is long-distance?" Gihon asked.

"Worldwide, if I scale it correctly. It would just be a matter of strengthening those quartz receivers to take in and distribute frequencies across oceans. Difficult, but not impossible. If Queen Edelein is willing, I could test my theory in Avalstice and set up transmitters between Zenluve and Ravencroft."

"I could talk to her," Gihon realized. "I could hear her. We wouldn't have to write, or wait ages for letters to be delivered."

"It'll take some time, though. I still have to perfect the technology, and get the appropriate permits to build the infrastructure in Ravencroft–"

"Granted," Gihon confirmed. "You focus on developing the alchemy, I'll arrange for construction to start as soon as you're ready. I'll write to Edelein in the meantime and discuss sending a team out to add your receivers to Avalstice's power supply. They don't use electricity as much as we do over there, but with the Society's interest in trading with Avalstice, it won't be long before they modernize. Excellent work, young Apocathra."

Luthro beamed at the praise from his master. He ran to Jana, taking the second stone from her hand, and disappearing into his office once more. Gihon turned around as well, before Mandus quickly stopped him.

"Nope, not you. You need a bath and a nap first," Mandus instructed. "Your work will be here when you get back. For now, the best thing you can do for Edelein is take care of yourself. Go get some rest, Gihon. You've earned it."

The familiar comfort of a high-speed Zenluvian carriage felt anything but assuring as it toted the Queen through her homeland. Edelein gazed out at the passing scenery, mind racing as sky-high trees drank in the sunlight above.

Across from her sat Ehret Zander and Zwitet Alett. The men seemed to be more relaxed now that they were in familiar territory, eager to return to their normal lives. Edelein, however, felt an anxious knot weighing heavily in the pit of her stomach.

"Eddie, are you feeling alright?" Alett asked, tilting his head. "We're almost home. Aren't you happy?"

Edelein shook her head. "Being home is nice. I'm only dreading the rest of it, is all."

Zander narrowed his eyes, his usual scowl deepening.

"Cub, I'll ask again. What did you offer in exchange for Gihon's life? This is unlike you. You lack your usual... fighting spirit."

The Queen looked down, avoiding eye contact.

"It's nothing. The Dirigent lives, and that is all that matters."

Alett offered a sympathetic look towards Edelein, before smiling brightly.

"I know what will cheer you up!" Alett beamed, gesturing towards the window. "Look at how many people are excited to see you."

Turning to where Alett was motioning, Edelein looked out at the passing streets. The carriage had just begun to enter the Upper District, a high-end region of Zenluve where top officials and nobles lived. Elegant half-timbered and white stone shops lined cobbled roads, ivy decorating each wall with accents of life.

People of all races and walks of life cheered as Edelein's carriage traveled through. The further in the entourage went, the denser the crowds became. Patrol officers dotted sidewalks and intersections, hands extended warily to keep the bustling civilians out of the road. Human, zoa, and elf alike shared waves and smiles, each face hopeful to catch a glimpse of their long-departed Queen.

A smile found its way to Edelein's lonesome face. Feeling the warmth of her people's love, the Queen waved through glass in hopes that they would know the depths of her appreciation.

"We're nearly home, Ed," Alett repeated with a reassuring grin.

Edelein nodded, recognizing the path ahead. The Upper District was the closest area to the Luvestein Castle, surrounding the thousand-year-old palace with natural elegance. Edelein's castle sat atop a large hill, Zenluve's topography only adding to the sheer opulence of her home.

The excited crowds thinned as Edelein's entourage began their ascent onto royal grounds, the area shifting into the off-limits privacy of the Luvemann family. The buildings began to bleed into a thinly wooded forest until nothing remained but trees and underbrush, a single winding road carrying the Queen up to her estate.

"At least the people are happy to see me," Edelein sighed.

"The castle staff will be excited to see you, too!" Alett added. "I bet Grand General Varden has missed you the most out of anyone."

Edelein laughed softly. "I've missed Grand General Varden, as well."

The carriages slowed as the road looped into a large ring at the front of the castle, grandeur greeting the Queen with a warm familiarity. Another large crowd was gathered at the castle's entrance, this time consisting of a hundred or so staff members standing behind dozens of finely dressed figures.

"The entire Royal Court is here?" Edelein exclaimed in disbelief. "I see the Clan Heads, the Guildmasters, and pretty much every person of noble blood that I've ever met."

"I mean, you are the Queen. It's not that outlandish for the Court to attend your return party."

"Are we meant to host one? Was there some gala I was supposed to be planning? I just wanted to go up to my suite and sleep for the next several days," Edelein groaned.

"I don't see Grand General Varden," Zander replied suddenly, confused.

"Wait, Zander is right. Where's Varden?" Alett asked.

As they spoke, the large castle doors swung open slowly to greet their mistress. An older elf stood upright with hands clasped behind his back, white and gold armor shining brilliantly in the sun as he stepped outside. The elf's hair was wavy and slicked back, grey strands highlighted against dusty, muted blond.

"Uncle Varden!" Edelein beamed.

Grand General Varden Windbough, the head of the Zenluvian military, was an elf nearing six-hundred years of age. With centuries of wisdom and experience, Varden was known not only for his prowess as a soldier but for rearing each Luvemann firstborn for generations. He was the man who taught Edelein the art of melee combat, and her father the masterful practice of archery. After Alderis' passing, Varden became even more of a father figure to the orphaned Crown Princess in her darkest hours.

"You still call him that, huh?" Zander said with a gentle sigh. "He's not your uncle, cub."

Edelein ignored Zander's comments, already stepping out of the carriage to greet Varden. She waved warmly at the crowd of nobles and staffers as she passed by, drinking in the sounds of celebration.

Varden approached Edelein, meeting her halfway down the deep blue carpet that had been rolled out to welcome her home. He bowed deeply. Edelein hugged him tightly in return.

"I missed you, Uncle Varden," Edelein admitted.

Varden laughed warmly, patting the lioness' head. "I missed you too, Eddie. I'm glad you made it back safely."

"Is everything going alright in Zenluve?" The Queen asked as she pulled away, addressing Varden more formally.

"I can give you a full briefing inside. I would like to hear every detail of your sojourn as well, so I've already called for a tea cart to be brought to your private garden. Leyline tea and an assortment of your favorite sweets. Though, if you'd prefer, I can have the tea sent out to your parlor room instead–"

"The garden would be wonderful. Thank you, Varden."

Butlers held open the ornate front doors of the castle as the Queen and her top general stepped inside, the six remaining Zengarde following closely behind. Looking over their numbers, worry clouded Varden's expression.

"Noentet Nephvir, did he fall in battle? Zextet Everett, as well?"

Anguished, Edelein nodded.

"The Winter Court came to collect their dues," Edelein confirmed. "I wasn't there to save Neph. Everett sacrificed himself to slay a dragon. I wish to honor them as heroes and host a memorial for them, as well as Sievtet Tyrus and Aktet Cyzen."

"The fae followed you to Caandemium?" Varden asked, shocked. "I'm… so sorry, Edelein."

The expression on Varden's face betrayed his curiosity regarding the mention of a dragon, yet he knew better than to ask for details from the grieving Queen.

The interior of the castle was even more opulent than the outside, with white marble foundations and columns accented by golden embellishments. Large windows filled the space with light. Embroidered azure drapery kissed the sunlight on the edges of each window, with carpets and tapestries to match.

Varden slowed his pace briefly to whisper something in Zander's ear, though the clacking of Edelein's heeled boots on cold marble drowned out the comment. Zander's face fell into a deep scowl in response. He nodded, barking an order at the others that stood behind.

"You're relieved of duty for the rest of the day. Return to your quarters at once," Zander commanded.

At Edelein's visible confusion, Zander approached her with

a salute.

"Grand General Varden will be filling you in on the current events of Zenluve in the gardens, as he mentioned. You will be given utmost privacy for as long as you need it. We will not disturb your rest and peace, though I am but a single word away at all times."

Straightening from his salute, Zander clasped a warm hand on Edelein's shoulder. His gaze turned sympathetic for a moment, before turning heel and disappearing quickly down a hallway that led towards the Zengarde suites.

As the hallway emptied, leaving Edelein alone with Varden, her eyebrows furrowed in deep thought.

"Did something happen, Varden?" Edelein asked. "Why did you send the Zengarde away?"

"I just assumed that after your journey, you would wish for a bit of peace and quiet. You know full well that your garden is not meant to be intruded upon by anyone without your permission, so I simply sought to relieve them of duty to allow them some much-deserved rest and to bring you a few moments of respite to catch up with me. Is this alright, Your Majesty?"

Edelein tilted her head, confused but in agreement. "I suppose that is wise."

A few moments passed in silence, the elf and zoa drawing closer to the royal gardens.

"How is the situation with the shadow-beasts?" Edelein spoke, breaking the silence.

"You don't wish for a cup of tea, first?" Varden replied, surprised by Edelein's newfound insistence of work.

The Queen shook her head, though she continued to walk towards the gardens. "I've been worried sick that more have appeared in my absence. Are there any more casualties related to phantasms?"

"Actually, none. For better or for worse, the shadow-beasts all but vanished when you left, Your Majesty. I've been trying my hardest to convince your more skeptical subjects that this is unrelated to your absence. There have been new problems to worry about, but thankfully, the shadow-beast situation has become manageable. They appear on occasion outside of the walls, but we have not engaged with them. Now that you've returned, we will be able to dispose of them properly, as well."

If they're appearing and being handled outside of the walls, does this mean there is a rogue alchemist practicing somewhere nearby? Edelein wondered. *Why would they stop attacking Zenluve upon my departure?*

"What of these new problems, then?"

Varden hesitated, thinking.

"A few things. There's been an uptick in zoa poaching and disappearances, and we've had no luck busting the ring yet. It may be related to an increase in vampire sightings, but there's no evidence to support the claim. Also, there's been an unfortunate new development in the thirteen-year-old cold case of Lylia Brightwood."

Edelein's eyes widened. "You have a lead on the Brightwood Massacre?"

"When Lylia first came to Zenluve, she claimed the assailant was a monster beyond her comprehension. We were unable to find any beast fitting her description and ultimately dismissed it as a one-time incident, perhaps involving hallucinogens or trauma rewriting her memory. Unfortunately, Lylia was right. A new species of beast has been seen more frequently, clearly not native to the Deepwood. They are intelligent and incredibly violent, and they match her description. We've lost a few patrolmen to them already. Whatever that thing was that killed Lylia's tribe, it has reproduced at an alarming rate. Speaking of reproducing at an alarming rate, there's one more thing I need to warn you of–"

Varden's words were cut off as Edelein pushed through the glass doors of her private garden. Surrounded by a medley of peony and rose, a single elegant ironwood table stood between two beautifully-carved chairs. The table was set with an array of cakes and pastries on a golden tower, teacups on either side and a pot in between.

The Queen's Garden was a restricted corner of the castle, an outdoor pavilion that only the royal family and their permissed guests were granted access to. Most days, Edelein would take her tea time in the gardens alone, enjoying the quiet birdsong with a cup of leyline tea and a stroll through its fragrant pathways.

This time, however, Edelein's private oasis was interrupted as she locked eyes with an unfamiliar figure. The man was sitting at the table quietly, but stood up as the Queen entered.

The gentleman was handsome by nearly any standard of beauty, with wavy blond hair and gentle amber eyes accenting a perfect porcelain face. A masterfully-tailored white suit hung gracefully from his square shoulders, the suit bearing accents of gold and blue that matched the halls of the Luvestein Castle. Most notably, however, were the leonine ears atop his head and a tufted tail that swayed behind him as he approached.

Varden put a wary hand out, extended towards the man.

"You are not supposed to be here, Klaus," Varden warned.

The man named Klaus swept Edelein's hand into his, bringing it to his lips and kissing the back of her glove. Feeling her demeanor falter, the lioness' next words were spoken not as the Queen of Zenluve, but as Edelein von Luvemann.

"Who the hell are you?"

I met a lot of really great people when promoting The Man in Red. Here is to hoping that I will meet many more through Soulweaver.

Thank you to my small-but-mighty community of supporters. You motivate me to keep writing, because I seek nothing more than to share my stories with you all.

Lately, I have been needing to trust God more with my time and my art. Here's to relinquishing control, something that is near-impossible for me to do. Trust the process.

Much love,
B.G. Lyrax

Crown of the Alchemist will continue with book three in 2027. Please look forward to it, and keep in touch via our social media for news and updates!
Join our free Discord community to discuss the story, get exclusive sneak peeks, and make new friends with other fans of COTA!

All links are available at bglyrax.carrd.co.

Visit cota.bluandgihon.com/read to check out the Crown of the Alchemist webcomic for free today!

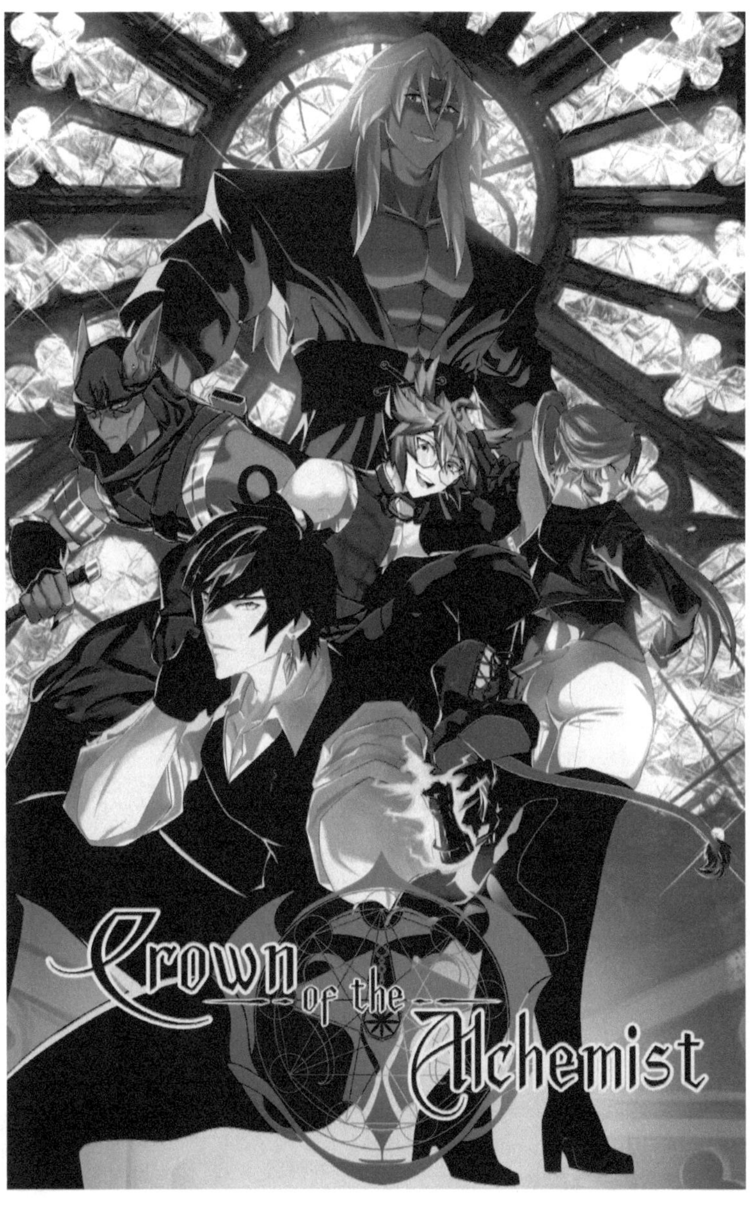

Finally, a huge thank-you to our Patrons who have supported our journey. There's been a lot of ups and downs from the day we first started to where we are now, and your support means the world to us.

If you'd like to receive exclusive benefits including extra short stories in the COTA world setting, supplementary reading, private AMA events with the creators, digital wallpaper downloads, and more, you can join today at

www.patreon.com/LYRAX

www.ingramcontent.com/pod-product-compliance
Lightning Source LLC
LaVergne TN
LVHW100512110826
845146LV00002B/610

* 9 7 9 8 9 9 3 3 0 4 8 2 3 *